THE
LEGACY
OF THE
Rocking K
RANCH

FOUR GENERATIONS OF
LOVE, LOSS, AND GRACE

MARY CONNEALY
D. J. GUDGER
BECCA WHITHAM
KIMBERLEY WOODHOUSE

BARBOUR
PUBLISHING

Prologue ©2024 by Kimberley Woodhouse
Eleanor ©2024 by Mary Connealy
Grace ©2024 by D. J. Gudger
Caroline ©2024 by Becca Whitham
Penelope ©2024 by Kimberley Woodhouse

Print ISBN 978–1-63609–739-8
Adobe Digital Edition (.epub) 978–1-63609–740-4

All scripture quotations, unless otherwise noted, are taken from the King James Version of the Bible.

This book is a work of fiction. Names, characters, places, and incidents are either products of the author's imagination or used fictitiously. Any similarity to actual people, organizations, and/or events is purely coincidental.

Cover image © Sandra Cunningham / Trevillion Images

Published by Barbour Books, an imprint of Barbour Publishing, Inc., 1810 Barbour Drive, Uhrichsville, Ohio 44683, www.barbourbooks.com

Our mission is to inspire the world with the life-changing message of the Bible.

Member of the
Evangelical Christian
Publishers Association

Printed in the United States of America.

PROLOGUE

By
KIMBERLEY WOODHOUSE

PROLOGUE

---◆◆---

PENELOPE
New York City, 1910

I am a writer. . . . I am a writer. . . . I *am* a writer. . . ." Tears streamed down Penelope Cooper's face as she left another publishing house after yet *another* rejection.

Not once had she allowed her emotions to get the best of her until today. But. . .she hadn't traveled halfway across America expecting to have her dream crushed over and over and over again. It was beginning to wear her down. Three weeks of the same old story.

Swiping at the rebel tears, she lifted her chin. Why was it women were only seen to be capable of writing gossip, advice, or society columns? Not one publisher saw fit to answer that question. Oh, they all raved about her writing and her short stories, but the fact remained, she wasn't a man.

Women were a greater risk for them. She understood that. People were more likely to plunk down their hard-earned money for a book by a well-known male author than they were for a book of Western stories written by an unknown *female* from Wyoming. Most people still called her home state Wyoming Territory, even though it had been a state for more than twenty years. If they even knew how to spell it.

5

She pushed the cynical thoughts away. It truly wasn't that bad, even if a good part of America didn't know all their states. The sarcasm in her swelled with each thought. She really should tame her mind. This was no way to accomplish her goal.

The problem was, after so much rejection, she tended toward pessimism rather than optimism. Growing up on the ranch, she'd gotten used to the men ribbing each other and using sarcasm to cope with the grief of the day.

But that wasn't how ladies were supposed to behave.

The question still hung in the air. . .how on earth was she going to find a publisher who would work with a woman?

Based on almost every rejection she'd received, if she wanted to have her stories published, the publishers needed her to be a man. Plain and simple.

Not that she wanted to be a man.

No.

God created her just the way she was. So why did He give her this creative gift of story—as her mama lovingly put it—if she wasn't supposed to use it? Would she really have to stoop to using a male name? That wasn't her first choice. But what else could she do? Now that she'd met with all these publishers face-to-face, they knew who she was. They'd read her writing. And not one of them had offered her the opportunity even if she *would* agree to using a male pseudonym.

Did that mean she wasn't good enough?

No. That couldn't be it. Each one had told her the stories were great, her writing stellar.

But the more she replayed the meetings in her mind, the more the real reason haunted her. Each man had been shocked by her boldness—as a woman—to request meetings with them and present them her work in person.

She hadn't had time to do things any other way. Was she supposed to go a different route? Why hadn't anyone told her? Maybe she should have taken the time to investigate the proper procedure to pitch to a publisher.

Ladies of the city behaved differently than ladies of Wyoming. That much was certain.

Botheration, this world was complicated and the rules of society and business even more so. Especially for a woman.

If she had the power to do so, she would change things in the world. Like making sure that every man and woman had the right to vote. Good heavens, women had the right to vote in Wyoming since 1869, before it was even a state.

She would also see that all people were treated fairly, no matter their class or station or ethnicity. And opportunities— including writing—would be open to anyone wanting to put in the hard work.

With a nod, new determination filled her, and she stomped her way up the sidewalk in Manhattan. She would not give up. No. Never.

The smell of freshly baked goodies wafted out of a shop somewhere ahead of her. Her stomach rumbled. When she came to the window for the small bakery and tea shop, she stopped and watched the proprietor fill the trays in the window with delectable pastries.

Licking her lips, Penelope was ready to reach into her handbag and lay out each and every cent she had for one of everything in the window. She placed a gloved hand to her lips and giggled. That wouldn't be good for her waistline or her budget, but a bit of tea and something tasty might help her collect her thoughts and positive outlook once again.

After ordering a cup of tea and a lovely, sugary confection

with cherry filling, she took her seat at a dainty little table by the side window, where she could enjoy her purchases and watch the people as they scurried about their afternoons.

The first bite had her mouth clamoring for more. If only she could sneak this home and work with her mother and grandmother to create a duplicate recipe. It was sheer heaven.

The pastry was crisp on the outside, tender on the inside, and held just the right amount of filling. The balance between the buttery shell and the tart cherries covered with a sugary glaze made her taste buds come alive. It was a good thing they *didn't* have this sort of thing back in Wyoming. She'd eat more than her share every day.

Halfway through the cherry tart, she leaned back in her chair and allowed her shoulders to slump. Even with the tantalizing treat in front of her, she couldn't erase the fact that today had been another negative response. A setback, as her grandma Grace would say.

But just like her own grandmother overcame all odds after a horrible bout with smallpox, Penelope was determined to overcome this insurmountable mountain as well.

Her entire family had cheered her on and paved the way for her travels to New York. Even the luscious sweet in front of her couldn't take away the immense undertaking before her. It wasn't within her power to change the world overnight. Gracious, she hadn't been able to change even *one* man's mind about publishing her stories yet. She released a long sigh.

"Such a despondent utterance from such a lovely lady." A man's voice enveloped in a rich British accent made her sit up straight and snap her gaze away from the window.

Swallowing her embarrassment of him finding her in such a casual manner, she could only blink up at him.

Top hat, black coat with tails, and the most pristine white shirt she'd ever seen clothed the man before her. "Would it be awfully untoward of me to request this seat?" He laid his hand on the chair across her small table. His deep brown eyes sparkled with a touch of amusement. "There isn't another to be had this afternoon."

His words forced her to pay attention to her surroundings. The shop had filled, and he was correct; her extra chair was the only one remaining. Penelope cleared her throat. "Of course, be my guest."

"Nicholas Allen Junior." He snapped his heels together and bowed.

Her lips tipped upward of their own accord. She'd never seen such a thing. Was this how gentlemen behaved in England? Back home, men simply removed their dusty hats. "Miss Penelope Cooper."

With a dip of his chin in her direction, he removed his hat and took his seat. "What, pray tell, has brought you to New York City, Miss Cooper?"

"Are all English gentlemen as inquisitive as you on their first meeting?" She took a sip of her tea, intrigued by this man and his forward behavior.

He released a slight chuckle. "Only when we meet a beautiful woman clearly untainted by the worldly pleasures of the big city."

"You try to sway me, sir, with your words." She quirked one eyebrow up at him. "What gave me away? That I'm not from the city?"

A slight smile formed on his mouth and produced small crinkles around his eyes. Clearly her senior by a good many years, he still appeared youthful and in the prime of his life. "While your speech is impeccable, your accent is not of New York—or

LEGACY OF THE ROCKING K RANCH

anywhere on the East Coast, for that matter." He met her stare with raised eyebrows of his own.

Was he thinking something else that made her stand out as an outsider? Was her attire not the latest fashion? Tempted to look down, she forced herself to ignore the impulse and held his gaze. "Thank you for the compliment. . .I think."

"Oh, it is quite the compliment, Miss Cooper." He crossed his arms over his chest and tapped a finger to his lips. "But you intrigue me, and I would love to know your story."

Her story? No one had ever asked her that question before. The words connected with the deepest longings of her heart. "I'm a writer, Mr. Allen." She dared to lay out the statement before him. "I came here from Wyoming to seek publication."

His eyes widened as his smile grew. "Wyoming, you say? Of the Wild West?"

It was her turn to laugh. "I'm not sure those of us who live there would classify it as the Wild West any longer, sir."

"Forgive me. But you must agree that it is still a fascination to be sure. One of the greatest, if I wish to be honest. . . . Hmmm. . ." He nodded to her, but the smile didn't leave his face. He sipped his tea and then lifted a linen napkin to his lips.

Penelope waited, as he clearly had something else to say. His eyes sparkled with what she could only guess was curiosity.

"Are you hoping to write for a women's magazine?"

"No." A little too much vehemence came out with the single word.

It seemed to amuse him even further. "Then a novel, perhaps?"

"Perhaps one day." How much should she tell this stranger? There was nothing wrong with honesty. Besides, he couldn't steal anything from her; he hadn't even seen any of her writing. "I've written over fifty short stories—Westerns, since that is what I know—that I hope will intrigue readers from the East."

"That is impressive. Impressive indeed." He leaned forward. "The people of England and Europe do love a good American Western. As I said, it is of the greatest interest to them."

His words brought the spark within her to a full flame. "Do *you* love a good Western, Mr. Allen?" She braved the question.

"I do. It is my favorite type of story."

The response was a balm to her soul. Maybe she was seeking publication in the wrong place. Perhaps she should send inquiries to England. There were many more women writers there. Her mind whirled with the possibilities. Even with all the rejections of late, God had seen fit to encourage her with this random meeting with a stranger.

"I see you appreciate my reply."

Brought out of her thoughts, she beamed a smile at him. "Mr. Allen, you've given me a great deal to think about. It was exactly what I needed to refresh my spirit after a trying morning."

His shocked expression made her want to giggle. "I'm glad I could be of help." He sat back in his chair. "But I'd like to be of even more help if I could."

Unsure of his intentions, Penelope's guard instantly went up. Why couldn't he simply have been a gentleman who sat down for a cup of tea?

"I see I've given you the wrong impression with my words. Forgive me, Miss Cooper. That was not my intention." He folded his hands in front of him. "You see, my father owns the British publishing company Allen and Tate. I'm in charge of acquisitions. If you'll allow me to see your writing, there's a possibility *we* might be interested in publishing your stories."

———— ••• ————

Eight weeks later

Penelope's fingers flew over the keys of her Underwood No. 3 typewriter. Four years ago, every member of her family had chipped in to give it to her for her eighteenth birthday. Each one of them had written her a note encouraging her to write her stories and get them published. They all believed in her ability and wanted her to succeed. That faith in her was what spurred her on day after day.

And now. . .she had the opportunity of a lifetime.

The past two months had passed in a surreal blur of excitement ever since she met Nicholas Allen Jr.

Not only did he love her writing, but his father did as well. But it wasn't just her short stories. As soon as they found out that she'd been born and raised in the Great American West, where there were still cowboys living and working on her family's ranch, and that her great-grandfather was part Shoshone Indian, they'd offered her a contract that very day to write the true story of her family. In her mind, it was a legacy of love. But to them, it was four generations that had come from the Wild West, wrestling against man and beast to tame the land.

Granted, the contract wasn't perfect. They wanted her to use a male pseudonym of which they would have control. But their excitement over the project overruled her misgivings. Especially since she'd be writing a true account, Nicholas Jr. was insistent that it would also help protect her privacy.

They'd paid for her small apartment and amenities, and a promised advance was coming this week.

After their initial talks, she'd had one stipulation that she'd insisted upon in the contract. That all native people—Indians—would be represented with respect. Even today, people feared the Arapaho and Shoshone or any of the other tribes of Indian descent. It didn't make a lick of sense to her.

Penelope paused her frantic typing. She sat back in her chair and flexed her fingers. How should she tackle the sensitive history of her home state? It wasn't pretty. Massacres had happened—by both white men and Indians. Land was taken from many tribes, and false promises of prosperity and independence fell through. Even now, people seemed to refuse to understand that white people had come in and taken land that didn't belong to them. Would they ever understand a wound of that magnitude?

Probably not. Such was the way of sin-filled humans.

Even so, she wanted to do what she could to portray everything accurately—with honor—and prayerfully open the eyes of those ignorant to the truth.

She winced. Perhaps that was a little harsh. But she was tired of hearing the derogatory statements toward people that were different. What if everyone knew *her* heritage? Would they treat her poorly as well?

Here in the big city, they prided themselves on being knowledgeable and always on the cusp of what was to be the latest and greatest. In all actuality, not only were people prejudiced against Indians or anyone with dark skin, but they were of Jews, the Irish, and many others. What did *that* say about their knowledge? Or of America? When this country was founded by immigrants?

It didn't make sense to her. The color of a person's skin shouldn't matter. Nor should their accent, where they were born, or what their lineage was.

Back in Wyoming, their neighbors didn't care about heritage or ethnicity. Everyone pitched in to help one another—especially if the winter had been especially difficult and long. Which happened a lot.

Of course, there still weren't a lot of people in Wyoming. Maybe the more it populated, the more they might struggle with attitudes of prejudice as well. People were first and foremost cursed with human nature. In their flesh, none of them were decent or good.

In truth, she'd withheld from the Allens that her own father was full-blooded Arapaho. While her dark hair and dark eyes might be recognizable once they knew her heritage, her lily-white skin was from her mother. Most people never knew that she was half-Arapaho unless they knew her family.

She turned her mind back to the story, and a deep sense of longing for home filled her. After sending a telegram followed by several letters, she knew her family would be rejoicing with her for the writing opportunity. But the more she wrote, the more she realized she wanted to go back home and hear every detail firsthand. It didn't matter that she'd heard the stories passed down multiple times. There were a lot of details she didn't know. Places she'd marked in the manuscript that she needed to fill in.

A knock at her door made her jump in her seat. How long had she been sitting, ruminating, and staring at the page in front of her?

She smoothed her hair, stood, and then smoothed her skirt as well.

Opening the door, she smiled. "Nicholas!" She welcomed him into the sitting room. "I wasn't expecting you this morning." With a hand to her hair, she prayed it was still encased in its chignon.

"I had to come see you as soon as I heard." His voice was a bit breathless, and he grabbed both of her hands in his. "I know these past few weeks have been a bit of a whirlwind, and we've shared countless hours together, but Father had a brilliant idea today that I'm hoping will thrill you as much as it does me."

Heart pounding in her chest, she stared up at the handsome publisher's son. What could it possibly mean? Nicholas had never taken her hands before, and the way he looked at her... Well, it was much more intimate than their friendship had allowed prior to this moment. "Go on." The words rushed out on a whisper.

"Marry me."

She sucked in her breath. What had he just said?

He held up a hand and led her over to the settee. "Allow me to explain." Once she was settled, he paced in front of her. "I've been far too busy with the business over the years to even pay attention to my surroundings, much less find a woman worthy of marrying. At thirty-eight years old, it's high time I settled down and had a family. While this might begin as a marriage of convenience, I think we could truly come to care for one another. We get along smashingly and have a great deal in common. You're the first woman I've even considered."

"Marriage of convenience?" Her throat squeaked.

He rushed on. "If we marry, Father thinks that it would be perfect for *both* of our names to be on the book. That way, there will be a male name on there for substance, and you won't have to use a pseudonym. You could use your *real* name. Well, your married name. After this first book, he wants to start expanding on all of your Westerns. If we write them together, he thinks we could make each one a novel length and release a new one every few months. Especially with what you have already written." His grin widened. "Just think of it. A husband-and-wife writing team. It would be exhilarating. Different. And gain everyone's attention almost immediately since you are truly from the Wild West we'll be writing about. It lends authenticity and even a bit of grit."

"Grit?" Her brain grasped for sound footing but found none as it swirled around. What was going on?

Her question went unanswered. "Truth be told, I already care for you, Penelope. I know we are a good match. We're good friends, are we not?"

She blinked. Nodded. They were good friends. But his words were just a bit too much to take in all at once.

"We can announce it to your family and back in England. In a few months, we'll travel back to Britain as husband and wife and begin our new life. Father has already arranged for me to train my replacement in acquisitions so that I can devote my time to *our* books. He's certain they will take the world by storm and become popular almost overnight. That is, once you've finished writing your family's story. It will be how we launch our writing team. He's already spoken to the *New York Times*, the *Post-Standard*, and the *New York Tribune* about it, and they are eager to not only host our advertising but to perhaps even do a write-up about the extraordinary husband and wife behind the story." The excitement on his face was evident.

Well, she hadn't expected *this* when she woke up this morning.

"Please. . .say something. Or have I completely overwhelmed you with my exuberance?" He sat next to her and reached for both of her hands again. "I truly care about you, Penelope, and only want the best for you. I hope you understand that in the depth of your heart."

Staring into his eyes, she searched for any glimmer of love. Each woman in her family had come to deeply love their spouse even if her great-grandmother and grandmother had also married in essence for convenience. Could she do the same thing? She did care for Nicholas. But could she love him?

In that moment, she realized he was holding out a beautiful

offering to her—a way to bring her dreams to life. Wasn't that just like love? They could grow to care for one another as well. Her thoughts whirled around her. The opportunity before her was incredible. She'd be a fool not to take it. "All right."

"All right?" He leaned a bit closer, the questions clear in his eyes.

"I'll marry you. Write the books. Move to England." It made her swallow hard. "All of it."

He pulled her into his arms, and she wrapped her arms around him as well. This was what she wanted.

When he released her, she held up a hand. "I have an enormous request to make."

A glimmer of hesitance flashed through his eyes. Tipping his head to the side, his smile slightly diminished. "Of course, my dear. What is it?"

"I need to go back to Wyoming to write the book about my family. To give it all the authenticity and accuracy as possible . . . . I need to go home."

"Is this about your great-grandmother?"

She'd told him about the telegram that told her of Great-Grandmother Eleanor's illness. It wouldn't be right to be dishonest. "In part, yes. I need to hear her story from her lips while she is still alive. But I have mountains of questions to ask *all* of them. I may know the stories like the back of my hand, but I don't know all the details. To do this properly, I need to know everything. The good, the bad, the joyous times, the hard times. From everyone's perspectives. Wouldn't you agree?"

His lips pursed for a moment as he clearly tossed thoughts around in his head. "I do agree with you. To make it the best possible, you need to return to Wyoming." He took her hands once again. "I will send the best photographer I can find to go out there with you. It might be a week or two later, but he can document the family ranch and area and assist you in any way that you need after he arrives. We can use the photographs in the papers here and in England to advertise the coming of the book. It's perfect! I don't know why I didn't think of it." He surged to his feet and rubbed his chin. "I wish I could go with you—I wouldn't want you to come into any danger—but I have a great many responsibilities the next few weeks."

"That's all right. I'll be fine in Wyoming on my own. I assure you." With a giggle, she came to her feet. A little thrill rose from her toes up to her scalp. Oh, how she'd missed her family! And now, she could share with them in person all the excitement for her upcoming stories and marriage.

God had paved the way for her dreams to come true.

Her family's legacy could touch the lives of people around the world. Four generations of her family still lived on the Rocking K Ranch.

It was time to go home and tell their story.

ELEANOR

By
MARY CONNEALY

CHAPTER ONE

—◆◆◆—

1850
Along the Oregon Trail in unsettled Indian Territory—
land that wouldn't be the state of Wyoming for forty years

Screaming did no good.

She knew it for a fact because she'd done a fair share of it.

Horror brought her to tears. They were leaving her. Out in the middle of the wilderness. Probably Indian Territory.

Her husband possibly dying. . .her daughter too.

Eleanor would live to bury them both, and then. . .a wave of fury swept through her. . .then she'd hunt down every one of these cowards and kill them.

No. No she would not do that. Definitely no.

Probably no. Probably she wouldn't be able to find them, so definitely no.

She was a Christian woman who had to dig deep to pray for those who abandoned her, left her very possibly to die.

Why didn't they just steal her cloak and slap her across the face while they were at it?

The wagons lumbered along. Each driver averted their eyes. They knew what they were doing, but they were scared.

Terrified.

So was she.

———————————

Ray "Wildcat" Manning rode toward the wagon train, smiling.

The sun rose bright. The sky was clear. And he was almost home. Three more days, five at the most, and he'd be done with this job.

Thirty covered wagons were hitched up and ready to go. He rode down the steep slope, glad these folks would go on to Oregon. He sure didn't want them here on the eastern edge of the northern Rockies. There were over one hundred people, all looking for farmland. They'd clog up the whole mountain if they stopped here.

He'd never cared much for crowds.

They'd go on with a trail guide eager to get to Oregon. He'd take his leave. Hightail it to the high-up hills and finally be done with his wandering. He'd wanted it for a while, and then the life had trapped him, because guides were badly needed and well paid.

And they earned every penny.

But it had suited him to rove the land back and forth. He'd been from Independence, Missouri, to Oregon every year for the last five. But no more. He'd had enough and found himself longing for the rugged mountains, the breathtaking views, the huge, antlered elk, and mostly his ma and pa.

His pa was a mountain man, his ma a Shoshone woman. Between the two of them, they'd taught him all he needed to know and then some about the frontier, especially the treacherous, magnificent land of mountains. The Rocky Mountains.

This time he planned to stay here in the Rockies and be able to walk for days without seeing another soul. Ride like the wind without wondering if he'd run across one of the little towns that looked to him like a wound on the otherwise unspoiled prairie.

He'd be able to breathe again in the land he loved.

His years of work left him with money in his pocket, and that would make life a bit easier. . .if riding five days to a trading post could be called easy.

He smiled at the thought, ran his hand over the bristles on his face. He'd shaved only a few days back. He was clean-shaven in the summer and grew a thick beard to survive the cold winter.

Now he rode down a long slope, leading his packhorse toward the hungry travelers. He expected to bring cheer to these folks because he brought food, fresh meat. The single deer wouldn't be much more than a bite for everyone, but it would be welcome.

Then he heard shouts and saw the first wagon roll out. The sun was just cresting the eastern sky in a wash of pink. They'd need a short day today because they were entering rugged territory. A short day today to get them to the base of a mountain trail, then a long, harsh day tomorrow.

They had all agreed it was best to take it easier today, which meant there was plenty of time to roast venison for everyone.

Instead, the lead wagon rolled, its wheels creaking, the oxen team leaning hard against the harness. The driver whipped the team hard and shouted with more urgency than necessary.

Then the next wagon moved, and the next. Wildcat picked up the pace. What in the world was going on? He wasn't the wagon master, but as the guide, he was the one who told the wagon master when to start each day and when to stop. That had worked since they'd started the trip. Why change now?

A dozen wagons were rolling now. That's when he noticed one wagon without a hitched-up oxen team. It stood as it had overnight, in a circle of wagons used to create a makeshift corral for the cattle and horses. The circle was breaking up. Everyone moved but that wagon.

Wildcat knew this train well. He knew exactly who was in that wagon. Eleanor Yates, her husband, Carl, and their daughter, Grace. A nice family. Wildcat had helped them maybe a little more than most wagons because Carl wasn't a particularly useful kind of man.

Making it as a farmer in Oregon was going to be all the city slicker could handle. But Mrs. Yates was a hard worker, and Grace was game. Carl liked to read and talk and dream out loud of outlandish greatness awaiting them all.

They'd make it. Wildcat figured Mrs. Yates would see to it. And maybe even Carl would set aside his strange impractical ways and amount to something. He'd surprise everyone if he did, but Oregon might make a man out of him.

Now, why were they staying by the overnight campfire while everyone else was moving? And why wasn't anyone helping them hitch up when they all knew Carl was sick?

Wildcat's stomach sank as he spurred his horse.

CHAPTER TWO

———◆◆◆———

Smallpox.

It was a killer disease and terribly contagious. Half those who got it died. Her beloved Carl had it. There was a good chance he was going to die. And these "good, honest folks" were going to make sure of it.

In a ringing voice that she'd never heard from her own lips before, a voice of pure hatred, she cried out, "You are all cowards before the Lord. Remember well this day when you chose to sacrifice a man, woman, and child to save your own sorry hides."

She'd had smallpox as a child and survived it. She'd told them that. She'd begged them to drive a distance but then wait for her there.

Two weeks, the wagon master said. Four, if Grace was only now exposed to it and came down with it two weeks from now. Then they had to wait for Grace's illness to run its course. They might be waiting for a month.

No, they couldn't delay that long.

But she'd seen it in his eyes. The delay was a huge problem, but fear was what drove him.

He said she could come along behind them if she stayed

well back. Didn't camp with them. Shared no food with them. She wasn't sure if she could survive under those conditions, but she'd decided to do that until Carl started coughing. He'd been coughing and feverish for three days. A cold, she'd thought. But this morning his coughing deepened until it hurt her ears to hear it. She'd gone to check on him and seen the spots.

Smallpox.

They'd heard there were cases of it in the last town. Wildcat Manning, their guide, had found that out and rushed them out of town almost before they'd gotten in.

All but Carl. He loved to meet new people. Talk and share a meal. Most everyone else had headed for the general store. Eleanor hadn't noticed Carl slip away, but she wasn't surprised. She hadn't expected any different.

But when they'd been dragged away by Wildcat's urgent warnings, Carl had been left behind.

Carl was brilliant. He wrote songs and poetry and essays with dreams of publishing stories about his life in the West in some magazine back East. He had made no arrangements to do it. He hadn't even gotten the names of publishers he could send his work to. But Eleanor believed in him. He had a gift, and he'd find a way to use it. He was so interested in everyone and everything. He'd spent their time in town talking, sharing ideas and dreams.

And now he had smallpox, and no one else did.

If more of the illness cropped up, would they leave other wagons behind?

Feeling nearly hysterical, she imagined this wagon train sprinkling abandoned families the length of the Oregon Trail.

The hysteria faded to numb horror as more wagons rolled by. Every last one of them chose their own safety over the life of her family.

And finally, the last. She watched it pass her. Her eyes locked on it, and she stood frozen in place. Carl's coughing echoed behind her, and she knew she had to tend him. Try and get his fever down. Bathe the terrible rash.

Pray.

———————

Whatever had caused these folks to pull out early, Mrs. Yates—he admitted he thought of her as Eleanor but never called her by her first name—was probably moving slow, trying to doctor her husband and make him comfortable before she took up the reins.

A slow start was Carl's way at the best of times. But he had a cold. Coughing, feverish. It'd been going on for two days. And the fool had taken to his bed as soon as he began ailing. Wildcat had helped out the Yateses more than usual while Carl was sick.

Then he heard the shouting.

And saw Eleanor standing with her hands on her hips.

Then this tough little pioneer woman, who kept her pretty blond head down and worked all the hours in the day and then some, stopped shouting and cried.

Something terrible had happened.

Wildcat spurred his horse.

———————

Stunned, frightened, she watched the last wagon trundle by.

A small child riding in the last wagon popped up and looked at Eleanor through the small opening left by the tightly drawn wagon tarp.

The little tyke waved forlornly.

Yep, "bye-bye" about covered it.

Then Eleanor heard pounding hooves, and she turned, expecting to see hostile Indians pouring down out of the hills toward her.

And instead, she looked at hope.

Mr. Manning. Wildcat, they called him. He'd been so kind. Helped Eleanor so much. Well, she'd send him on his way. Or rather, she probably wouldn't need to because he'd run right along with the rest of them.

She saw he drew a packhorse along, carrying the deer he'd hunted in the hours before dawn a couple of days a week.

He knew Carl was sick. He saw the train leaving. She almost expected him to turn and follow along. Abandon her too.

Instead he rode up, frowning. "What in the devil is going on?"

He saw Eleanor flinch.

He was getting better at watching his mouth around her. Oh, he didn't use profanity. He was a believer, and he wasn't one for taking the Lord's name in vain. But he had a rough mouth. Given to temper at times.

When it was deserved.

"Why is everyone pulling out but you?"

He saw her throat work, swallowing as if her whole body was bone-dry.

Then her shoulders squared. Her chin came up. Her eyes flashed. She'd been crying, but the tears seemed to have passed, because she looked in a rage.

"They are leaving, and right now, ahead of schedule, because Carl is covered with a rash this morning. He almost certainly has smallpox. You go too, Mr. Manning. Leave us. Save yourself."

Realizing the wagon train was deserting a helpless family made Wildcat so mad he almost drew his gun and started firing at the retreating wagon.

Of course the only wagon he could see was the last one. And a little girl was waving as she looked out the back.

Yep, that'd be plumb evil and pure stupid. He didn't consider himself to be either.

"Smallpox." His stomach sank at the word. He was the one who'd heard there were cases in the last trading post. He was the one who'd rushed everyone in the wagon train back, demanded they move on.

He was the one who'd found Carl Yates eating in the diner tacked on the back of the trading post, sharing a meal, talking and laughing with a man who had a cough.

Wildcat had dragged Carl out and gotten him going. It wasn't that easy because Carl had to lecture Wildcat on good manners and proper behavior.

Wildcat showed his appreciation for the lecture by not punching Carl in the mouth.

And now Carl had smallpox.

"I can't believe they left you." He looked after the train again, furious. "All alone out here with a sick husband and child."

"Cowards." Eleanor closed her eyes for a moment. Her jaw clenched so tight, he hoped she didn't break any teeth. "No, that's not fair. Smallpox is terrifying. I lived through a spell of it in my childhood. I had it. I remember the fear."

She said the words, but Wildcat could see the terrible effort it took for her to not call out to God to rain down fire on their heads.

"It's understandable that they left. Not kind. Not brave. Not right. But understandable. The wagon master refused to wait even at a distance. We got a late start out of Independence,

Missouri, and were slowed down by that week of hard rain west of Fort Kearny and flooding on the Platte River. We had more breakdowns than usual, he said, so we're going to be risking a late crossing as it is. We—they might not make it through the Rocky Mountains before the snow flies if they don't press on."

She almost kept the bitterness out of her voice. But he saw those eyes, that jaw. Her fists were clenched until her knuckles were white. She was furious and scared.

She stopped talking and almost panted for breath. Wildcat waited. She deserved to have her say, and he'd give her that.

The coughing broke through the brittle silence. Her head snapped around.

Turning his horse toward the wagon, he rode up, dismounted, lashed the lead horse to the wagon wheel, and headed for the back end.

"No, stay back." Eleanor rushed up and grabbed his arm. She pulled him back, and it worked only because he was turning anyway. She had a good arm for such a little thing. Blond like her little girl. Though Grace's hair was flyaway, white and fine, while Eleanor's made a thick braid of burnished gold that fell to her waist.

She was dainty, no more than five and a half feet. A whole head shorter than Wildcat. And she was slender but full of strength—add in determination. Her eyes were a rich, bright shade of brown that always made him take a second look.

Nothing like his black eyes and raven dark hair earned from his Shoshone ma.

Now, she seemed to be trying to overpower him. And the heck of it was, she was doing it to protect him.

He cut through any nonsense, any debate. "I've had smallpox. I've got scars but none on my face or not enough to mention.

It swept through a town I was in back East the first year I went back there, and I got hit hard, but I survived. I'm not likely to be in any danger, and you need help."

His eyes lowered to where she held his arm. "Now, let loose of me, and let's see what we can do to help your man."

And calling Carl "her man" was a good reminder of why he shouldn't enjoy that hand on his arm one speck more than necessary.

CHAPTER THREE

———◆•◆———

Eleanor boosted herself up to climb into the back of her covered wagon. Her hands shook, and she faltered. Then a strong grip around her waist lifted her in. She glanced back at Mr. Manning.

"Thank you." Then she turned back to Carl. Grace was at his head, curled up in a ball, sleeping, pressed against the front of the wagon. She was ten years old and a sharp-witted girl who'd learned the harsh ways of the frontier along with everyone else.

She knew what it meant to be left behind.

The only other folks who'd stayed behind had been buried.

Grace had been up most of the night tending her father. Eleanor and Grace had taken shifts, but Carl had tossed and turned. Any true, deep sleep was impossible.

When the other wagons had begun rolling, Grace had crawled into the wagon and stayed there. Now she'd fallen asleep.

It seemed to Eleanor that it was an act of hopelessness.

And for the first time this morning, Eleanor had some hope, all because one man had stayed behind and said he'd help.

Climbing into the tight confines of the wagon through the back, Eleanor saw Carl's eyes were wide open.

Her gasp came so loud that it pulled Carl out of the odd, dazed restlessness that seemed like he wasn't fully awake.

"What is it?" His voice broke. It was raspy and soft, as if he couldn't draw in enough breath to speak any louder. For a moment, his gaze was clear and knowing. It was the first time he'd been fully awake since this day had begun.

"I—I am sorry." She couldn't tell him the white of them had gone blood red. "The rash is worse."

Were these bloodshot eyes part of smallpox? She just didn't know.

Well, she did know. Because the ugly rash was spreading, and each spot was getting bigger with each passing hour, and the knowledge that there'd been smallpox at the trading post...there was every reason to believe that's what he had. The blood red eyes must be part of it.

Eleanor forced her face to a bland expression, hiding the horror of what she saw in Carl's eyes. "Let's see if we can get your fever down."

At her gasp, Mr. Manning leaped in beside her as sleek and fast as his nickname. She'd heard him called Wildcat.

He pushed her forward so she was near Grace. There was room for only the basin of cool water between her and Grace's sleeping form. Eleanor dipped a cloth in the basin and wrung it out.

Mr. Manning rested one of those strong hands on Carl's forehead, right where Eleanor wanted to press the cool cloth.

Irritably, she wondered if the man had to check for a fever himself, as if he didn't take her word for it. She hated the anger, directed at the only man who'd offered to help, and she prayed for forgiveness and self-control.

Then Mr. Manning eased back. She pressed the cloth to Carl's cheek, then his forehead, then his neck.

Carl seemed to fade away once he felt the cloth. Not awake, not asleep, but that in-between world he'd been living in for the last three days of his fever.

Eleanor said quietly, "Grace and I were in here with him all night, and Grace tended him most of the last two days while I drove the wagon."

Looking at her daughter, she said, "I'd send her outside to stay away from danger, but she's exposed. There's no sense pretending different. No sense taking drastic steps to avoid her father at this point."

Eleanor spoke and did her best to make it easy and calm when she wanted to scream.

But Mr. Manning, the man she'd probably choose to scream at, was their only hope. From terror, she'd veered directly to believing that with him here they had a chance.

And for that, just that chance, for the strength that grew in her backbone, the breath she now could draw in without wanting to scream it out. . .and whether Carl lived or died, whether any of them survived. . .for this one chance. . .she would praise God in heaven for Wildcat Manning every day for the rest of her life.

She wrung out the cloth and spoke quietly. "God bless you, Mr. Manning. Thank you for staying with us. Thank you for your courage."

Nodding, Mr. Manning said in an equally quiet voice, "When I had this, I was an adult. You said you had smallpox as a child. Do you remember all the details of this disease?"

"I remember a bit. I was five. Most of what I remember is, I suppose, talk I heard afterward. I have only a few clear memories. And of course, a few pockmarks scarring my neck and chest and. . .well, all over. They aren't bad like some folks."

He scooted back, as if he wanted as much space between her

and himself as he could manage in this tight place.

"There were a few—" He stopped as if he hated what he had to say, and Mr. Manning was known for being fearless and plainspoken to a fault.

Eleanor braced herself.

———————

He remembered a few cases like this. Especially the red eyes. A terrible version of smallpox. They'd called it red pox or bleeding pox. The doctor had some five-dollar word for it. Hem-something. Hemor-age smallpox? That wasn't quite right.

The name of it didn't make any difference. What it meant was, Yates was going to die—and die fast. That was the long and short of it. The ones whose eyes turned red like this were bleeding inside. They died within days, while most of the cases were strung out over a couple of weeks with the chance they'd beat the ugly illness.

Wildcat had never seen nor heard of a single patient surviving who had the bleeding pox.

Tending Yates wouldn't matter one speck. They'd do better to spend their time digging a hole.

He forced himself to go on, not sure if he should. "The red in his eyes, it means he's got a mighty serious type of smallpox."

He fell silent, feeling almost like the words rammed into a wall. He couldn't stand the look that was on her face. Grief. Already grief, and then that wiped away by denial.

"We'll have to care for him diligently then." She turned her back to him, wrung out her cloth. Yates tossed his head and moaned, and Eleanor shushed him and followed after him with the cloth.

"I'll get more water from the stream." A bucket hung from a nail on the inside of the wagon. "Then I'll get some breakfast on. I'll spell you caring for him while you eat. I got a deer, and I'll butcher it after you're done with your meal so we can make some broth and try to get your husband to eat."

Eleanor didn't look at him. Almost as if by giving her such bad news, he was the problem.

Well, women were notional. All folks were, really. If she needed someone to blame for this, and she couldn't bring herself to blame her half-wit husband, though honestly going to a diner and sharing a meal hadn't oughta get a man killed, then fine enough. He'd take the blame. He had the broad shoulders to bear it.

And Eleanor needed a pair of broad shoulders, for a fact.

CHAPTER FOUR

———◆◆◆———

The funeral began with Grace, in her beautiful little-girl voice, singing "Come Thou Fount." Grace had always held a tune as perfect and true as a golden sunrise.

Eleanor stood in silent misery, listening to the crystalline music as Mr. Manning shoveled dirt onto Carl's shrouded body. Her eyes burned with unshed tears. The song ended on a sob.

Eleanor pulled Grace close to her side and let her cry without trying to comfort her. Where could they find comfort? There was none anywhere in this harsh land.

The sobbing was the only sound that broke the silence...except for the shoveling.

For three days she'd fought for Carl's life. Three wretched days, all the hours there were. Coaxing broth and water down his throat in tiny sips. He couldn't take much.

The dry scratch as the shovel dove into the mound of dirt, then the dull thud of dirt hitting the grave, was like a madman screaming in her ear. It made no sense, but she thought the sound, mixed with Grace's sobs, would haunt her for the rest of her life.

Finally, the grave was full.

Mr. Manning said just above a whisper, "I'll leave you to your prayers for a bit, ma'am."

He walked away from the mound, shovel in hand. Taking care of everything like always.

Prayers?

It shocked her to realize that, since Carl had died, she hadn't uttered a single one.

As if she'd turned away from God.

Her arm tightened on Grace as she was stabbed with a reminder that Grace might yet catch this. They might still need a miracle.

"Let's each say a silent prayer, Grace. Though your song was like a prayer to me."

"Do we pray for Father's soul, Mama?" Grace called Carl *Father* because that was Carl's wish. And she normally called Eleanor Mother these days, but right now she went back to the more childish *Mama*, and it soothed Eleanor's aching heart to hear it.

"We believe a soul is lifted up to heaven at the time you die. Your father was a man of strong and true faith, and through faith we are saved. Our prayers can fly after your father, but he is in the arms of Jesus. Kneeling by the throne of God. Our prayers can only be sweet music to him and to God, much as your song. But he doesn't need our help now. He's walking with his Savior."

Grace nodded. "I think I'll pray for us then. That we can figure out what to do." She bowed her head.

And Eleanor thought how true that was. They needed those prayers. Including that Grace wouldn't get sick. And beyond that, they for certain needed to figure out what to do. Where were they going?

The wagon master was probably right. It was very late to try a crossing of the Rocky Mountains. And if Grace fell ill, it would be even later. They couldn't risk it.

The tears threatened, but she was too consumed with her worries to let them fall. She hadn't shed a single one since Carl's death. Instead, those tears hardened in her heart, in her belly, like jagged stones. And they cut and scraped. . .it felt right. Like she had something solid to remember Carl.

Pain.

--- * ---

Wildcat fed them. Hauled water. Urged sleep on them. For three days, he'd done everything practical to leave Eleanor free to tend her husband. Not that it was hard work. Meat was plentiful. No scouting the trail ahead. The horses grazed. Water was right at hand and plenty of firewood.

They were the easiest days of this trip so far.

If a man hadn't been dying and two females heartbroken, it would've been a vacation. He made no mention of that to Eleanor.

The woman hadn't slept more than a few broken minutes. She'd barely eaten. She was running on the ragged edge of collapse, and she either didn't know it or didn't care—he suspected it was the first.

He could barely stand to look at her anguish. Her pretty face had haggard lines in it. She didn't cry and, though he had no use for tears, that worried him some.

Her eyes burned with a fanatical determination to save Carl Yates. And the fact that it was hopeless only stoked the fire.

A tiny part of him knew no one—well, maybe his ma but certainly no other woman—had ever cared for him like that, and it stung. Well, no, *stung* was too strong a word. *Pinched.* That was better.

It made him wonder what his future held. But Wildcat wasn't a man to plan far ahead or to overly worry about anything. He figured he'd do what came next and let life unroll before him. He was a praying man, and beyond prayer and working hard to do what came next, he didn't see what else he could do or any point in fretting.

No, he saw a man who owned the love of a good woman, and it pinched.

Shoving the strange feeling aside, he smoked venison and put up enough food for a week.

He listened to Grace, a bright, spirited girl. Overly sheltered, in Wildcat's opinion. At her age, he was already hunting to feed his family. He was a crack shot too.

Now Eleanor coddled her, when to Wildcat's mind the tender care chafed and Grace wanted no part of it.

Grace had slept and eaten. Eleanor wouldn't take care of herself, but she'd care for her daughter.

All of this made Wildcat wonder, but it didn't worry him much. What did haunt his thoughts was that Grace was going to get smallpox.

Assuming—and he thought it was a good assumption—that Grace had caught this since Carl came down with it, Grace had about eight days. It'd taken five days for Carl to die from the first sign of fever to his last breath.

If Grace took two weeks for the sickness to hit, then they had eight days before they had to stop and care for a desperately sick little girl.

And the only place Wildcat knew of within eight days of here was his home. A home that was in about the exact wrong direction for folks heading for Oregon.

He would've taken them on west, except in eight days they'd be in the worst stretches of the Rockies. If they had to stop and care for a sick little girl for a week, they ran a good chance of being caught by winter. Wildcat could live through a winter in the high-up hills. He'd done it before.

He could build a shelter. Hunt for food. Even hike out across treacherous snow-covered trails in a land that stood on end more than it lay flat.

But Eleanor and Grace would be trapped in there. Wildcat considered if he could carry both of them up and down a mountain on his back and figured the answer was no.

One of them, maybe, but both? They'd be stuck on a mountaintop, and they'd be hard-pressed to survive until spring.

He needed to get moving, get Grace to his ma. Except no, he couldn't do that. He couldn't take a young girl with smallpox to his Shoshone people.

He'd kill them all.

He needed to get her somewhere with shelter. Where they could stop moving and care for her and hopefully save her.

The only place he could think of might well be the goad that broke through Eleanor's rigid control.

The break would come when she filled his backside full of buckshot.

The two of them came in from the lonely grave. Carl had died in the night. Wildcat had the grave dug before the sun was up, and they'd buried him with the breaking dawn.

And now, they needed to move. He hesitated as he studied Eleanor and tried to wrangle around in his head for words of comfort. Better maybe to just hitch up the team, toss them both bodily into the wagon, and drive.

Then Eleanor came up to him, her eyes still bone-dry and valley deep with pain. She said, "What are we going to do?"

"I've given it some thought, ma'am. And I can only think of one possible thing."

CHAPTER FIVE

———◆•◆———

S he saw it in his eyes.

He already knew what they had to do. She couldn't imagine what that was, because her thoughts were too muddled.

"Do you trust me to take care of you and Grace, Mrs. Yates?" he asked and stopped talking.

So different from Carl, who was a thoughtful man—educated, friendly. A man who liked to talk to her, talk through different ideas and hear her opinion, debate both sides, before deciding how to proceed.

It made something boil inside her that this man wanted her to obey without an explanation.

Then her head spun and her knees wobbled.

Grace cried out in alarm.

Without quite knowing how it happened, she was in Mr. Manning's strong arms being carried.

She couldn't scare her daughter. Grace had endured too much already.

A deep rumbling near her ear sounded like coming thunder. Her mind just wouldn't work. She couldn't make sense of the sound. Then she was lying down—on a hard surface but at least lined with thick blankets.

Another blanket covered her, and sleep pulled like an anchor on her ramshackle brain.

She felt Grace scrambling over her. Heard the sweet little-girl voice with such a gift for music. Then many sounds, lighter but just as fuzzy as the thundering voice. . .words of comfort. Grace lay down and wrapped her arms tightly around Eleanor, and it felt wonderful. Then a bit of time must have passed because she felt as if she'd slept then woken up when the world started jingling and rocking along.

It was like being held in her mother's arms, being rocked. Grace sang quietly with what might be bells, or maybe the metal of the harness, as background music.

The next thing she knew, she was waking up alone in a wagon that wasn't moving. She turned on her side, her mind still not fully awake, to see the sun setting out the back of the wagon. That meant they were heading east when they needed to go west?

But they were just sitting here. Eleanor heard the crackle of fire and smelled woodsmoke. She enjoyed the pleasant sounds and smells for a few long moments.

And then she remembered Carl was dead, and it struck her like an axe handle. She broke down and cried.

"Grace, wait." Wildcat stopped her from running to her ma when they heard the sobs.

Grace looked at Wildcat, torn nearly in half with the need to go to her ma and her natural inclination to obey her elders.

That gave Wildcat a moment to explain himself, which he didn't usually do.

"Your ma hasn't cried since your pa died. I think she needs to let her feelings out. She was so tired this morning. Hungry too, I reckon. But there was no chance to get any food into her before she fell asleep."

"I slept too." Grace's cheeks turned pink, as if embarrassed from all her talking.

"I was happy to see you two take a good long nap. You'd gotten a bit of sleep between spells of tending your pa, but your ma had barely slept in three days. She needed a day of solid sleep, and being bounced along on the back of a covered wagon didn't seem to be enough to wake her up.

"Now she needs to cry it out. Then we'll get some of this venison stew into her belly. She's gonna be mighty sad about your pa for a time. You too, most likely. But the worst will pass. I'll get you to my cabin. It's a mighty homely shack, but the roof doesn't leak. . .not much anyway. And it's got a stout door to keep the varmints out, the big ones anyway." He smiled. "You've been livin' mighty rough in this rolling tent of yourn." He pointed at the covered wagon. "My cabin'll be an improvement over a house that moves every day."

Grace nodded without responding. Wildcat wondered how long they'd be with him. He didn't see how they could go anywhere until spring. Maybe he could teach her to speak up a bit by the time they moved along.

If they moved along.

Wildcat had a notion about that too.

He served up a plateful of stew and tossed on the sourdough biscuits he'd made. He was a man who knew how to feed himself at a campfire.

Grace sat on a log he'd pulled up by the fire and ate her fill. He'd fed her jerky and hardtack when she'd finally roused a couple of hours ago. But the youngster needed solid food.

The twist, low in Wildcat's gut, was the only reminder he needed that Grace might be facing a bad sickness and he'd just spent one of the eight days he thought he had to roll them closer to his cabin.

He figured it for five long, hard days. He'd driven them hard today. Both women sleeping helped him push the team to cover a lot of miles.

When the sun was getting low in the sky, he knew he had to look for a water supply and shelter of some kind. If he drove on until full dark, they wouldn't be in a safe place to stop.

"I think she's done now." Grace was done too—her plate cleaned up, a smudge of stew on her cheek.

He pulled out his kerchief and dabbed her face clean. Was that right? Was he supposed to help her? She was old enough that she might be offended by someone wiping her face. He just didn't know.

It was done, so he fumbled his kerchief into a ball and wondered how a man could know the right and wrong of how to treat a girl child at this age. Heaven knew he'd never been around one.

His ma would know.

It struck hard at that moment how much he missed his ma. How much he wished she were here. If only he could go to her. Let her help him care for these two women. But the smallpox made that impossible at least for a time. And heading for his cabin put him a long way from the Shoshone winter hunting grounds. By going to his cabin, he'd made a decision that, should winter fall down hard, might well cut him and the Yates women off from anyone until spring.

Ah, Ma. He wished for her, prayed for her. And knew he had to stay away. To do otherwise might cost her her life, might cost her whole tribe their lives.

Kimama had been a gentle mother but wise and strong. She loved Wildcat's pa, but she knew him too. Had no foolish notions that he'd ever be a tender man, ever be around much.

They called Pa *Rock*, for the Rockies he loved. Rock Manning—his real name Ray, and Wildcat was honored to be named after him—was a mountain man. A good man as such wild men went. Sober and not given to consorting with women outside his marriage. He wasn't one to use ugly language, and he never raised a fist to Kimama, though he was known as a scrapper in the regular course of things. Rock had taught Wildcat all the things he needed to know about shooting, trapping, hunting, and fighting.

But true survival went deeper in the rugged mountains. And most of that, he'd learned from Kimama. Probably, truth be told, Kimama had taught Pa a lot too.

Pa had taught him to read sign. But the deeper skill of tracking came from his Shoshone ma and her people. They knew the mountains. Knew the way of all the animals that crept or crawled, swam or flew. They knew how to read the wind for approaching storms and sight trouble coming—whether wolves, a threatening snowpack that could lead to an avalanche, or a root or berry that could kill.

And she taught him to turn a buckskin into a warm coat. How to use an antler to tip a spear. How to turn a buffalo hide into a warm teepee. She'd guided him to the good food so abundant in the mountains. Nuts and berries. Roots and pine cones. She'd taught him how to rob a grouse nest for eggs and use a bow and arrow with deadly silent skill.

More than all of that, she'd taught him his faith. There'd been black robes, what the Shoshone called missionaries, who came to the village with the news of Jesus Christ. And they'd believed—Kimama with them. And she'd raised Wildcat in that faith. It was a faith that fit the harmony Kimama had learned in her high mountain range, and she'd passed it along in a way that Wildcat accepted fully.

Right now, if she were here, Kimama would know what to do. All Wildcat could do was stumble around, care for them, and keep them safe from the oncoming winter.

He wasn't looking forward to Eleanor finding out what he was up to. Her near to passing out from exhaustion had cut off any protest she might've made until they were hours and hours down the trail. Too far now to turn back.

But not too far for her to yell. Wildcat hunted for his backbone, stiffened it, then said, "Let's go get her then. The stew is ready, and I'd bet she's so hungry her belly button is rubbin' on her backbone."

Grace flashed him a shy smile. She was a solemn little tyke. And that had been true before her pa had sickened and died. She had that beautiful singing voice that seemed almost miraculous coming from such a little thing. When she sang, she came alive. Otherwise she tended toward silence.

And with her pa dying, now it was worse. So he cherished the smile without commenting on it, for fear it'd make her stop.

"We'll let her sit in the wagon and eat." Wildcat scooped up more stew and added a couple of biscuits. He poured a cup of coffee and said, "Bring the canteen. She'll be thirsty."

They went toward the silent wagon. No more sobbing, but Wildcat was afraid of what he'd find. Because not knowing whether or not to wipe a little girl's messy face now rose up as pure foolish pondering compared to facing a teary-eyed woman whose heart was ravaged with grief.

Planning to shove the plate at her and run, Wildcat squared

his shoulder, firmed his jaw, and rounded the back of the wagon.

———————

Eleanor smelled the food and heard the approaching footsteps.

Her mind was a jumble. Between the foolish tears. . .what a waste of time. . .and the hours of sleep, the grief, and her hunger, she was next thing to addlepated. No, not next thing to. She'd fully lost her wits.

And now someone was bringing her food.

She saw Grace first. Empty-handed but alive and smiling. Fine. Eleanor had vanished into sleep for the whole day, leaving her baby in someone else's care. But she was fine.

Next came Mr. Manning. What did they call him? Wildcat. That was it. It didn't suit him particularly, but she wasn't calling him by a nickname anyway, so she didn't have to manage that odd name.

He pressed a plate full of steaming hot food into her hands. Stew and biscuits. Then a cup of coffee. Grace had a fork and spoon. And she carried the canteen.

"Thank you." Her voice sounded like ten miles of rocky trail. She cleared her throat but didn't speak again. Instead, she reached eagerly for the canteen and drank deeply. The first swallow didn't make it to her belly. Or it felt like it didn't. Her mouth was so dry, her throat so parched that it seemed to soak the water up.

Mr. Manning unhitched the back of the wagon. The tightly drawn cover had been loosened already, and now he swung down the wooden back end, and Eleanor sat up and swung her legs over the edge—a much more comfortable way to eat.

There was plenty of water, and she drank until she could forget how long it had been since she'd had water.

The plate of stew came next. The first bite was hesitant. Not for fear of the food. Mr. Manning had cooked for them a number of times on the trip. He'd helped their wagon out more than the others. Eleanor knew Carl was a man of the city. He didn't know horses and wagons. He didn't know farming. But he was brilliant. He'd learned a lot about western ways on the trail west, and he'd have learned more once they reached Oregon.

But in the meantime, Mr. Manning had gotten them through a few times. More than a few.

Mr. Manning didn't speak. In fact, he picked up Grace as if she weighed nothing and set her beside Eleanor. It flickered through her mind that she didn't pick Grace up. She hadn't for years. Grace was a petite child. And thin, as everyone riding on a wagon across an entire nation was. It was a trip that stripped a person down to skin and bones.

Carl didn't pick Grace up either. It struck Eleanor as odd to see her half-grown daughter being picked up like a small child.

Mr. Manning had immense strength though—that was something Eleanor had noticed. The way his forearms corded when he picked up heavy logs and split them for the fire. The ease with which he carried buckets of water from a stream to the wagon.

Mr. Manning tugged on his hat and said, "I'll build up the fire. Call if you want more food."

He turned and walked the few feet to the fire. He'd built it small and hot and far enough from the wagon that there was no danger of fire.

Her horses grazed to the far side of the fire, picketed so they wouldn't wander off.

As she chewed, Eleanor wondered where they'd set up for the night. But even after a full day of sleep, she was still exhausted. And terribly hungry. She'd set aside questions until tomorrow. In the meantime, she'd pray for her little girl, begging God not to let the smallpox catch hold of her. And, if it did, that she'd survive.

CHAPTER SIX

"We're going where?" Eleanor's question nearly pierced Wildcat's eardrum.

She'd managed to get her meal eaten at least. Now he hoped the unsettling truth didn't make her belly uneasy.

"My cabin. My cabin near the Shoshone summer hunting grounds. The tribe will go south before the winter winds blow, so they won't be around. But we can make it through the winter in my cabin."

"I can't spend the winter in your cabin."

"Um...the word *can't* doesn't seem exactly right. Sure you can."

A low noise came from somewhere deep inside Eleanor. A mean noise. A noise that, for all his courage facing down a wounded grizzly or a rabid wolf, scared him a little.

"You're going to correct my grammar at a time like this?"

Wildcat's head itched at the strange question, and after he scratched a while, he asked, "What's grammar? Or do you mean grandma? An eastern way of saying it, maybe."

That noise again.

"Mr. Manning, I cannot—"

"Call me Wildcat. It's mighty strange being called mister all the time. Don't make sense to me."

"I can't call you Wildcat."

"If I tell you, you can, are you going to start talking about your grandma again?"

Eleanor's head dropped into her open hands.

"Do you want more stew? If you don't, I'll get your plate washed up and tend the camp." She'd set the plate and her tin coffee cup aside, so he took them without waiting for her head to come back up. She'd just start glaring and talking again. He decided he preferred her sitting like she was right now.

He had the fire built bigger. Not real big. A good woodsman knew how to build a fire hot and small. Less wood and less attention to the campsite.

A pot of heated-up water was ready so he could wash up. He was just about to open his bedroll and get settled in for the night—they had a long way to go tomorrow—when Eleanor came around the back of the wagon. She'd finally managed to crawl all the way out of bed.

"Mr. Manning—"

"Wildcat."

She gave him such a raging look, he was tempted to laugh. No idea why, but the pretty little thing acting like her temper made her the least bit threatening was just plain funny.

She pursed her lips as if trying to force her mouth to speak such a foul name as Wildcat.

Finally, drawing in a deep breath until her chest and shoulders lifted—and he probably shouldn't be looking at her chest—she said through clenched teeth, "Fine then. Wildcat."

He waited.

"I can't go—"

His hand came up fast, and he held it flat, palm facing her, to stop her.

She pursed her lips and breathed deeply again.

"It is improper for an unmarried woman and man to spend—to—that is, to live together in a cabin."

"Can't be helped."

Eleanor's shoulders sagged then. She might be out of air.

"Why aren't we going to Oregon?"

Wildcat's eyes flickered to Grace, who'd come around the wagon a bit slower than Eleanor but now stood quietly. The youngster didn't miss much.

He'd never considered other folks' feelings much. He was a straight-talkin' man. If he had something to say, he said it, and folks could like it, hate it, ignore it, or try to swing a fist. But that didn't make him change his blunt ways.

Now he took that quick look at Grace and wished he'd controlled his eyes better, because Eleanor noticed, and her brow furrowed. But that was all right. She just hadn't thought of what they had to do yet. Wildcat figured she'd get around to agreeing with him without him having to explain every bit of his decision. And he would have been glad to explain it.

But Grace.

Did he dare say right out loud what he was thinking? What had him making plans and pushing hard to carry them out?

Eleanor shook her head. It made Wildcat realize that she was still half-asleep. Still exhausted from her days at Carl's side. She really didn't know what he was doing. She hadn't thought of what lay ahead. At least not since she'd awakened.

"We couldn't go on west." Wildcat struggled to say what needed saying and not a word too many. "We'd've been deep in the mountains and pushing on toward fall. Your wagon train is taking a risk going this late, and we're a few days behind them. If. . .something. . ."

And dang it if he didn't glance at Grace again. It was like his eyeballs were completely out of his control. "If we had to stop. If something delayed us for a few days or even a couple of weeks—"

He saw the moment Eleanor figured out what he was saying and heaved a sigh of relief that he didn't have to talk about Grace getting sick right in front of her. If the youngster hadn't figured it out yet—or even if she had—there was no sense talking about what might happen. Best to pray for the best and prepare for the worst.

Wildcat wasn't sure where that was in the Bible, but it made sense to him.

"So we can't go west, and there's no sense going back east. Nothing there to go back to. We need a stopping place, and I could only think of one."

Eleanor nodded her head in the tiniest motion imaginable. Good thing Wildcat had a mighty good imagination.

"My tribe isn't all that close but for sure close enough to go to if we needed people for any reason." He couldn't think what reason that would be. He wasn't a man that needed much help.

Not to say they wouldn't help. He'd love to have his ma to hand. She'd be a source of comfort to the women—and strength if Grace got sick. But he wasn't letting anyone from the Shoshone tribe near a possible case of smallpox.

But he mentioned it, hoping it'd make Eleanor feel better to know others weren't so far away.

"Let's turn in for the night. We'll be starting early in the morning."

"I've slept all day." Eleanor paused to yawn, then shook her head. "But I think I'm tired enough to go straight to bed. I want to stretch my legs a bit, and then I'll sleep."

She looked at Grace. "Do you want to walk along with me?"

"I'll come too." Wildcat reached for his Sharps rifle—the finest gun ever made—and he'd found one before he'd headed for the mountains west to stay.

"Um, no, Mr. Manning...I mean Wildcat." Eleanor's cheeks turned a shade of pink that put Wildcat in mind of the wild roses that grew near his cabin.

"W–we need a moment." She stared at her toes as if she'd just discovered she had fifteen of them. Then she glanced up, met his gaze, and looked down again.

He figured it out.

"Oh, sure, ma'am...uh...that is, Eleanor." Blast it, he might be feeling a bit of heat crawling up his own face. "I'll just pour myself another cup of coffee."

And why was he babbling? She didn't care what he'd do. Only that she be allowed privacy, for the love of Pete, and that he keep his carcass here in camp.

Wildcat spun around to study the fire as if it might flare up and burn the wagon down. He heard Eleanor and Grace hurry away.

What was the matter with him? All sorts of things like this happened on the trail west. It'd never embarrassed Eleanor or him before.

Was it because they were alone with only Grace as company?

Wildcat got the camp set up for the night and was ready to climb into his bedroll beside the campfire when the womenfolk came back.

"Good night, ladies." He nearly dove under his covers. Then he listened to their few words of good night and heard them settle into bed in the back of the wagon.

It hadn't been as bad as he'd expected.

———— ···•·•··· ————

Eleanor was ready to grab her rifle and blast Wildcat Manning right off the seat of his horse.

Five days in the wrong direction.

She'd kept her mouth shut. . .well, mostly the whole time.

And then the cabin came into view.

A tinier structure she'd never seen. And her life hadn't been one of plenty.

Trying to figure out how to take back control of her life from this—this—this kidnapper roiled in her head and her belly. And she kept it all inside because of her fear about Grace. Five days since Carl had died.

He'd been sick for about five days before that, so ten days. She'd heard someone exposed to smallpox would show symptoms after a week or two.

That was now.

They'd know if Grace would be sick very soon.

And if she wasn't, then they could have gone on. Instead, they'd come here.

Now it was impossible to get through the Rockies before winter set in.

Which meant she was spending the winter in a one-room cabin with her daughter and this—this—this—Words failed her. None were enough. Ruffian. Hooligan. Half-wit. Mountain man.

She thought of her precious Carl. He was an educated man. He'd gone through high school and then had become a teacher. They'd married while he was teaching. Then he'd quit that to work at a newspaper. The work suited him, but he wanted to be in charge.

Eleanor worked cooking in a diner and made decent money, and they lived in the room above the kitchen for free and ate for free as part of her pay, so when Carl wanted to start his own paper, Eleanor had worked longer hours and supported him while he pursued that dream.

He was a wonderful writer.

The paper had failed, but Carl hadn't let it get him down, and he'd decided he might want to write a book. He worked at that while Eleanor tended the kitchen, and the diner owner let her stay late and come early and clean to earn more. She'd done odd jobs, taken in mending and a few other things to make ends meet.

When Grace had come, Eleanor had found she was allowed to keep the baby with her while she worked so Carl could have peace and quiet.

He'd gotten a few magazine articles published, and the book came along nicely, but before he'd finished it, a dream had awakened in him to go west. He thought there'd be great stories to be told out west. He'd awakened a dream in Eleanor to have their own land, their own cabin. They'd live off the land and not need any money so she wouldn't have to work anymore.

And now her dream was dead along with her husband, and she was moving into a cabin with a man who wore his hair pulled back and tied with a leather thong. He shaved about once a week, and it looked as if he'd missed a week or two. He didn't share his thoughts. He took charge and didn't even consult Eleanor. He was in all ways the exact opposite of Carl.

Oh, Wildcat knew the mountains. She knew he'd be able to find them food and keep the cabin warm. How much wood could it possibly take to keep such a small building warm?

He lightened her load, she'd give him that.

But he was no Carl Yates, and her heart ached to think of

her dreamer husband gone too soon, and here she was stuck in this wilderness with a barbarian.

She fought down the urge to scream and, yes, maybe shoot Wildcat Manning's backside full of buckshot, as he rode horseback ahead to his cabin. He glanced back over his shoulder and smiled.

"We made it. We're home."

She managed not to growl at him as she brought the wagon along.

The cabin stood in a clearing.

One room with a shanty built over the front door. One room? How could she spend the winter in a cabin with one room with a man not her husband?

It didn't bear thinking about. So, of course, she could think of nothing else.

Except Grace.

Under all the upset, probably causing the upset, was her worry for Grace.

At least they'd found a—what had Wildcat called it?

Then she remembered.

A stopping place.

This was biblical, wasn't it? To follow the path God laid before her. To follow His will, not her own? Or was this the story about wandering into the wilderness for forty years as punishment for lack of faith? She needed to pull out her Bible and read just as soon as she wasn't falling asleep before her head hit the pillow, as if she had a pillow.

She pulled up close, unable to speak, for fear of what would come pouring out of her mouth.

Wildcat rode on past the house and turned his brown gelding loose in a small corral built of saplings strapped together with woody vines. With the saddle and bridle off, the horse shook its head and whickered, then lay down and rolled in the dirt as if to wipe away the feel of the leather.

Eleanor's horses were sturdier, small draft horses with no breed she knew of. One a mostly white, blue roan, the other brown with a long cream-colored mane and tail.

She knew they'd be enjoying the freedom in just a few minutes, and, she had to admit, it would be because Wildcat would remove the harnesses, turn them loose, make sure they were fed and watered.

Yes, he was a good man. Just so very different.

Then he came to the wagon and reached up for Grace, who reached down for him. He lifted her down while Eleanor clambered down from the high wagon seat.

She felt a twinge when she heard Wildcat's kind voice talking to Grace and Grace's sweet reply. They'd come to love each other in these few days. Grace turned to Wildcat with all her questions, when she used to turn to Eleanor.

Then Wildcat's voice cut through her jealous musings.

"Grace has a fever."

CHAPTER SEVEN

———◆•◆———

Wildcat lifted Grace and cradled her in his arms.

Eleanor came rushing toward the back of the wagon.

"No, go get the door open. Grab my bedroll by the door and spread it on my bedstead."

He walked fast as he talked. And he examined Grace's flushed face. He'd known from the minute he saw her that she was sick. Then he'd asked how she felt and rested his hand on her forehead.

Grace had smallpox.

His jaw set in a tight grim line, he moved fast, but Eleanor moved faster. She had his blanket and was inside. But the time he got Grace in, Eleanor was spreading the blanket on his bed. Dust everywhere. But there was no time to tidy up now.

He lay Grace down. "I'll get water and get a fire going." He stepped out the door and got his canteen. "In the meantime, try and get as much water into her as you can."

Then he jerked his kerchief out of his back pocket. "Bathe her forehead with this. I'll set things up."

And set things up he did. For a couple of hours he worked, twisting every bit of speed out of every move he made.

Eleanor stayed at Grace's side, talking to her, trying to keep her fever down with cool water, and urging her to drink.

Wildcat started with prayer and kept asking God to spare Grace while he built a fire. He'd hauled extra wood in the wagon today because he knew they'd get home late, and he wanted a fire without having to chop wood. He'd need more wood very soon, but for now he was glad he could make short work of getting flames crackling in the hearth.

Then he rushed to the spring to get water. His bucket as well as his cook pot were thick with dust, so he had to wash them out. He soon had water heating.

Next, he knew right where to go to get willow bark. Gathering the bare minimum—he'd get more later—he brought it back and steeped the fever-reducing tea.

Then he poured the hot water into a kettle, set it to the back of the fireplace, and started dinner. He'd laid in supplies at the last trading post, the one with smallpox, before he'd rushed everyone out of the place. He had flour, sugar, yeast, and coffee. He'd managed a few cans of peaches and a few other favorites. But he had to travel light, so there'd been little in the way of variety.

He got stew bubbling, then went to unhitch Eleanor's team and settle them in the corral. He hauled in most of what was in the wagon, chopped wood to keep the fire going all night, and fetched more water from the chilled spring so it was always cool for Grace's face.

He was hours trying to get the worst of the dirt driven out of his cabin. He was a tidy man, and he would've cleaned up once he got here, but usually he was a few days about it. Now he wanted it as clean as possible for Grace's sake.

There were other remedies and medicines in the forest. Once Eleanor and Grace were eating, with Eleanor urging bits of the sauce from the stew into Grace, and the cabin clean, and more willow bark tea brewing, Wildcat went out to find more medicine. While he was out, he brought down a couple of rabbits. He'd set snares as soon as possible so he could save on bullets.

Through all of this, Eleanor stayed at Grace's side, kneeling on the floor by the bed, wringing out the cloth he'd found among her things, then pressing it to Grace's forehead, cheeks, and neck.

Such a devoted mother. Eleanor's eyes had flashed with pure terror when Wildcat told her Grace had a fever. But she hadn't wavered. She'd fought down the fear to hide her worry from Grace and kept her attention on her child, as she'd done with Carl.

She was the finest kind of woman.

Thinking that, as he ran to do three days' worth of work before he slept the first night, he felt the ache in his heart for his ma. Ah, how he wished Kimama was here. She'd keep calm. She'd be thinking. If there was a treatment to be had in nature, she knew of it.

He hoped he was doing all he could, but he would've been so happy to have that wise, steady woman at his side.

But to bring her here was to ask her to die. He wouldn't do it.

The sun sank behind the mountains. He brought more tea to Grace, who dozed off and on. But when she was awake, she spoke clearly if a bit fretfully. The fever wasn't high enough to torment her.

Two days or three for the spots to pop out.

Then a day more to see if it would be the awful kind of red pox. Then, if she didn't have that, another week at least to let the illness run its course.

And Eleanor had barely rested from staying up so long caring for Carl.

He knew she'd let him do all the work to care for them, except tend Grace. But she couldn't do it, not again. Not so soon after her most recent ordeal.

He planned to sleep on the ground out by his shanty of a barn. It was big enough to keep his horse inside with room for a feed bunk, and he put up a couple of stacks of prairie hay once it dried in the fall.

It was time to be doing that. Well, another week wouldn't matter. The tall blue stem and grama grass would still be there. Snow would come but not quite yet. They had time.

It was at that moment he realized he had another mighty big job to do. He had to build on to his cabin. He couldn't spend the winter in a shanty-barn with no fireplace. And he couldn't stay in that one room cabin with Eleanor.

And he saw no way to avoid spending the winter with her.

With a silent shake of his head, he squared his shoulders, lifted his chin, and added to the long, long list of things that needed to be done before snow drifted to the top of his cabin.

And none of that could be dealt with while Grace was so sick.

But it'd get done. Wildcat didn't know any other way but straight ahead. So that's how he'd go.

Just as soon as he did one crooked thing.

He had to trick Eleanor into letting him take a turn with Grace. And it probably had better be tonight before she got so sick Eleanor wouldn't be able to draw herself away.

Eleanor was battered still from Carl's death. She felt like a wire strung so tight the smallest pluck sent her vibrating. A single harder hit would snap her in two.

She knelt by her precious girl. One child. That's all they'd been blessed with.

Grace now fought for her life. Eleanor did everything she could to keep her little girl's spirits up. Grace had watched her father die only days ago, and she knew full well she had the same disease.

It took only a short time before Eleanor realized while she was battling to control her terrible fears for Grace's sake, her daughter was doing the same thing for her ma's sake.

"Your fever isn't very high. Not as high as your father's was. You'll have a milder case than he did."

"I'm going to be fine, Ma. I'm sorry for the nuisance of coming down with this. And I'm sorry to cause you such worry. It doesn't feel as serious as Father's. Remember, his fever was high right at the beginning. He wasn't able to talk to us, not rationally."

Wildcat handed her a cup of steaming tea. "It'll bring the fever down. Willow bark tea."

Eleanor didn't have the strength to challenge him on what exactly this was. And he seemed sure. With some misgivings, she coaxed Grace to drink every drop.

Then Eleanor had a tasty stew set before her along with a bowl of thick broth for Grace. Wildcat muttered, "Starve a fever and feed a cold. That's what I've been taught, so no heavy food for Grace. Plenty of water though, and the tea every few hours."

It was surprisingly good, with chunks of meat and vegetables that weren't exactly what Eleanor was used to. Deer meat, most likely. But there hadn't been much in the way of vegetables left in her wagon. Had Wildcat stored things at the cabin before he'd left? It was well seasoned and cooked to a perfect tenderness. Eleanor hadn't even watched him cook it.

And now it was handed to her. Carl had never done such a thing.

He would have, he just didn't know how.

She shoved her questions and doubts aside and saved her energy for tending her child.

"Thank you. This is delicious. I appreciate it so much."

Then she kept urging spoons full of broth on Grace and getting as much water into her as she could. Finally, Grace lapsed into a deeper sleep.

"Eleanor." Strong hands rested gently on her shoulder. "I've spread a blanket by the fire. Lay yourself down a while. I'll watch over your sleeping angel and wake you if she stirs."

"No, no, I don't dare." Somehow, she was on her feet. Her knees ached. She swayed. A solid arm came around her shoulder.

"Come now. It's nearly dawn. An hour of sleep will keep you going. And if she stays sleeping longer, you may get more rest than that. She's only at the beginning of this. You have to keep up your strength for when it turns."

He didn't say turns…what? Turns into that red pox he'd talked about. What Carl had? Yes, she'd need her strength.

"I know you're right. But you need sleep too."

"I sleep, Eleanor."

She found herself guided to a pallet he'd made up on the floor and wondered if he'd really slept. It seemed as if he'd always been there with fresh water and food. But then she'd paid very little attention to him. As she stretched out on the floor, her head was swimming with exhaustion. A blanket settled over her and tucked around her as if she were a child.

CHAPTER EIGHT

————◆◆◆————

The pox erupted on day three of the fever. It sickened Eleanor to see so many of the ugly little blisters. Grace clawed at them, and Eleanor battled to keep Grace's hands from them.

"Don't scratch." How many times had she said that? Dozens. Hundreds maybe. Grace was in a stupor, and aside from mutterings that made little sense and moans of pain, she hadn't spoken much since yesterday.

————◆————

On day seven, Wildcat, who'd been seeing to all their needs, even seeing to it Eleanor got at least a bit of sleep every day, said, "She doesn't have the red pox."

He'd almost said it three days ago. Then he'd fought hard to keep his mouth shut two days ago. Yesterday had been near impossible. Only the terrible fear that he'd say something and get Eleanor excited when she was so exhausted kept him silent.

But no more.

Today he was sure. "Hemorrhage pox, I think they called it. She'd show signs by now. In fact, Carl showed signs the first day the rash broke out. Grace has been covered by the rash for four days. She definitely has the less serious kind."

"You mean the kind that is only deadly half the time?" Eleanor let bitterness seep into her voice.

"Hush now, Ellie." He rested his hand on her back, wishing he could hold all her fears. "My ma, her Shoshone name is Kimama, always said the sick ones can hear, or she believed it was at least possible they could. Don't speak of things that are discouraging to Grace."

Eleanor rinsed her rag and nodded. In the moment when Eleanor turned her attention away, Grace scratched at her face in her feverish sleep. Eleanor caught her daughter's hands and held them in one of hers while she worked.

Wildcat saw several of the pox broken open. They were such ugly blisters, each with a little dimple at the center after they were a few days old. When one of them broke, Wildcat saw a wound so deep it was like the blisters were coming from deep in her body.

She had them the worst on her face, but she had them everywhere. Wildcat didn't watch when Eleanor bathed her under her clothes, but he'd seen her arms and neck. And she had pox inside her mouth. He wondered if she had them all the way inside. On her heart and stomach, her brain and backbone. They seemed like wicked little sores that might reach that far inside.

———————————

On day ten the fever broke.

Wildcat didn't wake Ellie to tell her. Plenty of time for that in an hour or two. And the fever might come back up. So the worry then would return. For now, he let Eleanor get in four solid hours. Grace was sleeping comfortably when Ellie stirred then surged out of the covers and rushed to Grace's side. Every time she'd awakened, she'd done this. As if terrified that Grace would die while Ellie slept.

Every time, the sweet girl was still breathing.

When Ellie got to Grace's bed, Wildcat had been kneeling at Grace's side. He scooted back and said, "She's going to make it. The fever is down."

"She's beaten it?" Ellie turned to Wildcat.

He'd noticed that she'd become more and more dependent on him. Every decision he made. When she wanted something, she asked him, not even attempting to get it herself.

When she had a worry, she'd tell him as if asking for him to handle whatever was bothering her or sometimes to give her permission to handle it herself. He'd known her all the way out on the wagon train, and this wasn't like her.

Between exhaustion and worry, she'd become sluggish, her brain barely capable of wringing out a cloth or restraining Grace's fretful hands. It was even mostly Wildcat's job to lift the child high enough so she could sip willow bark tea and water and broth.

Now she was asking him if it was all right to hope.

It twisted Wildcat's heart to see this strong woman brought so low. And as she'd depended on him, he'd stopped thinking of her as Eleanor and begun to call her Ellie. She hadn't complained about it. He hoped she didn't start, because it suited her.

"Starting right now, you can set aside your worry and just get her to eat and drink. To keep her from scratching until those pockmarks go away. Because the worry she'll—"Wildcat cut off what he was saying and glanced at Grace. Sleeping but maybe able to hear. "Because she is going to get well. She needs time to heal, but all other things you're fretting over, you can stop now."

Then he grinned, and Ellie grinned then smiled wide. They

knelt there, side by side, grinning like fools, then Ellie flung her arms wide and grabbed him around the neck and hugged him. He laughed and stood with her still clinging to him and swung her around in a circle.

In the pleasure of the moment, he didn't quite realize just how close he held her.

"Ma? What's going on?" Grace spoke from where she lay, with a slurred voice but clear and more alert than she'd been for near a week.

Ellie gave a gentle cry of delight, let Wildcat go, and sat on the side of the bed to talk to her daughter.

"I've got chores," Wildcat said as he ran outside, away from a moment that he didn't think Eleanor had even noticed. But Wildcat sure had. He'd held a beautiful woman in his arms. She'd been all gleaming happiness and joy. It was a pure pleasure.

Wildcat had noticed he had a woman in his house. Of course he had. But any concern he'd had about that involved figuring out a place for them all to sleep. His cabin was one room. Grace and Ellie would need their own. It might not hurt for him to have one too. That'd been his thinking.

But no more.

He had a woman, and while she'd laughed and hugged him, while he'd whirled her around, he'd decided he was keeping her.

A widow of two weeks.

Wildcat didn't figure it'd go down right with her. He didn't figure she'd fall right into line with his thinking. But they were getting married.

And they had to do it fast, before his Shoshone people and the Black Robe parson who lived in their village headed to their winter hunting ground. He had to figure out just the right way to tell her that this was her new home permanently.

CHAPTER NINE

———◆◆◆———

Getting over smallpox was a slow business, but Ellie... She stopped at the name. She'd come to think of herself as Ellie. That's what her folks had called her as a child, but Carl had said her name was elegant and he loved saying the whole thing, Eleanor.

Being called Ellie, well secretly she loved it. It touched a sweet spot in her heart. And in some ways, it was a break in her life. An after. The before was Carl, the after was alone with her daughter. A new name gave her a way to protect wonderful memories.

Shaking off the thought, Ellie considered Grace's slow healing. The fever broke a week ago. She was shaky, but Grace was regaining her strength and showing interest in this strange little house they were living in.

And she was restless. Restless enough she'd gotten out of bed and insisted on getting dressed and sitting at the table.

Eleanor had given her a small breakfast of bread soaked in warm milk, and she'd eaten every bite to the sound of a hewing axe—Wildcat working as he did every daylight hour.

"Can I just go outside for a while, Ma?"

"Aren't you afraid a tree will fall on you?" She smiled at her daughter, fighting back the worry over the slow healing of those pockmarks. They'd get better, surely they would. Right now her face was badly scarred. Her beautiful little girl had to heal from these marks.

No, stop it. Sometimes survivors of smallpox were scarred. Ellie knew that; she'd seen it. But they lived. God had given her a miracle, and Ellie would not lament that it wasn't the exact miracle she'd hoped for.

The fact that she did lament was shameful, and when she became aware of her stomach twisting worry over the scars, she'd shake her head and stop. She'd go back to praising God that Grace had survived this dread disease.

"What is he doing today, Ma?" Grace had so many questions. She peppered Wildcat with them when he came in for meals.

"He's cutting down trees. He plans to build two bedrooms onto the cabin. He says we just won't fit in here, and there's no way to leave, no people except his Shoshone tribe nearby."

"But they're fine people, Wildcat said. We could go see them if we want to. We could even live with them for the winter instead of making Wildcat do all this work."

"Yes, we'd be safe with them. His ma is Shoshone. He said when you're up to traveling, we'll ride over and see them if the winter weather holds off." Ellie didn't want to go, and it wasn't because she was afraid of the Shoshone people. Wildcat trusted them, and Ellie trusted him. It was because a long ride, even in the mild weather, would be too hard for Grace.

"It's only September, Ma. It can't be winter."

Shaking her head, Ellie said, "It's hard to believe, but we're up really high and a fair piece north of where we lived. He said snow comes early and stays late up here. I believe him. But I think it might be best for you to avoid travel of any kind for now."

Ellie patted Grace's hand, noticing the scars. And the trembling. Grace was definitely not up to anything strenuous. Not until she'd fully regained her strength.

"Well, I'd love to meet his family. That should be so interesting." Grace was out of bed, sitting at the tiny table in the tiny kitchen in the tiny cabin. Ellie wished Grace would just take a few more days in bed, but Grace had insisted to the point that Ellie was afraid the upset would harm her.

She averted her eyes from the scarred face, and hands, and arms. Scars everywhere, so much worse than Ellie had expected. But Grace would heal. Surely she would. And these pockmarks would go away.

She wouldn't even think of them as scars, for heaven's sake.

Her daughter just wasn't fully healed. She would be fine and whole again if Ellie just kept her safe, made her rest.

Losing Carl had been hard and heartbreaking. To lose Grace on top of that was unbearable.

There, on the spot, Ellie took a silent vow to God that she'd protect her precious, fragile Grace with all her strength.

———◆———

The tyke needed fresh air and sunshine. Wildcat didn't figure she was up to chopping down trees, although Wildcat had done plenty of chopping at ten years old. He'd start her on splitting logs in a couple of weeks.

But she could carry kindling in and lend a hand while he set the walls in place.

She could groom the horses and check their hooves. She could hunt for walnuts and ripe berries and gather pine tips for oil. He could teach her how to set a snare for rabbits and how to fish in the stream. Plenty she could do, and she'd have fun every minute of it.

Staying to the house wasn't good for a youngster.

"Grace, you up?" He juggled an armload of wood so he could open the door and shove it as it dragged along the floor. He was mighty proud of the wood floor he'd laid in this one room. Eventually, he'd do it with the two new rooms too. Maybe over the winter when the snow was as deep as the rooftop.

They'd be living high, for a fact.

He tried to control his pride, sin that it was.

"Can you get the door closed? No sense letting flies in." He noticed Ellie had a restraining hand on Grace, who was up and dressed and looking fit if a little gaunted up.

Then Ellie rushed to the door and closed it while he stacked the split logs in the wooden crate he kept by the fireplace for just this purpose.

"How are you doing on the cabin?" Ellie sounded chipper and interested when he was mighty sure she'd like to run screaming out of here and not stop until she caught up with the wagon train.

But she was stuck with him. And he had to pick the right moment to tell her she was staying.

Forever.

She seemed like a reasonable woman, so she'd see they had no choice. But he didn't know much about women outside his tribe, and most of them let you know they were upset with you by drawing a knife and threatening you.

He liked that. He approved of anyone letting him know exactly how they felt. It saved him the trouble of guessing.

Ellie hadn't drawn her knife yet. He didn't think she even had a knife. It seemed unlikely, but he'd noticed many of the women on the wagon train didn't carry knives or guns.

It'd be a wonder if any of them survived.

"I'm ready to start raising the walls." He turned to smile at the womenfolk he'd corralled. "I can use a hand. The work goes a lot faster if you hold logs in place once I lift them, while I get the other side done."

"I'll be glad to help." Ellie turned to her daughter. "You'll be safe in here alone, won't you?"

"Both of you would be better. It's heavy work. Might be too much for just one of you."

"No, Grace isn't up to it yet. She's still shaky."

"She's probably shaky from not eatin' much for two weeks and not getting on her feet for just as long. Girl needs to be outside, bending and stretching, working up an appetite."

Ellie turned her eyes on him, wide with fear. "She can't do that. She's sick."

Wildcat studied Ellie's fear. That's what it was. Coddling the girl was wrong, he was sure of it. But he understood the inclination. Maybe gradually they could ask more of her.

"When the winter comes, every step outside will be hard work. Let her come outside and sit in the sun while it's shining. She may not be up to work, but she's beyond lying in bed all the day."

Ellie hesitated, but it worried him. He hated seeing Ellie hover like this. Then she said, "I guess being outside won't hurt her. For a short time, as long as it's warm."

Wildcat got Grace's coat off the hook. He looked around at all the things Ellie had unpacked from the covered wagon.

"It's nice to see all the things brought in and set out. My house has never looked so much like a home."

CHAPTER TEN

———◆●◆———

E llie let Grace do more than she probably should have. It was getting harder to protect her girl as she regained her strength.

The first day, she went out and sat in the sun on a flat-topped boulder. The second, she walked around, pet the horses, and even went back inside to sweep out the cabin.

The third day, she pushed Ellie hard, and Wildcat taught her how to wrap a thick rope around felled trees, then tie the rope to a saddle horn and drag in lumber while Wildcat and Ellie did the building.

By the end of the week, Grace was helping brace up the logs when Wildcat would put one corner in place, then turn to the other corner. He rigged things so the horse helped pull all the heaviest weight, and it wasn't too strenuous. Still, Ellie worried.

By the end of the second week, they'd had snow two nights and both rooms were up. He'd built the rooms so the fireplace was open to both of them and the main cabin. One good fire would warm the whole house. Once the roof was up and secure, he moved the bed into one of them for Ellie and Grace. Wildcat had been sleeping outside.

The fireplace was in the center of the wall, so he was putting two doors in, one to each bedroom, on either side of the fireplace. They'd have some privacy and good warmth. Ellie couldn't help but admire his skill at building.

"Grace, I cut more logs late last night, slender saplings. You heard where I was chopping."

"Sure, do you want me to bring them in?"

"Yes, they're what I'll use to lay a floor. So bring them up close and make a stack. That's a job I'll leave for the winter."

Grace went back to a job Ellie had decided wasn't too hard, while Wildcat worked on the door.

As her daughter went out, Ellie wondered how much Wildcat knew about the aftereffects of smallpox. The scarring was terrible, but Grace's health seemed decent.

"When you had this, how long did you take to heal all the way?"

Wildcat paused in his work to look at her. She saw such kindness in his eyes that it scared her. Why would that question make him want to be so careful and kind?

"I worry about her breathing. She struggled with it. Could her lungs have damage that she'll struggle with the rest of her life? Could she have damage to her heart? And if she does, might doing heavy work lead her to harm?"

Ellie held the door in place. It was swung open into the new room Wildcat would sleep in. He stood in the open doorway and studied her for too long. She wanted to know everything he could tell her. At the same time, she dreaded any bad news he'd add to her worries.

He gave his head a tiny shake, then turned back to his work. The man wasn't one to ever shirk when there was a job to be done.

"Let me finish this last hinge, then I've got something to talk to you about." He worked, tightening the leather strip that would keep the door in line.

When he was done, he set his tools aside and surprised her by stepping into the room and closing the door. Why would he do that?

It occurred to Ellie that she'd never really been alone with him. The wagon train was always around them, then Carl, finally Grace.

Did he have terrible things to say that he didn't want Grace to hear? She wished she'd never asked.

"I'll be calling these rooms done by the end of the day. Laying the floor is a job for the winter when it's too hard to get outside."

"It's a nice addition to your cabin. Thank you for doing all this work to make a place for Grace and me."

He was a nice man. Hardworking. His hair had grown long enough most days he pulled it back with a thong at the base of his neck. His eyes were black as midnight. His Shoshone heritage shown through. He was tall, much taller than Carl, and broad shouldered from long hours of hard work.

"That's what I'm hoping I've done, Ellie."

"What you've done?" Ellie wasn't sure what he meant, and Wildcat wasn't a man to talk in circles. He said few words, only the ones that needed to be spoken. And he was direct. Nothing like Carl, who liked to debate and discuss.

"Yes, I hope you can see a place for yourself, Ellie. Because..." He looked straight into her eyes as if searching for something inside her. "Because I want you to stay with me for good. I don't see a way to spend the winter together in here with you if we're not married."

"M–m–married? But I was just widowed barely two weeks ago. I can't—"

"Don't say no." He cut her off. "Don't say you can't. You're not ready to find a new husband yet. How could you be? But a woman alone doesn't make it out here. And I can't get you through the mountains to Oregon until spring. And once you get there, you'll most likely have men lining up to marry a pretty woman like you."

"I come as a set, and Grace may have problems all her life."

"Scars, I reckon. But maybe they'll do some healing yet. But they matter none to me. Grace is pure of heart and voice. She's a delight. You coming as a set is the best part of you marrying me."

"Wildcat, I—I—I—"

He leaned down and kissed her. The surprise of it froze her in place. Then his arms came around her waist and pulled her close.

It was so strange to let a man touch her this way. Confusing and unpleasant and. . .pleasant. She really hadn't touched Carl much for a long time. He wasn't a vigorous man and rarely came to her in the way of a husband. That was one reason they'd never had more children. He'd rather talk about ideas than feelings. Being held this way was wonderful. As if she'd been thirsty and Wildcat offered her a fountain that quenched her heart and soul.

He raised his head, and she realized she was standing on her tiptoes as he moved away. As if she was chasing after him. Oh, not as if. She was definitely chasing after him. Her arms were around his neck. He was no stranger. She'd known him for months on the wagon train and considered him a friend. Then she'd been as good as living with him since Carl died.

She knew his character. His respectful treatment of her and Grace. His hard work, most of it done strictly to take care of the Yates women. A man she liked and respected. Add a kiss to that mix, and she could see being with him. It could work.

It wouldn't be love, not like the love she'd shared with Carl with all his dreams and ideas. Carl had been an extraordinary man.

But for very common-sense reasons, she could see herself being with Wildcat for the rest of her life.

"Where would you go? Especially after spending a winter here with me. You'd never be able to admit you did such a thing. And you'd have to tell Grace to lie so no one would know."

Ellie opened her mouth to tell him the idea had merit. "I think—"

"When I brought you here..." He stopped her from talking, almost as if he didn't want her to say yes. Except that wasn't it. He was afraid she'd say no. "I knew we'd have to marry and do it soon. My people will leave to migrate to lower lands soon, and we need to see the missionary who travels with them to bless our union."

"Wildcat, I—"

"We could be married in the way of my people, the Shoshone." He interrupted again. "But I think it would be better for a parson to say the marriage vows."

She grinned.

He stopped talking. Then he said, "You're going to say yes."

Nodding, figuring he couldn't talk over that, she watched those black eyes spark with happiness. He still had his arms around her, so he swooped her up and twirled her in a circle. Then, lowering her slowly to the floor, he kissed her again, deeply, with a joy she'd never felt from a kiss before.

"We'll go in the morning. We can make the trip and be home in one day if we start early. And we can take a few long breaks so Grace doesn't tire out, though I think she's feeling much stronger now." He kissed her again. "She's mending, Ellie. She made it through."

At that, Ellie hugged his neck tight and drew his head down for another kiss—one that was her idea this time.

They were still kissing when they heard Grace ride up on her horse.

Ellie pulled away, shocked at herself. "What are we doing?"

"We're getting married. Tomorrow." Wildcat held out his hand.

Ellie reached with hesitant movements. As she slid her hand into his, she said, "I admire and respect you, Wildcat. And clearly I like kissing you."

"I'd say that's right." He grinned and arched his brows.

"But Carl hasn't been gone long enough. I don't feel right marrying so soon. I'm afraid. . ." She drew in a deep breath, hesitant to say what was on her mind. "If we're to marry, we have to be honest with each other, don't we?"

Wildcat's eyes widened, and he looked scared for the first time since she'd met him. "I'm not sure that's necessary, no."

Ellie thought of all the long talks she'd had with Carl, discussing everything that came into their heads. Wildcat was a quieter man. No doubt about it.

"Yes, it's necessary." She went on quickly, not wanting a debate over their mutual honesty or the lack thereof. "And because it is, I have to tell you that I fear thoughts of Carl will be between us. It really is too soon for me to remarry."

She shook her head as she thought how outrageous it was to marry this fast. But the cabin and the winter—it was impossible for them to make any other choice than to marry.

"I said yes. And I mean it. But you could be hurt by me if my thoughts go to another man. Or if I want to speak of him, especially to Grace. I want you to think whether this is the right decision for you. We could put off the marriage for a time, somehow."

She wasn't sure how. But surely they could think of something.

Wildcat said, "I've thought of it. I'm ready. If you accidentally call me Carl, I'll keep my poor delicate feelings to myself and try my best not to cry."

Ellie snorted, and then she laughed out loud. "I appreciate that. I felt I needed to speak of it, but if you're sure, then yes. I'll marry you."

He grabbed her and kissed her hard and fast, then stepped away and said, "Let's go tell Grace the good news."

CHAPTER ELEVEN

———•◦•———

G race slid down from her horse when they came around the cabin. Her eyes flickered between the two of them, paused to look at their clasped hands, then flickered between them again.

The little girl might not like a new pa. She might have the same confused feelings as Ellie had. He thought of the joke he'd made of it with Ellie, but if Grace didn't want to make a family here with him, it'd hurt. It bothered him that he came a definite second place to that worthless Carl Yates.

Didn't these two know Wildcat would take care of them a whole lot better in this frontier life than Carl Yates ever could? Hadn't they noticed in the last two weeks when he'd worked himself to the bone taking care of them?

Wildcat decided it was Ellie's job to share this news. He'd been dragging her along behind him. Now he stopped, pulled her forward, and just next thing to ducked behind her.

He didn't really duck. That would be cowardly. But he did give Ellie the lead and let her talk. He let go of her hand and maybe stood so her shoulder was in front of him.

"Wildcat and I are getting married." Ellie went forward to meet Grace. "We'll marry tomorrow. He will guide us to his

Shoshone village, and the missionary there will perform the ceremony."

As Ellie talked, Grace lifted her hands to press against her face, both palms flat on her cheeks—a strange gesture that Wildcat couldn't read, and he was mighty good at reading folks. Of course, that was mainly men. He hadn't had much practice with youngsters.

Ellie reached her daughter. "We'll head over in the morning. It's a distance, but we can get over and back in one day. And we can take it slow so you don't get overtired. We'll head out—"

With a worried glance back at him, Ellie went to studying her daughter's strange silence, the way her fingers began to spread wide over her face so she watched her ma like a prisoner looking out from behind bars.

"What is it? You like Wildcat. Is it too soon? Do you want me to—"

"I won't go." Grace spoke from behind her hands.

"Th–the village folks aren't dangerous." Ellie looked back and gave Wildcat a stern look. He could read that rightly enough.

He came up to Grace. "You're safe with me, Grace. I won't let any harm come to you."

The little girl shook her head, still with her face covered.

"Don't you want me to marry your ma?" He'd thought Grace liked him.

"Go. Get married. I'll stay home."

Ellie gasped quietly. "We can't do that. You'd be here alone for hours. A young woman shouldn't—"

"I'd like to stay here." Her words were muffled by her hands. "I'd be happy to have you two marry." She looked at Wildcat between her fingers. "I'd be proud to have you for a pa, and I like this land, this cabin, these mountains all around us."

Ellie reached up so her hands pressed on Grace's, now there were two layers of hands on the little one's face.

"Then what is it? I think you'd enjoy seeing an Indian village."

"And you'd like my ma, Grace. She's a wise and kind woman. She'll be your grandmother."

"She won't like me."

"Of course she will," Wildcat protested.

Ellie wrapped her arms around Grace and said quietly, "Why do you say that?"

There was another long silence, and it crept into Wildcat's head what the problem might be.

Ellie whispered, "Is it that you're still not feeling well? We can wait a while until you're feeling stronger and until the pockmarks heal all the way."

Silence reigned, broken only by a soft autumn breeze that swept across the grassy mountain meadow like the hand of God. It was a beautiful place.

Grace wrenched out of Ellie's arms and turned her back. "They're not gonna heal, Ma."

She wrapped her own arms tight as if hugging herself. Grace's voice rose to a near shout. "You act like I'm still sick, but the only thing that's sick about me is these scars. I'm healthy and well, rested and fit. But I've been feeling these awful bumps all over my face and today I went and looked at myself in the stream. I can see well enough to know I'm ugly!"

Grace dropped her arms and turned to face Ellie. Tears streamed down her face. "I'm surprised even you, my own mother, can bear to look at me. So, yes, I want to live here where I never have to let anyone see me. I won't go with you and let all those Shoshone people see that I'm a monster. I won't make another person see me looking this way."

Ellie stood frozen. Wildcat could see that she had no idea what to say. How to make this better for Grace.

Wildcat came up beside Ellie, then went on past and hugged Grace.

He'd never once in the whole journey seen Carl spend time talking with the girl or working beside her. He hadn't been cruel; he'd just ignored the youngster. And he'd certainly never given her a hug.

Wildcat said clear as the wide mountain air, "Now you listen to me, Miss Gracie. You are not ugly."

Putting his hands on her shoulders, Wildcat pushed her back to arms' length and looked her right in the eye. "You could never be ugly because you have the most beautiful heart I've ever known. And you sing with the voice of an angel. You do not know if these scars will last. Sometimes it takes a stretch of time for healing to be finished, so give yourself time. But whether they get better or not, your ma and I love you. We know your goodness. We know how smart you are and how able and strong."

He shook her shoulders just a bit, careful not to scare her. "You beat smallpox. And not too many can say that. But you can, I can, your ma can. We stand here on this majestic mountain, part of the stone backbone of America, and all three of us, soon to be the Manning family, are its match."

He pulled her back tight and hugged her for a long time. Ellie came up, and he drew her in so that he hugged them both. He gradually felt Grace relax a bit, then he let her go. "We're going to see my family tomorrow. You're part of that family. They will love you, and if they ask about your scars, you'll tell them the hair-raisin'est tale of how you battled through one of the worst sicknesses known to man and beat it. You bear the marks of it with pride. You're part of a family of fighters. Warriors. The

Mannings don't let anything get the best of us."

Grace watched him. Her eyes burned with the inner strength he knew she possessed. Yes, she was afraid. Yes, she was so sad to think she'd always be badly scarred. But there was fire there. Strength. Intelligence.

He saw those things battle, and he saw them win.

She jerked her chin. Her voice wobbled, but she sounded solid when she said, "I did beat it, didn't I?"

"You did. And the day may come, like it did for your ma and me, when surviving smallpox is a gift from God on high. You'll be able to stay and help if you come upon someone suffering with it when others need to flee. It's hard to see it now, but good can come of this. Good *will* come of this because you've come through, and you're all that is good, Gracie."

Wildcat turned so he could put his arm across Grace's shoulders on his right and around Ellie on his left. He looked between them, then focused on Grace.

"So you like the idea of me marrying your ma and staying here?"

With a nod, Grace said, "I like it here. Surely this is the most beautiful place on earth."

"I thought so when I built my cabin here. I've got a plan to bring in some cattle, build up a herd. I think we could drive a few to a spot along the Oregon Trail and make a good living selling beef to hungry pioneers. It'll take time and work, and the winters up here are fierce, but it's a likely place."

"D–do you want me to call you Father?" Grace sounded unhappy with that idea.

Wildcat was stumped. He looked at Ellie.

Ellie shrugged then leaned forward so she could see Grace. "I think you should keep the name *Father* for when you think of your real father. That name is special. But I don't know about calling him Wildcat."

Grace giggled. "That doesn't sound right."

"Or Mr. Manning."

"Nope." Wildcat shook his head and started guiding the women toward the cabin. He thought the three of them should take some time and talk over several things to do with their new life. "If you wanted to, you could call me *Pa*. Most folks out in the west call their fathers that. We'll think of me as your western pa and Carl as your eastern father. It'd be a good idea, if you're agreeable."

Grace rushed for the door and opened it for them. She grinned. "Pa sounds right. Yes, that suits me, Pa."

"It suits me too. Now, let's talk about what you can expect at my village."

There was coffee still hot, and Ellie poured them each a cup, Grace included. The coffee was too weak to carry much but heat, so Grace had taken to drinking it on the way west.

"You really grew up in an Indian village, Pa?" Grace smiled when she called him that and sounded fascinated. She cupped her hands around the coffee and paid strict attention.

"Nope, my pa was a mountain man. A fur trapper and pathfinder. He explored these mountains until he knew them as well as any white man alive, I reckon. My ma went along most of the time. Ma taught him the ways of living with the wilderness instead of fighting it."

"What does that mean?" Ellie asked.

Wildcat reached out and rested one of his big rough hands on Ellie's soft, delicate one. "Stick around up here with me, soon-to-be Mrs. Manning, and I'll teach you. It's a rich and generous land. A place where folks can thrive if they respect the weather and all that can go wrong, and get ready for trouble before it comes."

They settled in and talked. Wildcat said more words in that one coffee break than he usually said in a month. But he enjoyed it. The women acted as if every word was important and they didn't want to miss a single one.

The coffee gone and Wildcat talked out, they got back to work. He had a lot to do today to be ready for tomorrow and becoming a married man.

CHAPTER TWELVE

———◆◆———

"What did you say your mother's name was again?" Ellie was getting nervous. Carl's mother had never approved of his marriage to Ellie. And she'd said it plain many times, and Ellie had bent over backward to keep the woman happy. Now she had another mother-in-law to please.

"It's Kimama. When she was young, it was said she was a delicate thing who loved to dance about. They called her Little Butterfly. In Shoshone that's Kimama. She is a small-built woman." Wildcat looked at Ellie. "But she is strong. She can drag an elk home, cut it, skin it, cook it up, and make a tent out of its hide and spear tips out of its antlers. She knows plants, the ones to eat, to avoid, to use for medicine and flavoring. She knows how to survive a blizzard, find her way through rugged mountain trails, and bring down a stout tree.

"There is so much to know about this land. I still learn from her all the time. She's going to be happy to see me wed, and she'll be delighted to have a granddaughter."

Grace had grown quiet as they neared the village. Smoke puffed out of the pointed tops of the Shoshone teepees in the chill of midday. People were moving around the camp.

Ellie saw Grace move one hand to cover half her face, then pull the hand away. Then later, her hand would creep up again.

The urge to protect her girl was so strong, Ellie had to clamp her mouth shut to keep from demanding they go back. They had to get through this, they had to go to the village to get married. Then they'd go home, and Grace would have time to heal more fully and learn to accept the scars that remained.

A cry went up from the village, and a form broke free of the small settlement. One form, small enough Ellie couldn't make out a face. But it was a woman, running with the grace of a deer in full flight. Or a butterfly fluttering on the wind.

The woman called out, "Wildcat, my son."

It was Kimama. Another person broke from the group, and a third and fourth. Soon a group was running and shouting. Wildcat spurred his horse with a laugh and galloped forward, leaving Ellie and Grace to come along at a walk.

When he neared the woman, still in the lead, he swung off the horse even as it stopped. He was on foot when the woman threw herself into his arms.

Then he was swallowed up by talking, laughing people, all speaking in a language Ellie couldn't understand. Wildcat spoke rapidly to them. A reunion. She knew he'd been gone at least the last few months as he'd ridden with their wagon train.

Finally, he made a broad sweep of his hand toward Ellie and Grace, who were closing the space between them. Ellie fought down the urge to pull her horse to a stop, maybe wheel around and run. And if she was tempted to do that, she could only imagine how Grace felt.

Glancing at her daughter, she saw a hand over Grace's cheek again. Ellie doubted Grace even knew she was doing it.

Wildcat came to Ellie and said, "Ma can speak some English.

And several of the villagers can. What they can't understand, I'll translate." He plucked her off the horse and set her afoot. Then he lifted Grace down. He leaned low and said something to her Ellie couldn't hear. Grace straightened her spine, lifted her chin just slightly, and faced the village.

Kimama came up close to Grace, caught her hands, and said, "Granddaughter. My oldest son, Wildcat, is the last to give me a grandchild."

"The last?" Ellie said, looking at her soon-to-be husband. "You have brothers and sisters?"

"Yes, a passel of them. My pa was Kimama's second husband, so I had three brothers older than me. And she married again after Pa died, and there were two more."

Wildcat gestured at the crowd gathered and rattled off names and how they were related to him. Ellie hoped she wasn't required to remember any of it. Maybe with time and practice.

"And finally, he marries." Kimama turned to Ellie with a bright smile. "May I hug my new daughter?"

There was only time for a swift nod, and Ellie was nearly swallowed by the strong arms of this beautiful woman. She saw a resemblance to Wildcat in the shining smile, the dark hair, the angular cheekbones.

Kimama was slender and not overly tall. She was dressed in a buckskin tunic, her legs wrapped in some type of fur-lined moccasins with long thongs of leather wrapped around them to keep them up. If Ellie had thought at all about how native folks dressed, she hadn't really considered winter. The clothing looked warm and comfortable.

And then, before she could do more than take a sweeping look around, she was standing in front of a man narrow as a rail, wearing a long black robe. He had a circle of hair surrounding a bald dome and a bright smile.

They were married with only the slightest of vows.

Ellie spent an hour in Kimama's teepee over a fine meal. Extra food was brought in by the village women, who turned out to be family. They were his sisters or married to his brothers. There were a few very young adult women who were nieces and some closer to Grace in age. Also a few babies were brought in to be admired. Wildcat delighted in all of it.

Grace was included to the extent she could be with the children, but they couldn't speak to each other. From where Ellie sat across the fire from her daughter, she saw Grace's hands go to her face several times. Were the children commenting on her scarred face? Or was Grace just self-conscious as she'd been during the ride in?

Then the children finished their meal and ran out of the teepee to play. Ellie saw them gesture to Grace to come along, but Grace shook her head and stayed by the fire. The parson had joined them, and when the children left, he moved to sit beside Grace and visit with her. He was a jovial man with an air of serenity that made Ellie wish she could get to know him better.

But her meal was focused on Wildcat and Kimama. Kimama was kind and seemed delighted that her son had married.

Ellie had wondered if Kimama would be unhappy with her son for marrying outside the tribe until she remembered Kimama had done the same. There wasn't the slightest hint that Kimama was other than delighted.

She promised to come and visit when they returned from their winter hunting grounds.

Then the newly minted Manning family was on the trail home. "We'll make it there before darkness catches us."

Grace didn't make any mention of how the day had gone for

her, but she pushed to keep up the pace for home as if she were desperate to get back. They rode fast enough that there was little time for talking.

CHAPTER THIRTEEN

———◆◆◆———

Winter came down hard on the Manning family.
They were cut off from everyone and everything.

Wildcat loved it. He hiked into the deep snow to tend his horses. The three horses, his and the two Ellie had brought with her into the marriage, were all the animals they owned.

He'd set up trap lines in the woods at some distance to the house, and he checked them every day, hiking for hours in the deep snow. To his delight, Grace went with him some of the time. She seemed to delight in the wilderness, and she learned when to talk and when to be silent. He built her a bow and arrow, and she was learning to use it to fetch a rabbit. He let her handle his gun and load it, but he liked the silence of the woods, liked to see if he could sneak up on the wild critters. Shooting a gun ruined that, and he saved it for when it was really needed.

Then he came home to work on laying floors and building furniture. They had two bedsteads now. And a third chair for the table. He built a wooden chest for Grace's things and let Ellie have the one he used. His clothes could be handled by hanging them on a few elk antlers on the bedroom walls.

He brought down enough elk and deer to make warm coats

for Ellie and Grace and sturdy moccasins and gloves. Ellie and Grace worked with him like hardy pioneer women. They were handy with tools and swift with a needle and thread. It made all he needed to do easier, and having their smiling faces greet him each morning and Grace's beautiful voice soothing his soul each night made life a delight.

And the greatest delight was finding out the mysteries of a wife. The warmth of her in his arms, someone to hold close and show him the ways of married life in the night, were a wonder.

The days were their usual fight for survival—a hard fight but one Wildcat knew how to win.

The nights were a glory.

The snow came in feet, and Wildcat stayed more to the house. He turned the horses loose in a sheltered canyon with a tight fence across the mouth. The north side of it stayed clear, the tall grass fodder for the winter. A spring gushed out of a crack in the rocks. Wildcat had lived here long enough to trust that there'd always be water for the horses.

"Wildcat," Ellie whispered after they'd settled in for the night, "we need to talk about Grace."

The wall between the two bedrooms was built of small saplings, the gaps chinked, so they weren't easily overheard, but Wildcat whispered even more quietly. "What about her?"

Ellie moved close, then closer. She rested her head on his shoulder as she was inclined to do. He slid his arm under her shoulders, pulled her tight, and struggled to keep his mind on what Ellie wanted to say.

He was afraid he knew.

"She's n–not—" Ellie's voice broke. She turned her head so her face was pressed against his chest, and he pulled her fully on top of him. Her arms went around his neck, and she cried quietly.

Even in her tears, she didn't want Grace to overhear.

"She's as healed from the pox as she'll get." Wildcat ran his hands down Ellie's back, then up, soothing her as sorry as she was, but maybe more accepting for a hard turn of fate.

Ellie nodded, her face still buried against him.

He let her cry. The tears hurt him. Made him ache with the wish he could fix this for her. He'd done everything he could to care for Ellie and Grace almost since the wagon train had set out from Independence, but he couldn't fix this.

Maybe he could help her another way though.

When her tears ebbed, he leaned down and whispered into her hair, "Since we've been back from my Shoshone village, she's almost never referred to it."

"She touches her face though. Presses a hand over her cheeks like she did that first day."

"Yes, once in a long while I see her do that, but not often. We'll give her all the time she needs to get used to the scars. Time will pass, and she'll adjust to it, think about it less. We have no visitors, and I don't see us getting any, except maybe my ma come spring. Some of my family."

"We could ask them not to come here. We could let Grace have privacy."

"Let her hide, you mean? From everyone, forever? It's not a good idea, and even if it was, it wouldn't be possible."

Ellie was silent. Wildcat felt the war raging inside her because he knew she wanted to protect Grace with all her strength.

What he didn't know was, did protecting her mean allowing her to cut herself off or forcing her to face the world boldly with her scars?

He was sorely afraid Ellie would choose somewhere in the middle. She wouldn't let her hide, but neither would she encourage

LEGACY OF THE ROCKING K RANCH

acceptance of her appearance. If Grace didn't find a way to be bold in her scars, life would always be a struggle.

"Maybe not forever, but for now, just for now, let her choose to stay to herself. As she grows up, she'll mature and grow wise. Maybe we should start reading the Bible at night before bed. We've been spending time in prayer and with the Good Book on Sunday mornings, but maybe we all need a deeper understanding of prayer and God's guidance. I'm thinking of Grace, but I may need it more than she does."

Ellie lifted her gaze to meet his, almost asking permission to feel as she did.

"Reading the Bible and praying is always a good idea. We'll do that. But we also need to talk about Grace being grateful."

Ellie sniffed. "Grateful she is badly scarred? Grateful her father is dead?"

The words hit like knives. Because, of course, for Wildcat to be married to Ellie, Carl had to die. And no woman with her husband little more than a month dead, already remarried, thinks that's a fine thing.

Wildcat knew he couldn't expect Ellie to be happy she was married to him. But would the day ever come? Or would Ellie always see their marriage through the eyes of grief? As her taking a second husband to survive but never to love?

Because he knew he didn't dare hope Ellie would love him, at least not for a long, long time, he didn't comment on that part of what she said. He couldn't bear to think of his life going on like that. Instead, he thought of Grace.

"Grateful for life. Grateful she overcame such a dreadful illness. Yes, there is a lot to be grateful for."

Ellie looked at him. Deep in his eyes. Not like she was searching for his true feelings or trying to know what he really thought, but rather as if she looked long enough, hard enough, she could see past his common-sense words to find what she wanted to hear.

That he'd allow Grace to hide away up here forever rather than love herself as she was.

"We just love her, Ellie. We accept the scars, and we look at her every day until they are so much a part of her that we only know her as beautiful. We don't even notice the scars. Because she is a beautiful little girl. Inside and out. Those scars may be a burden for her when she meets new people, but anyone worthwhile will see past them to our beautiful daughter."

Ellie frowned, but no more tears spilled. Wildcat circled her waist with both arms to hug her close, expecting she'd stretch out on top of him for a while and use his body as a warm, comforting pillow.

Instead, she stretched up just enough to kiss him.

Quietly, against his lips, she said, "I know you're right. I know it's just a simple truth that any worthy person will see how beautiful she is. But right now, it's hard for me to see it, and that's a terrible sin."

"It's not sin. It's love. It's a mother's love and the wish that our children faced no pain. Don't add the weight of calling your sorrow a sin. You love Grace. So do I. There's no sin in that." He wanted to say, "And I love you," but he lacked the courage.

He could face down a hungry grizzly, but he couldn't risk saying I love you to his own wife. He knew she couldn't say it back. Maybe not ever but for certain not now.

To silence his mouth before he could say words that might break his own heart, he kissed her back. She must have wanted to end this talk too, because she joined with him in the kiss with all her might.

And for a time, they drove back the grief and loss, the scars and fears, their turmoil and worry turned to passion as they enjoyed being a married man and wife. Trouble would find them tomorrow. That was life. For tonight, they held each other tight.

CHAPTER FOURTEEN

———— ◆•◆ ————

W e're reading the Bible before bedtime from now on," Ellie said, settling into the rocking chair Wildcat had just finished this afternoon.

He hunkered down on the floor beside the fireplace. Grace had her own chair, small, just right for her. That had been one of the first things he'd finished, and it gave him deep pleasure to see his two womenfolk on chairs he built and under a roof he'd provided.

The lantern was turned high. It hung from a hook on the ceiling just a bit to the right of Ellie.

"Wildcat, why don't you read to us tonight?"

There was a sudden tension from the man who'd relaxed back to sit on the floor. "Uh, no. You read. I like hearing your voice of an evening."

"But I like hearing your voice too. And I always read. I'd like you to take a turn."

He was sitting right near the fire. He'd stay here until he built himself a chair, and he had other things that needed doing first. So every night he perched here, leaning against the hearth. And that might be why his face was suddenly hot.

He'd been shaving, though he liked a beard in the winter. So if he wasn't hot, as he very much feared, but embarrassed, then he might be blushing.

And the thought that he might be made his face even hotter. He looked down at his hands as if they were the most interesting things in the world. And more than that, they were his tools. They were his talent. They were his education.

No sense making more of a fool of himself by denying what must be clear as a mountain spring.

"I can't read."

Silence fell over the room—a silence broken by the crackling of the fire. A silence that would be all that came from him if he tried to read.

"I couldn't read until I was eighteen years old, no, nearly twenty-one. I started when I was eighteen." Ellie's quiet voice made his heart pound so loud that he felt it in his ears.

"You're so smart, Ellie. You and Grace." He was able to lift his head now to look at her.

"I am smart. And that's why when Carl married me and found out I couldn't read, he taught me. And I learned easy because I was smart."

"I figured you for an educated woman. Didn't you go to school as a child? You lived in a city back east, didn't you?"

"No school would take a poor child, and Pa had no coin to pay the fees. And anyway, Pa saw no reason to waste time in study when there was work to be done. I grew up baking in the back of my father's general store. I was seven when my mama died. She did baking for the store, and it was a big part of our business. We sold bread and rolls, some cookies and biscuits, quite a few different things, to the bachelors in the small town in Indiana where we lived. And it was taking every waking moment for Pa to run the store as it was, with Ma helping so much. He needed me. And Pa couldn't read, neither could my mama overly. None of us gave it much thought."

"Ellie, I haven't heard you talk much about your childhood. Carl was such a reader and talker." He was always reading or talking when there was work to be done. "I figured you and he were both well-educated folks."

"I met Carl when he got the job of teaching our school. By then I did more than baking for Pa. The store was struggling, and what we earned was barely enough to pay off a loan we had. I worked so we could live after the bank took every week's earnings. I did some cleaning at the boardinghouse and for several private homes. There was always mending to take in. The school board hired me to tidy up the school once a week. I met Carl, and we married right away."

"You fell in love with him that fast?" Wildcat kept his voice even, but again he was compared to Carl "the Half-Wit" Yates and somehow found himself the lesser in Ellie's eyes.

And hers were the only ones that counted.

"We got married and went on as we had been. Him teaching. Me working for Pa and cleaning and mending for others. At first Pa kept the money I made at the store with my baking, and Carl got the money I made cleaning. But then Pa remarried, and it was to a woman who was a fine hand with bread and biscuits. So, I left the store work to her and found more jobs cleaning and mending. I didn't have to share my work hours with Pa; it was all for my husband."

"For your husband? Don't you mean for *you* and your husband?"

Ellie shrugged one shoulder and gave a shy smile. "Yes, that's what I mean."

But Wildcat wondered why she'd said it the way she had.

"Then Carl left the teaching job because he got an opportunity at a newspaper. Our room was provided by the school, but I was cleaning and doing some cooking at a diner, and the owner gave us the room above stairs as part of my pay."

"Carl owned a newspaper?"

With a shake of her head, Ellie said, "Not at first. He was hired to write for one, but he wanted to be his own boss, so we picked up stakes and moved to a town some distance away without a newspaper and he started one while I went back to work, another diner. Another room we were lucky enough to get. The paper failed, but Carl had loved it. That's when he decided to write a book."

Wildcat ground his teeth together and didn't ask any of twenty questions he had—well, one hundred questions, honestly. Just how hard did Ellie work? Who had paid the money to start up a newspaper? It sounded like the only real money coming in— With a mental shake of his head, Wildcat quit trying to form questions he could use to make her admit her husband was a shiftless skunk who couldn't or wouldn't hold down a job.

And now the skunk was dead. Which for the most part Wildcat approved of, because he wouldn't likely be married to this beautiful woman if Carl hadn't turned up his toes. But Ellie spoke of him with stars in her eyes. She had a dreamy sound to her voice as if she wanted Wildcat to write a book too. And with the skunk being dead, it was likely Ellie would hold him in this almost worshipful regard for the rest of her life.

He wondered if she ever thought of herself. He wondered how a woman who'd worked so hard all her life could grow up to not recognize when another person wasn't working. Had her father been shiftless and lazy? Was all her work at his general store the only work that got done?

ELEANOR

Wildcat knew one thing.
He was in love with his wife.
And she was in love with her former husband.
It looked like that would remain true for the rest of his life.
It was all he could do to not howl at the moon like a lobo wolf.

CHAPTER FIFTEEN

W ildcat was learning to read.
Ellie sat beside him and helped him sound out the words.
They had a McGuffey Reader. Ellie had brought it west with them,
because Ellie had always hoped there would be more children.

Now she used it, and within a couple of weeks, Wildcat was
doing a fine job of reading simple things.

The snow came more every day. They'd be stuck inside most
of the day very soon, so Wildcat worked hard outside in the
ever-shorter days.

One morning he warned them he might be gone overnight,
and when he'd returned, three days later, he'd driven five long-
horn cattle before him. He'd herded them in with the horses and
announced with some pride that today he was a rancher.

He brought in enough meat to salt away or cure or pound
into pemmican so that they were set for winter. He built a small
stone smokehouse and smoked fish and hung the fish on a line
inside the cabin.

Ellie considered it a very strange way to decorate her house,
but she didn't mention it.

The additions he'd put on the cabin had their floors laid

already. They had enough chairs for all three of them to sit at the dinner table. And he'd built two more rocking chairs so they could spend their evenings in front of the fireplace.

He'd brought in a wild hog, and they'd rendered the fat and made lard and candles and cured bacon and ham. Living with Wildcat in charge of food made their lives a never-ending feast.

In the evenings after his long, hard days of work, he studied reading.

"You're picking this up fast. It's a pleasure teaching you."

Grace had slumped a bit in her rocking chair and slept by the fire. She ended up doing that most nights.

"I–I've wanted to ask you something." Ellie twisted her hands together in her lap and seemed to hold his gaze only by pure force of will.

"What's that?" Wildcat looked back, one brow arched as if he was a little afraid of what she might say.

Glancing down at her fingers, Ellie seemed able then to ask, "Would it be all right if I started calling you Ray instead of Wildcat?"

He blinked. "What makes you want to do that?"

Lifting her chin, she said, "A wife should call her husband by his real name, not a nickname."

There was a startled silence, then he said, "Wildcat is my real name. Ray was my pa's choice and Wildcat my ma's. Wildcat stuck."

Reaching out one hand, she rested it on one of his wind-chapped cheeks. "If you wouldn't mind, I'd like to call you Ray."

His eyes narrowed, and he took a quick glance at sleeping Grace. "Is it because Wildcat is too Indian for you? Are you sorry you're married to a man who's half Shoshone?"

Ellie's eyes narrowed right back. "I am *not* sorry I married you. It seems to me the life you grew up in only makes you a better man—and that most certainly includes the Shoshone blood flowing in you. We are blessed that you came and stood by us when the wagon train abandoned us. Seriously, beautifully, brilliantly blessed. I l–lo—" She fell silent. She couldn't force the word love past her lips. Not when she knew he'd only married her out of a complete lack of options.

He'd given up his chance to find a woman he loved, a woman raised in the mountains or maybe a Shoshone woman who knew this land and this life and would be a true partner for him. Instead, he was stuck with her. She worked hard every day to make him glad he picked her, or rather to accept that he was stuck with her.

She was falling in love with him, but she couldn't tell him. Couldn't land the burden of her feelings on him when he'd never be able to honestly return the words. She would not add to the weight of caring for her and Grace.

"I thank you for everything. And you have my deepest respect, *Ray!*" She emphasized his name. "I'm calling you that from now on." She stood so suddenly the rocking chair skidded away and rapped into the wall with a load crash.

Grace jumped, groggy and confused.

Ray. . .she was calling him that now. It touched something in her to have her own name for him. Something private between them.

He'd get used to it.

Ellie went to Grace and urged her to her feet. "Let's get to bed now, honey."

This was the usual way they ended the night. They all went to bed early and got up late. Sun to sun, that's how Ellie thought of it.

Ray called it "can see to can't see." He claimed they'd be working hard in the long days of summer, but as the days shortened, they needed to save on candle wax and get under the blankets so they could save on wood for the fire.

The additions to the cabin were built so both bedrooms shared the fire and were reasonably warm, though there was a definite chill by morning when the fire burned down to embers.

Tonight as every night, Ellie guided the sleepy Grace to her room, then left her alone to change into her nightgown and slide beneath the covers. The girl said her own prayers and reminded Ellie often enough that she was growing up and could handle most of the care of herself alone.

When Ellie went to her own room, Ray had already slid between the covers and pulled them up to his ears.

Ellie soon joined him, and as usual he wasn't asleep.

He rolled over and pulled her into his arms. "I don't mind if you call me Ray. I'm sorry I accused you of something I know isn't true of you."

Ellie snuggled close, rested her head on his strong shoulder, and tried to work up the nerve to add another burden to her husband's overburdened life. The burden of love.

CHAPTER SIXTEEN

W ildcat watched in wonder as his beautiful wife lifted herself onto one elbow so she looked down at him, lying flat on his back. The room was dimly lit by the crackling fire. It made Ellie's blue eyes dance and glow. She was beautiful, for a fact. And it was a wonder to him that she'd ended up married to him.

She lay on his right side, so he lifted his left hand, reached across and rested his big, roughly callused fingers gently on her cheek. Soft, despite the wind and weather and her hard work at his side, she was still soft and sweet-smelling and all woman. A wife he didn't deserve and would never have gotten if not for the terrible circumstances.

And it struck him that he was a weakling and a coward. But not because he felt less for not being able to read. No, it was because he hadn't taken the risk, the terrible and bold step in faith, that she so richly did deserve.

Even if she didn't feel for him what he felt for her, she needed to know the truth.

"I love you, Ellie."

She jumped as if someone had stuck her in the backside with a pin.

LEGACY OF THE ROCKING K RANCH

His heart sank until it was nearly under the bed, on the floor, because the way she acted could only mean she didn't feel it back. Didn't expect or want his words.

"You do?" She sounded nervous, as if she had no idea what to do with words of love.

Wildcat fought down his despair. This was his act of courage. To give with no hope of getting in return. He would've rather faced a wounded grizz, but he didn't have that choice.

"Ray, I love you too." She leaned down before he could quite understand what she said. Her hand came up to his cheek. Her lips met his.

The kiss blurred his thinking for a bit, then her words soaked in his thick skull and he jerked back.

"You don't have to say that. I didn't tell you to wring those words out of you. I know you're not done grieving for your husband. . . ."

She rested her fingers on his lips, and he stopped talking. The words were hard to get out, so it was no hardship to hush.

"I am still grieving Carl. Losing him isn't exactly real to me yet. For him to die, then the urgency to get here before Grace got sick, then the fight for her life, then our marriage and through it all, and still now weeks later, you've been so busy building and tending everything. It's hard to remember life before I came here."

She shook her head as if to rid it of confusing thoughts. "My main feeling for you has been guilt."

"Guilt?" Wildcat scowled. "You didn't do anything wrong."

She kissed what had to be a deep frown. "I know that. But I trapped you into this marriage. We had no choice."

"We had a choice."

"What else could we have done?"

"I don't know. But we didn't try that hard to think of anything. Leastways I didn't. But that's cuz I wanted to marry you something fierce."

Her expression lightened until she glowed as warm as the fire. "Thank you, Ray. I like hearing that. Because I've been feeling like you stood up and did what you believed was the right thing to do without having any say in the matter."

He growled. "If I hadn't wanted to marry you, I'd've probably figured a way out of it."

She laughed, then threw her arms around his neck and landed on top of him. "I do love you, Ray. Wanting to call you by a name only I use is part of that. I want to be special to you."

"We're laying on my bed, you right on top of me." Wildcat wrapped his arms around her waist and held her tight. "Not much that's more special than that."

She laughed and buried her face in the crook of his neck.

Finally, she raised her head and looked down. Now her face was in shadows. But she was close enough he could see her shining eyes and her beaming happiness. He slid one hand up her back, to the nape of her neck, and pressed so her head lowered and their lips met.

When the kiss ended, he said, "I do love you, Ellie. I grew up in a wild place, and all my learning is how to survive out here. But it's giving me great pleasure to learn to read, especially having you teach me."

"I love having something to give to you, when you give me so much."

Shaking his head, murmuring, Wildcat kissed her soundly. "You've given the most, Ellie, my beautiful bride. You've given me sunlight on a cloud-covered day with your smile. You've given me warmth in the deepest winter. All of that and more."

He hugged her tight. "So much more. Most important of all, you've turned a ramshackle cabin where I spent little time into a place I now recognize as home."

They whiled away the hours of the night. There was a lot ahead of them. They needed to turn wild country into a ranch. They needed to help Grace accept her new truth. The scars she'd need to learn to bear. They needed to nurture their love and grow in faith that went beyond earthly things.

Together they built a home and laid a foundation upon which they built a legacy of love.

Mary Connealy writes romantic comedy with cowboys. She is a Carol Award winner and a RITA®, Christy, and Inspirational Reader's Choice finalist. She is the bestselling author of the Wild at Heart series, Trouble in Texas series, Kincaid Bride series, Lassoed in Texas trilogy, Montana Marriages trilogy, Sophie's Daughters trilogy, and many other books. Mary is married to a Nebraska cattleman and has four grown daughters and a little bevy of spectacular grandchildren. Find Mary online at www.maryconnealy.com.

GRACE

By

D. J. GUDGER

This book is dedicated to my father, Robert H. Yetter who inspired my love of history. He wanted to visit Fort Laramie the next time he came to Wyoming, but he's with Jesus.

CHAPTER ONE

---•••---

July 25, 1865

Three miles east of Willow Creek, Dakota Territory

D id that fool just sentence himself and his men to cer-
tain death?" Captain Winfield Cooper of the 11th Ohio
Volunteer Cavalry pulled his horse alongside Lieutenant Henry
Bretney's.

"I'm pretty sure he did." Bretney stared ahead. "I'm thinking
we go back and try one more time."

"Agreed." Winfield wheeled his horse around while Bretney
commanded the others to stay put.

Both men spurred their horses to a gallop. It wasn't far, but
time was of the essence. A morning telegraph from Platte Bridge
Station warned of growing Indian activity. The Kansas men at
the fort were on edge.

Within a few minutes, the outlines of the army wagons
appeared in the gloaming. Orange light from the fire reflected
on the white canvas covers.

"Sergeant, Captain Cooper and I insist you join us. Our men
will make sure you will arrive at the fort by morning."

Sergeant Custard glared at them over his handlebar moustache.

"I ain't goin' nowhere. Gotta give the critters a rest."

Winfield slid off his mount and marched to the Kansas man. "Be reasonable. You know very well the Indians are agitated and eager for conflict. It's suicide to travel during the day." He bent down and picked up a still warm skillet. "We'll call our men back and help get you on the way."

Custard grabbed Winfield's arm. "Now lookit here. You Ohio fellows are skeered. We will go on, and if you want to be safe, you'll wait 'till morning and go with *us*."

Blood pounded in Winfield's ears. Nobody called him a coward. Especially some lower-ranking sergeant. He tore his arm from the man's grasp and wagged a finger in his face. "You're making a big mistake," he hissed.

"Captain, let it go," Bretney called from his horse.

What if he pulled rank? "Sergeant Custard, I command you to pack up your boys and come with us."

Custard put his hands on his belly and laughed. "You ain't got no authority over me, Ohio boy."

"Leave him be, Captain. His fate and the fate of his men are now in his hands."

Taking a deep breath and letting it out slowly in the sergeant's face, Winfield leaned in closer. "You better pray to the good Lord for mercy. The blood of those men is on your hands." He rose to full height, brushed his sweaty palms against the rough wool fabric of his pants, and returned to this horse.

"His pride will be the end of him and his men," Bretney said while Winfield mounted.

"That's what I'm most afraid of."

Winfield, Bretney, and their men rode in silence through the dark night. The cool mountain air was a welcome relief. All around, the glow of campfires lit up the night. There were thousands of

Indians in the vicinity of the fort.

"This doesn't bode well," Bretney whispered.

"No. The fact that they are resting means they likely have something planned for tomorrow. I think we need to hurry and warn Major Anderson at the fort." Cooper gave a signal with his hand, and the group broke into a flat-out run. It seemed like an eternity before they thundered across Guinard's Bridge.

Once in the confines of Platte Bridge Station, Winfield and Bretney raced to the major's sleeping quarters. The man snored like a bear. "Wake up." Winfield grabbed the man by the shoulders and shook him so hard his teeth rattled.

"What the—"

"Sir, you need to send reinforcements to bring Sergeant Custard's supply train in. You're surrounded by thousands of Indians. He only has twenty men."

The major looked up with wild eyes. "Do you know what time it is?"

Winfield glanced at Bretney, who stood there wide-eyed. "These men will die." He finally broke the silence.

"We'll worry about it in the morning. Let me sleep." Major Anderson pulled his wool blanket tighter around him and rolled away.

"We best sleep outside on the parade grounds, just in case. I'll tell our men." Bretney spun on his heel and left the room.

Winfield clenched and unclenched his fist. What was wrong with the Kansas units? Did they not care about human life? A snore ripped through the night air as if it answered his question. Best get outside and get what little rest he could in case of a night raid.

Streaks of sun pierced through Winfield's eyelids. He bolted upright. Must be about five thirty or six. The bluffs surrounding the fort were quiet. Time to get up and talk some sense into the major if that was possible.

In the mess hall, a familiar form caught Winfield's attention. "Lieutenant Collins. How was the trip to Fort Laramie?"

The young lad, barely over the age of nineteen, flashed a wide smile. "It was great. I picked up a new uniform in anticipation for my promotion."

Winfield slapped him on the back. "A well-deserved one."

The conversation was interrupted by Bretney stomping toward them. "Can you believe that good-for-nothing Anderson? I offered to take up to a hundred men to get Custard. He refused. Know why?" He ran a hand through his hair.

Caspar Collins shook his head. "No, tell us."

"His excuse is that the Kansas boys muster out on the fifth of August. He doesn't want to get them killed." Bretney balled his fists.

"He'll get us all killed and then some if he ignores the threat surrounding this fort."

"You talking about me, Bretney? I told you I'd give you twenty men." A red-faced Anderson joined them.

"That's suicide," Bretney roared.

"I'll do it." Caspar Collins threw his shoulders back and lifted his chin. The foolishness of youth. What was the lad thinking? "I'll do it on account of you giving me more men. Say, a hundred."

Winfield smiled. Caspar was smart for his age. Well educated. Well respected by everyone, including some of the Indian tribes.

The major folded his arms. "Twenty."

"I don't mean any disrespect, sir, but twenty isn't enough."

The high-pitched sound of war whoops cut through the morning air. Winfield's heart pounded against his ribs. What was the major's problem? "Caspar, don't—"

Anderson's cheeks puffed out, and his eyes became slits in his face. "Do you mean to disobey my command? Do you make a habit of insubordination, Lieutenant Collins?"

Caspar took a step back and looked the major in the eye. "Sir, I *never* disobey a commanding officer." He turned to Bretney. "May I borrow your brace of Colts?"

"What is going on here?" Winfield got in Anderson's face. "You have no authority over my man!"

"Back off, Captain, and mind your own business. This is my outfit. I call the shots."

"You're going to get them all killed." It took every ounce of control not to slug the man.

Meanwhile, Bretney unholstered his pistols and handed them to Collins. "You don't have to do this, you know."

Lieutenant Collins nodded.

"Caspar, listen. This is nuts. You know that, right? You are just a kid. You have a whole future ahead of you," Winfield pleaded. Unfortunately, Anderson outranked him.

Blue eyes the color of the western sky took on an unshakable sincerity. "I must at least try. It's the right thing to do."

He put a hand on the boy's shoulder. "May God be with you." Caspar nodded and headed to the bunkhouse.

Two hours later, the boy, clad in his new uniform, high atop an iron gray horse, led a group of Kansas men across the bridge. He smiled around the cigar in his mouth and waved to Winfield and Henry Bretney.

The events that unfolded that day shattered Winfield in ways he never imagined.

CHAPTER TWO

June 1867

Fort Laramie, Dakota Territory

Heat seared Grace's back as if an iron, out of the flames, pressed on her. Swirls of dust rode the violent winds whipping the laundry on the lines, threatening to undo all her hard work.

She lifted a shirt out of the water, placed it at the top of her wash board, and scrubbed down.

Up, plop, scratch, splash.

I must get home. The words repeated in her mind with the rhythm of her movements.

Home...

A place so precious, she'd never leave again—no matter what her parents wished.

They loved her and wanted her to find a life of her own, so they paid for fare to send her east to stay with her grandparents. After some lessons on how to be a lady, they hoped she would find a loving husband, someone who needed a mother for a house full of children. All impossible. The smallpox that robbed her of her father and almost took her life wreaked havoc on more than her skin.

Scarred and ugly, there was not a man alive who'd propose to her. Unless he was blind. And there were no blind soldiers at this post.

Sweat rolled from her brow into her eye. She swiped her face with her hand after dropping the shirt into the tub. Grace didn't mind hard work; she only minded being around people. What she needed was to go home, see if she could file for 160 acres of land, and run her own cattle ranch. It was what she knew. She didn't need anyone to help.

Grace picked up the shirt and resumed her rhythm at a much faster tempo.

"These better be done by tomorrow." An officer stood before her, his arms loaded with dirty laundry. He stared off into the distance at a point somewhere above her head as though looking her in the eyes might somehow infect him with smallpox. Grace tucked her chin to her chest. She bit her lower lip, locking in the snide comment bouncing around on the tip of her tongue at his impoliteness.

Plop. The trooper deposited his load on her to-be-washed pile. "Better not find any holes in mine." As silently as he approached, he slipped away. Rude. Rude. Rude. A smile or simple hello would've been nice. Maybe he had a lot on his mind. But then he greeted another laundress. Grace's insides flopped like wet mud. Why did he choose her to do his wash when he seemed to hold her in contempt?

She slammed the clothing into the tub, splashing water all over her hot, tired body. Why did she have to be the fastest, most efficient laundress at the fort? Oh. Right. Her lack of social life aided in that accomplishment. She had nothing to do *but* laundry and mending.

Sighing, she plunged her hands into the wash water, curling her fingers around the shirt at the bottom of the tub. She leaned forward on her knuckles. Upon arriving at Fort Laramie a month ago, she sent the first of many telegraphs telling her parents she wouldn't be continuing to Philadelphia. After a few weeks on the stagecoach, she'd had enough of folks and their mean ways. By the time she reached the fort, she wanted to go home and stay.

Forever.

Each week, Grace relayed a new telegraph message to South Pass City.

Pa hadn't responded.

To be fair, he didn't have a reason to travel seventy miles to the relay station. He wasn't expecting to hear from her soon.

Pulling the shirt out of the water, Grace wrung it out and examined the stain. A bit of bluing would make it as good as new. She set it next to the wash tub and went in search of the blue dye used to make dingy white resemble freshly fallen snow.

Clunk!

Water exploded all around her. She cried out and covered her left eye. It felt as if someone lit it afire. She rubbed and rubbed. Tears mixed with sudsy water ran down her cheeks.

Laughter. "Looks like a drowned rat."

"Yeah! You flipped the tub."

"You owe me a penny."

Grace blinked and blinked. The stinging subsided a bit. The voices sounded like the Barlow boys. She gritted her teeth and shook her head. Taking a deep breath, she turned to face them. Something bumped her foot. She glanced at the muddy ground.

A sudsy ball rested next to her boot.

She picked it up and assessed the damage in her area. Sure enough, the tub was upside down. The pile of laundry from the soldier lay scattered in the mud along with the shirt she spent half an hour scrubbing to remove a stubborn stain. A groan escaped her lips. She tossed the ball and caught it.

"That's mine. Give it back." Abe, the oldest boy, crossed his arms and scrunched his face. His brothers, Brett and Caleb, stood next to him, dark eyes flashing.

Grace turned the ball in her hand. This wasn't the first time the kids on Suds Row targeted her workstation. She was tired of it. Rocks, snakes, kicked buckets. . .all things to make her job even more unpleasant. She tried to ignore them, hoping they'd get bored and leave. Well, that strategy didn't work.

She squeezed the ball between her hands. She'd have to work late to catch up. "If this ball's yours, then what's it doing in my workstation? Hm?"

Abe slid a glance at Brett. "You still owe me a penny."

"But ya didn't get *her*. You were s'possed to hit her in the head." Brett pointed a bony finger at her face. Caleb snickered.

"I flipped the tub up into the air. That should be worth *two* pennies." Abe shoved Brett, then returned his gaze to her. "Now, gimme my ball."

Grace tucked it under her arm. "You were trying to hit me?"

"Yeah. Of course. You're so ugly, we thought it might be an improvement. You could scare the stink off a dog with that face. Looks like someone ran it through a meat grinder." The elder brat lowered his arms and doubled over in laughter.

"Well, to me, your face looks like a cow stepped on it." Caleb put fisted hands on his hips, flaring his elbows out as if trying to make himself larger.

"Reminds me of when the cat threw up on my bed." Brett shouted, slapping his brothers on the back.

Anger flared through her veins. Grace's skin burned hotter

than if she wore a black shirt in the blazing sun. While on the stagecoach, she discovered anger served her better than embarrassment. "Where's your mother? I want to talk to her."

"Don't waste your time, Meat Face." Abe crossed his arms. "Our ma, she said you don't belong here. I heard her telling my pa she wishes you'd fall into the river and drown so she don't have to look at you anymore."

Enough. Forget turning the other cheek. These little hooligans needed to learn a lesson. Grace wanted to show them she wasn't going to be trifled with. She bolted out of her work area, held the ball out in front of her, let it drop, then kicked it far over the kids' heads. It arced high into the sky, hit its apex, then descended toward the latrine. It landed in the middle of the lake of human muck oozing from the overused structure.

Bullseye!

Years of playing ball with Shoshone children paid off.

Abe's mouth dropped open, forming a tall O.

"Go on. Get your ball and go home." Their mother could deal with the messy clothes.

Grace wiped her hands on her apron, turned, and marched back to her laundry station. She looked around and spotted the bandanna she used to wipe sweat off her face. Picking it up, he made a triangle, then tied it behind her head so the longest edge rested below her eyes—bandit style. Most of the time, she took great care to hide her face. But that day was so hot, she felt as if the bandana suffocated her. She removed it. Grace pressed the bonnet lower on her head to conceal her profile. This had to do for now.

She stooped down to sort through the fallen clothes. Which ones needed rewashing and which ones needed spot cleaning? The officers paid her good money to keep their clothes clean and in one piece. She wasn't about to let this incident defeat her. The empty wooden buckets lay on their side. It meant she had to get more water from the river. She'd have to build a fire to heat the copper. It took hours for the water to reach temperature. If she got to it right away, she might squeeze an hour or two of sleep before her workday started tomorrow. She fetched the yoke, hooked the buckets on each end, then set it behind her neck. Even without water, it was uncomfortable.

The boys lined up near the latrine, arguing over who'd pull the ball out of the smelly mess. A spring in her step, Grace sauntered upriver with a smile on her face.

Close enough to enjoy the boys' bickering, yet far enough away to avoid notice, she grabbed the first bucket by the handle and dipped it into the Laramie River. A cloud of dust on the opposite bank caught her attention. Probably another large wagon train coming in. What if she could get on with them as far west as Sweetwater? That small flicker of hope died out. They'd likely require a hefty fee. She spent most of what she earned trying to get messages back home. If she didn't receive word soon, she'd need to figure out how to make the trek alone.

She could do it.

A mountain man had raised her.

Grace set the full bucket on the bank before grabbing the empty one. She dipped it into the swift, cool current. "I could do it. On my own, I could get out of here. I don't need Pa to come for me." She spoke to the river as if it had ears to hear.

"You want to get out of here?"

Grace jumped. The handle of the bucket slipped from her hand, tumbling downriver. She lunged for it, belly flopping into the water. Her fingers closed around the wire handle, but the bucket was full. It dragged her. No, no, no. She couldn't afford to lose the bucket. She struggled to her knees, grabbed with her other hand, holding the bucket in place. Somehow, she had to get it above the rushing water to empty it out.

"Let me help."

A man stooped in the water next to her. He didn't seem to care that his wool uniform would weigh more when wet. His hands found purchase on the bucket's handle. Grace let go and stumbled out of the river.

She fought her way back to the bank, skirts sticking to her legs as she crawled ashore. Grace picked up her skirts from the bottom and stared, wringing the water out. Only then did she take notice of who startled her, causing this mishap. It was Captain Winfield Cooper.

Figured.

Even though he was probably the only person on site who treated her without malice, he had a bad habit of sneaking up on her and then attempting to engage in conversation. It was annoying because she always had to scramble to conceal her hideous face. If he saw, he'd likely treat her as poorly as the rest of them did.

Captain Cooper lifted the bucket out of the current with ease. Grace turned her face away since the wet handkerchief clung to her throat. The water exposed her face. She tugged it up over her nose.

"That was refreshing." The bucket appeared at her feet.

"Thanks."

"Before our unexpected swim, what did I hear about you wanting to get away?"

"I need to get back to work." There was no way she was going to burden him with her sob story. She needed to get that fire going.

"Let me help." The bucket disappeared. "Ah, there's the other one."

Grace wrung another section of her skirt so it wouldn't weigh her down so much. "I can manage on my own, thank you."

"I'm not pressed for time, and I cannot leave a damsel in distress."

"Watch your tongue. You don't know to whom you speak." No one ever called her a damsel before. In fact, she couldn't recall if anyone ever referred to her as a woman. The best thing that could happen would be for him to go away and leave her alone.

He grunted. Then, his booted feet took off in a quick step. Was he gone? She dared not look. Grabbing the empty yoke, Grace made her way back to her copper.

Double-quick crunch steps grew louder. "Where do you want the water?"

Grace gritted her teeth so hard, pain shot up the side of her jaw. How dare he think she needed help? But there he was. Trying to patronize the poor, faceless laundress. She sighed. The water was here. Might as well not waste it. "In the large copper kettle." She kept her back to him. Hopefully, after pouring the first two buckets of water, he'd leave.

"Before I oblige, I want to know what you meant when you spoke of getting out of here."

For heaven's sake. "I'm going home." Now go away.

"Home? I'd say I'm ready to go home myself, but I'm not sure I want to call Ohio home anymore. These big skies and open prairies of the west are seductive. I'm thinking, when I muster out in a week, I'd like to stake out a hundred and sixty acres in the territory."

"That's nice. I really need to get back to work."

Water poured into the kettle. "That's nowhere near enough. Allow me to fetch more." The soles of his boots made a *squish-crunch* sound as he departed for the river. Grace put her hands on her head, turning a circle. Imagine the talk if the others saw an officer carrying water for her. She had to get him to leave her alone. Besides, she could do the job faster by herself.

He made it to the river in record time, filled the buckets, and trotted back. Why was he being so kind? What did he want from her?

Well, he would not get it. She was *not* that kind of girl.

"I've returned." *Splash!*

"I appreciate your help, Captain, but you really must go."

The sound of the Barlow boys yelling at one another about smelling like human refuse intruded upon the pause. Grace snorted.

"You all right?"

"It's nothing." She could get written up or worse yet—fired. She needed this job until she planned a way to get home.

"It was nice talking to you." Captain Cooper's inflection rose a bit at the end, as if he were unsure.

Grace busied herself with a bar of soap to make her refusal to face him seem less offensive. "Thanks again for the help."

He sniffed a few times. "Oh, I smell like a dead horse in this heat. I'm sorry you had to endure my odiferous presence. It was nice talking to you. I'll be back tomorrow." The sound of boots crunching on gravel receded.

Captain Cooper puzzled her. He left without making any requests other than her cleaning services. She wondered what he would think of her if he ever laid eyes on her pox-pitted face. He'd probably join the Barlow boys in kicking balls into her wash space.

Winfield looked over his shoulder. The laundress tossed the bar of soap from hand to hand, peering at him over her scarf. Every time he saw her, she wore a scarf or other covering and took pains to avert her face. Sometimes she would only engage in polite conversation from behind sheets on a line. Was she hiding some kind of disfigurement? Was that why others treated her poorly?

He'd seen how she was shunned. Left out of social events. Rarely did he notice her away from her station. He couldn't recall seeing her doing anything other than laundry and mending at her workstation, which happened to be set apart from all the rest. While the others shared resources provided by the quartermaster, this woman seemed to have to make or buy her own.

He went out of his way to treat her with kindness. Because of the scarf, it was unclear if he ever succeeded in making her smile at one of his silly jokes.

She had to be lonely. Her awkwardness made him want to make her life better. Just like how he enjoyed helping new troopers find confidence. He hated seeing people in positions of disadvantage and challenged himself to offer words or acts of encouragement. But how could he help her? He was leaving for South Pass City in a week.

Without his permission, an unwelcome memory shoved aside pleasant thoughts of gold mining. Winfield's breaths became shallow. His chest labored to suck in air. Not now. Not now.

The tension eased. Air rushed in. Hoo boy. That was close. His emotions nearly burst from their locked box. A good soldier—especially a captain—didn't allow the realities of the battlefield to ruffle him. He blinked a few times, pasted a smile on his face, and waved at some troopers fanning themselves with their kepis.

Winfield picked up his pace and headed to Old Bedlam, a large, white, two-story officer's quarters sporting covered porches on each level. He needed to go through and sort his belongings. What was his versus what belonged to Uncle Sam?

One week until he was a free man. His mood lifted like a raptor on a warm breeze.

Now, what would he do with all that gold?

He'd likely join up with some of the renowned mountain men to scout out an appealing parcel of land. Then he'd build himself a cabin using his own hands with trees he'd cut down and prepare himself. Once that was complete, he'd build fencing and acquire cattle.

Before the army, he assumed he'd settle one day and have a family. But all that changed. What woman would want a man who woke up in a cold sweat in the middle of the night shouting the names of men lost to brutality? War was all he knew. He'd be better off alone with his memories.

He entered his quarters. Not much cooler than outside, but at least he was out of the sun. He stripped off his jacket and hung it on a hook and then sat on the bed and yanked off his boots.

Mountain man. It was a rather nomadic life. Would that be a good fit for him?

Winfield chuckled to himself. He didn't have to figure it all out in the moment. He had time. And he had a plan for the immediate future. And that future was striking it rich in that new lode rumored in South Pass City.

———————

Hands gripping the sides of her bonnet, Grace raced to the sutler's store. She ignored soldiers and settlers while weaving her way toward the post office. Ordnance Sergeant Schnyder poked a finger into the chest of a young man. "I spent hours sorting and organizing the mail, and you have the *gall* to trot on in here, rifling your filthy paws through it, wreaking havoc. I'll have you fitted with a government watch."

The trooper winced with every jab. He didn't take a step back, as if holding his ground would prevent the sergeant from attaching a cannonball to his ankle.

"Now be gone with you, and don't you dare creep in here and touch my mail ever again."

The soldier saluted. "Yes, sir." He scurried out like a frightened rat.

The sergeant muttered to himself, stroking his mustache. Grace wasn't sure if he didn't see her or was ignoring her. "Excuse me."

Sergeant Schnyder stooped and scooped up about a dozen envelopes.

Grace slid closer to the counter. She kept her face turned to the side, chin tucked to her outside shoulder. "Sergeant Schnyder, have you received correspondence for Grace Manning?"

"Can't you see I'm busy?"

Searing heat bubbled in her chest. Regrettable words pounded on the backside of her teeth, desperate to lash out. She swallowed them. Hard. "Please take a moment to look. Then I shall be on my way."

"I don't recall any letters for you."

Grace sneaked a glimpse at him. He was bent over the mess on the floor. How could he know? No use pressing the issue. She spun on her heel and hurried out through the sutler's, nearly knocking over a knot of small pioneer children.

"Mommy, what's wrong with that lady? Why's her face covered?"

"Don't ask such questions. It's not polite."

Grace lengthened her strides and ran smack into a woolen blue wall. She stumbled backward and landed hard on her behind. On the first bounce, she looked up to see Captain Cooper reaching toward her. She pulled her hands in to cover her face. Too bad it didn't make her invisible.

"Hey...um...you? Hey you." Amusement colored his tone.

How could she work her way out of this encounter? She was in a compromising position.

"Let me help you up." Hands cupped her elbows and lifted. Her hands tore away from her face. She tried to resist, but he was too strong.

"Please don't."

"Are you hurt?" His voice was close. Too close.

"No." She rolled away from him to her knees, removed her hands from her face, and pushed up to stand. Without another word, she lifted her skirts and took off toward the river at a sprint. He'd better not follow.

At the river's edge, she slowed to a trot. She needed to be alone. The shore was empty. A large cottonwood tree stretched its branches high and wide, blocking the sun's light with its green canopy. Leaning against the rough bark, she slid down to sitting and then tore the bandanna from her face so she could breathe. She pushed her bonnet off her head to allow the breeze to cool her.

A bit of driftwood floated by. Too bad she couldn't build a raft and float home. If only it were so simple.

Grace undid her hair, letting it fall loose over her shoulders. She dug her fingers into the sandy soil until they curled around a smooth rock. She launched it toward the river, where it landed with a *plop*. She picked up another and tossed it a bit harder. It landed in the middle of the swirling current. Grace crawled on her hands and knees to the edge of the water and let it mesmerize her. She needed to clear her mind and come up with a plan. It was obvious her father wasn't receiving any of her telegraph messages. If he had, he'd have responded to her by now. Her parents believed she was in Philadelphia with her grandparents, learning how to live in civilization. Mother told her she'd be schooled in something called elocution and manners—both sorely lacking in the wild western territories. Wouldn't her parents be shocked to see her marching up to the hand-hewn cabin, rifle slung over her shoulder, wearing men's pants? Imagining the horrified look on her mother's face made her laugh out loud.

"What's so funny?"

Not again. Grace propped onto her elbows, putting her hands over her face.

"I came to check on you and make sure you weren't hurt."

"I'm fine. I need time alone if you don't mind."

"Are you trying to avoid me?"

That was blunt. And yes. She was. "I have a lot on my mind." Her voice was muffled by her hands.

He dropped to the ground next to her. "I'm a good listener."

She twisted away from him. "I don't doubt that."

"Do you have a complaint against me? Every time I try to strike up a conversation with you, you turn away. As you are right now. What have I done to offend you, Hey You? Why are you lying there like a child with your hands over your face?"

She'd just ignore that last question. "I'm not a sociable person. I grew up in the wilds, a daughter of a mountain man. My manners are lacking. Forgive me."

"A mountain man, you say? I'd like to meet him sometime. Perhaps he can advise me on how to live out the rest of my days."

Despite the heat, chills ran up and down Grace's spine. No way was she was going to get close enough to this trooper to introduce him to her pa. "If you don't mind, I really would like to be left alone."

A deep exhale. "Should you need me, I'll be in Bedlam." The leather of his boots creaked as he rose. Grace waited until she no longer heard his footsteps before lowering her hands.

That was close—too close. While she longed for friendship, she knew it would be over when he saw her face. She stared at her reflection in the calmer water along the shoreline. The memory of seeing her face as a ten-year-old girl rushed back.

Monster.

That word had filled her head when she saw her reflection in the water back then.

For a while, her mother assured her the scars would lighten and be less noticeable. But it never happened. Her face was as pitted as a dead tree assaulted by woodpeckers.

She rocked back onto her heels. She had to get home on her own. Pa taught her how to survive in the woods.

Before she could leave, she needed supplies. A rifle, knife, knapsack, and provisions. Unfortunately, the sutler's prices were too dear for her income. She suspected her pay was lower than the other laundresses. Perhaps she could visit one of the Laramie Loafer tribes across the river to trade, but she had nothing to trade with them. She owned nothing of value. Nobody wanted a ragged change of clothes.

Her only option was to save money and take on extra mending. But that would take time. She wanted to leave now and get away from the cruelty. Grace balled her fists and pounded them into the sand. She had to find another way home.

CHAPTER THREE

———◆◆———

G race knocked on the frame of the quartermaster's door. He
 sat at his desk, coat hung over the back of his chair, sleeves
of his white shirt pushed up to his elbows. Beads of sweat rolled
down his bald head. He swiped at his eyes and grunted what she
took to be an invitation to come in. "Sir?"

He looked up at her. "What do you want?"

"I'm here to give two-weeks' notice." She hoped that was
enough time to prepare for her journey.

"Notice of what? Get to the point. Can't you see I've a mountain of work to do?" He motioned to the pile of folders teetering
on the edge of his desk.

Heat built up under her scarf. "I'm leaving, sir."

"Leaving? That's it?"

"Yes, sir."

He stared at her for a moment. His eyes narrowed. "Off with
you now." He flicked the fingers of his right hand at her.

"But—"

"What do you want? Me to cry a torrent of tears? Now get
out of here and get back to work." He picked up a folder from the
top of the pile and slammed it on his desk, muttering to himself.

Grace watched him for a moment.

"I said, go back to work."

She spun on her heel and fled to the one place she felt comfort. The river.

A large white pelican floated downstream as Grace paced along the riverbank, wringing her hands. Did the quartermaster even hear her? What would happen if she up and left in two weeks' time? Humpf. Who'd notice she was gone? At least she didn't have a set schedule. Could it be a mercy the quartermaster ignored her resignation?

She stopped and closed her eyes to take a mental inventory of her few belongings. She had her Bible, a traveling outfit, and the ragged dress on her body. Living on a homestead didn't require a plethora of clothes. Upon arrival in Philadelphia, her grandparents would have outfit her with proper attire. One thing was for sure. What she had was not what she needed to survive an almost two-hundred-mile trek home.

Perhaps she could trade the traveling clothes for an old rifle. But the only people who would trade with her were the Indians. They had little to no need for a dress unless they traded it with some immigrants.

Nonetheless, she had to start out on her own and pray the good Lord would see her through.

Opening her eyes, she scanned the shore for a river rock. A flat, rounded rock lay against a piece of driftwood. Perfect. She stopped and scooped it into her hand. She checked to see if anyone else was around, then positioned the rock between her thumb and forefinger before letting it fly.

One, two, three. . .woo! Twelve skips. Pa would be proud.

"Impressive."

Captain Cooper. Grace snatched another smooth rock. It fit

in her palm. She took her time, turning enough to acknowledge him while hiding her face.

"Did your mountain man father teach you to skip rocks?" Cooper leaned against a cottonwood, arms crossed, face hidden in the shadow from the brim of his hat.

"Yes." She gave it a toss and caught it.

He gestured toward her. "Should I be worried?"

"Only a man with ill intent would ask such a question."

Cooper pushed away from the trunk. He seemed to be a bit off balance. Ha. She knew it. He was a scoundrel.

"Trust me, Captain, you don't want to test my aim."

"I assure you, I mean no ill. You are clearly misunderstanding me. I—"

"Then why are you so *nice* to me? No one else is. No one is nice to me unless they want something from me. And for the record, I am not for sale." She turned and threw the rock as hard as she could. It landed with a *sploosh* near the opposite bank. She needed to give a display of strength should he try to overpower her.

"Whatever gave you that idea? Let's talk about who is misreading whom, shall we?"

How dare he? She spun to face him, no longer caring.

He whipped off his hat and slapped it against his thigh. "I am a God-fearing man who believes in treating all beings, human or animal, with dignity and kindness. How could you draw such conclusions about me? My *intent*, miss, is to treat you with the respect you deserve as one created in the image of God. Nothing more. Nothing less."

Grace's heart thumped in her chest like a Shoshone war drum. Oh boy, she'd found his trigger. He didn't like his character questioned. She felt bad. "I–I'm sorry."

He approached the water while maintaining a respectable

distance from her. With his boot, he scraped around the river rocks, then bent to grab one. "This will do." With a flick of the wrist, he sent the rock skipping across the water.

Fifteen.

He looked at her and flashed a grin. Was he challenging her? Grace couldn't allow herself to be bested by Ohio Boy. Without a word, she grabbed a rock and let fly.

Eleven. She stomped her foot. Needed a thinner, lighter rock. Aha. She found one. She hooked it with her finger and threw again.

Sixteen.

Victory. She wiped her hands on her skirts. Now what? An awkward silence hung between them.

Captain Cooper settled his hat back on his head. A river of sweat rolled down his face into his mutton chops. "I'm mustering out next week. I'll need to turn in my uniform—clean. After that, I'm considering heading to South Pass City. I heard gold's been discovered."

Grace gasped at the mention of South Pass City. It's where her pa would go to pick up mail or receive messages.

"Are you all right? I can't imagine you'd miss me all that much." He smiled.

Think. Think. Think. How could she tag along? It appeared as if he was leaving when she was supposed to. What if this was an answer to her prayers? Should she ask? What should she say? Would it come across as being too forward? Especially after the recent verbal altercation.

What did she have to lose? Worst thing he'd say was no. And then, maybe she could stalk him and his crew. "May I travel with you?"

Cooper's eyes widened. His mouth dropped open. He toyed

with a brass button on his wool coat. "You want to travel with us?"

"I'll introduce you to my pa. He knows the area better than anyone." Might as well give some incentive. The captain said he wanted to meet her father.

"I'm sorry. I don't believe it's a wise idea for an unmarried woman." He did an about-face and walked away. All hope sank like a boulder dropped in the river.

CHAPTER FOUR

———◆••◆———

An anguished cry rivaled the sounds of the river and the fort as Winfield sped away from the laundress. His heart ached for her but taking a lone female on a weeks-long trek with a bunch of untoward, rowdy men was incomprehensible. Improper. She had to wait for her father to come to her aid.

Now the uncomfortable question was, how could he face her again to have her clean his uniform? Hopefully, by then she would calm down. Women's emotions led them to irrational thinking sometimes.

Over the next few days, the remainder of Company G arrived from their posts to muster out. Winfield spent his time preparing for his journey. Rumors of gold in South Pass City intrigued him. He remembered the one time he tried panning. After hours of dipping his pan and swirling the water along the riffles, a few tiny gold flecks winked at him in the sun. That discovery made his heart race with excitement. He wanted more.

Talk of a lode near South Pass took his mind off the horrors of war and the mundane day-to-day of frontier life. Winfield paused with a horn of gunpowder in his hand. His mind filled with images of himself walking into the assayer's office, arms loaded with bottles full of heavy golden chunks. Oh, the good he could do with that kind of money.

But he had to muster out first. The face of Caspar Collins filled his mind followed by the men in Sergeant Custard's ill-fated wagon train. No. No. Enough of that.

Winfield pressed his hands against his head. He couldn't let his thoughts stray. Now, what else did he need to do before entering civilian life?

The uniform. He had to get it to the laundress. Question was, would she clean it after he shot down her hope of getting home?

It was the right thing to do. The trail was no place for a woman, let alone one so skittish. Rather than leading his men, he'd have to spend all his time protecting her from them. They would never get to South Pass City. He didn't want to be responsible for a life he wasn't sure he could save.

He draped his uniform over his arm. Better see if she'd take it.

As he approached Suds Row, he heard shouting. Words most troopers shied away from blasted from the lips of women. He picked up the pace.

A metal washtub flew by his head, missing his ear by less than a quarter inch.

"Take that, you conniving little thief!"

To his right, the faceless laundress cowered against the side of a wash shed. The tub was only a few feet short. Obscenities assaulted his ears.

"Captain. This woman needs hung. She done stole *my* soap. Little, no-good, sneaking—"

"Enough!" Winfield assumed a commanding pose and stared down at the woman.

"She's the one who ya should be lookin' at."

"Your soap? From my understanding, your soap is supplied

by the quartermaster. Therefore, you don't own it. Now go back to your station before I have you put in a government watch."

"You wouldn't dare."

"Ma'am, are you being insubordinate to a commanding officer?"

She narrowed her eyes and glared at him for a moment before picking up her skirts and scurrying away.

The laundress was curled into a ball. Her hands over her head, body shaking. He knelt beside her, uniform slung over his arm. He put his hand on her back. She rolled away.

"Don't touch me!" Her head jerked around, eyes wide and wild. The lower portion of her face was covered by her scarf.

"What happened?"

She scrabbled out of reach. "What do you care?"

"Did they hurt you?"

She shook her head, eyes darting back and forth like a caged animal.

Winfield let out a huff of air. He flashed a tiny smile to put her at ease. "You know, I could order a nice, heavy ankle ornament on your behalf for your friend over there." He bobbed his head in the direction of the woman he chased away.

The eyes shrunk to normal size. She pushed to a sitting position. "All you men mustering out. . .so many uniforms. Ran out of soap. The others get soap from the quartermaster—"

"You're not provided with soap?"

"No, sir. I must make my own. Sometimes the others let me buy bluing for a hefty price."

He rubbed his hand over his face. "If I get you soap, would you wash my uniform?"

She looked down and scratched at her thumbnail.

"It's the last time."

She pushed to her feet. Her hair fizzed around her head like a white-gold cotton ball. "Get me soap, Captain Cooper. I'll have it done by morning." She turned to head to her lonely workstation.

"Wait!"

She turned to face him, scarf swaying where it hung below her chin.

He stared for a few minutes as his mind raced. How could he, an honorable man, allow her to remain in a state of abuse? Also, how could he, as an honorable man, ask her to travel with a bunch of ruffians for weeks? Her virtue and reputation were at stake.

"Must not be important." She crossed one foot over the other.

Winfield reached toward her and blurted, "I'll figure something out to help you get to South Pass City and even home." Dear Lord, make a way clear because he had absolutely no idea how he'd do it. Maybe find some kind pioneers willing to take her? But who would guarantee they'd treat her right?

"I appreciate the sentiment. But I'll manage on my own. I always do." She took off toward her station at a sprint. Her sobs riding the hot summer wind.

Later that night, he sprawled on his bed, studying the wood grain of the ceiling. He spoke to a few travelers in the sutler's store, but most were men headed west for the gold fields in California. The few families he encountered couldn't afford to take on another mouth to feed.

Leaving her behind wasn't an option. He had enough blood on his hands.

Knock! Knock!

The door flew open, hitting the wall. He never bothered to get the doorstop fixed. Oh well.

"Captain Cooper." Private Lloyd burst into the room, breathing as if he'd run around the parade ground ten times. Winfield sat up, then stood.

"Private, you know better than to crash in here before I answer your knock."

The younger man stiffened to attention and saluted, knocking his kepi askew. "Sorry, sir. But I was comin' to tell ya the guys and I are all having a meetin' outside the mess about our trip. We wanna make sure we're ready to go an' strike it rich."

Winfield pulled his coat from its hook on the wall. "One more day and we'll be civilians."

"Yes, sir. I can hardly wait myself. Wearin' a heavy wool coat in the middle of summer blazes is for the birds."

Lloyd stepped aside to let him leave his room. He trotted alongside Winfield like a puppy.

"Captain's here," Private Lloyd announced. The group snapped to attention and saluted.

"At ease." Would they shed all the pomp and ceremony on the trail?

Maps were laid out. Routes planned. Provisions and gear catalogued.

As the group wrapped up, Winfield posed the question banging around in his mind. "How would you feel if a woman traveled with us? She needs to get to South Pass City."

"I don't know about that, Captain. Ain't it kinda improper? Besides, depends on who it be."

Of course, they would have to ask. "The laundress, uh. . .the one who covers her face." His cheeks burned. He still didn't know her name.

"Her?"

The group erupted into laughter.

"She's a little crazy." One trooper circled a finger around his ear.

"Only way I'd get comfortable with a woman around was if

she were someone's wife an' he was with her. Only way it'd be proper an' all," Private Lloyd offered.

A buzz passed through Winfield's body as if he were struck by lightning. Surely there was another way.

"I ain't opposed. Could give us some evening entertainment, if ya know what I mean," another man sneered.

"Shut up, Novak." Lloyd moved toward the man with a raised fist.

"Attention!" Winfield barked the command. The men snapped to. He needed to think this through. He laced his fingers behind his back and paced. Lloyd's words marched in endless file through his brain. Marrying her would make it legitimate. But then what? He was going to the mines. He made another lap. What if it were nothing more than a business proposal? They could always have it annulled in South Pass. He stopped. That was it!

But how could he get her to agree to this harebrained plan?

He needed to get her some soap and his uniform for the ceremony. He'd feel things out and ask in the morning when he retrieved his uniform.

CHAPTER FIVE

◆●◆

Grace rose from her cot, blinked, and rubbed her eyes. They felt full of gravelly sand from down by the river. Between the tears and staying up all night to work on uniforms, she was exhausted. She stumbled into her work area to lean on the table to prevent tipping over.

Captain Cooper and his men were headed to South Pass City the next morning. Grace decided she would hide in the shadows and follow them. She accepted the fact she'd likely never make it home. Her family would be left to wonder about her fate. To them, she'd have disappeared into thin air. Her mother would blame herself for sending Grace to her death.

She flipped over the washtub and plopped down. One thing was clear. She wasn't staying here. Closing her eyes, she opened a conversation with Jesus. After all, she'd be seeing Him soon.

A voice interrupted her prayer. It was too early for any of the men to come pick up their wash. She hopped to her feet with a wobble and looked for some kind of weapon. The bar of soap Captain Cooper brought the night before was missing. Of course it was. They couldn't leave her alone.

The paddle for swishing clothes. That'd work. It might be

another laundress coming to steal the rest of her supplies. No one could bully her if they were dead.

"Hey, Hey You! It's Captain Cooper."

Grace cupped her free hand over her brow, squinting into the rising sun. A form jogged toward her.

"I know I'm a bit early, but I need to speak with you."

Early. That was an understatement. What could he want? She still didn't trust him as far as she could drop-kick him like the Barlow boys' ball. Resting the paddle on her shoulder, she stepped out of her workstation.

Captain Cooper slowed. "Ah, good. I have a proposition to make."

Pinkish gold sunlight popped over the eastern horizon, stabbing her bleary eyes. "If you wait out here, I'll get your uniform."

"We'll get to that, but I need to ask you something first."

Grace pulled the paddle off her shoulder and smacked the handle against her palm. "Ask away."

"Will you marry me?"

A bison rammed into her chest at a full sprint. The paddle fell to the ground. "You're making fun of me." Her voice cracked.

"Hear me out. It's not what you think. You asked if I'd let you travel with me and my men to South Pass City. As you know, your reputation would come into question. A single woman traveling with a group of single men. It's scandal material."

"But—"

"Listen to me. Think of it as a business deal. Once we get to South Pass City, we can have it annulled and you can go your way and I will go mine—after we get ahold of your father, of course. What other option do you have?" He removed his hat. His thick mustache twitched as he waited for her reply.

What other choice did she have? Death? Was God answering

her prayer by providing her a way out despite its unconventionality?

"I—I don't even know you. You don't even know my name."

"What is your name?" His eyes pierced her to her soul. They were not the eyes of a man making jest. What did he want from her? This couldn't be genuine kindness.

She turned away from him and hugged herself. No. This was insane. She was not about to marry a strange man just to get home. "I can't." Tears pooled in her eyes. What if this was her only chance?

"You have to. I can't leave you here."

"I *have* to?" Grace whirled to face him.

"Yes." He stared at her unblinking. "I've seen how they treat you. I wouldn't allow my horse to stay in these conditions."

"I'm not a horse." Anger rose, clogging her throat.

"I didn't say you were." Captain Cooper broke eye contact and scanned her space. "Where's the soap I brought you last evening?"

"It's—It…disappeared," she whispered.

"That is why you must marry me. I will get you home to your father. You have my word. I will expect nothing of you. It's strictly business."

She either accepted and traveled under the protection of the group, or she sneaked along like a common thief, sure to die. "Fine. I accept." She crossed her arms and looked away. "Now what?"

"Tell me your name. Hey You won't work for the legal documents."

"G–Grace Manning."

"Well, Miss Manning, I must go to the chaplain to get the papers drawn up. We need to make this legal by evening since we depart early tomorrow."

The impulse to run and hide caused her knees to shake. "I will prepare once all the uniforms are picked up."

"I'll see you later in my office." He left.

Grace put her hands over her face and turned in circles. Her heart pounded like the hooves of a galloping horse. Her mind raced. What did she agree to?

By evening, she'd be a married woman.

She righted her wash tub and fetched the buckets to fill with water. What was she doing? She didn't have any soap. She didn't have to do any more laundry. She was headed home to her mother and stepfather.

When she was a child, Grace's family had headed west. Her city-slicker father wanted to try his hand at farming in Oregon. Along the way, she and her father contracted smallpox. The rest of the wagon train left them to die along the trail. Ray Manning, one of the guides, stayed behind. Grace's father succumbed to the illness, leaving her and her mother.

To save Grace's life, Ray took her mother to his cabin. Ray married Mother to keep things proper.

All these years later, Pa and Mother were *still* married and loved each other. What they meant to be convenient became the real thing.

Unlike her mother, Grace had an exit plan. Marrying for love was not possible. How could she possibly love someone else when she didn't love herself?

She was disfigured. Hideous. A monster. No man would willingly spend the rest of his life with her. No matter how nice he was.

This arrangement was merely a vehicle to get her to where she wanted to be.

Home.

Then she could make a life for herself. By herself.

CHAPTER SIX

Late June 1867

Fort Laramie, Dakota Territory

G race hid in the shadows while the other laundresses picked her workstation apart like vultures on carrion. She hugged her few belongings to her chest, making sure no one looked in her direction, then dashed into the building. Fortunately, the offices were labeled.

Captain Cooper greeted her and introduced her to the chaplain. The marriage was little more than putting signatures to paper. The chaplain must have been briefed on the circumstances because there weren't any vows or flowery words exchanged. Grace was relieved.

The men shook hands, and the chaplain left.

Grace studied the toe of her boot, hoping it would embolden her to speak.

"Congratulations, Mrs. Cooper."

Oh. He—her husband—addressed her. She nodded, biting her lip. Words lodged in her throat. She opened her mouth and took a deep breath, hoping that would help. "Um. . ."

"Yes?"

She still couldn't bring herself to look at the man standing in the room with her. "Do you think it's possible to leave tonight? I don't want to waste any time getting home."

"That's not possible. We still have some last-minute provisions to procure."

"But I already vacated my space and have nowhere to spend the night." The words tumbled out like rocks off a ledge.

"You can stay in my quarters. I planned on bunking in the stables with our horses. We'll leave at dawn." His tone was matter-of-fact. Grace prayed the floor would swallow her. What would people think if they saw her enter and exit his room?

"Grace...if I may call you that...are you all right?" There was a hint of concern in his voice. She peeked up at him.

"It—it feels so wrong."

"If it will help, we can wait until the dark of night. You need rest. This journey won't be easy."

Grace snorted. "I am aware of that, Captain Cooper. I traveled here to begin with."

"Please call me Winfield."

Footsteps pounded down the hallway and the door flew open. A red-faced man stood panting in the entry to the office.

Captain Cooper ran his hand down his face and sighed. "Lloyd, how many times—"

"Sir..." His voice trailed off as he looked from Grace to the captain. "What's she doin' here?"

A smile pulled at the captain's lips. It didn't reach his eyes. "Let me introduce you to my wife—Grace Cooper."

"So, it *is* true. Me an' the guys heard rumors, which is why I came. They called a meetin' at the stables and wanted to know if it was true or not."

The Lloyd fellow's eyes looked her up and down like he was

an auctioneer and she a beef cow. His eyes didn't project disgust; he just seemed curious. But the others? How would they respond? What if some of them were the mean ones?

"Well, Grace, it's time to inform the men that you will be traveling with us."

Grace groaned. But there was no way out.

After a quick jaunt to the stables, the captain made his announcement.

"Yer what?"

"Captain, you gotta be hornswoglin' us."

Captain Cooper took her hand. Grace flinched. No man other than her father and Pa ever touched her hand. She fought the urge to pull away.

"You gotta be kiddin' me," one man said, spitting a slimy stream of tobacco into the dirt. "Her? Scarf Face?"

The entire group broke out into laughter. Grace tugged her hand free, spinning on her feet to flee. This was a bad idea.

Strong hands gripped her shoulders. They pulled her into an awkward side hug. "The Bible tells us not to judge a man. . .or woman by outward appearance. Grace is my wife, and I expect you to treat her with respect or you'll get Chicagoed by me personally. Understand?"

The men fell quiet. Only the wind and ambient sounds from the fort wafted around them.

"Yes, sir," they cried in unison. "Nobody wants t'get beat that bad."

From the look on his face, he was serious. He seemed intent on keeping her safe.

"Tomorrow morning, we leave at first light. Let's make all the final preparations so we may depart without delay."

"Aren't ya gonna take some *honeymoon time*?" one man snickered.

Her feet itched to run. Run as far away from Winfield Cooper as possible. Surely he wouldn't expect. . . That was not part of the deal! It took every ounce of her strength to remain rooted to the ground.

"Mind your own business and go get ready."

The men paused.

"Now." The captain surged forward. They scattered like roaches in sudden candlelight.

Grace and her new husband stood in strained silence.

Captain Cooper cleared his throat. "Well, that was awkward."

No kidding.

"I meant it when I told you this is an arrangement for your protection. I expect nothing from you. However, our marriage is official, and it would raise eyebrows if we didn't share the same quarters tonight—"

She hopped farther away. "But you said. . ." What was she thinking? "I—I can't."

"I'll sleep in the closet if that'll make you more comfortable. I'm also willing to linger about until you fall asleep and rise before you awake to give you privacy."

He assumed she'd be able to fall asleep. He knew nothing about her. She was used to sleeping with one eye open in case someone sneaked into her quarters to wreck her work or steal from her. She hadn't slept soundly since leaving home.

"Grace?"

She closed her eyes. It bothered her that he used her name. He used to call her Hey You. It felt comfortable. More. . .distant. He asked her to call him Winfield. There was no way. She could only think of him as Captain Cooper.

"Grace?"

Again, what other option was there? The marriage had

to appear believable to preserve her purity. What a paradox! "All right."

He cupped her elbow with his hand and led her to his quarters. Catcalls and whistles rang through the parade grounds as they walked. Morning couldn't arrive fast enough.

CHAPTER SEVEN

Late June 1867

Winfield knocked back his third cup of the strongest black coffee known to man. The plan was to creep to the closet in his quarters after Grace fell asleep so he could rest before embarking on their journey to South Pass City. Problem was Grace never fell asleep. She sat rigid against the head of the bed, knees pulled tight against her chest, eyes darting about as if she expected bears to burst out of the floorboards. Winfield wandered the fort, avoiding detection lest someone question the legitimacy of the marital arrangement.

He didn't expect it to be this difficult. How much more would it be on the trail?

A hint of crimson appeared on the eastern horizon. Better get Grace moving so he could ready himself and the men and depart by sunup.

He knocked on the door in Bedlam. Grace opened it a crack and peered out. Her face covered in layers of a bonnet, scarves, and a bandanna. How could she breathe under all that material?

"I need to come in and gather my belongings."

The door opened wide, and Grace positioned herself behind the door.

"Did you get any sleep?" Winfield gathered the few remaining items lying about into his bundle. He pulled his rifle off the wall and checked to make sure his Colt was in the holster.

Grace shook her head.

"Ready? We're meeting the boys at the stables. We purchased horses from some Loafers. I'm assuming you can ride?" She could probably ride better than most cavalrymen.

Another nod.

Irritation roused in his chest. He was doing this for *her*. He didn't have to invite her along and marry her to make it possible. The least she could do was talk to him. "Did you lose your voice?"

"I have little to say."

"Aren't you the least bit excited about going home?"

A nod.

Time was wasting. "Let's go. We are going to be late." He opened the door and held it for her. She slipped by without as much as a glance or thank you.

This was going to be a long, arduous journey.

Winfield's horse stumbled and let out a low whinny. They weren't quite to the designated camping spot, but if they continued farther, his horse wouldn't make it. He threw his leg over the horse and hopped down. After lashing the reins to a sage bush, he called out to the party. "We need to stop here. My horse is beat." He looked down the trail. Grace lingered about two hundred yards away.

The boys dismounted and began looking for a lower spot with the tiniest modicum of shade. Trees were not in abundance in the Dakota Territory.

"Are you coming?" It was hard to hide the annoyance in his tone.

Grace's horse danced in place, still a good two hundred yards down trail. They could not continue like this. It put the entire group at risk, and they'd never make their destination.

No answer. Winfield took a moment for deep breaths. This was not an insubordinate trooper; this was his wife. He couldn't yell and threaten punishment. He had to find a balance between being gentle yet firm. His new wife was more skittish than a baby bird. If the boys saw him treating her harshly, they would follow suit. It was up to him to set the tone with her.

Rather than giving an order, he walked at a slow pace to her. He took hold of the bridle and led the horse to camp.

She didn't resist, nor did she speak. "You don't need to be afraid."

"I'm not afraid."

"You hung back from the group all day long. So much so, we need to stop miles from our planned camp."

"I prefer to be alone."

"About that. There are a lot of threats along this trail. We need to stick close together. When you lag like that, you put yourself and the boys at risk. Not to mention, my poor horse has to travel double the distance going back and forth."

They stopped out of earshot of the group.

"I'm not used to being around groups of people. Maybe this was a mistake." She pulled her mount's head sharply to the right. Winfield let go.

"What are you doing?"

"This is a mistake. I—I can't. . ."

"You can't go back."

"Then I shall go it alone. I'll pay you for the horse and the provisions once I settle." She kicked the horse into a trot.

"Stop!" Winfield tore off after her, diving for the reins. He halted the animal.

"Let go." She kicked harder. The horse reared. She held on as if one with the beast.

"Listen, Grace *Cooper*, when I signed those papers, I made a promise to protect you. Isn't that why you agreed to this arrangement in the first place? When I deliver you in one piece to South Pass City and into the hands of your father, you will never have to lay eyes on me again."

The horse landed. Grace made clicking noises with her tongue and patted his neck. He calmed, pawing at the ground. "I want to sleep apart from you men."

Winfield pulled his hat off and wrung it in his hands to keep from wringing her neck. "You realize the boys and anyone else we meet must believe we are married. You act as if I am revolting."

"You assured me nothing would be expected—"

"Let me rephrase. Nothing of the ah...marital duty or expression is required. However, what is required for your safety and virtue is to at least pretend I am tolerable."

"Nonetheless, I wish to bunk with Peaches here."

"Peaches? You named your horse Peaches?"

"Do you have a problem with that?"

"You're diverting. You will sleep alongside me, or if you prefer, you can cozy up to Private Lloyd over there."

The former private looked up from building a fire ring. "Sir?"

Winfield leaned in, positioned his hand vertically to his mouth and whispered. "He has the worst hygiene in the entire unit. His smell alone will keep any predators away, human or beast." He gave his armpits a quick whiff. "Me? I bathed in the river last night while you slept. But those are your choices."

Grace's eyes narrowed to the point of almost disappearing in the shadow cast by her bonnet. Did she get the humor? Was she angry? Bewildered? How does one read a faceless woman?

She hopped off Peaches. "Fine. But if you pull anything, I'll break your nose."

He had to turn away to hide the smile. This woman was all or nothing. "Yes, ma'am."

In truth, she had nothing to worry about. He was a man of his word. With the deadly threats lurking in the frontier, he'd likely spend most of the night on watch.

CHAPTER EIGHT

Early July 1867

Oregon Trail, Dakota Territory

Grace stroked Peaches' muzzle while the boys cooked some awful-smelling stew over the fire. Every now and again, one or more would look in her direction, say something to a buddy, and then snicker. She felt more comfortable with the horses.

Captain Cooper tried to coax her over. He had a point about their marriage appearing real, but he didn't know how hard it was for her to be around people—especially people who were mean to her at the fort.

The urge to hop on her horse and take off alone was strong. Spending the night in the captain's quarters at Bedlam left her nauseous and exhausted. She didn't even want to lie down on the bed. It felt wrong. So very wrong. And having to lie down alongside him that night felt wrong. She didn't know if she could bring herself to do it. But she had to. She had to if she wanted to return home.

"Food's ready!" the Lloyd fellow called out. "Come and get some of this fancy meat biscuit soup."

"What's a meat biscuit?"

"The advertisement said it has the nutrition of five pounds of fresh beef."

Grace frowned under her scarf. That didn't sound appetizing. The sutler's store sold all kinds of gimmicky items to weary overland travelers. Meat biscuits sure sounded like one of those items. Maybe it was better than what the men were used to eating?

She meandered through the sagebrush to the fire. Captain Cooper approached Lloyd with two tin cups in one hand and two spoons in the other. She hung back. Would requesting to eat with him apart from the others uphold the facade? She steeled her nerves to ask once he was served. She was not used to taking initiative with others aside from her family.

Lloyd slopped a brown mushy-looking substance into the cups. Cooper searched for her in the circle, then seemed to look beyond. She gave a little wave. He headed toward her.

"Why—why don't we sit over. . ." Why couldn't there be a tree for shade? And why was she so nervous? "What about that rock?" She pointed.

Cooper smiled and took the lead. She sat, and he handed her the steaming cup of scary meat biscuit soup.

"I figured eating together would uphold our charade."

"It will. We need to appear to have a conversation."

Oh. How was she supposed to know what a former cavalry captain wanted to talk about? Grace lifted the cup under her scarf to blow on it. It didn't smell like any meat she recognized.

"Tell me about yourself. Now that we are, for all intents and purposes, married, it would be nice to know a little bit about you." He scooped a spoonful of soup into his mouth. He grimaced, then swallowed.

"There's not much to know. I grew up on the plains at the base of what is now known as the Bridger Range, named after the famous mountain man, Jim Bridger."

He stirred the spoon in his cup. "So, what did you do?"

"What do you mean?"

"Did you attend school? Who were your friends? You know, normal growing-up kind of things."

Grace let out a laugh. "How long have you been in the territory?"

"About four years."

"You are asking if I went to school?"

"Well, I mean, I suppose if you grew up in the middle of nowhere, you wouldn't exactly attend school."

"My father—not my stepfather—was a highly educated man. He brought a collection of books with us. My mother taught me. I can read and write in English and Latin."

"Really?"

"Why are you surprised?" What did he think? That she ran around in the wilds wearing bearskins, foraging for food, and grunting?

Captain Cooper scratched the back of his neck and examined the sky as if he were making sure it was staying in place. "Ah, growing up in a town with excellent schools, I never thought about what it was like on the frontier. I guessed. . . I don't know what I guessed."

"What about you?" Reciprocation seemed the next logical move.

"I grew up in Hillsboro, Ohio. I'm an only child. My mother died in childbirth. My father never remarried. I did the normal boyhood things: hunting, fishing, teasing girls. I volunteered during the war, hoping to fight back east, but we were sent west instead."

"Lookit the lovebirds!"

"Hey Cap, you and the wife gonna help with cleanup?"

The captain knocked back the rest of the soup and wiped his mouth with the back of his hand. Grace had yet to taste hers. He gestured at her cup with his spoon. "You better eat up. I know it's pretty awful, but you're going to need all the energy to travel in this heat."

"You act as if I have never made a long trip. How do you think I got out here?" Memories of traveling with freighters prickled her mind. She shuddered. The oxen or mules received better treatment than she did.

"It appears civility wasn't included with the English and Latin." He rose. "I best help the boys and get our bedding out for the night. Looks like it should be a clear one."

Oof. That stung. Was she truly so abrasive?

Cooper hopped over a sagebrush and joined his boys, slapping several on the back. Her soup was cooler. She turned away from camp, removed her scarf, pinched her nose, and downed the stuff. It was foul indeed. She didn't know how anyone could claim it tasted like beef let alone hold any nutritional value.

The next few days were repeats of the prior. Grace attempted to keep up with the group, which meant enduring sly ridicule and snide comments when the captain wasn't within earshot. She did her best to ignore them but hoped at some point she could take revenge. Nothing humbled a man like a bull snake in the bedroll. Most thought they were rattlers. She'd have to pay extra-close attention at camp to see if she could catch one stretched out in the sun. Then again, Cooper would be furious. One thing was clear—he demanded respect toward everyone. Even her. Probably from her as well.

On the eve of the fifth day, things changed. Her usually jovial, talkative husband grew quiet and even pensive. He ignored the ribbing from his boys and gave her clipped one-word responses whenever she tried to strike up conversation to keep up the facade and make life on the trail less miserable. All her efforts were in vain. Cooper seemed more and more distant. As if he were afraid of something.

The closer their little band got to where Fort Caspar once stood, the more sleep eluded Winfield. One night out from that dreadful place, Winfield waited until Grace was asleep and sat by the fire. Private Lloyd dropped onto the ground next to him. "Tomorrow we're gonna go by the bridge."

"I know. I'm thinking about a detour." He stirred the embers with a stick.

"You know Red Cloud and Crazy Horse is out there. Besides, there ain't no other place to cross. This is the most dangerous area. Between here and Sweetwater. I don't think there's many guarding the wires now that we're out."

"Every time I go to the bridge, I'm overcome with a sense of dread. My stomach kicks like a wild horse with a thorn in his side."

"You and he were close. I remember. He was a good kid."

"And then there was Custard. Why didn't he listen? I *told* him. Bretney told him." A log popped, sending sparks swirling into the black velvet sky.

"Ain't your fault, Cap. None of it were. The Injuns was all stirred up like angry hornets."

"You know if I see any, I will kill them," Winfield spat the words out.

"I hear ya. They are a pestilence."

"What they did to him. . ." He let his words trail off. "I can't go back there." His voice hitched. Emotions long buried gushed to the surface. "Worst part is he actually respected them. He and his father spent years building a relationship. He was fluent. The Lakota taught him themselves. I don't understand." Winfield buried his face in his hands to hide the tears from Lloyd. "I've never been given to hate anybody, but I hate them. God forgive me."

CHAPTER NINE

———◆•◆———

Early July 1867

Near Fort Caspar, Dakota Territory

After Captain Cooper and Private Lloyd went to bed, Grace bid her time trying to count stars. She knew they were beyond number, but that never stopped her from trying to count. It reminded her of how big God was. She needed to take her mind off the conversation she'd overheard.

When a hint of light glowed on the eastern horizon, Grace got up. Captain Cooper snored about a foot away. His arm was on part of her blanket. She dug her fingers into her scalp. Now what? She was married to a man who planned on killing the next Indian he saw. What if Pa was the next Indian? Would the captain put a bullet in his head? What about his conviction about respect? Hate and respect didn't mix. She had to do something. But what? Maybe a morning ride would clear her head so she could muster up the courage to confront her so-called husband.

Lifting her skirts, Grace tiptoed around sagebrush, careful not to step on dry twigs or foliage. The horses nickered as she approached. Putting a finger to her lips, she shushed them as if they understood. She worked fast saddling her horse. After untying Peaches, she put her left foot in the stirrup.

"Where do you think you're going?" She let out a yelp. Peaches hopped to the side. Grace went down hard, her foot stuck in the iron. Winfield Cooper ran to the horse, calming him. He tied him to a bush and freed Grace's foot.

She scrabbled away from him as he approached. "Stay away."

"I want to help you up."

"No. Leave me be."

"Grace, what's gotten into you?" He rushed in and tried to catch her under the arms, but she rolled out of reach.

"You're nothing but a bunch of hateful killers. I—I want nothing to do with any of you." She flipped to her knees and pushed to standing, brushing bits of sage and dirt off her skirts.

"What are you talking about?" He stepped closer.

"Keep away."

"Grace?"

"I heard you and Lloyd talking about how much you hate Indians and want to kill them. I want nothing to do with you."

"Grace, be reasonable—"

"Me be reasonable? I'm not a cold-blooded killer. I'll have you know that my stepfather is half Shoshone. That tribe has practically adopted me. How dare you?"

"I don't have a beef with the Shoshone—"

"You both said you hated all Indians and want to see them all dead. I want nothing to do with you. Now leave me be."

By now, all the men were awake and gathered in a knot.

"I don't want to be married to someone who can wish death and destruction upon another human being. What if you turn murderous toward me?" She ran toward her horse, yanked the reins from the bush, and leaped on his back as she learned from her Shoshone family. She gave Peaches a kick, and the horse bolted away from Cooper, galloping down the trail. Tears blurred her eyes. She needed time to think before finishing the confrontation.

How did she not realize the reason most of those men were out west was to deal with what they called the Indian problem. Frankly, the white settlers were the problem. If they didn't make and break treaties or go on murderous rampages like Chivington did a few years back, maybe they could've gotten along.

The sun hovered over the horizon, a giant orange-red ball. It was to her right, so she headed north. She'd gotten off the trail a bit. She pulled the reins to slow her horse. It was a miracle Peaches didn't trip or break a leg during the flight. She'd been careless, putting her horse at risk. Grace turned the horse until the sun was behind her and to the right. A cloud of dust appeared to the southeast. Grace squeezed her legs, prompting Peaches into a trot. She rose in the stirrups to lessen the impact on her bottom from the choppy gait.

She glanced over her shoulder. The dust cloud was bigger and nearer. Surely Winfield Cooper wouldn't come after her now. Hadn't she made it clear she wanted nothing to do with him? She called him a murderer.

What if it was a band of warriors or a hunting party? She'd welcome that. She knew enough sign to communicate with several Plains tribes. Perhaps they could get word to Pa's tribe?

Whomever it was, Grace decided not to show any fear. If it was her so-called husband, she'd tell him she'd talk when she was ready.

"Grace!"

Her heart sank. It was the captain.

His mount skidded to a stop in front of Peaches, causing the palomino to rear.

"I told you to leave me alone. I need time to think." She didn't look in his direction. She maintained her focus on the trail ahead and wheeled her horse to move around his.

"Stop. Will you?"

"I'm not one of your men. You have no authority to command me."

"I'm your husband."

"On paper. It's a business deal that clearly isn't working."

"You can't go off by yourself. It's not safe."

She yanked Peaches' head hard to face him. "Safe? Aren't you one to talk? Apparently, you and your 'boys' have no compunction for slaughtering innocent people because you don't like them."

"You don't know what you're talking about!"

"I don't? Why don't you just admit the only good Indian is a dead Indian? You make me sick."

"Do you have any idea what happened at Platte Bridge?"

"No, but I'm sure you and your ilk brought it on yourselves. I've heard about what your soldiers have done to my people."

"Your people? You're as pale as they come! Your hair is so blond, it's almost white."

She leveled her gaze at him. "Look, Captain Cooper, I may have been born of white parents, but the Shoshone tribe is my family. They accept me as I am."

"Then why are you alone?"

Grace felt as though an arrow pierced her heart. While the Shoshone tribe was kind, she never felt she could move into the village. Words evaded her.

"One of my best men and friend was murdered at Platte Bridge." He hopped off his horse and approached. "It wasn't fair. Caspar didn't deserve to die. I won't even tell you what they did to him." Cooper choked on his words, leaned away from his horse, and dry heaved.

He was upset. Something tugged at her heart. Something forced words out of her mouth in a hoarse whisper. "Tell me."

Winfield Cooper wiped his mouth with his sleeve. His eyes wide. "I don't talk about it to anyone."

She nudged Peaches closer to where he stood. "You're the one reminding me I'm your wife. Now I'm reminding you. Tell me."

Cooper's face went through a series of contortions. This display of emotion made Grace's insides squirm. She wanted to kick her horse and take off running again, but something held her back. Deep in her gut, she knew she needed to hear what he had to say.

Bracing himself against his horse, he gazed into the distance. "There were supply wagons. A few men and myself came upon their encampment as we headed to Platte Bridge Station. Despite our warnings of ambush, the sergeant scoffed and called us cowards. I keep asking myself if there was something more I could have done. Made him listen."

Grace swung her right leg over Peaches' rump and dismounted. She stood arm's length from the captain. "It's not your fault he didn't listen."

"Lieutenant Bretney and I even went back a second time." His voice cracked. "They were killed and tortured. All of them."

She closed her eyes. None of the Indians she knew could be capable of such things, could they? But then again, all men inherited the sin nature from Adam and Eve. No man was above evil acts. "And—and Caspar?" Cooper flinched at the mention of that name. "Tell me about him."

"The next—the next day his body was found on the bank of Dry Creek." Captain Cooper took several deep breaths. He clenched his hands. "There were twenty-four arrows in his naked body. They—they wrapped him in. . .telegraph wire." Silence.

Grace's feet moved her close. She put a hand on his shoulder. "Go on."

Deep blue eyes, the color of a late summer sky, bore into her. "This isn't fit for a woman."

Fear crawled along the surface of her skin. She shivered despite the heat from the rising sun. She needed to understand where the hate came from. If it remained hidden, the hate would fester over time. It had to come out before she introduced him to her pa in South Pass City.

Cooper didn't break his gaze. "The back of his head was caved in. His brain, heart, and bowels were removed. His hands and feet. . ." a sob broke his stream of words, ". . .were cut off. I don't remember if it was that night or later, but a warrior could be seen from the fort wearing Caspar's new uniform jacket, dancing." He turned away and buried his face against his horse's neck. His body shook.

She let her hand fall away. That explained his odd behavior the past few days. She put her hands to her face. What should she say? Anything that came to mind seemed trite.

"Grace, I know it's wrong to hate, but I can't get past the depredations. We lived in a kill-or-be-killed world. It does things to a man."

"Enough to go back on your word?"

Winfield Cooper spun around. "What's that supposed to mean?"

She shrank back. "Your promise to keep me. . .us safe to South Pass."

"I am a man of my word." He sighed and pulled his hat off his head.

"Every man has a breaking point. I hope and pray your hatred for the Indians isn't yours, Captain."

"I pray so too, Grace. And please. Call me Winfield."

CHAPTER TEN

July 1867

Fort Caspar to Sweetwater Station, Dakota Territory

Winfield pulled himself onto his horse. Today was the day he had to face what was now known as Fort Caspar. Sleep steered clear all night as dread kept him in a choke hold. Staying atop the horse was going to prove a challenge.

Through the course of the morning, the pressure in Winfield's head grew and grew. Would his neck shoot it off like a cannonball out of a howitzer?

The men in the group appeared to sense the gravity of the situation. No one spoke. The only sounds were the wind and the crunch of horses' hooves on the hardpan.

When the low, long log buildings came into view, Winfield's heart beat harder and faster. Phantom sounds of war whoops and yells filled his mind. Smoke from rifles and the *zing* of arrows overwhelmed his senses. He squeezed his eyes shut and shook his head as if that would clear the memories.

"Captain, are you all right? You look as though you might fall off your horse." Grace's voice cut through the war in his mind. Revealing his struggle with her last night wasn't easy, but in this moment, he was grateful for the conversation.

He grunted and sat taller in the saddle.

"So, this is it. I remember passing through here on my way east. I had no idea—"

"Please, Grace. Not now." Winfield dug his heels into his horse, and the beast took off at a gallop toward the bridge. Near the fort, a sentry waved him down. He pulled on the reins and stated his party's intent to cross the bridge. The opposite side of the North Platte was where his friend fell. His plan was to give his horse his head and let him race until they were well past the spot. Given that the fort was occupied, he wasn't worried about Grace or the men.

Private Lloyd pulled up alongside. "You gonna wait for the rest, Cap'n?"

"I need to get through here as fast as possible. I'll wait for you a few miles upriver. Heeya!" He squeezed hard into his horse and burst forward through the familiar parade grounds then thundered across the bridge. The horse surged up the bluffs on the opposite side. Hot wind whipped Winfield's face. His eyes watered. He told himself it was from the wind and dust, but his heart revealed otherwise as a soul-shattering sob burst from his mouth. He was likely in the very spot Caspar took an arrow to the face while saving one of the Kansas men. Why did such a good man have to die? One so young and full of promise?

Anger toward Major Anderson flared. He and Lieutenant Bretney stormed into Anderson's office when they found out Caspar was lost. Bretney didn't hesitate to accuse the man of cold-blooded murder. Winfield backed him up. The major had no business ordering one of *his* men to certain death.

The horse raced on, hooves eating up the gravely dirt and sagebrush. White lather appeared on his coat. In this heat, Winfield knew it was time to slow down, but the speed, the risk was cathartic.

But not cathartic enough.

The Indian scourge needed to be eradicated. Maybe then he could move beyond the past.

———————•———————

Grace was surprised she hadn't melted after a long day of being beaten by the sun. A sullen Cooper dismounted at a place he called Willow Springs. It was barren, rocky, and full of sagebrush. Private Lloyd told her this was where the captain and Bretney found Custard camping. She figured this would also be a difficult night for their leader. He blamed himself for the death of all those men.

Cuing off Captain Cooper, the men remained silent and pensive as they set up camp. No one ribbed her about her scarf or lack of affection toward her husband. It made life easier for her.

While dining on hardtack soaked in bacon grease, a lone figure approached. He or she took lurching steps and appeared to be carrying something or someone in their arms.

One man grabbed his rifle, chambered a round, and pointed it at the person. "Who goes there?"

A weak reply came in the language of the Plains tribes. A woman. She sounded Arapahoe.

All the men set aside their supper and took up arms.

"Put those away." Grace got up and stood in front of the business end of the rifles pointed at the woman. "She appears to be alone."

"Could be a decoy," Captain Cooper stated, lifting his rifle to his shoulder and putting the woman in his sights.

"It's a woman and child. Put your rifle down." Grace grabbed the end of Cooper's Spencer and pushed the barrel down.

All the men froze, and all eyes fixed on their former captain.

"Git yer woman outta the way. You 'spect us to be kilt?"

"I've heard of such things. Send a lone woman in and ambush the entire camp. Dismember and scalp everyone. Including women." The former trooper glared at Grace with narrowed eyes. "Want me to go into detail? Some bore holes in the head while the person was still alive. Pack it with gunpowder and BOOM!" He swung his arms in a wide circle. Carbine going for a ride in his right hand.

"Enough!" Captain Cooper barked. "Grace, go see what she wants. You know how to communicate?"

Grace released her hold on his gun and nodded.

He regained his sight. "I'm not lowering my carbine until we know for sure she is alone and it's safe."

Grace called out a greeting, making a sign with her hands. The woman tried to hurry but stumbled and fell to her knees, jamming the bundle against her chest. She hit the ground hard, then tipped forward onto her face. Grace lifted her skirts and sprinted to the woman. She rolled her over. Her eyes were swollen, and fresh blood flowed from her nose. It looked like she was injured before she fell. A young child, no more than three years old, let out a weak cry from the bundle of skins.

"Lakota and Cheyenne. Bad ones. They attacked my village." She struggled to get her words out. Grace knew enough language to understand. There were some similarities, as many languages came from Algonquin.

"She's alone!" Grace yelled to the men. "She's hurt badly. I need to look."

"We ain't gonna have no Indian in our camp."

Captain Cooper waved his carbine. "Send her away."

"She has a child. Have you no heart?" Grace noticed a fresh bloodstain on the woman's abdomen. She gently prodded around the deerskin dress to find an arrow embedded deep in the bowel area. The fletched end was broken off. There was little hope for the woman's survival. Grace wondered how far she wandered like this.

"Grace, you are putting all of us in grave danger. Send her away."

"My son. Please. Take him. I am not long for this world." Her dark eyes took on a glassy stare. Her breathing became shallow.

Grace stroked the woman's hair. "I need help! Anyone here have medical skills?"

No one moved. Not even the captain.

"I won't let you die." Grace spoke in Shoshone and used sign language.

"Promise. He is the last of our tribe." The woman's eyes fluttered. She was unconscious.

"I promise." Grace wiped the tears burning her eyes. She glared at the boys all hiding behind their stupid guns. Why wasn't anyone coming to help? "She's unconscious. I need help moving her near the fire. I need to look at the child. He isn't making any noise."

"I hope he's dead," someone growled.

The captain appeared by her side. "Grace, they're going to die. We best leave them. Apparently, there is a raiding band in the region."

"I'm not leaving them. I refuse to be like those cowards in the wagon train who left my family to die." She leaned low until her scarf brushed the woman's ear. "I promise I won't leave you or your son." She hoped the woman understood enough of what she said.

She gently unfolded the woman's arms from around the boy

and took him into her arms. He was floppy and listless. Small and thin. Probably needed nourishment. When was the last time either one of them had eaten?

The Indian woman's eyes fluttered open. She lifted her arm toward the boy, but the life went out of her before she could touch him one last time.

"Grace, leave them." A hand rested on her back. She shrugged it off.

"The mother is dead. Are you happy?" She struggled to her feet, child pressed against her chest. "Now I need something to feed this child. He may be dehydrated. I need to save him. I suggest you and your 'boys' bury her."

"We—"

Grace cut the captain off. "It's the decent thing to do. If anything, do it for me." Grace ran to the campfire and searched for something the boy could ingest. Hardtack hardly seemed appropriate. She had a hard time biting through the rock-like square.

The men grumbled as Captain Cooper summoned them to the dead Indian woman. She'd have to wait until they finished lest they use her request as an excuse to leave the woman for the wildlife.

"Hey Captain, your wife is using our provisions for that savage." One of the men complained as she laid the boy by the fire to search through the sacks.

Hardtack. More hardtack. A meat biscuit. Moldy bacon. Wasn't there any powdered milk? If she had some, she could soak the hardtack to soften it. She doubted coffee would be a wise choice. She'd never cared for a small human before. Only animals. Sighing, she grabbed a square of hardtack. She could smash it between two rocks and put it in his mouth. But what if he choked? He needed to be awake to take solid food. That much she knew.

She decided to grab one of her bandannas, soak a corner in water, and put it in his mouth. Maybe that would rouse him.

Back by the fire, she sat cross-legged on the ground and pulled the boy onto her lap. She grabbed a nearby canteen and wet her bandanna, then placed it in his mouth. He turned his head away.

"Come on, little guy, you need something to wet your whistle." After some coaxing, he let it rest, then sucked for a few moments. His eyes opened and, upon seeing her face, he startled, arms and legs weakly pushing her away.

"You need to eat," she said in the language of the Shoshone, hoping he'd understand. Grace picked up a rock and smashed the hardtack. She pinched some small crumbs and put them on his lips. His tongue poked out and licked them off. "Yes, yes. That's it."

The sound of rocks being moved and piled filled the night air. She hoped their efforts were enough to avoid conflict. The Indians were particular about burial.

Little Guy's lips were clean. She gave him more smashed hardtack. Hope filled her heart. Maybe he would regain his strength.

"Well done, my brave boy." She froze. *My. Brave. Boy.* That meant he was hers. She promised his mother who just died. Now, she was his mama. Which meant. . .

Grace's heart skipped a few beats.

Despite the warm evening, she broke out into a cold sweat and shivered as the stiff wind from the north hit her damp skin.

Her marriage was to be annulled upon arrival at South Pass City. Now she had a child—albeit not from the usual means of conception. She'd be an unwed mother. Her reputation and virtue would be ruined.

So what? It wasn't like there was anyone around the homestead to pass judgment.

She would take the baby, raise him as her own on her own piece of land. The only problem was that he was Arapahoe. Not Shoshone. There was prejudice between tribes.

So what?

The good Lord would make a way for her and Little Guy.

She wrapped her arms around his bony frame. He struggled. "Shh. It's okay. I'm going to take care of you now. Shhh."

"Why is that thing still here?" An angry member of the group stormed toward her.

"We ain't travelin' with that thing."

"Hey, Captain, what are we going to do with it? Why don't we bury it with its mother?"

Anger boiled from Grace's gut up to her mouth. "He is not an it. And he stays."

"If he stays, I go. Who's with me?"

"Everyone needs to calm down. Let's think this through," Captain Cooper called out over the din of growling men.

"Ain't nothin' to talk about."

"That thing's gonna draw attention to us, and we'll all be scalped in our sleep. Indians will assume we stole it."

"He's not an it!" Grace clamped her mouth shut and pressed her free hand over her scarf.

"Why should we listen to you? You who won't even show your face. What're you hiding?" The former trooper lunged toward her, hand extended. Grace lurched out of reach.

"Don't you dare touch my wife."

"Your wife, eh? Sorry, sir, we aren't buying it anymore. Do you know what she's hiding? Far as we know, we're all gonna be infected with some kind of ailment."

Private Lloyd slouched toward Captain Cooper. "Sir, I don't

mean any disrespect, but here's the deal. Either the Indian goes or we go. And we'd like you to come with us."

"You are suggesting we leave a woman and child behind?" Cooper's voice rose nearly an octave and cracked on the last word.

"Not exactly. She can come with us if she leaves it behind."

Grace pressed Little Guy closer. "I'm not leaving my son behind." These men were monsters. "You all go ahead. But know that someday you will have to stand before a Holy God and account for your actions."

Lloyd looked to Cooper. "Sir?"

CHAPTER ELEVEN

$\cdot\cdot\cdot$

July 1867

Willow Springs, Dakota Territory

Winfield's gut clenched when Grace used the words *my son*. If the Indian was her son, and he was her husband, then logic dictated that it was his too. But it wasn't. It couldn't be. This arrangement was supposed to be temporary. He was supposed to mine for gold at South Pass City. Not settle down and raise a family. At least not yet—or ever.

"Lloyd speaks for all of us, sir. Either she leaves it behind or she gets left."

He held out his hands. "Let's be reasonable here."

"Sir, we're all mustered out. You don't have authority over us anymore."

He looked over at his wife, her ice-blue eyes snapping from above her scarf. The Indian boy looked from Grace to him with bottomless black eyes.

Winfield took in a deep breath. There was only one right thing to do. "Feel free to go. You're welcome to spend the night and leave in the morning." He paused for a moment. "Whatever you choose will not be without consequence. Your honor and character are on the line. I despise these Indians as you do, but I—I will not abandon my wife."

"Captain Cooper!" one man exclaimed.

"Let me make something clear. If any of you says anything derogatory or dares to lay hands on my wife or that child, you'll answer to me." Winfield put a hand on the handle of his Colt. He'd defend Grace to the death. He needed to show her she could trust him and that he was a man of his word. He couldn't let his hatred cause him to break. He'd figure out what to do with the boy in South Pass.

Private Lloyd made eye contact with every member of the group. Something unspoken passed between them. "We'll sleep on it and let you know in the morning."

Winfield scrounged around in the dark for more fuel to add to the fire. The men settled in their bedrolls. Grace sat on a flat rock, arms wrapped around the child, trying to keep him warm despite her own shivers. Once the child fell asleep, he figured he would have a difficult discussion with Grace. Her rapid attachment to the Indian boy would complicate her life once they went their separate ways in South Pass City. They needed to find someone to take him.

He returned to the fire and fed sage twigs into it one at a time. The wind whipped the flames one way then another, swirling dirt and dust all around. He'd never seen such relentless wind until he came to the Dakota Territory. And the summer winds were nothing compared to the violent winter gusts, so strong they could blow over a horse.

"I think he's tiring." Grace kissed the boy's forehead. "I hope he can sleep in peace."

"I'm sure it will be fine."

Grace's head popped up. Her narrowed eyes reflected the growing flames. "*He* is *not* an it."

Winfield sank to the ground, folded over, and put both hands behind his head. "About that."

"I'm keeping him."

Winfield closed his eyes and let out a sigh. "Don't you think it would be better to find a family to take him? Someone with children or the need for a farm hand?"

"I promised his mother I'd care for him. I won't break my word." Grace's voice shot up in pitch. Groans rose from the dark forms in the shadows. She nestled her face against his head.

"I bet the minister in South Pass City could connect us with an orphanage."

"What do you care? When we get to South Pass City, you'll go your way and I'll go mine. I'm keeping little. . ." She paused. "Raymond. His name is Raymond after my pa, who adopted me when my father died."

"A single woman can't raise a child alone."

"Captain Cooper, why do you have so little confidence in me?"

"I wish you'd call me Winfield."

"What's the point? We're—we're parting ways soon." Her words were muffled by the Indian's thick black hair.

"Why would it be so terrible if we part as friends?"

"Now that I'm a mother, I don't have the energy or resources to invest in a friendship. I need to plan for his future—our future."

Suddenly, Winfield felt a wave of sadness break over his soul. As difficult as things had been, Grace didn't deserve a life of solitude and loneliness. And her fierce loyalty to a child she'd only known for a few hours moved him. He couldn't help but admire her for it.

He buried his face in his hands. How could he abandon her in South Pass City? She wanted what he did—a plot of land on which to run cattle.

"You're awfully quiet."

The fire snapped and crackled. A dust devil swirled the smoke like a mini tornado. "I'm trying to figure out what to do."

"Stick to your plan. It's what you want."

"You know you won't be able to tame him."

"What's that supposed to mean?"

"He'll grow up to be a murderous savage."

Grace stood up and within two steps was looming over him. "How can you say that? You call yourself a man of God?"

"I do."

"A true man of God would not abandon a human life regardless of parentage. Raymond is a human being created in the image of God Himself. Just like you. Just like me."

Winfield flinched. Grace's words stung as if she'd reached out and slapped him across the face. The judgment he passed on the Indians was based on his experience. He viewed them as the enemy—including this boy.

"You best get some sleep, Grace."

"I'm not tired, and I need to keep Raymond warm."

Winfield put his hands on his knees and pushed to standing. He shook his head while feeling around for his blanket. Once found, he placed it around Grace's shoulders. Not a sound.

The fire burned bright. He needed rest. Winfield stretched out on the ground, carbine at the ready. He fell asleep with a myriad of prayers for wisdom.

CHAPTER TWELVE

———•◆•———

July 1867

Oregon Trail, Dakota Territory

S tray wisps of hair whipped around Grace's face, sticking to her eyelashes and getting in her mouth. No matter how she tried to secure her baby-fine hair, it slipped out in the wind and assaulted her face. She didn't want to think about the knots. She'd likely have to cut them out when she returned home.

Raymond bolted upright, head knocking into her jaw. Pain shot through her mouth as her teeth crushed her tongue. He cried out for his mother, eyes wild. Terror tremored through his thin frame.

"If you don't shut that thing up, I'm gonna put a bullet in its head," a voice called from the dark.

Blinking back tears from the pain, Grace faced the direction of the voice. "You'll have to put a bullet through me first."

"Nobody is going to shoot anyone else." Winfield popped up from his spot by the fire. "The next person who speaks ill toward my wife or—or the. . .child will be cast from this group. I'll make sure your reputation follows you wherever you go. Any questions?"

Grumbles and mumbles rose from all around.

Grace studied the silhouette poised with his hand on his Colt. He appeared to be ready to kill anyone who threatened her. *Her.* Why?

Something cracked in her granite heart. An unfamiliar emotion swelled in her breast. No! She imagined a fist pounding it back into the depths. In a few weeks, she would be on her own. She needed to part ways with the captain. Besides, she needed to care for Raymond. The boy caught a glimpse of Cooper poised to shoot, and he thrashed out of her arms. She didn't have the strength to hold on to him. "No!" She bolted after him in the dark. What if one of the men took aim? She called after him in Shoshone, but he either didn't understand enough or chose to ignore her in his flight.

"Which way did he go?" Cooper appeared alongside her.

"Put your pistol away," she hissed. "That's what seemed to set him off."

There was a snap, a thud, and a sharp cry. Grace lifted her skirts and plunged into the pitch black. "Raymond, I'm coming!" How could she assure him that he was safe with her?

Hysterical sobbing and broken words sliced through the night to her left. She changed course and headed in that direction, sagebrush slicing her legs.

"I found him!" Cooper called out seconds before the boy let out an ear-splitting scream. "Ow! He bit me!"

"Back off." Grace cupped her hands around the boy's slimy face. "I'm here. You're safe with me." She pleaded with God to help the boy understand. He threw his skinny arms around her neck.

"Raymond and I can't travel with those men. I don't trust them not to follow through on their threats. He needs to come to terms with his loss and learn to trust me. Perhaps you can spare some provisions, and he and I will venture alone. It's for the best." Grace's heart pounded against the weight of her son. Could she make it home with a young boy? He was apparently afraid of the white soldiers. She couldn't imagine what his young eyes had seen.

"Grace, have some reason. It's not safe."

"For whom? Raymond's not safe with your boys threating to shoot him like an animal. I'd rather take my chances alone. Let me have Peaches, a carbine, and a week's provisions." She turned to face the glow from the fire, but a hand latched onto her arm.

"I can't let you do that." He spun her to face him.

Raymond pressed his face into her neck and squeezed so tight, she could hardly breathe. "It's the only way. Raymond. . ." She tried to loosen his squeeze. ". . .is terrified of them—of you."

He let go of her arm. "Grace, you're shivering. Let's get back to the fire."

A chill swept her body. In the heat of the moment, she hadn't realized how cold she was. "There are too many ears over there. We need to resolve this here and now."

"I made a promise to get you home. I intend on fulfilling it."

"What about them? Your boys?"

"You're my priority. I will send them on their way, give them a head start. When we arrive in South Pass, I'll help you find a home for. . .him, and we'll contact your father."

Grace huffed. "While I'm grateful you recognize him as a boy, I have no intention of giving him up."

"Grace." He groaned. "Please think this through."

"I have, and I will not change my mind. Ever."

"Let me ask you this." The captain took a deep breath. "Are you doing this because you need companionship? That's quite a burden for a small child."

Heat swept her cheeks. What gave Cooper the right to judge

her motives? "Now you're worried about him? I don't understand you, Captain Cooper. But I can assure you of this. I will love Raymond and give him the best life I know how. My pa will support me."

"And your mother?"

Why was he asking so many questions? Why did he have to complicate things? It's not like they were actually married. They would be going their separate ways shortly. What did he care? But that question shook her resolve. What would Mother think? She was so by-the-rules.

She'd worry about that day when it came. Grace brushed past the captain, carrying Raymond to the warmth of the fire in hopes its light would chase away the nightmares.

CHAPTER THIRTEEN

July 1867

Oregon Trail, Dakota Territory

G race brushed past without a word. Cradling the boy, she settled by the fire, stroking his head, whispering in his ear. In the mere hours since the Indian came into camp, Grace said more words to him than she had said to everyone on the whole trip. Would she let the boy see her face? It was obvious she preferred Indians to her own kind.

Something pinched Winfield's heart. Did he really view Indians as something other than human? The only experiences he had were violent. Did little Raymond feel the same about him?

Raymond.

Winfield tilted his head up toward the night sky splashed with more stars than he could ever count in a lifetime. What just happened? In an instant, the boy went from being nothing more than a savage Indian to Raymond. A boy with a name. A boy who didn't deserve Winfield's ire.

"I think he's finally asleep." Grace's voice was soft.

The fire dimmed. "There's no way I can convince you to give him up." It came out as a statement rather than a question because

Winfield knew the answer.

"He's lost everything. How can I put him through that again?" Grace lifted her head. Orange light flickered in her eyes above the dirty scarf. "I'm all he has." She paused. "You wouldn't understand anyway."

Why did women resort to that deflection from conflict? "Try me."

"You realize he's Arapahoe."

"He's an Indian. Aren't they all the same?"

Grace's eyes narrowed.

"That was out of line. Go on." Why did his mouth outrun his brain at times?

"Where I live is Shoshone territory. The two tribes are hostile toward one another."

"How will they be able to tell?" Genuine question, right?

"Your hatred jades your judgment, Captain Cooper. I truly believe it's best Raymond and I travel on our own come morning. Now, if you'll excuse me, I need to get some rest so I can take care of my son." She rested her chin on Raymond's head and closed her eyes.

Winfield poked at the dying embers until faint light glowed on the eastern horizon. The boys stirred in their bedrolls. Not only did Grace want to get away from them, she wanted to get away from *him*. Knots formed in his stomach. It felt as if he swallowed a box full of nails.

No question, the men had to proceed on their own.

But Grace?

Until South Pass City, she was his wife. He was responsible for her safety and the safety of her new charge. He ran his hands through his hair and down his face. He had to convince her and Raymond to allow him to accompany them. Such a tall order.

"Cap'n?"

Winfield twisted to see Lloyd standing over him. "Just want to let ya know one more time that we'd like ya to come with us. But if you don't, I understand." He cut his eyes toward a still sleeping Grace. "You've always been a man of your word."

This was it. The choice. Go with his men or stay with a woman and child who didn't want him around.

"Let me fetch some paper from my saddle. I'll send a letter of recommendation with you in case our paths don't cross again." He groaned to standing and made his way to the pile of tack. Who knew what would befall any of them. The letter would assure his men could find gainful employment in South Pass City.

Within an hour, they were gone.

"You shouldn't have stayed." Grace smashed a square of hardtack between two rocks. Raymond sat alongside her, wide eyes watching Winfield's every move.

"I made a promise—"

"I release you. I see your intent, but for the sake of Raymond, it's best you leave us and catch up to your boys."

"You know I can't do that." He locked eyes with her.

"Why not?" she challenged.

Why not? He gazed down the trail. Dust rose into the morning air. They weren't far away. But it was as if his feet were nailed to the ground. He blinked a few times and refocused on the woman and terrified child before him. "Leave no man behind." He choked out the words. "If I wouldn't leave one of the boys behind in the heat of battle, why would I leave you and Raymond behind? I have to stand before a Holy God one day and account for my actions. I want Him to be pleased."

Grace dropped her gaze to the boy beside her. He trembled like an aspen leaf in a stiff breeze. "You said his name."

"Is—is there any way you can let him know I won't hurt him?"

"Honestly, I'm not certain he knows I'm safe. I'm sure at this age, he recognizes I speak an enemy language. Our best bet is showing him we are safe."

Warmth spread across Winfield's chest. Grace spoke the words "we" and "our." Perhaps there was hope for comradery for the remainder of the journey. And maybe during these last weeks of travel, he could figure out how to help her devise a plan to raise Raymond.

———— ◆ ————

Grace sneaked a look at Captain Cooper as he prepared the horses. Something shifted in the man. He acknowledged the boy was human by using his name. He also backed down regarding pawning Raymond off on some strangers who wouldn't love him like she already did.

How was that even possible? Not even a day had passed, yet her heart bonded to the terrified child.

Raymond sat next to her, back ramrod straight. His dark eyes were wide, following every move of Cooper.

"It's okay," she whispered in the language of her tribe while stroking his head in what she hoped he felt was soothing. He glanced at her, so she smiled and nodded. Pinching her fingers together, Grace pantomimed eating. But would the scarf cause confusion?

Noticing Cooper's back was turned, she lifted her scarf and brought her fingers to her lips then chewed and swallowed the imaginary food. Raymond imitated her gesture. He didn't seem to react to her scarred face.

"Hungry," Grace said in English. Raymond stared. She needed

to be patient and give him time. She picked up some of the crumbs from smashed hardtack and put them in her mouth. Raymond followed suit. "I know it's not tasty, but it will keep your belly full." She patted her stomach.

Cooper marched toward them. "Horses are ready. Raymond can ride with you on Peaches."

Grace stood, extending her hand to her son. "Up?" He popped to his feet. Grace moved closer and took his hand. "Horse." She pointed at Peaches with her free hand. Raymond nodded. She led him past the captain, who ruffled the boy's hair. He flinched. "It's okay. He won't hurt you." If only he could understand.

While they plodded along, Grace pointed out anything and everything that wasn't a sagebrush or rock, speaking the English word in Raymond's ear. No matter what she tried, he didn't make a peep.

As the sun slid past its apex, they entered a rocky stretch of trail. Grace lurched to one side then the other, holding on to Raymond as Peaches picked his way through. A faint vibration undercut the *whoosh* of the hot wind. Like someone shaking a tin can partially filled with sand. Peaches' mane rushed toward Raymond's face while Grace lost grip and tipped backward. The horse screeched and twisted on his hind legs.

"Raymond, grab his mane!" The cantle dug into her back, her feet pulled from the stirrups. Grace pawed at the air, but it was in vain. Sharp pain exploded in the back of her head before a screaming Raymond crashed on her chest.

The sky blurred, and the light of the sun was like a dagger to her eyes. Someone shouted. The captain? It sounded hollow and far away. Was this how it ended?

An equine scream tore through the air. Winfield whipped around in his saddle. Peaches hopped on his back legs, while the front paddled the air in front of him. Grace yelled something then toppled off, landing on her head. Pulling his horse's nose to his right knee, Winfield wheeled the beast around and charged over the few yards in time to see Raymond land hard on Grace.

Winfield threw his right leg over the rear of his animal and landed on the rocky ground with a thud. The unmistakable sound of a rattle froze him where he stood. A snake!

Peaches landed on all fours, then bucked and hopped like he were on fire. He needed to get to Grace, who wasn't moving or moaning. Raymond, on the other hand, rolled off Grace, took one look, lifted his face to the sky, and let out a wail.

Giving the snake a wide berth and never taking his eyes off it, Winfield worked his way to his fallen wife and the boy.

Grace lay still. Blood pooled on the rocks under her head. Her scarf had flipped up, exposing deeply scarred and pitted skin. The left side of her lips twisted into a grimace from deeper scarring. So that's what she'd been hiding.

Raymond's wails rose in pitch, interrupting his thoughts. From his movements, the boy didn't appear hurt. Winfield drew close and put a hand on his shoulder, giving it a squeeze. Raymond quit howling and looked up with wild eyes. He stabbed a finger at Grace's supine form. "I'm going to help her." He prayed he could. Her lack of movement tied a hard knot in his stomach. He let go of Raymond's shoulder and knelt next to his wife.

"Grace." He shook her shoulders.

Nothing.

"Grace, can you hear me?"

Nothing.

Raymond dropped to his knees and pressed his head on her chest, sobbing. A slight moan escaped her lips.

"Grace!" Relief washed over him like a cool wave from a mountain lake. His fingers fumbled to remove the scarf. He balled it in his right hand, lifted her head with his left, and pressed it against the back of her head. Before he could roll her over, he needed to make sure she wasn't injured elsewhere. He'd seen men thrown from horses lose the use of arms and legs.

Grace's eyelids fluttered but never fully opened.

"Before I can roll you over to check your head, I need to know if you can wiggle your feet?" He remembered hearing doctors asking that question. He shifted his gaze to her boots. Her right foot twitched, then the left. "Did that hurt?"

A moan. He needed a clearer response. "Blink once if that hurt, twice if it didn't."

Her eyelids squeezed down once. He needed to do a more thorough check for broken bones. "You're not going to like this, but I must check for broken bones. Please know that my intent is pure."

A single tear rolled down her cheek and mixed with the blood and dirt. Winfield tapped Raymond on the shoulder then pointed to Grace's head. He stroked her hair a few times. He took Raymond's hand and used it to stroke her matted hair. The boy shuffled into a better position and caressed Grace's hair and face. He didn't seem bothered by her scars.

With gentle hands, Winfield checked her arms and legs. He moved bigger joints then smaller ones, all the while watching her face for any reaction. He judged he could risk rolling her over to examine her head.

Once again, he garnered Raymond's attention then pantomimed rolling with hands suspended over Grace's body. The boy nodded. Winfield's heart skipped a beat. It was the first communication without feral fear.

Swallowing hard, he rolled his wife onto her stomach. The scarf fell off, revealing bloody, matted hair and fresh, bright red blood. Using his fingers, he moved the hair around to reveal a large gash. The only course of action was to rinse it with water and stitch it up, then pray God would protect her from infection. "Raymond." His voice cracked. The boy locked eyes with him. He pantomimed drinking from a cup. Without a sound, the boy scampered for a canteen. It was at this moment Winfield noticed Peaches writhing on the ground. The boy froze a few feet from the palomino then looked back at Winfield. The boy seemed to know what needed to be done and went to Winfield's horse for the canteen. He also brought the Spencer.

Within moments, it was over. Peaches suffered no more. Now to return his attention to Grace.

Wordlessly, Winfield and Raymond worked together to rinse the wound, and Raymond cradled Grace's head as Winfield stitched the skin closed. Grace's whimpers tore at Winfield's heart.

"Raymond. . ." she croaked, reaching toward the boy's face.

"He's fine. You broke his fall."

Heat rose into his face, and something pricked his eyes. He turned away to rub them. What was this emotion flooding through him like a wildfire? Grace was badly hurt. He couldn't lose her. Not now. But what to do? She was in no shape to travel.

Grace's lips trembled as tears etched trails down her dusty temples.

Now what? The man with all the answers was at a loss. He needed a wagon to lay her in. It could be days before they saw anyone. His only option was to leave her with the boy and ride like the wind to find help. Even then there was a risk of her not surviving being so exposed to the elements. And Raymond? How could he communicate with the boy about what needed to happen next?

CHAPTER FOURTEEN

---◆◆◆---

July 1867

Oregon Trail, Dakota Territory

Grace felt like her head was an anvil in a blacksmith's shop. Pain pounded and pounded, never diminishing. Never ending. Raymond's wide-eyed face hovered over her own. His chin quivered. Was he worried about her?

Contracting her stomach muscles, Grace tried to sit, but the pain that shot through her back arrested her movement. Not good. "Help me up," she muttered through gritted teeth. She needed off this bed of hard, sharp rocks. She had to get Raymond home to her parents. "These rocks hurt too much."

"I'm not sure that's a good—"

"Just help me." She exhaled the words in a rush while lifting her arms toward Cooper.

"I need to protect your back, so don't be offended when I come in close and ask you to put your arms around my neck."

Grace's heart thumped harder. Why couldn't he just pull her? There wasn't any point in arguing. She didn't have the strength, and what if there was something wrong she wasn't aware of? "All right."

Cooper leaned in, wrapping his arms around her, pressing his chest against hers as a brace. "I'm going to help you sit up while keeping your back straight."

He smelled of horse and sweat. Grace held her breath until the pain from sitting tore it from her mouth. She panted through her mouth, trying to avoid inhaling his stench.

"Next, I will reposition and help you to your feet. I'm sorry if this hurts."

She nodded. The sooner she was in a more comfortable spot, the sooner. . . Her thoughts dropped like a rock when she saw Peaches motionless on the ground. "P–Peaches!" she cried, pulling away.

"Rattlesnake. It had to be done." The captain pulled her to him. The fight melted out of her, and tears flowed.

Something tugged at her skirt. She looked down. Raymond. He made a sign she interpreted to convey sorrow. "H–horse." It was the first word he'd spoken since they found him. What were they going to do now without a second horse? She knew she couldn't walk. Her injuries were too severe.

"Let's find a less rocky place to sit you down. I wish there was some kind of shade. May have to build you a shelter."

Cooper's words collided in her mind. What was he saying? Between the throbbing in her head and the pains all over her body, concentration eluded her. "Need to go home." Her legs buckled as the world tilted.

"Grace—Grace!" The captain's voice was sharp in her ear. It felt like he hit her with it. "Stay with me."

Grace felt her feet dragging along the hard ground until she was lowered amid waist-high sagebrush.

"Listen, I'm going to leave Raymond here with you. He seems capable enough to watch over you while I'm gone. I need a wagon to get you to South Pass City."

"Pa. . .get my pa." Talking hurt. She hoped he didn't have more to say.

"I'd prefer to go to—"

"Please. Home. . .is closer." She knew it was. What was the name of the mountain range that shadowed the homestead? Grace fought through the fog and prayed God would bring it to mind. "Bridger. Mountains. Copper Mountain. Tallest. Home. . .in the valley." Sleep pulled at her like a strong ox. "Take Raymond." She had to give her son a chance at life in case she didn't make it.

"He stays with you." A gust of wind blew dust and sand over them. "Grace, I. . ." Hands cupped the back of her head. Her face pressed against his shirt.

Wait.

Her scarf! It was as if a bolt of lightning surged through her. Despite the pain, she thrashed to pull away. "Wh–where's my. . . scarf?" Panic rose in her throat, squeezing off her air supply. The captain's arms tightened like a vise.

"Grace, settle down." Another squeeze.

"My face—don't look at me. Please don't look at me." She pressed her face into his chest, flattening her nose. Hard sobs wracked her body. The captain was bound to detest her and abandon his quest to help save Raymond.

"What kind of man do you think I am? You should know by now."

"I'm. . .a. . .monster."

"A man or woman's worth isn't measured by what is seen on the outside. It's measured by what's in the heart. And Grace, you. . ." His voice cracked. "You have a beautiful heart. Here you are, seriously injured, and your concern is for Raymond, who you've only known for a full day, if that." His chest rose and fell.

"I'm going to lower you down so Raymond and I can create a makeshift shelter. The sooner I leave, the sooner I'll be back."

As Grace tried to relax on the spot where she fell, she forced one eye open. The captain's head blocked the intense summer sun. Would it be the last time she'd ever see him?

CHAPTER FIFTEEN

---◆◆◆---

Late July 1867

Off the trail, Dakota Territory

Winfield didn't waste any time securing blankets to the sagebrush to create a semblance of shelter for his wife. The boy caught on quickly and helped. Indian children were ages ahead of white children in practical knowledge. When he was Raymond's age, Winfield cared more about playing with blocks and his friends than being helpful. His own needs were his priority as a young child.

Once the shelter was crafted, he made sure Grace had a full canteen of water and plenty of hardtack. He saddled his horse and secured his own provisions. He prayed Grace's homestead wasn't too far away and that he could find it with her minimal directions.

Before he mounted, he knelt alongside the boy. "Raymond, I need to get help for—for your mother." He pointed toward Grace. He doubted the boy understood a single word. "I will be back soon. Take care of her." Again, he pointed and made like he was eating and drinking. The boy cocked his head to the right, squinting his eyes. Was he confused?

The sun angled toward the west. Winfield didn't have much time to sit around and play charades. He had to trust Raymond would figure out what needed to be done. He patted the boy on the head then pulled himself onto his horse. He dug his heels in, and the beast took off. *Lord, watch over them while I'm gone.*

A few days passed, and Winfield had yet to come across a living soul other than the animal type. Every day he was away from Grace and Raymond, the less likely they'd survive. Grace would sacrifice herself for Raymond. And then what? He wasn't fit to raise a child, let alone an Indian child who didn't speak English.

Winfield sat on his horse, peering into the distance. He prayed help would come for Grace's sake. A cloud of dust appeared on the horizon. It couldn't be the wind because the air was unusually still. Could it be a wagon train? Digging in his heels, his horse lurched into a full gallop toward the wagon train. Praise the Lord!

As he approached, several horses with riders crested a small hill. Dark brown skin glinted in the sun. Winfield pulled the reins. His horse skidded so hard, he almost sat on his haunches.

Indians!

His carbine was with Grace.

Winfield's blood ran cold. Should he turn and run? Or stand his ground?

One Indian in the lead raised an arm and pointed at Winfield. They spotted him. He braced for an arrow through the heart. Hopefully, death would be quick so he wouldn't feel them cutting him into little pieces.

Nothing happened.

If they meant to kill him, he would be dead by now.

They thundered closer and closer.

He had to show he meant no harm. He remained on his horse and raised his arms in the air, hoping they understood.

In seconds, a band of Indian men surrounded him—braves? Circling. Examining.

"I mean no harm. I need help." Probably useless to speak. He doubted any of them knew English.

"What help?" A heavily painted rider asked, trotting closer. "English?"

The man laughed. "Yes. Speak English. Not too good, but enough."

Sweat, not from the heat, poured down Winfield's face in rivers. "My wife is hurt bad." What should he say about the child? He needed to keep it simple. There was no time or reason to go into the complexities of his relationship with Grace. "Her son. . .our son is with her. He's a little boy." His nerves buzzed while those words sunk deep into his heart. Hopefully, these guys were trustworthy and not hostile. After all, he prayed for help, and here it was in a most surprising form. Winfield took deep breaths to soothe his nerves. What if he took a band of killers to Grace?

"Lead us to her. We will help." The leader smiled, his eyes kind. "I am Jumps on Horse."

"Winfield Cooper." *Lord, please don't let this be a mistake. Help me put aside my hatred for the sake of my wife.*

"Let us go, Winfield Cooper."

Winfield turned his horse to the southeast, where he left Raymond and Grace. They rode hard for hours, stopping every so often to give the horses a break. They stopped for the night. Great. What if they killed him in his sleep? Then what would happen to Grace?

"Winfield Cooper, you look like you see a bear. Why so afraid?" Jumps on Horse left the others, who lounged around a blazing fire.

Was it that obvious? His fear of them? How did he get out of this conversation? "I'm tired."

Jumps on Horse shook his head. "No, not tired. Fearful. You afraid of us?" He smacked a hand to his chest and let out a loud laugh, which shook Winfield to the core. "I see white man shake." Another loud laugh.

Winfield pulled his hands behind his back, lacing his fingers together. Images of Caspar's mutilated body filled his mind.

Jumps on Horse moved in close until their noses almost touched. It took every ounce of control to not back away. "I see eyes of man who saw war." Several minutes passed as the Indian leader stared into his eyes. The Indian slapped a hand on Winfield's shoulder, causing him to yelp and jump back. "Good for you, Winfield Cooper, we are what you call the good guys. Me? I like white men...for dinner! Come join us." Jumps on Horse flashed a set of straight white teeth. "Don't hold what others did against us." He turned and jogged to the fire.

Conviction burned over him. Not only were these men civil, kind, well-spoken, perceptive, and willing to help a stranger, Jumps on Horse had a sense of humor—something many whites lacked. In that moment, it was clear Winfield could not hold the depredations by other tribes against these men. He didn't want Chivington's murderous atrocities held against him because he wore Union blues and was white. *Lord, forgive me.* He breathed as he approached the fire.

The night passed without incident. Winfield surprised himself by sleeping deeply with both eyes closed. Jumps on Horse and his band of hunters made him feel at ease. Not once did he feel like any of them held his past as a soldier against him.

Before the sun peeked over the horizon, the group set off. Winfield guided them based on landmarks or topography he noted on his way for help. By high noon, the tattered blankets from the makeshift shelter came into view.

"Grace!" he called out before the group reached range of the carbine she had. The last thing he wanted was for a rescuer to be shot.

No reply.

"Grace!" Surely she heard him call unless she'd gone foraging for something.

The Indians held back as he hopped off his horse and carefully picked his way toward the shelter. His heart leaped into his throat and nearly stopped when he saw a pair of feet. A weak cry from Raymond reached his ears.

"Grace!" He broke into a run and motioned for Jumps on Horse and the others. "Please God, let her be alive."

Grace lay on her back. Raymond was on the ground beside her, his head on her chest. He panted in the heat. Winfield tore away the blanket. He dropped to his knees and put his ear near her mouth. A tiny puff of hot air brushed his ear. "She's alive, but barely. Do any of you have water?"

Jumps on Horse knelt beside Winfield. "Sings Like Meadowlark." His voice held a note of recognition mixed with surprise. "Grace Manning. We grew up together."

Winfield blinked a few times. Shook his head. Was he hearing correctly? "You—you know my wife?"

The Indian looked Winfield up and down. "She skips rocks very good. And kicks hard when mad." Jumps on Horse chuckled and put a hand on Winfield's shoulder. "Don't make her mad enough to kick you, Winfield Cooper. You will limp for days." He pointed at the boy. "Arapahoe." The word fell from his lips like a lead cannonball. The brown lips curved down into a severe frown.

Panic fluttered in Winfield's chest like a wild goose. "Yes, but will you help?"

"We will help her."

"What about Raymond?"

"No."

Winfield rocked back onto his toes, squeezing the top of his hat on his head. What happened to the forgiving spirit Jumps on Horse seemed to demand from him last night? What could they hold against a boy too young to have committed any crime? His own hypocrisy rended his heart. "Look, the boy... He's—he's Grace's...." Words formed a logjam in his throat. What he was about to say would change the trajectory of his entire life. He breathed a silent prayer, and peace washed over him. He opened his mouth, and the words tumbled out. "Raymond is our son. He is the sole survivor of his group. Grace and I..."

Jumps on Horse's mouth relaxed. "Say no more, Winfield Cooper. If he is Grace's family, he is ours. We will help. You were quick to not hold sins of other tribes against mine. I do the same." He put a hand to his chin and seemed to examine Winfield like a man trying to read small newsprint. "I approve of you. You make Grace a good husband." He flashed his bright smile.

Jumps on Horse spoke to his band in their native tongue. Two teens close to him slid off their ponies. After a few moments of intense conversation and hand waving, the teens tore off in separate directions, scouring the ground.

"We need to make a...sled. I fear Sings Like Meadowlark may fall off horse."

Another Indian approached with a skin full of warm water. He handed it to Winfield, who tipped it to his wife's lips.

"Attend to her, Winfield Cooper, and we prepare for journey home." Jumps on Horse strode away.

"Hey, buddy." Winfield ruffled Raymond's hair. The boy cracked open one eye, then the other. He bolted up, pointing at Grace. "She'll be all right, I promise."

He pointed and grunted, tears rolling from the corner of his eyes. How was he supposed to communicate?

"I can help." One of the teens who had been sent for sled materials towered behind him. "I'm Chases Girls. When I was little, I liked to chase girls around the village. I like languages and know a little Arapahoe, Cheyenne, and Lakota Sioux." He squatted next to Winfield and spoke to Raymond, who calmed down after a few phrases. "I told him we will help his mother. She will be fine."

Relief flooded Winfield's body. He lowered himself until his face hovered over Grace's scarred one. "Hang on, Grace. You're about to go home. We're about to go home." He planted a gentle kiss on her hot, dry forehead. Then he focused on getting water through her parched lips.

Grace was positioned on the makeshift sled the Indians crafted for her. Using rope, they created a harness to tie to a sturdy pony. An Indian teen took hold of the pony's halter and led. Winfield hoisted Raymond onto his horse and mounted behind him. They followed the sled to make sure Grace didn't fall off.

"I have good news to make Winfield Cooper glad." Jumps on Horse lived up to his name and sprung onto his horse's back. "I know how to get to Sing's Like Meadowlark's home where Wildcat lives." He dug his heels into his horse's sides. "All will be well. Our way will take only one sleep."

CHAPTER SIXTEEN

Late July 1867

Home

Bumping, sliding, rocking. Where was she? Last thing she remembered was Raymond's little face hovering over her, his tears dripping onto her face as she sang to him.

Raymond!

Grace's eyes popped open. The bright sunlight hurt her eyes. She squinted hard and noticed a horse with two forms towering above her. She contracted her stomach and tried to sit up, but the hammering pain in her head caused her to drop back down with a cry.

"Stop! She's awake!" It was her husband's voice.

"Raymond." Her son's name rasped from her throat.

"He's with me." Two heads hovered above her own. A warm hand touched her cheek. "Oh, Grace, I was so worried."

"Look like we have happy family reunion, Sings Like Meadowlark."

She recognized that voice. It was one that teased her through-out her childhood. One who was on the receiving end of her swift kicks. "Jumps?"

"The one and only."

"Where am I?" She tried to sit up again, but gentle hands held her down.

"Home, Grace. Jumps on Horse tells me your family's homestead is only a mile or so away. We made it, Grace. We made it home."

We? "But—but what about the gold?"

"You're quite perceptive for a woman with a bad head injury. Most of my men who took a hit like that wouldn't remember their own name let alone what day it is." A deep sigh. "I'm afraid you're stuck with me, Grace. I've decided I can't let you raise Raymond alone. He needs a God-fearing father, and you need a husband whether you realize it or not."

"I agree with Winfield Cooper. He's a good man, Meadowlark."

"But—"

"Shhhh." He pressed her finger to her lips. "There will be plenty of time to discuss things once you are recovered, but for now, let's press on and get home."

Hot tears pricked her eyes. Was this real? Was she about to see Mother and Pa after all these long months? She knew Pa would be ecstatic, but what would Mother think, seeing her in this condition with a—a husband and son in tow? "One request. I want to sit up to see. I want to see home."

"I put you on my horse, Meadowlark. I'll make sure you don't fall off."

"Since when have I ever fallen off a horse?" She tried to laugh, but the pain cut it short.

"How do you think you got that hole in your head?"

Cooper and Jumps cradled her head and helped her to stand. Opening her eyes was difficult, but she fought through it. In no time, she was on the horse.

The stout cabin made of hand-hewn logs came into view as the shadow of the Bridger Mountains closed in on them.

A wooden door creaked. Someone either entered or exited the cabin. Grace's heart sped up. "Pa! Mother!" she called out, wishing she could put the pony in a gallop. Her pain held her back. She wanted to enjoy the unexpected reunion, not pass out.

"Who's there?" It was Pa's voice.

"Grace." Her throat ached. "Pa, it's me. I've returned."

"Gracie? How can that be?" The figure of her pa grew larger. "Ellie, come on out here. You'll never guess what the cat drug in!" Puffs of dust rose around his pounding feet. He slowed. "Gracie, what in tarnation happened to ya?" His eyes scanned all those accompanying her and stopped on Winfield and Raymond. His mouth opened and closed, then opened again. "Who's that?" He pointed a gnarled finger at Winfield.

Grace felt her scarred lips tug into a smile. "Meet my husband, Captain Winfield Cooper. And "—she gestured to Raymond—"that's our son, Raymond."

Pa's mouth hung slack. He could catch a barnful of flies.

Mother stepped out of the cabin. She shielded her eyes with her hand. "What's all the fuss? Ray, who's there?"

"You won't believe it, Ellie. It's our Gracie. She's come home. And she's got some guests."

Mother lifted her skirts and ran toward them. "Grace, what are you doing here? You're supposed to be in Philadelphia." Mother tried to sound annoyed but failed.

Grace shrugged. "Let's say I got a little homesick."

"We got ourselfs a son-in-law and grandson to boot!" Pa put his hands on his belly and howled in laughter. "Our Gracie. Always full o' surprises."

Mother's hands fluttered to her chest, and she gasped. All the color drained from her face. Jumps on Horse ran over and put an arm around her. "No need to worry, Missus Ellie, I approve of this Winfield Cooper as husband for Meadowlark."

"How—How—" Mother stood there, mouth flopping open and closed, repeating the word. She looked like a bigmouth bass.

A large, strong hand closed around Grace's. "So, this is home."

She tilted her sore neck to gaze upon her husband. "Yes, Winfield, it is."

Her husband blinked a few times. "Did you—did you just call me—"

"Winfield. Yes. If you're not going to go traipsing off to the mines in South Pass, I might as well use your name. Captain Cooper becomes a mouthful after a while. Especially when one has a splitting headache."

"Speaking of that, we best get you settled so you can recover."

"Recover? Whatever happened to my Gracie?"

Jumps on Horse approached Pa and thumped a hand on his shoulder. "Long story, Wildcat. We get Meadowlark and her family settled, then we speak of it over tea." His eyes twinkled in the sun. "Or do you have coffee? It's been many, many times since I had strong white man coffee."

The entourage proceeded to the cabin. Winfield and Raymond hung back with her.

"Winfield, are you sure about this? I know how you feel about..." She trailed off, letting her gaze fall on Raymond.

"Mrs. Grace Cooper, I've never been surer about anything in my life."

D. J. Gudger spends much of her time dodging the Wyoming wind, ducking into historical museums and archives, and imagining life on the frontier prior to modern comforts. When not in a library or at her computer, D. J. can be found paddling the river in her kayak, hiking, walking her psychotic freak-biscuit of a dog, or in the pool determined to hit her two-mile goal. Her ridiculous love of books almost flattened her son when overburdened shelves collapsed on him during his birthday party. Her husband implemented an immediate ban on physical books. Undeterred, D. J. finds creative ways to sneak books into her home and pushes her Kindle to its limits. You can connect with her at www.djgudger.com and www.facebook.com/darciejgudger.

CAROLINE

By

BECCA WHITHAM

"The real aim of this bill is to get at the Indian lands and open them up to settlement. The provisions for the apparent benefit of the Indians are but the pretext to get at his lands and occupy them. . . . If this were done in the name of greed, it would be bad enough; but to do it in the name of humanity, and under the cloak of an ardent desire to promote the Indian's welfare by making him like ourselves, whether he will or not, is infinitely worse." —Senator Henry M. Teller (Colorado)

CHAPTER ONE

——◆◆◆——

November 1886

You throw the best parties in Washington, DC."

Caroline Forrester smiled at the compliment, but her heart sank deeper with every such accolade. How many more parties before her father released her from this prison to do the thing she wanted to do—save lives as a medical doctor. Five parties this week. Five! Each one more exhausting than the last.

"I don't know how you do it, my dear," Mrs. Wilson, a large woman with an even larger heart, chuckled. "Ned and I were here on Monday, and I just can't believe how different the drawing room looks tonight compared to then."

Caroline cast an approving eye over her work. Waiters wearing colorfully beaded vests served delicacies on handwoven baskets in support of her theme for the evening, Indian artistry. On Monday the theme centered around the Indians' skill with horses. Tuesday, their unique foods. Wednesday, poetry and music. Yesterday, their clothing. The poor waiters endured an abnormally hot November night wearing buffalo skin caps and coats. She smiled at the senator's wife. "Oh, you know me. I can't ever throw the same party twice."

"Well, you're a genius at it. If you ever decide to leave your father's side, I will hire you in an instant to plan all my parties." She leaned closer to Caroline's ear and patted her shoulder. "Although I don't know what good it will do. My Ned says this General Allotment Act fixes the Indian problem, and I believe he's in the majority." Her gaze moved to somewhere behind Caroline. "Please excuse me. I simply must speak with Senator Teller's wife." And with a swish of purple silk, she was gone.

Really? All her work—all her father's work—this past week was for naught? Not one mind changed?

Caroline allowed herself an instant to close her eyes and gather a small measure of composure amid the throng surrounding her. A pinch on her bottom popped her eyes wide open. She knew before her gaze collided with the leering Congressman Snelling's that he was the culprit.

"A good party, Miss Forrester, though I think my favorite was last night's." He leaned close, his breath coated with rum. "I enjoy watching people sweat."

"I will ask you again to keep your hands to yourself, Mr. Snelling." She refused to call him Congressman, a title he clung to almost as tightly as his alcohol.

His beady eyes narrowed to slits. "You can ask all you want, lovely girl, but your father needs me more than I need him. I will continue to come to your marvelous parties and continue to behave however I please." He wrapped his arm around her back, his hand reaching for her breast.

She jerked sideways and whispered, "How dare you. My father will—will—"

His chuckle sent shivers of revulsion along her neck. "Will what? He's too wrapped up with his Noble Savage"—he threw a contemptuous look at Raymond Cooper, her father's new legislative aide—"and wooing me to vote for his lost cause to care what happens to you." He tapped his finger on her nose. "And you care too much about what people think to cause a scene, which is why you always whisper your unfinished threats."

Before she could formulate a scathing response, he turned and walked away, the leer on his face replaced with a charming smile he painted over the true nature of his soul.

The air in the crowded room disappeared. For the first time in six years, Caroline abandoned her role as hostess for the safety of her father's library.

If only Papa would honor his word and allow her to attend medical school. People were dying out in the real world while she planned useless parties. No more. She no longer cared that women doctors were scandalous creatures who faced life's challenges without a husband and children. That opportunity passed her by when Edward ended their engagement.

We aren't meant to be, dearest.

Were crueler words ever punctuated by an endearment?

Caroline swiped away the tears wetting her cheeks. Whether from heartbreak, frustration, or humiliation, it mattered not. She was done. No more excuses. She would find a way with or without her father's help to get to medical school. Dr. Caroline Forrester would make a difference—a real difference—in the world.

———•———

"May the Lord preserve us from legislators whose only qualification is their good intentions."

Raymond Cooper kept his face impassive as he watched the reactions of the ladies within hearing of Senator Forrester's impassioned pronouncement. He was, after all, just the senator's aide and—for lack of a better term—his "case in point." A Harvard graduate, Raymond hoped to attend the law school there but was detoured when the senator requested that he come on staff specifically to help defeat the General Allotment Act.

A few ladies darted fearful glances at him as though he wore buckskin and feathers rather than a black suit and tie. He fixed his eyes on a gilt-framed portrait of the senator and his daughter hanging in the foyer of their Dupont Circle mansion. Painted six years ago when they'd first come to Washington, DC, it captured Senator Forrester's still handsome visage, though his hair was more salt than pepper these days, and his daughter's blond radiance. Raymond pretended to be captivated. No point in upsetting the society ladies in front of him by daring to look them in the eye like a normal man.

"But Senator"—a tall brunette with too much rouge on her negligible cheeks placed a hand on her thin chest—"every member of Congress should ground his work with good intentions."

Raymond's lips twitched. He couldn't help himself. The dramatic sighs of assent by the gaggle of women surrounding his senator simultaneously put him in mind of cats circling a bowl of cream and of his literature professor flinging his arm in the air to quote the famous proverb, "The road to hell is paved with good intentions."

"Do you mock me?"

It took an instant for Raymond to realize the question was directed at him. *"Mais non, madam."* He used French on purpose. It always created confusion when an Indian savage spoke that most refined language. "I agree wholeheartedly with you." He waited for the woman's brows to settle back down to their normal height. "Except I believe what Senator Forrester said is that, if those are a congressman's *only* qualifications, we are in trouble as a nation. Because, as is the case with the General Allotment Act, good intentions do not always equal good law."

"Well said." Senator Forrester patted Raymond's shoulder. It was a planned gesture. One they had repeated several times—and would again—as part of their show of force at this past week's parties. "Now, if you will excuse us, ladies, Mr. Cooper and I need to mingle with the rest of our guests."

Raymond dipped his head in a polite bow and followed Senator Forrester to the next group of people, this time men, where they repeated the same song and dance while emphasizing that the General Allotment Act broke treaties signed with Indian tribes across the entire nation.

After three more such reenactments, Senator Forrester drew Raymond to a secluded corner of the drawing room. "Have you seen my daughter?"

Raymond looked around the crowded room. "Not recently."

The senator sighed. "That girl." He pointed a finger at Raymond's nose. "Stay here. Do not try to fight this battle without me. We're in this together, remember?"

"Of course, sir." Raymond pointed to the ground. "Right here."

Forrester's face split into a charming grin. "You're a good man, Raymond Cooper." After another pat on his shoulder, the senator waded back into the fray.

Raymond stood alone, watching the sea of humanity ebb and flow around him as though he stood atop a small island. "*Together*, my cat's hind foot," he muttered too low for anyone else to hear. The expression came from his grandfather, after whom he was named. Pappy had a way with words, part of his Shoshone heritage, that used descriptions rather than outright statements. A cat's hind foot was bent. Crooked. Which was another way of calling something a lie.

A snippet of conversation drew his attention.

"...agree with you. We must do something about the Indian problem. I'm just not sure that giving them homesteads is the answer."

Raymond swallowed down his hatred of the term "Indian problem" and waded back into the fray. "Gentlemen, I'm so glad you came tonight. Can I get you a refill?" Without waiting for a reply, he lifted his left hand and waved over a waiter carrying champagne. "It's not a matter of giving people a homestead claim; it's a matter of keeping our word." Raymond lifted two glasses from the tray and held one out to Senator Mobley. "America needs to honor its treaties. Don't you agree?"

Mobley's face flushed. "Excuse me, I see that my wife needs me."

Raymond backed up a step to allow the senator to pass, glancing right to assess Mrs. Mobley's apparent insurmountable need. The woman was deep in conversation with another lady and, when her husband broke into their conversation, scowled at him for an instant before pinching her lips into a smile. Raymond squeezed his toes inside his black patent leather shoes. It was a trick his grandfather taught him. *When you want to run, boy, you squeeze your toes so they can't move. Stand, my boy. Stand for as long as you can.*

A swell of longing caught Raymond in his chest. Pappy had been Raymond's best friend growing up. Half Shoshone, he too navigated a world where he didn't belong. At least not until he married Granny E and, together, they'd carved out a place of their own.

Raymond turned back to Senator Lennox. "Champagne?"

The balding man shook his head, his jowls jiggling. "No, thank you...Carter, is it?"

"Cooper, sir. Raymond Cooper. We met last week when—"

"Yes. Of course. I'm sorry. Please excuse me." He waddled away. At least he hadn't trumped up an excuse.

Raymond pressed his lips together to keep from saying something he shouldn't. Several heads turned his way. Wide eyes, censorious frowns, and pitying glances had him guessing the cause until a woman dropped a contemptuous gaze to his hands.

The champagne glasses! One in each hand. Although not a drop was missing from either one.

"And that, my friends, is precisely why we need to pass this legislation." Her sharp voice overpowered the string quartet playing in the ballroom.

Raymond uncurled his toes and lifted his head, righteous anger heating his whole body. "I wonder, madam, how well you would fare if someone took away your home, your land, and your means of putting food on the table. I know men who have turned to drink for far less reason, don't you?" He turned his gaze to her husband, whose cheeks were mottled red from years of overindulgence.

Her face paled then suffused with bright color. She opened her mouth, but her husband put his hand on her arm and pulled her closer to his side. Not because he feared what Raymond would do—no one cared what the Noble Savage had to say—but because Senator Forrester wielded power within the party.

Raymond turned and marched away. He replaced the champagne glasses on a waiter's tray, remarking that neither had been touched.

Loudly.

How much longer should he stay where he wasn't wanted? And not just in this house but in Washington, DC, on the East

Coast, or anywhere but the place he grew up and worked so hard to leave. At least his adoptive parents had *wanted* him. He loved them too, but to live near the Shoshone as an Arapahoe was intolerable. The two tribes were sworn enemies from before white men ever invaded their land. Being raised away from his or any other tribe alienated him even more. So Raymond ran as far and as fast as he could for college. But four years of undergraduate work at Harvard earned him no friends and very little respect, despite his stellar grades. His application to law school languished in a desk drawer needing the force of someone like a U.S. senator to back it.

It was easy to understand how he'd gotten where he was. The question was where to go next. Raymond doubted his position with Senator Forrester would last after the vote on the General Allotment Act concluded. The senator was a good man, but he was also practical. What use was an aide who was excluded from conversations? And if he couldn't prove his worth as an aide, would the senator help him get into Harvard Law?

He had three weeks to figure it out.

———————◆———————

"Will you honor your word or not, Papa?" Caroline flung the question at her father's back as he closed the library door, shutting out the noise of their party.

He turned around, his cheeks red and his expression grim. "That's not fair, Caro."

"You're right. It's not fair. You promised you'd let me pursue medical school. For six years, I've been your political hostess, helping you win favor. How many more parties must I throw? How many more pinches on my arms or leering glances down my bodice must I endure?"

"Who dared to—"

"All of them!"

Papa's eyes narrowed to slits. "Cooper?"

She shook her head, heat flooding her cheeks. Raymond Cooper was the most confusing man she'd ever met. He held himself aloof from everyone. His expressions were always...perfect. He smiled when it was appropriate, frowned when the topic of discussion warranted it, and laughed at jokes, yet no emotion ever touched his eyes.

Except once.

He'd come upon her when a drunk senator had her cornered and was trying to persuade her to kiss him. In that moment, a fire burned in his eyes that both thrilled and terrified her. He'd stepped between her and the senator and snarled, "You will leave Miss Forrester alone now and forever more, or you will discover just how savage an Indian can be." The senator hadn't bothered her since. If only Raymond Cooper had noticed other, more odious attentions. Though not tall, he had an imposing air about him.

Realizing she'd spent too long thinking about the man, she looked her father in the eye. "No, Papa. Mr. Cooper has been a perfect gentleman."

Papa's shoulders slumped in relief. "We need to get back to the party."

"Not until we settle this. I want to *help* people."

"You are." Papa stepped deeper into the room. "Do you not understand what's at stake tonight? The General Allotment Act is bad law. Senator Dawes and several of his supporters have noble intentions, I'll give them that. However, attempting to 'civilize' Indians by forcing them to become farmers or ranchers..." He shook his head, his hands fisting. "Not only does it go against their culture, it breaks our word by stealing millions of acres from their reservations. It must be defeated. People will lose their land, our nation will lose a bit of its soul, and we have no way of calculating the lasting damage twenty, thirty, or a hundred years from now."

Caroline's temper rose. "You speak of our nation losing its soul by failing to keep its promises. What of your soul? And what of the people dying because there's no doctor to heal them?"

"I want more for you, Caro."

"I know what you want. And it has nothing to do with me pursuing my dream of becoming a doctor and everything to do with a husband for me and grandchildren for you."

Papa rubbed his scalp, small tufts of salt-and-pepper curls standing on end as testament to his frustration. "Edward Harrow was a fine man, but he's not the only man in the world."

Caroline sniffed and pressed a finger under her nose. "He was for me."

Papa stepped closer. Held out his hand. Dropped it when she didn't reach for it. "I have done all in my power to empathize with your loss, but it's time to throw some cold logic on your fiery heart. The notion that there's only one person in the whole world for you is utter nonsense. Edward ended your engagement because he recognized that you and he wanted very different things in life."

The sting of his rejection felt as fresh now as when he'd asked for his grandmother's ring back seven months ago. "There will never be another man for me."

Papa lifted both hands and shook them at her. "There's no reasoning with you. How will you become a good doctor if you are so convinced of your own opinion that you refuse to listen to anyone else?"

Caroline set her jaw. For years she'd listened to excuse after excuse about why she wasn't ready to leave home yet. "You speak of there being more than one man for me, but what about you? Mother's been gone for ten years. Lois Ambercrombie would happily marry you and host your social gatherings." They wouldn't be as good as Caroline's parties, but that shouldn't matter. It *didn't* matter.

"We have strayed from the point of this discussion." Papa gripped the silk lapels of his dinner jacket. "I have kept you close not because I don't intend to honor my promise but because you aren't ready for life as it is rather than life as you want it to be."

"How do you know what life I'm ready for when you won't allow me to pursue anything beyond this?" Caroline waved a hand, her wrist swirling to indicate more than just the four walls of the library. "And what's so wrong with the General Allotment Act, anyway? It will give those poor people land of their own. It will give them a reason to get up in the morning and work rather than drink their sorrows away."

"You're wrong." Papa turned to leave.

"Why? Because I don't agree with you?" Caroline raised her voice, but her father didn't turn around. "What if it's you that's wrong? No one agrees with you, Papa." He put his hand on the doorknob and flung the door open. Her frustration boiled over, and she shouted, "I think the General Allotment Act should pass!"

Light bulbs flashed. Papa slammed the door closed as quickly as he'd yanked it open and turned to glare at her.

Caroline slapped a hand over her mouth. Oh dear!

CHAPTER TWO

———— ◆◆◆ ————

R aymond arrived at the Forrester mansion early the next
morning. "I'm here as requested."

Jeffreys, the butler, let him in. Not one trace of a week's worth
of parties remained. No scuff marks marred the gleaming marble
floors, and the family's personal paintings had been restored to
their places. The only remnants were wooden crates stacked against
the wall, presumably containing the borrowed Indian-themed
paintings waiting to be returned to their respective various gal-
leries. The staff must have worked all night to restore order.

Jeffreys took Raymond's coat. "They're waiting for you in the
breakfast room, sir."

"Thank you." Raymond turned toward the back of the house.
He'd almost reconciled himself to being called *sir* after four
months of practically living at the Forrester home. The door to the
breakfast room was ajar, but he knocked just the same. "Hello?"

"Come in, Cooper." Forrester and his daughter were seated
on opposite ends of an oak table that sat eight people. Their
food was half-eaten, and a couple of newspapers rested at their
respective elbows. A bold black headline proclaimed, "Society
Hostess Revealed as a Fraud" over a large picture of the senator

frowning, his hand on the door to his library, with his gawking daughter in the background. The subheading was too small to read, but Raymond knew what it said. "Senator Forrester's Daughter at Odds with Her Powerful Father over the General Allotment Act Despite Parties Aimed at Defeating It." He'd read the paper before his summons appeared.

Forrester waved his hand at an empty chair. "Have a seat. We have much to discuss."

As soon as Raymond sat, a footman placed a plate of eggs, bacon, buttered toast, and orange slices before him, then made way for a different footman to pour a cup of coffee. "I already ate, sir." True, it was only dry toast and a lukewarm cup of coffee, but still.

"Then eat again, because you're going to need some sustenance." Forrester looked over the top rim of his reading glasses at his daughter. "I'd like to introduce you to my hotheaded daughter. You've met the composed society princess. This is her alter ego and the reason we're gathered here this morning."

Miss Forrester crossed her arms over her chest and huffed.

Raymond bent his head and prayed over his food, hiding his expression. The criticism was harsh but not undeserved. A better man would keep the smirk from his face.

He was not that man. Not this morning.

Once he had control of his facial muscles again, Raymond lifted his head. "Do you have a plan, sir?"

"Of course." Forrester picked up the paper and slapped his hand against the headline. "This requires the personal touch, so Caroline will visit every senator and congressman's wife from whom she can wrangle an invitation to tea over the next three weeks, and you will accompany her."

Raymond stopped chewing his toast. He swallowed then washed down what got stuck in his throat with coffee. "Me?"

Forrester pinched his bottom lip between his thumb and index finger for a moment, a sure sign that he was worried. "I'll be busy tackling the issues head-on with those senators whom I think can be swayed. The point of your visits will be twofold. First, Caroline needs to assure her friends that she spoke out of frustration with me, which is true, and that she doesn't believe what she shouted...er, said. Second, we need to make your people as a whole nonthreatening."

"So I'm to be the gentleman entrusted to see your daughter safely around the streets of Washington, DC?"

"Exactly."

Raymond wiped the corners of his mouth with a linen napkin. "That's not why I came to the nation's capital, if you don't mind me saying so."

"Don't mind, just don't agree." Forrester set down the newspaper. "And if you think I didn't hear about you losing your temper with the Gerrards last night, think again."

Whatever remained of his earlier smirk disappeared. "I apologize, but it wasn't without justification."

"Doesn't matter." Forrester pointed a finger. "Your job is to help me help your people. Accusing sitting U.S. senators of drunkenness—justified or not—is counterproductive, and you know it. Therefore, you will escort Caroline around town and be a perfect gentleman to make up for your ill-timed and gracelessly uttered truth. Unless you have a better plan."

Raymond shifted his gaze to the senator's daughter. Why wasn't she jumping into the conversation? Surely she had objections. "Not off the top of my head, sir." He returned his attention to Forrester. "But I've studied this act inside and out. I know it better than you do, if I may be so bold."

"You may, but there are two ways to win arguments: logic

and passion." Forrester pushed his half-eaten plate away. One of the footmen whisked it off the table before he'd returned his hands to his lap. "You and I have argued logically for the past four months. We've made our case, for the most part. Now it's time to attack from the other angle."

Raymond looked again at Caroline Forrester. "Pardon my bluntness, but this isn't a job for someone who just plans parties all the time. What can you do that your father and I can't?"

Her smile reminded him of the first time he tasted penny candy. "Why, I'll be charming and winsome and remind all those wives that they never, *ever* want to be on the outside looking in at a Caroline Forrester party. Then we'll leave them to work on their husbands. Never underestimate the power of the woman behind the man, isn't that what you always say, Papa?"

An undercurrent of something passed across the table. If forewarned, Raymond could have caught it with his bare hand.

"And if we"—Miss Forrester waved her hand between herself and Raymond but kept her eyes on her father—"manage to turn the vote, you'll honor your promise to send me to medical school?"

Raymond's eyes widened. "You want to be a *doctor*?"

She turned icy blue eyes on him, and he repressed a shiver. "A frontier doctor, to be specific. Now, pardon *my* bluntness, but what's that to you?"

He dropped his shocked gaze to the food in front of him. What the woman wanted to do with her life was none of his business. She just didn't seem hardy enough to pull weeds from a hothouse garden. He pictured his no-nonsense grandmother and his solitude-loving mother. Those were women who'd not only survived but thrived in the harsh Wyoming Territory. Caroline Forrester, with her soft hands and coiffed hair, would last three days on the frontier.

If that long.

How had it come to this? He was a Harvard graduate. Top of his class. And now he was relegated to escorting a lovely but deluded young woman around the city, hoping to persuade some women to sway their husbands into voting the right way.

"I can see the objections forming in your head, Raymond." Forrester rarely called him by his first name. "So let me make you a similar deal to the one I made with my daughter. If you and she can turn the vote, and I warn you now that it's an uphill battle, what do you want in return?"

Raymond looked his mentor in the eye. He'd hoped for this since coming to the capital. "I want you to sponsor my application to Harvard Law School."

Forrester stuck out his right hand. "Done."

They shook hands, and a weight lifted from Raymond's shoulders. All his work, every sacrifice, and the unrelenting fight to prove himself against men who deemed him inferior after one look at his brown skin, was about to pay off. Except. . .

He looked over at Miss Forrester. A headline swam across his mind. "Senator Forrester Creates Circus Show to Defeat General Allotment Act" with the subtitle "The Lady and Her Pet Savage."

Senator Forrester stood. "I'm off. You two feel free to finish breakfast and strategize your next three weeks of campaigning."

As soon as the door shut behind him, Raymond turned his attention to the daughter. "Before we go any further, I need to know one thing. What do you think about the General Allotment Act?"

Miss Forrester's shoulders hitched a fraction higher. "That I had better campaign against it if I ever want my father to honor his word and send me to medical school."

CHAPTER THREE

———◆◆◆———

Raymond ground his teeth together. "Do you have any notion what's at stake for hundreds of thousands of people besides yourself? Do you ever think of anyone but yourself?"

Her eyes flashed. "Of course not. I slept a grand total of twelve hours this past week making sure every single person who came to our parties would have no complaints and, therefore, no reason to vote against my father because lack of sleep is fun. In fact, I've done it for six years because, oh my, it's just my faaaavorite thing to do."

He shot her a glare.

"Oh, and let's not forget that I want to be a frontier medical doctor because it sounds so glamorous and easy."

Raymond might have found her sarcasm funny if the stakes weren't so high. "Are you done?"

"Being insulted? Yes, I am." She raised her eyebrows, the ice in her eyes replaced by a blue fire.

Raymond rubbed the back of his head. "Fine. Maybe I was a little harsh."

"Maybe? A little?" She leaned back in her chair and cocked

her head to one side. "How nice of you to admit your possible miscalculation."

When did Caroline Forrester turn so bitter? She'd always seemed unflappable. "All right. Let's try this again." Raymond leaned forward and stuck out his hand. "Hello, Miss Forrester. My name is Raymond Cooper, and I'm here because the federal government wants to rescind their promises to hundreds of thousands of people. I'd like to stop that. How about you?"

Her lips twitched, and the hostility in her eyes faded. She stuck out her hand and shook his. "It's nice to meet you, Mr. Cooper. I'm Caroline Forrester, and I've never had a man ask me my opinion before now, so forgive me if it takes a moment to catch my breath."

Raymond let go of her hand. "No one? Not even your father?"

She scoffed. "Least of all my father."

He sat back and took a sip of lukewarm coffee. "What do you know about the General Allotment Act?"

"That I can't possibly have an informed opinion because I'm just here to plan parties."

Raymond bit back a scathing response. He deserved that. In recompense, he schooled his features and tried again. "I am in earnest. I would genuinely like to hear your thoughts."

Her tongue peeked out between her lips, as though she wanted to retort with something biting but was reconsidering. She looked away for a moment before focusing her attention back on him. "All right, here's my assessment. While I think it's important that we honor treaties with the Indians, I also think those treaties need to be reevaluated in light of ongoing circumstances. I know Senator Dawes. He's been a guest here many times. He's always seemed both reasonable and conscientious about his voting. Knowing his character, if I were a senator, I'd be inclined to vote yes on anything he proposed."

"He's a good man, no doubt about it." Raymond watched to see how his assessment of the man whose bill was diametrically opposed to his reason for being in Washington affected her.

She frowned. "Then what, as you see it, is the biggest problem outside of breaking signed treaties? Because, frankly, giving each man a hundred and sixty acres to farm or three hundred and twenty for ranching seems fair, considering it's exactly what white homesteaders get when they prove up a claim."

Raymond fingered the rim of his coffee cup. "I see several problems, but I'll limit myself to the top three. First, no one who has proposed it has asked the various tribal leaders what it will do to *their* people. Outsiders who've observed a limited number of tribes are pushing this as though one solution fits all situations. Indians live in community. Families aren't isolated units. What belongs to one belongs to all. Cutting up their land into individual plots not only robs them of millions of acres of reservation land but destroys their traditional means of providing for each other through roaming hunts rather than farming or ranching. Those are white man customs, not Indian ones. The outsiders pushing this act think Indian traditions and cultures are inferior for being different, but who's to say individualism is better than community or vice versa?"

She nodded. "All right. I can see how one tradition isn't necessarily better than another, but there are some things that are undeniable truths. For example, it's Indian tradition to believe in multiple gods rather than the one, true God. Is it not our Christian duty to teach them the truth?"

"Teaching is one thing, forcing is another thing." He kept his eyes on her to gauge her reaction. "In my view, it's no different than the Spanish Inquisition, where belief in God was forced via torture."

Her tongue peeked out again. "I want to argue that such atrocities would never happen here, but. . ." She chewed her bottom lip and looked away.

Respect for her honesty lowered his animosity. "Which brings me to my second objection. In order to prove up a homestead claim, white settlers must show that their land has buildings and crops or cattle on it. Those are tangible things. The General Allotment Act says that an Indian must prove he has adopted the habits of civilized life to gain full rights as a U.S. citizen and land owner. What makes a man civilized? Who gets to judge that? It's an intangible, moving target. Such vague wording leaves room for legal interpretations that make me shudder. What's worse, whether it aims to or not, the result will obliterate Indian culture."

"Which, as you've already said, should not be forced." She pinched her bottom lip, an exact duplicate of her father's mannerism. "I'm almost convinced, so I am most curious to hear your third point."

He pushed his half-eaten plate away. "For better or worse, America is my home. Her future is my future. At a little more than a hundred years old, she's a child compared to other nations. As such, her personality must be carefully molded. If she becomes a nation that dishonors her word at the earliest opportunity, what will become of her in years to come? The General Allotment Act is, in my opinion, a seminal moment. First, America will either honor her word or break it. And second, a government deciding to eliminate an entire class of people's beliefs is a slippery slope."

Caroline tilted her head to one side, a frown on her face. "Explain, please."

He leaned forward, crossing his arms and resting them on the table. "The pilgrims who first came to America did so to practice their religion free from government persecution. England is a civilized nation. So is France. Yet in their history, they have both persecuted people whose beliefs differed from the governments' official religion. What if, in years to come, America follows that same path?"

"Again, I want to say that would never happen here because the Founding Fathers specifically protected the right to practice religious freedom into the constitution, and yet. . ." She trailed off once again.

He sat back in his chair, watching the play of emotions across her face.

She frowned and looked him in the eye. "Those seem quite rational, so why are so many people for it?"

"Depends on who they are." Raymond looked her in the eyes. "I sincerely believe Senator Dawes thinks he's doing the right thing. I disagree with him, but I don't doubt his character. Some others have endured or heard stories of atrocities and want to wipe out any trace of threat, although they conveniently forget that atrocities have been committed on both sides. But the strongest support comes from those who see millions of acres and"—he pressed his lips together for a moment to keep from saying something he shouldn't—"are just plain greedy to grab it."

The fire was back in Miss Forrester's eyes. "Then you and I had better see to its defeat."

———————•———————

Ezra Smith loved nothing more than pulling off a grand scheme where he was the primary beneficiary. He poured himself two fingers of whiskey without offering any to the grimy men standing in front of the paper-littered desk. "And you've seen the gold for yourselves?"

The dark-haired brute pulled something from his pocket.

Ezra tensed and walked back to the mahogany desk where a gun resided inside the top right drawer. He'd just reached the burgundy leather chair when a shiny object landed atop the files.

"There's more where that came from." The other brute, this one with red hair, pointed a dirt-caked finger at the walnut-size gold nugget, which rolled to a stop two inches from the edge of the desk. "And Myron here"—he tilted his head toward his companion—"has the geological survey proving there's a vein of gold just waiting to be dug out."

Ezra held out his right hand and snapped his fingers. Something flickered in the dark man's eyes before he complied with the silent demand and handed over the survey. Ezra perused it. "If I discover you're lying to me, you'll find yourselves face down in a creek somewhere." It was an empty threat but one they'd believe, coming from the office of a U.S. senator.

Redhead's lips tilted in a lopsided grin. "We wouldn't dream of it, boss."

Ezra sipped his whiskey. Ten in the morning was a little early, but he liked toasting his successes. "How many people have you lined up to claim Indian land once the General Allotment Act passes?"

"Twelve."

"You're pretty sure of yourself, boss."

The two men talked over the top of one another.

Ezra looked to Myron Whatever-his-last-name-was first. "Make it sixteen, two more on each end of this vein"—he pointed to the geological map then shifted his gaze to the right—"and I'm very sure. The act will pass, and this land will open up to people who know what to do with it."

Myron held out his hand. "I'll be takin' that back now." He pointed a look at the gold nugget.

Ezra smiled. "No you won't, because I'm having this tested to make sure you aren't lying to me."

"Sixteen is a lot, boss." Redhead hooked his thumbs in his front belt loops. "It'll cost extra."

"How much?" Ezra slipped the gold nugget into his pocket and withdrew a felt bag stuffed with hundred-dollar bills.

"Six hundred."

"Four." Ezra withdrew a hundred dollars and tossed it on the desk like he had plenty more. "And that's all you get until I've verified your gold nugget and your map. Now get out."

Myron snatched the money from the desk and shoved it in his jacket pocket. Redhead looked ready to protest.

Ezra sat back and picked up the whiskey glass. "Do you wish to argue with me?"

"No, sir," Myron answered and grabbed his friend by the arm. "Let's go."

"But we said—"

"Let's *go*."

Something about their exchange made Ezra's hackles rise. "Is there a problem?"

A look passed between the two degenerates. Redhead's shoulders slumped. He gave his companion a slight nod. "No problem, boss."

"Good. Now get out." Ezra waited for them to leave before crossing the room and locking the office doors. The stench of unwashed bodies filled his nostrils. He took a sip of whiskey to drown the scent and returned to his desk. A smirk lifted the corners of his lips. He'd been too late for the California gold rush, too sick to trek all the way to Alaska, and too late arriving in Montana to benefit from the riches lying inches underground. But none of that mattered now because this time he was early.

No one else knew that land had gold. Those idiots who'd carved up the land for reservations failed to check. All he had to do was pay a few people to claim homesteads then sign them over to him and he'd own every ounce.

He raised his glass again and clinked it against a brass picture frame holding his parents' wedding portrait. "And you thought I'd never amount to anything."

CHAPTER FOUR

———◆◆◆———

Caroline gripped her fingers inside her mink hand muff and lengthened her stride to keep up with Raymond. "If this is going to work, you have to be nice."

"I was very polite." The chill in his manner was worse than the blustery fall air.

She rolled her eyes. "Yes, but polite and nice are two different things. At least they are the way you do it."

Raymond slanted his head to look down at her. "And how else would you have handled that woman?"

A gust of wind whipped amber and scarlet leaves across the sidewalk. Caroline watched them tumble over the top of each other while formulating her reply. Mrs. Heath was a cantankerous woman under the best of circumstances. When surprised, her temper worsened, as demonstrated by her reaction to Raymond's appearance in her parlor. "While I agree that calling you a savage was unwise, she did temper it with 'noble' the second time."

Raymond huffed. "If someone called you a beautiful spinster, how would you react?"

"Are you calling me beautiful?"

"Don't change the subject." He placed his right hand on top

of his black fedora. "I neither called you beautiful nor a spinster, I asked how you would react to the moniker."

"I wouldn't turn into a stone statue." Caroline turned left to cross the street.

Raymond followed, angling his elbow toward her. He waited for her to take his arm and for traffic to clear before stepping into the street. "Which still doesn't answer what you would do."

"You are impossible."

"Why? Because I want a real answer rather than one of those polite evasions you're so good at doling out?"

Caroline clamped her lips tight. She withdrew her hand from his arm and stuffed it back inside the warm muff as soon as they reached the opposite side of the street. "I've never met a man as determined to ignore social niceties as you."

His left eyebrow lifted a fraction higher than his right one. "I do not ignore them. I simply don't have time to spend an hour on them before getting to the point."

"An overstatement to match my exaggeration, sir?"

"We have four blocks to go, which affords me the time to indulge in hyperbole."

A burst of laughter escaped before she could stop it. "A hit, sir. I acknowledge it."

Raymond chuckled, the sound warm and pleasant in her ear. "Does your father know you indulge in fencing terminology, Miss Forrester?"

"He does not, and I'll thank you to keep it to yourself, Mr. Cooper." She withdrew her right hand from the muff once more and curled her fingers around his woolen sleeve. "If you were half this charming in Mrs. Heath's parlor, she might have liked you very much."

"Doubtful."

"No, really. She enjoys a good verbal battle, and you are one of the few men in the city who could keep up with her."

"In spite of my savagery?"

Caroline's ire returned. "She didn't mean it like that."

"Of course she did, and no amount of your sugarcoating it will convince me otherwise."

Caroline pinched his forearm.

"Was that supposed to hurt?"

"You're impossible."

"I believe we already established that." He tipped his head to look at her, a glint of humor in his near-black eyes. "What we haven't established is how you'd respond to being called a spinster. You hoped I'd forgotten your lack of response, but I haven't."

A strange wish that Raymond Cooper forget nothing about her passed through her mind.

They crossed another street. Brown and ruby leaves clung to tree branches bordering the sidewalk in defiance of the wind. The mood between them shifted, or maybe it was just hers that changed. "I suppose you deserve an answer, but having never been called a spinster before, I'm not certain how I would respond."

"That's fair." He guided her around a pile of wet leaves.

Sudden insight made her breath hitch. "Fairness matters to you, doesn't it? More than to most men, I mean."

"It should matter to everyone."

Caroline drew him to a halt. "I've been in this city for six years, and I can tell you that men are motivated by many things, not all of them fairness and justice."

"Is that a warning, Miss Forrester?" He stared down at her, his face stoic but with an emotion in his eyes she couldn't quite place.

The urge to cup his cheek, to hold his gaze until she understood him, and to ease the pain she instinctively knew resided in his soul rooted her to the ground. "I suppose it is in an indirect sort of way. My father wants justice for your people, but—"

"Whoever *they* are."

Confusion jolted through her. "What do you mean?"

He looked away, breaking the connection between them. "Your father talks about 'my people' as though I understand and represent the interests of a host of diverse and sometimes warring tribes. That would be impossible even for someone born and raised within their tribe."

"And you weren't?"

This chuckle was full of irony. "No, my dear Miss Forrester, I most certainly was not."

"How did I not know that?"

His gaze returned to her, and she heard what he was too polite to put into words.

"Because I never cared enough to ask," she whispered.

He looked at the ground.

"I'm sorry, Raymond. Truly." She reached out to touch his hand. His eyes returned to hers, a wariness in them that twisted her heart. "I'd like to hear about it now, if you're willing to tell me."

He lifted his chin, pointing to the path ahead of them. "We only have two blocks left."

"Then give me the short version so I at least have *some* understanding before we meet Mrs. Adkins."

His eyes narrowed as though assessing her interest, or maybe her worthiness, to hear his story. "All right then, here's the short version."

She relaxed, pleased that whatever he'd seen in her resulted in him sharing his unique upbringing with her. The two blocks flew by as he talked about his adopted parents who raised him on the outskirts of an Indian reservation where his Arapaho blood made him an enemy of the Shoshone who dominated the land. "And when the government, in its infinite wisdom, placed the Arapaho on the same reservation as the Shoshone, it only made matters worse."

"You're certainly one of a kind." She meant it as a compliment, but the way he tensed told her it hadn't been received that way. "What? Did I say something wrong?"

"We're here." He assisted her up the steps to the brownstone.

"This discussion isn't over."

That polite mask of indifference she hated settled over his countenance. "It is for now."

⸺ ⸱ ⸺

Outside of an occasional head nod and "Yes, of course," Raymond contributed nothing to the conversation in Mrs. Adkins' parlor. Caroline kept up a constant stream of nonsense about the weather, the senator's health, the grandbabies back home, and the difficulty of retaining good help. He ground his teeth in frustration. Why had Senator Forrester condemned him to this torture?

Caroline finally rose from the red, shiny sofa with legs no sturdier than a spider's. "Thank you for having us. Mr. Cooper and I are grateful for your warm hospitality on this blustery day."

Raymond looked over at Caroline. They'd not uttered a single word about the reason for their visit. A warning look from her clamped his lips over his protest until they were back outside and walking away from the house. "What was that?"

She took his arm. "You were about to undo all the good we'd done."

"What good? And why am I even here if we're never going to bring up the Dawes Act?"

"Poor Raymond." She patted his arm like he needed consolation rather than answers. "Senator Adkins and his wife are tricky. They never discuss politics in social situations."

"That's not true. I heard him pontificate with the best of them just last week."

"You didn't let me finish. They don't discuss it unless *they* want to. You must wait for them to bring it up, otherwise you're ruined." Caroline slowed her pace and sent a quick look over her shoulder. "It does concern me though. Papa will need to know."

Raymond scratched his forehead, the knot in his stomach twisting tighter. "Need to know what? It's like you have this secret code that only women understand. I swear, I'm as useful as a porcupine at a ball."

She patted his arm again. "On the contrary, you proved yourself a true gentleman by inserting just enough 'mmm-hmm's' and 'uh-huh's' to show you were paying attention without taking over the conversation."

He shook his head. "And how is that helpful?"

She tugged on his arm to draw him to a halt. "You really don't understand, do you?"

Raymond thrust his hands into his coat pockets so he didn't fling them in the air out of frustration. Some passerby would see an Indian threatening a white woman, and he'd be in jail faster than oil got slick.

"Poor Raymond," she repeated. "Do you remember what Papa said when he sent us on these missions?"

"Yes, but what good does my escort provide if we never get to the point?"

"Your escort *is* the point." She raised her eyebrows at him. "You just spent an hour in the parlor of the queen of the Washington, DC, social circle."

"I thought you were the queen."

Laughter bubbled out of her, lifting her head toward the sky. When her neck returned to its normal position, her face sobered. "Oh. You were serious."

"Yes." Her expression confused him. "What? I've been to at least twenty parties since arriving here, and yours are unparalleled."

She inclined her head like a queen would. "Thank you, kind sir, but I'm twenty-two and unmarried. That disqualifies me from reigning over the social scene here. Not to mention, Papa is only a junior senator. Senator Adkins has been here for almost thirty years."

He scratched his forehead again. "Adkins doesn't have near the power in the Senate as your father does, despite his years."

"Yes, but his wife does. At least in the social sphere."

He looked back at the brownstone. "Really?"

"Don't let their modest home here fool you. She comes from an exceptionally wealthy background and has been cultivating her circle for three decades." Caroline turned and started walking again, so he held out his arm for her to take. He liked how it felt to be trusted.

And how it made several men passing them look at him twice.

He kept his face impassive lest the appreciative glances at Caroline and shock at seeing him as her escort turn threatening. He pondered Caroline's words for several minutes. "I still don't understand how my presence in her parlor is such a coup."

She tilted her head to look up at him. "Because she let you sit *in* the parlor."

Her words punched his gut. "Was I supposed to sit on the porch steps like a dog? Because that's the proper place for a savage like me?"

Caroline yanked her hand away from his arm. "That's not what I meant."

"Really?" He peered down at her. "Then what, pray tell, did you mean?"

Pink crept up her neck and into her cheeks. She looked away.

Raymond stopped walking, holding his ground both figuratively and literally. She wasn't going to wiggle out of answering him.

Caroline stuffed her hands inside her muff and looked at the ground for a long moment. When she raised her head to look at him, there was contrition in her eyes. "I'm sorry, Raymond."

"Sorry for what?" He should let her off the hook with the apology, but the fire in his belly needed more.

Her eyes darted from side to side. "Can we finish this conversation somewhere warmer?"

He was plenty warm. But she had a point. Stares from passersby were growing hostile.

He nodded and they continued walking. In silence. For the thoughts raging inside his mind were not fit for polite company, and she was likely trying to come up with words that would somehow gloss over the prejudice he faced every moment.

There were no words for that. And for some reason, it hurt worse coming from her.

CHAPTER FIVE

————— ◆•◆ —————

M rs. Mallory did *not* know how to throw a party. Caroline studied the ballroom. If she'd planned tonight's festivities, she'd have cut the guest list by half. People should be able to see all the way through a crowd rather than being confronted with a wall of fabric. Then there were the perfumes arguing with the pomades over the right to do battle with the floral arrangements. And the poor waiters had lost three trays of *hors d'oeuvres* already to dancers, large gestures, and a young lady's rather suspect fainting when a handsome young man was near enough to catch her.

"I can see your mind spinning."

The familiar voice sent a shiver down her neck. She lifted her lips in a forced smile, braced herself, and turned around. "Edward. How nice to see you." The lie fell from her lips with surprising ease. He was the opposite of Raymond Cooper in every way imaginable. Edward was tall and blond with blue eyes that never settled into place, and his shoulders sloped as though he'd spent so much time bending down to speak with people that his posture was irrevocably bent.

He grinned in that familiar way that had always turned her

heart upside down. "It's lovely to see you too, my dear. How have you been?"

Terrible. The word formed in her thoughts without any assistance, but was it true? She spouted off the expected, "Fine, and you?" while she examined her soul. Had it really been so terrible without Edward in her life? He loved these kinds of parties. The more the merrier, he always said.

"It's been a long time." He took her elbow and guided her toward the ballroom door. "Would you care for a breath of fresh air?"

Caroline nodded, wondering why he asked if he meant to drag her out the door before hearing her answer. "Do you suppose we've topped eighty degrees in here yet?"

He chuckled, the warmth of it adding to her discomfort. "Not quite. Give it another five minutes or so." He guided her through the throng, taking his time to chat politics with everyone in their path.

She'd forgotten how he tended to ignore her while he discussed topics he judged too complicated for her to understand. But after spending a week with Raymond, who didn't shy away from any topic with men, women, servants, and senators alike, she recognized how demeaning Edward's attitude was.

"I believe the problem isn't with the intent of the law," she inserted into a lull in the conversation between Edward and Congressman Hess, "but rather with the unforeseeable consequences of vague language regarding civilizing the Indians."

Congressman Hess frowned. "I've heard you've become quite the campaigner on your father's behalf." His gaze shifted to Edward. "I'm not sure how I feel about women meddling in men's work, Harrow. You?"

Edward pinched her elbow. "Miss Forrester meant no

disrespect, sir."

"Hm." The congressman looked down his long, somewhat bulbous nose at her. "Next thing you know, women will be campaigning for the right to vote. Then where will we be?"

"Better—" she began.

"—better not find out, eh, Congressman?" Edward finished for her.

Only he didn't finish *for* her but *against* her. Which, now that she thought about it, he'd done quite often during their courtship. It had never bothered her before, but it sure did now. She fumed silently while the two men wrapped up their conversation. They were still five feet from the door with at least two more couples to get past, but Edward must have sensed her willingness to thrust her unwanted opinions into a new conversation because he guided her past them with nothing more than a polite acknowledgment of their existence.

Once they were in the foyer, he released her elbow and turned her until they were face-to-face. "You can't really intend to spend your days campaigning with a—a—" Edward looked past her shoulder.

"A savage?" Raymond appeared at her side, the tension rolling off him in waves as palpable as if they stood at the ocean's edge.

She put her hand on his arm to steady him.

He shook her off. "That's what you meant, isn't it, Mr. Harrow?"

"That's not what he meant." Caroline grabbed Raymond's wrist and held on. "Edward is far too gentlemanly to describe another gentleman in such terms." She turned her gaze on her former fiancé. "Aren't you?"

"Of course." He bowed to her, tipped his head in what was almost a polite nod at Raymond, and then flicked his gaze away from them. "I see Senator Adkins. Please excuse me." He rushed off before Caroline could utter the polite niceties expected of her.

"What did you ever see in that man?" Raymond jerked his arm away and stalked toward the doors to the veranda.

She lifted the edge of her skirt and followed in his wake at a more sedate pace. When he pushed the doors open to the terrace overlooking the garden, she disregarded propriety by following him. Cold air sent a shiver down her neck, but rather than returning to the safety and warmth of the ball, she closed the veranda doors and hurried after Raymond. "Why did you assume Edward was going to call you. . ." She couldn't say the word, knowing how much it bothered him. "Has Edward ever called you that before?"

He flung his arm toward the mansion. "I'm sick and tired of being the savage, even if it is sometimes preceded by 'noble.' A noble savage is still a savage."

"I understand."

"No. You really don't."

"Then explain it to me." Caroline swept some dirt from the stone balustrade and sat. She'd wiggled out of finishing their conversation from the day after visiting Mrs. Adkins, but she wanted to finish it now. Unpleasant as it was going to be, it was better than what was going on inside the mansion behind them.

He turned his head to look at the doors. For a moment, she thought he'd leave her stranded on the terrace. But he didn't move. Nor did he speak. He just stood there contemplating the french doors as though they held the answers to life. Just as she was about to say she could sit there all night, he said, "I've never told you about my mother."

"You did. A little, anyway," she qualified.

He scratched his jawline. "I consider them to be my parents, given that I have no memories before they adopted me." He breathed in then let out the air in one big whoosh. "My mother was badly scarred by smallpox when she was a child. She wears a scarf to hide her face when she goes somewhere unfamiliar. People are often cruel with their stares and words."

Her heart tightened imagining it.

"I was about twelve when my grandparents and father came down ill. My mother and I needed to drive to the nearest fort, which was a three-day journey one way, for medicine. I'd never been off the Rocking K Ranch since arriving when I was probably about three years old."

Caroline cocked her head. "You don't know how old you were?"

"I still don't know."

She blinked at him. "Really?"

"My Indian mother was dying. Sharing my birth date with the white woman she was trying to convince to take me wasn't high on her list of priorities at the time." The sarcasm in his voice no longer bothered her. It was just his way.

She patted the balustrade, hoping he'd come sit beside her.

He remained standing, his face turned away from her, either unseeing or ignoring her invitation.

"Go on."

He shifted his weight from his left foot to his right and back again. "I knew I was an Indian, that my skin was darker than both my parents and my grandmother, but my grandfather was part Shoshone, so there were multiple skin tones in the family. I never thought anything of it." He shifted his weight once more. "We arrived at the fort as a wagon train was heading through."

Her heart squeezed tighter, her imagination already conjuring up the story. "What happened?" she whispered, unable to hold back her morbid curiosity.

"There were a few families with boys about my age." He

turned his head and gave her a wry grin. "Or at least as close as we can conjure. My mother decided to make the day I came into her life my birthday so we could have parties."

Caroline chuckled. "I can already tell I'd like your mom very much."

Surprise flitted across his dimly lit features. "I think you might."

Would she like me? The thought startled Caroline. No, not the thought. She always wondered if people liked her. The stunning part was how much the opinion of this unknown woman mattered.

Raymond dropped his gaze to the empty place beside her, took a deep breath, then sat down. His warmth eased the chill on her right side. "I'd never met boys my age. I'd never met anyone, really, so I'd never experienced rejection before."

She reached over and placed her hand on his forearm, an inadequate gesture of sympathy but all she could offer in the moment. He didn't pull away, which meant either he was so lost in his story that he'd not noticed or he wanted her comfort.

The thought sent a ripple of pleasure up her arm straight to her heart.

"I won't speak the names they called me. Suffice it to say I'd never experienced such hatred nor heard such vulgarity."

The part of her that longed for children wrapped invisible arms around the boy still inside the man sitting next to her. "How hard did you hit them?" She tried to inject some humor into the question, but it fell flat.

He shook his head. "I didn't move. I stood there. I had no idea what to do. Then Mom came to stand next to me, and those horrid brats turned their vitriol on her. They picked up rocks and threw them at her." The muscles beneath her fingertips hardened. "I knew *exactly* what to do with that. It took four full-grown men to pull me off them."

"Good for you." She didn't usually advocate violence, but she wanted to smack those terrible boys herself.

"That's what I thought." Bitterness soaked each word.

"You were defending your mother." She squeezed his hand, stunned when he gripped it with the strength of a drowning man.

"And I was proud to do it." There was a catch in his voice. "There's something inside me that flares up when I see people treated unfairly. I don't fully understand it, but I can't control my need to fight against injustice or defend the weak. Only when we got home, my father. . ."

Oh dear. She shifted on the balustrade so she could see his face better. "What happened?"

"I was so proud." He shook his head, his eyes focused somewhere in the past. "I made the boys who hurt my mother pay. My father had been a soldier. He taught me to defend what was right, so I was sure he'd be proud of me too."

Caroline sucked in a breath and held it.

"But he took me outside, walloped my backside, and told me I couldn't act like a savage."

"Oh no." Caroline pressed her left hand over her mouth. Tears pricked her eyes. Poor Raymond. No wonder he hated that term.

"He meant well, and the thing is, he was right. If my son raced away from a bleeding woman, I'd give him a walloping too. It's just. . ."

She placed her left hand over their joined ones. "That's one of the words those boys called you, isn't it?"

Raymond's nod was barely perceptible. "My father has no idea how much he hurt me."

"You should tell him."

"Why? To make him feel as badly as I did? No." He shrugged his shoulders. "It's better left alone."

"But it sets you off every time you hear it."

"That's not his fault."

Caroline held back a huff at how quickly he went from confiding to confrontational. "I didn't say it was."

"Then what are you saying?" He yanked his hand away and crossed his arms over his chest.

Caroline pulled her hands into her lap and gripped them together. "I'm just trying to help."

He bowed his head and tented his fingers over his face.

She patted his shoulder. "I'm sorry. You were right. I don't understand."

He huffed. "No, I'm sorry." He stood up and faced her. "I appreciate that you're trying to help. I do. I just don't think telling my father he unintentionally poured salt into an open wound does anything helpful. He did what he thought was right, even when he took me to the reservation once the Arapaho tribe was resettled there."

She hated to but couldn't stop herself from asking, "What happened?"

Light from the mansion behind them filtered through the bare branches and cast claw-like shadows across his face. "I'd never heard the Arapaho language, so I couldn't understand a word said, but their contemptuous snarls made the meaning clear."

"What did your father say?"

"He wasn't there. He was inside conducting business."

Caroline waited for him to answer the unasked question, but he never did, so she prompted him. "What did he say when you told him?"

"I didn't."

She couldn't hold back a huff at his succinct and entirely unfulfilling answer.

He must have understood her frustration because he added, "It wouldn't have helped."

"Then what would?" She stood and took a few steps to bring their faces within inches. His cedar and citrus scent filled her senses. "Tell me how I can help."

He stepped away from her. "There's nothing you can do."

His withdrawal hurt. "Because I know nothing of real-world problems, only the petty concerns of a woman who does nothing but plan parties?"

"I shouldn't have said that. I didn't know you then."

She should let it go, but spending so much time with him had rubbed off on her. "Yet now that you do, you're still shutting me out."

"It's better that way."

"For whom? Because it's not better for me, and frankly, I don't think it's better for you either." She placed a hand on his lapel, his heartbeat strong beneath her fingertips. Her own heart raced at the audacity of her action. "You're so convinced that everyone is against you, you refuse to see. . ."

"What?"

She lifted her face an inch. "Me."

Raymond took a step back. "You?"

"Is that so hard to believe?" She dropped her hand back to her side, her expression difficult to read in the darkness.

He swiped a hand over his face. "It's not a matter of belief."

She cocked her head to one side. "Then what is it?"

He looked up at the night sky. A few stars testified to the existence of millions more invisible in the city. "I'm Arapaho raised by white parents on an isolated ranch in the middle of Shoshone country. The Shoshone—at least most of them—hate me for being Arapaho, the Arapaho hate me for not being part of their tribe, whites hate me for being Indian, and Harvard classmates hated me for daring to prove I was as smart if not smarter than they. I'm alone in this world. No one understands what it's like to live as I have done."

"Of course not." Her agreement shocked him. Most people glossed over his isolation with the verbal equivalent of a pat on the head. "No one else is you. But no one else is me, either, and you have no idea what my life has been like."

He snorted and jutted his chin at the mansion. "You have at least seventy people here tonight who understand your life."

"Not the part that matters." Her voice was pitched low, almost a whisper. As though she was ashamed of something.

It caught him by surprise. His feet moved a step closer to her without a conscious thought. "Tell me."

Caroline turned away from him and walked toward the steps to the garden.

He followed. When she shivered, he shrugged out of his dinner jacket and placed it around her shoulders.

"Thank you." She pulled the lapels around her neck. "Let's get a little farther away from the house. I don't wish anyone to overhear."

Intrigued, Raymond held her elbow to assist her down the stairs and across the cobblestone walkway into the shaped hedgerows.

"What do you know about my mother?"

The question surprised him. "Only that she died when you were about thirteen or fourteen years old."

Caroline's pace quickened. "You asked me what I ever saw in Edward Harrow."

What did that have to do with her mother?

As though she'd heard his thought, she answered, "Please just give me a moment. This is a long story and it's all woven together."

"Of course." A small bench appeared along the path. He pointed at it. "Is this far enough from the house for your comfort?"

She nodded and they sat. She gripped her hands together, and the urge to place his hands over hers nearly overpowered him. She took a deep breath, held it, then let it out with a whoosh. "My mother didn't die. For all I know, she's still alive and living in Italy somewhere."

Raymond turned on the small bench, his knee bumping into her leg. "What?"

"She left us for her soulmate, Pablo Something-or-other. They met at a party my parents were throwing for one of Papa's friends who was running for governor of New York."

"You lived in New York? Sorry"—Raymond sat straight forward again—"I didn't mean to interrupt."

"We don't talk about those days on purpose. After Mother left, Papa sent me to boarding school while he made a new life and a new name for himself in Vermont."

Raymond's heart pinched. Leaving home, although the very thing he wanted, had been a challenge. But he'd left at eighteen with the blessing and love of his family. "How old were you?"

"Almost twelve." She began to pick at the edges of her left thumb with her right hand.

His fingers itched to touch her, so he leaned forward and focused his eyes on the ground. "Go on."

"Before she left, Mother told me she'd married my father before she'd had time to explore the world. She said my father wasn't her real husband."

Raymond twisted to look at her. "What on earth does that mean?"

Caroline picked at her nail with more determination.

Unable to stop himself, he reached over. Her hands were cold.

She turned her hands and gripped his. "I didn't understand then, but I figured it out a few years later. She believed that, if you were with your one true love, then life would be easy. Apparently, life with my father had gotten too difficult, therefore he couldn't be the right one for her. Ergo, he wasn't her real husband."

Raymond wished the woman were here so he could talk sense into her.

"When she met Pablo, he swept her off her feet. He was her one true love, she said, and I needed to believe her. Otherwise, she left because she wanted to." Caroline's grip was so strong, his pinkie finger was going numb. "And no matter how many times she said she wasn't leaving *me*, she was only leaving my father, it amounted to the same thing. She didn't love me enough to stay."

After a minute, Raymond prompted, "And how does this tie into Edward Harrow?"

"Seeing him tonight, I don't know. It's a little fuzzy in my head."

"Just talk it through. I'm listening."

She sighed. "Thank you."

They remained silent, the moonlight and breeze weaving some sort of spell around him. He was holding hands with a beautiful woman who seemed content, maybe even happy, to be with him.

As he was with her.

Which was dangerous.

Only. . .no one observed them, so there was no one to throw stones, either literal or figurative ones. He gave himself permission to enjoy the moment, for it would only be a moment before the illusory bubble encasing them burst.

"I promised Edward I would always love him." She broke into his reverie. "If I don't, does that make me as faithless as my mother?"

It was a rhetorical question, so Raymond debated for several seconds before saying, "But he was the one who broke off the engagement, wasn't he?"

She nodded. "I know that technically releases me from whatever promises we made regarding our future, but. . ." She sat straighter. "I won't ever be like my mother. I refuse to put anyone through what she did to us."

Raymond knew the answer before asking, "So you'll never love another man?"

"I don't know. I don't think so. Like I said, it's fuzzy."

"He's not worth it."

Her vise-grip on his hand loosened. "I'm beginning to see that."

He debated a moment before adding, "And letting go of him doesn't make you like your mother."

"Maybe not, but. . ." She pulled her hand from his.

And the fragile bubble burst.

CHAPTER SIX

———◆◆◆———

Caroline turned up the collar of her fur coat, but the frosty December air snaked down her neck whenever the wind gusted. "I'm glad we only have a week left before the vote. The weather gets chillier by the day."

Raymond, who seemed unaffected by the cold in his gray wool coat and top hat, kept his gaze straight ahead. "We need another month, and even then I doubt it would be enough time."

"You're such a pessimist." Carolyn lifted her chin toward the house they'd just left. "I think we persuaded Mrs. Adkins."

He cut a glance at her. "Perhaps. Or else she simply gave in to your persistence."

She pulled him to a stop and turned him to face her. "Why Raymond Cooper, I do believe that's the nicest thing you've said to me."

He snorted, laughter filling his eyes and twitching his lips.

Her heart warmed. "You're allowed to laugh, you know."

A full smile bloomed on his face. Gracious, the man was handsome without that perpetual scowl.

She let go of his arm, and they continued on their way.

A loud crash and shouting interrupted the quiet morning.

"I think it's up around that corner." Raymond quickened his stride.

She matched his pace then let him go ahead when she saw the crowd. A tall man with impressive sideburns approached. His gaze flitted between her and Raymond as his nostrils flared. Having seen the same reaction too many times, Caroline summoned her sweetest smile. If her mother taught her nothing else of value, she was right that more flies were caught with honey than vinegar.

But the tall man's scowl deepened. As Raymond raced past him, he spit on Raymond's shoes.

Caroline gasped. Raymond continued on as though nothing had happened. Maybe he hadn't seen it. When the tall man neared her, she said, "That was most ungentlemanly, sir."

His face contorted with hatred. He then called her a name she'd never heard and spit in her face.

Disbelief and rage warred for supremacy as she wiped the spittle from her cheek.

"People like him ought to be hanged," he snarled.

Caroline straightened to her full height. "You mean Harvard graduates and senatorial legislative aides? Why, that would condemn half the city." Perverse pleasure filled her chest at his shocked expression. "Probably even you."

Before he recovered, and before Raymond turned around to wonder what had become of her, Caroline stalked away. Her heart raced at both her exertion and audacity. Words she wished to hurl at the terrible man swirled inside her head as she followed in Raymond's wake.

Equine screams scraped her eardrums. "Have you got them?" she heard him ask.

An affirmative answer.

Raymond made a sharp right turn and came to a sudden stop. "Whoa, boy."

Caroline followed in his wake then peeked around his left shoulder. A black horse tossed his head, eyes wild.

"Shh. Calm down. It's just me." Raymond grabbed the horse's bit, pulling down his head to stroke his muzzle. "That's good. Just relax. I've got you."

Caroline pressed a hand to her galloping heart and stepped sideways to get a better view of the damage. She should help too. With the people. She planned to be a doctor, after all.

A crowd blocked her view of someone who, given the stooped shoulders of those surrounding, was lying on the ground. Taking her cue from Raymond, she pushed through them intent on helping.

Blood.

So much blood.

Caroline's vision went blurry. Humming in her ears grew louder as minuscule spots swirled in an ever-tightening circle until the world went black.

"Hey," she heard before her spiritless legs wilted.

An instant before she lost consciousness, she felt strong arms sweep her up. The smell of cedar and citrus with a hint of horse announced her rescuer. She was safe.

"Make way!" Raymond swung Caroline sideways as he maneuvered them through the gawking crowd. Frowns, averted eyes, and muttered expletives confirmed his fear that he, a savage, would dare touch a white woman. Fortunately, they were a mere two blocks from her home. He outpaced his expectation that, at any moment, a mob would form around them and lynch him for his audacity.

He took the granite steps to the front door two at a time and didn't bother to ring. He bent low enough to grasp the brass doorknob, turned it, and breathed in sweet relief when it turned.

"Mr. Cooper?" Jeffreys pulled open the door. "What happened? I saw you coming."

"Thank you." Grateful the butler's demeanor held no hint of contempt, Raymond pointed his chin toward the parlor. "I'll set her down in there. Some water, please."

"Of course, sir. For you as well?"

"Yes, thank you." Raymond turned left.

As he tilted toward the sofa, Caroline's arms wrapped around his neck. "Not yet. You smell good."

He jerked upright, tightening his grip so he didn't drop her.

"Yes," she murmured then sighed with what sounded like contentment. She tilted her head so her lips brushed his neck. "This is nice."

Raymond turned to see if any staff had observed. Tolerant of him as the senator's aide was one thing. Discovering that Miss Caroline wished to remain in his arms? That was a horse of a different color. But, Lord have mercy, she felt good.

He closed his eyes and savored the moment, even though loneliness pinched the edges of his joy.

How long had it been since anyone had touched him with affection? Senator Forrester occasionally clapped him on the shoulder, but the contact was brief. The last time anyone wrapped their arms around him and held on tight was when he left for Harvard four years ago.

Though he'd not forgotten how good that felt, he'd relegated it to the edges of his life as nice but not necessary. A mistake.

But one he could *not* rectify with Caroline Forrester.

He leaned over the couch and pried her arms from around his neck. She sighed again. This time with what sounded like disappointment, but he couldn't be sure.

He refused to be sure.

"You're safe, Miss Forrester." He finished removing her arms from his neck and stepped away from the couch.

Rapid footsteps announced Jeffreys' return. "Water, sir." He held out two cups as though expecting Raymond to administer the liquid to the lady.

He took one cup and retreated to the fireplace.

Jeffreys pinched his eyes tighter for an instant before understanding dawned on his face. "Very good, sir." He pulled a chair closer to the couch, sat, and held the cup to her lips. "Miss? Can you drink something?"

Raymond watched from the safety of ten feet away. Only it wasn't safe. Green-eyed jealousy reared its ugly head for how near Jeffreys sat, for how he lifted her head to help her drink, for the rim of the cup touching her lips.

Raymond turned away from the view to no avail. The images remained fresh in his mind, stirring up longings so primal he gripped the mantel until his fingernails imprinted in the painted wood. He should go back outside and let the mob beat him bloody. That would cure him of this nonsense.

"Raymond?" Caroline's voice reached across the room to caress him.

Pleasure vibrated down his spine. *Lord, help!*

He drained his cup, set it on the mantel, and then turned around. "I'm here, Miss Forrester." He forced his limp legs to walk closer and schooled his features with every ounce of self-control left in his depleted reserves.

"There you are." She smiled at him with genuine affection. "Thank you for being my hero."

Lord! I said help, not more.

He pressed his lips together and forced slow, steady breaths in and out of his nose.

She sat up with the butler's assistance then dismissed him with her gratitude for the water. "I'm fine now, thank you, Jeffreys. Mr. Cooper and I need to talk privately. Please see that no one disturbs us."

"Very good, miss."

Jeffreys retreated, closing the parlor doors behind him, before Raymond recovered enough equilibrium to open his mouth. "We shouldn't be alone, Miss Forrester."

She frowned at him. "We've been alone for the past two weeks."

"In public." Needing a barrier, he pulled the chair back to its original place four feet away and stood behind it.

"Pshaw." She flicked her wrist like his concern was nothing more significant than a fly. "My father trusts you, and you're the most honorable man I've ever met."

Did she know how much he needed to hear such words? His parched soul drank them in, filling the cracks formed over years of drought. Though her father often offered encouragement, his words lacked the power of those uttered by a beautiful woman whose warmth lingered on his body.

His self-control evaporated like morning mist. He stood defenseless against her. Whatever she asked, he'd move heaven and earth to lay at her feet.

And then both he and she would pay for it with their lives.

———————•———————

"We need to talk about what just happened." Caroline tucked a strand of hair behind her left ear. It had come loose when Raymond swooped her into his strong arms. Never in her life had she felt so—so— What? She couldn't find the right word.

He stared at her, his gaze hot.

Something flickered in her soul. It grew warmer. Wider. It spread down her arms and through her torso. All the way to her toes. She shrugged out of her fur-trimmed wool coat while trying to place the emotions throbbing through her veins. Desired, yes, but not in the way she'd come to expect from the men who usually surrounded her father. Because Raymond protected her honor. When he held her, she'd felt. . .

Aaargh!

Safe was too tame a word. Nor did it capture the underlying power of Raymond Cooper.

"You wanted to talk?" his voice interrupted her wild thoughts.

"Yes." She tossed her coat on the seat beside her and stared at it. Looking at Raymond when the mere sight of him made her blood roar was. . .unwise. Now there was a good word. "I, uh. I've never fainted before."

"Ever? Or just at the sight of blood?"

"Ever. I've never even come close." Not even when Edward pulled her into his arms, declared his undying love for her, and then kissed her for almost a full three seconds. She'd counted them, waiting to feel the unnamed emotion currently rampaging through her body.

"Have you ever seen blood before?"

"Of course." She shrugged one shoulder, an involuntary

response to the half lie. "Just never that much of it in one place."

"Ah. I see." His tone filled in the part she'd left unsaid.

"I don't want my father to hear about this." She braved looking at his face.

He tilted his head, his black eyebrows high. "Do you honestly think you can keep it from him?"

She cut a glance at the parlor doors. "Probably not." She crossed her arms over her chest. "I don't want to give him more ammunition in his fight to keep me from medical school."

His eyebrows twitched higher.

"Let me guess, you agree with him. You don't think a woman has what it takes to be a doctor either. Well let me tell you something, there's no—"

"Don't put words in my mouth, Miss Forrester."

"Oh, for crying out loud, can you please call me Caroline?"

He mashed his lips together.

"Am I so abhorrent to you that we—after all we've been through—can't even claim the simplest measure of friendship?" She pulled her arms closer, her fingernails gouging into her biceps through the peach satin sleeves.

"Abhorrent?" He tossed his head back and laughed in what she could only describe as astonishment and frustration. "That's not a word in my vocabulary when it comes to you, Miss Forrester. And"—he held up a finger to stop her from objecting again— "Miss Forrester it is and always shall be." His expression turned serious. "You aren't stupid. A little naive, perhaps, particularly when it comes to your desire to be a frontier doctor, but never stupid. You understand the world and why we can never be more than the senator's daughter and his aide."

"It shouldn't be that way." Tears gathered in her eyes. Why? Because they couldn't be friends? Because stupid men spit their prejudices? Because good men let those same prejudices make them too uncomfortable to confront injustice head-on? No. It went much deeper than that. So deep that it took her breath away.

Cherished.

That was the word she'd been looking for. Raymond Cooper cherished her.

And her fight to become a doctor paled to insignificance compared to convincing him that they belonged together. Which they did. She'd known it since the Mallorys' party but had been too afraid to let go of the romantic notion that Edward was her one and only to see it until now.

She stood and walked toward Raymond. "If people like us don't fight for how the world should be rather than what it currently is, who will?"

He shook his head. "Maybe in a hundred years but not now."

Caroline gripped the edge of the chair, leaning her knee on the seat so her face was mere inches from him. "Why not?"

He held himself rigid. "And you can't ever, *ever* be in my arms again."

She put her hand on his. He jerked it away. "Or tell you how good you smell?" She was pushing the boundaries of propriety, but this was war. She wanted this man more than anything she'd ever desired in her life. She'd fight for him with every weapon at her disposal.

Because *he* was that "more" her father wanted for her. Becoming a doctor was her consolation prize for losing Edward. Her way to make up for being unlovable to the one man she thought held her every hope.

He didn't.

She almost laughed at how silly that sounded now, but the moment was too solemn. Raymond needed no excuse to run away.

"If you won't fight for the way things should be, why are you in Washington, DC? Isn't that the whole purpose of being here?"

"That's different." He looked away, a sure sign that he didn't believe the words he was saying any more than she did.

"I won't give up on this, Raymond." She waited until he turned his head to look at her. "And yes"—she put a finger on his lips to both silence him and because she wanted to know how they felt—"Raymond it is and always shall be."

He jerked away, stumbling in his haste to fling open the parlor doors and run away.

She smiled. Had she won this round? Maybe. Maybe not. The fight was a long way from over, but at least she knew what she was fighting for.

And it was good.

CHAPTER SEVEN

———◆•◆———

Ezra Smith tore the report in his hands in two and slammed the pieces on his desk. The vote on the Dawes Act was next week. If the rumor mill was right, several sure yeses had slipped into the no column with a few more wavering. All because Gerald Forrester stuck his nose where it didn't belong.

Ezra curled his fingers, imagining that do-gooder's neck between them. Forrester needed to back down. He'd lost his wife before coming to DC, but that daughter of his would be an acceptable substitute. A few threats to her well-being with an anonymous note saying she'd best keep quiet ought to do the trick.

He opened the drawer holding his personal stationery, lifting the pages until he reached the blank ones underneath and wrote, *Tell your daughter to shut up, or I will close her mouth permanently.* He used block lettering to disguise his normal flowing cursive writing. When the ink was dry, he folded the missive and addressed it to Senator Gerald Forrester. Ezra tucked it beneath some of his other correspondence that would be picked up, sorted, and delivered by senatorial pages.

Of course, there might need to be a show of strength to back up the threat. But if a letter delivered via the Senate's interoffice mail didn't convince Forrester, killing that stooge he employed to safeguard his daughter as she meddled would do it.

Ezra mentally counted his remaining funds. He'd paid to have the geological survey authenticated, then paid again to keep the man's lips sealed. He'd paid even more for the same authentication and silence on the gold nugget.

Should he do the killing himself? He owned a gun but had never used it except to make threats. Poison might work. That Forrester gal was always throwing parties, so slipping a little something into her constant bodyguard's glass shouldn't be too hard.

While it was always better to hire someone so his hands were clean, good help cost good money. He needed every penny to pay for homestead claims, train fares, mining equipment, and a list of other things that seemed to grow rather than shrink with every passing day.

He stared at the wedding picture of his parents. *"You ain't nothin' but a lazy cheat that wouldn't know an honest day's work if it bit him on the leg. You'll never amount to nothin' but a two-bit fool, and that's the truth."*

"You're wrong." He picked up the picture and used his sleeve to wipe away a smudge on the frame. "And I'll prove it to you no matter what it takes."

———— ◆ ————

A change of clothes and a few hours with Jane Eyre and Mr. Rochester restored Caroline's equilibrium. When she heard her father arrive home, she set aside her novel and checked the mirror over the mantel to make sure no vestiges of her afternoon ordeal showed on her face.

The library doors flew open. "Caro!"

She spun around, her hand over her chest. "Papa. Whatever is the matter?"

He closed his eyes for an instant and took a deep breath. "I'm just glad to see that you're home safe."

She balled her hands into fists. Raymond must have tattled on her. "What did you hear?"

Her father frowned. "About what?"

Hm. Maybe Raymond hadn't said anything. She flattened her emotions and slid a layer of polite interest over the top of them. "You seem upset."

He glanced at an envelope in his hand. "I'm fine. Everything is fine." He rearranged his expression to match his words. "Please have cook set back dinner until seven, and have Jeffreys send a message requesting Raymond join us."

Her heart skipped with pleasure. "Of course. Anything else?"

"No, no. That will be all." He crumpled the envelope and shoved it into his pants pocket. "I have just a few minutes of work to finish up. I'll see you at dinner."

Caroline nodded then followed him out of the library to speak with Jeffreys.

Ninety minutes later, she was checking her reflection again, this time in her bedroom mirror, to make sure she looked her absolute best. She'd chosen a sky-blue satin dress saved from being too dressy for an in-home dinner by its plain lines and limited beadwork along the neckline. She'd asked her maid, Molly, for a simple hair arrangement with a loose bun and a few large curls pulled out to frame her face.

Molly wove a matching blue ribbon through the bun, leaving long tails to drape over Caroline's shoulder. "Matches yer eyes, miss."

"Indeed it does." More ammunition in her war to convince

Raymond that they belonged together. After a thank you to Molly for her hard work, Caroline pinched some color into her cheeks and headed out the door.

The look on Raymond's face when she walked into the formal dining room was worth every tug on her corset and scrape of hairpins on her scalp.

Even Papa noticed. "Why, Caro. You look lovely."

She walked over to brush his cheek with a kiss. "Thank you."

Raymond's torso turned to continue watching her, but his feet didn't move.

A giggle formed in her chest. She ruthlessly kept it from escaping her lips. The war was far from over, but she'd drawn the first blood. "Raymond. It's good to see you."

His eyes darted to her father as though expecting a reprimand for her casual use of his first name. No reprimand was issued, but it didn't ease his frown. "Miss Forrester, thank you for the invitation."

She smiled at him as she glided to her chair. Did men have any idea how much effort went into gliding? But when he moved to pull the chair out for her instead of her father, the strain was worth it. "Thank you, Raymond."

"Stop it." Though soft, his words were clipped and harsh around the edges.

"Never," she responded, her voice gentler than his. She snuck a peek at her father. His frown was aimed at the door to the kitchen rather than at her and Raymond. She tilted her head to look up at him to gauge his reaction to her next salvo in this war of theirs. "Do you really wish to fight me on this?"

Red crept up his neck as he frowned daggers at her. "Nothing good can come of it."

Triumph lifted her heart. He cared about her! Otherwise,

why would he be fighting so hard against her? She grinned. "It already has."

He let go of her chair and strode to his, the veins in his neck visible above his white celluloid collar.

She turned her attention to her father, who hadn't moved since she came into the dining room. He was still frowning at the door. "Papa? Is everything all right?"

"Yes. Yes." He ambled to his chair opposite her at the table and sat down. Raymond followed suit. As soon as they were all seated, the servants arrived with the first course. Two bites into the turtle soup, Papa set down his spoon. "Actually, no. Everything is not all right. I'm afraid I have some bad news."

Caroline set down her spoon and gripped her hands together in her lap. "Are you ill? You seem pale."

"I'm fine." He glanced down at his soup before turning his attention to Raymond. "But I'm afraid we've lost our battle against the Dawes Act. Without Adkins on our side, we won't turn his cronies."

Raymond cut a look at her, shock splashed across his features. "I thought we'd turned Mrs. Adkins."

"We did." She tore her gaze away from him to focus on her father. "He should turn at least three more just by declaring, and we have a whole week to work on the others. We're close, Papa. Very close."

He shook his head. "No. It's over. I talked with Adkins today. He was temporarily swayed but has reverted back to a yes vote. I'm sorry." He stood and tossed his napkin beside his soup bowl. "You're welcome to remain for dinner," he addressed Raymond, "but you'll no longer be escorting Caro around town."

She gasped in protest. "No, Papa."

He glared at her. "What did you say? Never mind." He held

up his hand to forestall any further comment from her. "You will do as you're told, or I will rethink my decision to send you to medical school."

"But, Papa—"

"The term starts in February, so you'll be quite busy packing." He wiped the corner of his mouth with the back of his hand. "That is all. Good night."

Caroline watched him hurry away, her jaw unhinged. The moment the doors closed behind him, she swiveled her neck to see Raymond's reaction.

His jaw was clenched tight.

"This isn't over." It couldn't be. Not when she'd just figured out that nothing—absolutely *nothing*—mattered more than being with Raymond Cooper.

He pounded his fist on the table, sloshing soup over the edge of his bowl. "I told you nothing good would come of your unwanted attention."

Unwanted stabbed her in the chest, a wound deeper than when Edward ended their engagement. Caroline ground her teeth together. "You think this is my fault?"

"What else could it be? We were turning the tide, we both know it, but then you had to ruin it with your silly romantic fantasies."

Her lungs seized. Words crashed into each other inside her brain.

"This was important. Not just politically but to me personally." He stood and, like her father, tossed his napkin on the table. "Goodbye, *Miss Forrester*. Have a nice life."

He was gone before she recovered. With a screech of frustration, she threw her napkin toward the door. It missed, landing instead in her father's soup.

CHAPTER EIGHT

———◆●◆———

Raymond strode down the hall toward Senator Gerard's office, the last one on his list saved for the last day before the vote. He'd spent the week pounding on doors to no avail. Without Senator Forrester or his daughter at his side, no one cared that he was the sole person in Washington with a personal stake in the General Allotment Act's passage or defeat. All his logic and passion meant nothing once people saw his skin.

Alone took on an extra layer of meaning.

But he refused to give up. He'd made a commitment to fight against the bill and fight he would. Even if no one else stood with him. And even if it meant humbling himself before the man he'd publicly shamed for being a drunk at a party.

If only he could summon the same courage and humble himself before Caroline. But then what? The woman plagued him, body and soul. No matter what she thought, there was no happily ever after to their story. He saw it even if she didn't.

Still, he should apologize for saying she'd caused her father's change of heart when he knew it wasn't her fault.

What was to blame? The promise of a committee chairman-ship? A block of votes for a bill Forrester cared about more than the General Allotment Act? After all, it was only a bunch of savages being double-crossed and looted.

Raymond turned a corner and pressed his back against a wall. If Caroline were here, she'd tell him he was letting righteous anger cloud his judgment. Often the prejudice he faced was real. But once in a while, he imagined persecution where none existed. She'd taught him that.

He took a deep breath and pressed on.

Muffled shouts grew louder as he approached Senator Gerard's office. The man's secretary had his ear pressed against the double doors. Raymond's nostrils flared with disgust. "What's going on?"

The senator's secretary jumped away from the doors, his pasty white skin turning a little pink. "I don't know what to do."

Raymond heard Senator Forrester's voice. "I know it was you. Do you deny it?"

"I have no idea what you're talking about!"

"I'll have you impeached for this!"

Raymond caught a smirk on the pasty man's face. "What do you know?"

The smirk was replaced with a look of deep concern. "Just that Senator Forrester barged in here without an appointment, and the two of them have been in a shouting match ever since."

Raymond narrowed his focus. "And why does that make you happy?"

The little man put his hand to the side of his mouth and whispered, "Gerard's not exactly the easiest man to work for, if you understand my meaning."

Raymond raised his eyebrows and stared at the secretary. It seemed like a reasonable explanation, but his skin tingled, every nerve on alert.

The man should be ashamed of himself for spying on his

employer. But rather than exhibiting any signs of embarrassment, he blatantly pressed his ear against the door while keeping his eyes on Raymond. After a moment, he straightened and ambled back to his desk.

"What? Can't hear anything?" Raymond let disapproval drip from his words. He walked past the man and knocked.

"Come in."

He opened the doors and walked in. Senator Forrester looked ready to burst, and Senator Gerard's cheeks were almost as red as the carpet. "Gentlemen." Raymond dipped his head in a polite bow. "May I ask what's going on?"

Gerard pointed a fat finger at Forrester. "This maniac broke in here to—"

"—I didn't break in. I just didn't take your secretary's no for an answer."

Gerard glowered. "*Broke in* to accuse me of threatening his daughter."

Raymond jerked his attention back to Forrester. "Caroline was threatened?"

Forrester kept his eyes on Gerard but nodded. "And I have it on good authority that two unsavory types were seen leaving this office a few weeks ago." He slapped the back of his right hand into the palm of his left. "The exact type of men who'd be hired for such violence."

"And I tell you I never met with such men. I wouldn't—" Gerard stopped mid-sentence. He glanced over at his well-stocked liquor cabinet. "Is it possible?"

"What?" Raymond strained against his impatience to punish whoever imperiled Caroline.

"I swear someone's been drinking my whiskey." Gerard looked toward the open doors. "Smith! Get in here! Now!"

A growled expletive from outside was followed by sounds of frenetic shuffling.

"He's making a run for it." Raymond raced outside. Smith was running down the hall. Raymond sprinted past him and blocked his path. "You aren't going anywhere until we get some answers."

Smith raised a gun and pointed it at Raymond. "Get out of my way."

Forrester hurried down the hallway, coming up behind Smith. "Are you the one who threatened my daughter?" From the way he approached, Raymond could tell he didn't know Smith had a gun. "I'll have your head for this!"

Smith swung around.

Bang!

Forrester dropped to his knees then fell face down.

Torn between apprehending Smith and checking on his mentor, Raymond chose Forrester and let Smith run past him. "Someone get help," he shouted at no one in particular as he ran back toward his friend. Gently, he turned Forrester over. Blood dripped through his fingers but, thank goodness, they were pressed to his shoulder and not a more vital area. "Are you all right, sir?"

Forrester nodded. "I'll be fine. Get to Caro. Don't let her out of your sight."

Raymond hesitated.

"Go!"

A crowd had gathered. A tall bald man pushed through them. "I'm a doctor."

Raymond stood and let the man tend to Forrester then, with one last look between him and the doctor, committed his mentor to God's care and dashed out of the building and into the first available carriage. "DuPont Circle! And hurry!"

CHAPTER NINE

———◆•◆———

C aroline sat at her dressing table while Molly worked her magic. "I don't know why I'm so nervous."

"Mm-hm." Molly twisted tendrils of hair around the curling tongs. "I'm sure and certain ya don't." Her Irish brogue was thicker when she was amused. And it was thick today.

"It's not like I've never spoken to the man before today."

"Mm-hm," Molly repeated.

Caroline plucked at the lavender fringe decorating her sleeve. "I might not even see him. He's coming to check on my father."

"A'course he is."

The fringe began to fray, but rather than leave it alone, Caroline pulled harder. It would need to be trimmed off anyway, so she might as well ruin it entirely. "Why is he coming? I mean, I know to check on my father, but is he planning on staying in Washington or is he going back to Wyoming? With the Dawes Act passing, will he have to go home? And does he still blame me for that? He's not an unreasonable man, at least not usually, but he was so angry. He can't still blame me, can he?"

"Don't know, miss, but pullin' at that there sleeve a yours ain't gonna be a'helpin'." Molly slipped the curling tongs down and waved her hand to cool off Caroline's hair.

"I don't know what to say to him. Or if I should say anything at all."

Molly set down the curling tongs and crossed her arms over her chest. "And just what would you want to be sayin'?"

I love you. I miss you. Don't ever leave me again.

But she'd never summon the courage to say it. What if he repeated that her attentions were unwanted? She'd crumble under the weight of his rejection.

"He won't ever be proposin' to ya, miss. That's for sure and certain." Molly cocked her head to the side, a red curl escaping her linen cap.

"Who said anything about..." Caroline trailed off at the look on her maid's face. "Why not? What's wrong with me? Why does no one want me?" Bitterness clogged her throat as tears fell from her eyes.

While Edward's rejection still stung, it was a mere prick to her ego compared to the consuming pain of losing Raymond. He'd ridden to her side and stood guard for a week until her father was released from the hospital. Hope nestled in her breast that he loved her as much as she loved him during those precious days. But the moment her father returned, Raymond left and she'd not seen him since.

Three agonizing weeks of waiting, hoping, and praying.

Molly kneeled beside the chair. "Ain't nothin' wrong with you, Miss Caroline. That man loves you. Every soul in this house knows it. He's as fine a man as I ever did know, and that's why he won't ever be askin' you ta marry him."

Caroline wiped at her cheeks. "Why not?"

Molly shrugged. "It's the way of this sorry world, ya ken?"

"You mean because he's an Indian and I'm a white woman?"

"Mm-hm." Molly took Caroline's hands in her freckled ones. "You've never faced what people like him—people like me—deal with every day. The Good Book doesn't say that perfect love be castin' out hate. No. It be castin' out fear. So for as long as people fear the Irish, the Indians, or anyone else takin' what they consider ta be rightfully theirs—whether it be jobs or land or anythin' else—there'll be no love between people like God intended. Now maybe things be different out there in Wyomin', but here?" She shook her head. "Being with you wouldn't be good for Mr. Cooper's health, if 'n ya ken my meanin'."

Caroline gasped. And though she wished it weren't true, she wasn't stupid. A little naive, perhaps, as Raymond had once said, but never stupid. "People need to stand up against such bigotry."

"Mm-hm. And maybe you be the one ta do it." Molly raised her brows. "But not here. Maybe in Wyomin' but for sure and for certain not here. At least not in the here and now."

Raymond had said something similar. She'd dismissed it as fatalistic then, but now? "Wyoming." She breathed it in like a prayer. "I expect life would be very different there."

Molly snorted. "I expect that be what's called an understatement, Miss Caroline." She gripped the edge of the dressing table and pushed herself off her knees to finish curling Caroline's hair. When she was done, instead of stepping away as she usually did, she bent down so her face was visible in the mirror. "Since we're bein' honest, Miss Caroline, I'd like ta be sayin' one more thing ta you."

Caroline looked the young woman in the eyes. They were of a similar age and met when Papa hired staff for the DuPont Circle mansion as soon as they arrived in the city. Molly had pledged to remain with Caroline for the duration of her stay in Washington as Papa's political hostess. How much had Molly sacrificed? Had any beaus come and gone while she waited on Caroline?

A soft expression filled the maid's face. "You've been lookin' for love and approval all kinds a ways ever since I've been knowin' ya. Some of them have been good, but some of them. . ." Molly made a face.

A mental image of Edward Harrow flitted through Caroline's mind.

"You throw the best parties in the city 'cause you think that will be makin' people like you. You thought bein' a doctor out in the frontier would make people be likin' you. And you hung on to that Edward fella 'cause he's well-liked around here and you thought that'd make people be likin' you too."

Caroline's heart warmed with conviction. Unable to form words, she nodded her agreement with the criticism.

"If'n ya choose Mr. Cooper, people aren't goin' ta be likin' ya. Matter a fact, some people are goin' to be hatin' ya."

The image of the tall man who spit on her filled her mind.

"Are ya ready for that?" Molly placed her hand on Caroline's shoulder. "Don't be answerin' too quick-like. You be sure and certain before ya go chasin' after that man. He's got his own hurts, that's clear as clear. And it's not right ta dangle happiness before him then snatch it away 'cause ya suddenly realize ya aren't up to what lovin' a man like him means."

Caroline lowered her gaze to her lap. How much of her mother resided in her soul? Could she remain faithful?

"Now, hear me," Molly broke into Caroline's thoughts. "It's going ta take remarkable courage ta let go of lovin' the world ta love one man. I, for one, think you're a remarkable woman, Miss Caroline, but you got ta be thinkin' it too."

Raymond pulled the lapels of his overcoat tighter over the scarf doing a miserable job of keeping the bitter wind off his neck. December was going out kicking and screaming.

Was it a sign? An answer to the prayer uttered a hundred times in the last few weeks to stay or go?

The Dawes Act had passed. Once Christmas break was over, President Cleveland would sign it. Very shortly after that, Raymond would either need to be in Wyoming to claim cattle-grazing land and prove he was civilized or remain in the nation's capital fighting against more than just bad laws.

Was he, like the wind, kicking and screaming against the inevitable?

The Forrester mansion loomed before him. Still on the senator's staff, he'd responded to a summons to come. To be dismissed? He and Caroline had failed their assignment, after all. And he still hadn't apologized for blaming her. Instead, he'd rushed to her side after her father was shot. Let her cry on his shoulder. Accompanied her to the hospital. Escorted her back home. Stayed at the house but kept himself aloof until her father came home. And in all that time, he never told her how sorry he was because he feared she wouldn't accept it. What if she saw into his soul and recognized him for what he truly was?

A savage.

He'd raged against the term for years, but when push came to shove, he was the very thing he hated. He dreamt of wrestling Smith's gun away and shooting him with it. He hounded the police for reports and lost his temper when they admitted the man somehow slipped out of the city. And exploded after the General Allotment Act passed, calling men fools and worse.

Were it not freezing cold, he'd draw a deep breath to prepare himself for whatever battle loomed behind the massive doors. He settled for a brief pause before ringing the bell.

Jeffreys swung open the doors. "Welcome, Mr. Cooper. The senator is in his study." He stepped back to allow Raymond entrance then held out his hands to accept Raymond's coat, scarf, and gloves.

Laying his hat atop the pile, Raymond took the deep breath he'd denied himself outside. "In case I lack the opportunity to say this in the future, thank you for always making me welcome, Jeffreys."

Surprise flitted across the black man's face. "Thank you, sir."

"May I ask you a question?"

Jeffreys schooled his features into mild curiosity. "Of course."

Raymond looked around the opulent foyer. "Why do you stay here?"

The butler's eyebrows drew down. "Here in the city or here as the family's butler?"

"Both, I guess."

His brow cleared. "Because this is where I know." Jeffreys cut a glance toward the door indicating the city beyond. "And this"—he looked around the foyer—"is what I'm good at."

Before Raymond had time to digest the wisdom of that simple statement, he was escorted to the study.

"Ah, Cooper." Senator Forrester stood up from behind his desk, his arm in a white cloth sling. "Thank you for coming."

The door closed behind Raymond with a barely perceptible click. A small but telling example of how the butler was indeed good at his job. "May I ask the purpose of this visit?" His words came out more clipped than he'd intended.

Forrester indicated the chair across from his desk with his good hand. "Have a seat. We have several matters to discuss, not the least of which is your future on my staff."

Foreboding curled Raymond's toes. "Then I prefer to stand, sir," he added almost as an afterthought.

"Oh, do be reasonable, Cooper. This isn't the Inquisition, you know."

Chastised but still feeling justified, Raymond took a seat.

"We haven't really chatted since this," Forrester tipped his head toward his sling. "I wanted to thank you for staying here and looking after my daughter while I was incapacitated."

"It was my pleasure, sir." Too great a pleasure. For that week, the rest of the world stayed away, and it was easy to pretend that he belonged not only in this city but in this house. With this family. With Caroline.

Forrester drummed his fingers on top of his desk. "I'm sure you were somewhat confused by me practically forbidding you to campaign against the Dawes Act."

"I assume it has something to do with the threat against your daughter." Raymond relented. "It's understandable, sir."

Forrester picked up an envelope and tossed it toward Raymond. "Here."

As Raymond read the threat to Caroline's life, fury rose in his chest. "I can't believe the police let Smith get away."

Forrester shook his head. "I console myself that the Lord will exact an appropriate vengeance."

"You'll forgive me for wishing it came at my hands." Raymond imagined curling them around Smith's neck and squeezing for the hundredth time. Or maybe the thousandth.

"As any man should, particularly one who loves Caroline."

A slight lift in his tone of voice allowed for both a statement and question.

Raymond sucked in another breath, this one as shallow as if he were still outside in the cold. "Are you asking if I love your daughter?"

A smirk answered. "That's not in question. However, I do wonder what you intend to do about it."

"Nothing." Raymond tossed the offensive letter on the desk with the casual dismissal denied his soul at the crushing decision. "She's better off without me. Which I guess means I'm no longer welcome on your staff."

"Before you fire yourself, let me outline your choices as *I* see them." The emphasis felt like a chastisement, as though Raymond was too stupid or selfish to see what was obvious to the senator. "Why do you think I sent you here immediately after I was shot? Why you and not, say, John Watson?"

Watson, who was also on the senator's staff, was a former soldier with shoulders almost too wide to fit through a door.

"I'll tell you why," Forrester continued before Raymond had a chance to answer. "Because for all his physical strength, he lacks the moral fortitude I want in a man protecting my daughter."

A painful sliver of hope pierced the protective shell encasing Raymond's heart. "Are you saying. . . ?" He couldn't finish the sentence because, should the answer be yes, it opened the door to his wildest dreams. The one where he and Caroline lived happily ever after with her father's blessing on their union.

And he'd accused *her* of silly, romantic fantasies.

"Listen, Raymond." Forrester leaned forward, winced, and sat back again so his injured arm wasn't pressed against the cherrywood desk. "I hope I've proved to you that I'm more interested in the color of a man's soul than the color of his skin.

I am proud to have you on my staff and would be proud to call you my son. But. . ."

The qualifier hung in the air between them. Raymond curled his toes inside his shoes.

". . .you have to decide where you can do the most good with your life."

What did that have to do with loving Caroline?

"I can see that you're confused, so let me clarify." Forrester waved his index finger between the two of them. "You and I are made of the same stuff. We see injustice and our insides burn to fight against it. The real question is, where will your fight do the most good? My place is here," he tipped his head toward the window, "in the Senate."

Raymond's blood fired up. "And mine isn't?"

Forrester didn't move. Didn't answer. Just stared at Raymond over the files scattered across his desk.

Raymond scratched his jaw. Some of the fight melted inside his soul. "Sorry. I can't help myself sometimes."

"You'll get better with age." Forrester smirked again. "But if you're anything like me, only by a little bit." He sobered and continued. "Sometimes life gives us very clear right and wrong choices. Not this time. This time there's only the choice you make and what you make of your choice. So again, you must decide where you can do the most good."

More tension drained from Raymond. He slumped into the chair. Jeffreys' words came back to him. *This is where I know, and this is what I'm good at.* There was undeniable logic in his straightforward wisdom. Raymond slumped into the chair. "So you're saying I need to go home? Take the fight there?"

"Where's home?"

The question straightened Raymond's spine again. "Excuse

me?" How many times had those two words crossed his lips in this conversation? He wasn't normally such a dunce.

"More importantly, *what* is home?"

The temptation to say *excuse me* again was nigh impossible to hold back, but Raymond managed. "I don't understand the question, sir."

"I didn't either the first time someone asked it of me. And I'm afraid I'm going to do the same thing and ask you yet another question instead of answering you." Forrester pinched his bottom lip for a moment before continuing. "My soul grew more by wrestling with this question than by having it answered for me, so I will ask you to search until you are satisfied with your answer."

"With such a preface, I tremble at the question." Raymond's attempt to infuse the conversation with humor tipped the senator's lips but failed to lighten his own soul.

"Then here's the question: Is home where people love you or where you love people?"

Raymond squinted with confusion. The obvious answer was both, so why did the senator consider it such a monumental question? What was he missing?

"I'll leave you alone to wrestle with that and with the ramifications of your choice should my daughter be at your side." Forrester came around the desk, pausing long enough to squeeze Raymond's shoulder and add, "Whatever you decide, be sure to say goodbye before you leave today. To me and to Caroline."

A moment later, Raymond was alone with his thoughts.

On the one hand, the senator's question was simple to decipher. Or at least what should be the correct answer. Home was where a man chose to invest his time and energy—in other words, his love. If he did that in Wyoming, he was fortunate enough to have family who loved him there. Home, then, would be both where people loved him and where he chose to love people. But Caroline on the Rocking K Ranch? She'd never survive the isolation.

On the other hand, if he chose to remain in Washington, a future with Caroline was equally impossible. He might gain a measure of influence over years of working on Forrester's staff, but the instant he stepped over Charles Darwin's evolutionary line deeming him subhuman because of his darker skin tone, it would be lost. More than that, being with him would endanger her life. General opinion might one day change to tolerate their union, but some people would always oppose it. Violently. Which meant that, no matter what he chose, one thing was irrefutable.

When he said goodbye to Caroline today, it would be forever.

Raymond slid off the chair to his knees. "Lord," he gripped his hands together, "if there be another way. . ."

CHAPTER TEN

— ◆◆◆ —

E zra lowered his binoculars and checked his map again. Small tents dotted the land that was supposed to be his. *All* his. He shoved the binoculars back into his saddlebag and dug his spurs into the horse's sides. It leaped to a gallop, but Ezra used his whip anyway because an uncomfortable notion had taken root in his mind. He headed for the largest clump of tents, hunting for a land claim office.

Moments after shooting Senator Forrester, he'd boarded a train heading west. Newspapers informed him that the Dawes Act had passed as he travelled. The nearest train stop left him miles from his final destination, so he rented two horses with the last coins in his purse and headed out.

The farther he rode away from civilization, or at least what pretended to be, the greater his fear that he'd made a colossal mistake. Even were it summer with warm breezes instead of bitterly cold, snow-covered December, the barren landscape was inescapable. There was nothing here. Nothing! The smattering of trees wasn't enough to build shelter or stoke fires, there were no stores to purchase materials, and until riding up to what should be his land, he'd seen no men who'd be looking for work once he dug enough gold from the ground to pay them.

The reservation hadn't even been broken up yet, so why were white settlers already here? In the middle of winter. He had nowhere else to go, having burned every bridge to get here. Were these wretched souls in the same situation?

Hostile stares greeted him as he reached what could only be described as squatter tents. "Excuse me," he called to a young woman whose eyes were on him rather than looking at the horses like food. "Where's the land claim office?"

A grim look settled on her gaunt features. "Ain't one. Don't expect a place like this"—she turned her neck left and right taking in the barren landscape—"is what you'd call high on the list a places where people are gonna need a land claim office."

Such an understatement deserved no response. He scanned his surroundings. Some of the others had thick coats and winter boots, but none of them had a beaver-skin hat or woolen gloves like his.

The girl's eyes narrowed to slits. "You got a claim too?"

"Too?" His breath puffed white and dissipated.

She waved her arm, the tattered coat flapping in the wind. "All of us gots one. Paid good money for 'em too 'cause there was gold, they said."

Ezra's breath hitched. "Who? Who said?"

"I don't know. A couple of men."

"What did they look like?"

She shrugged. "One had dark hair, the other was a redhead. They talked my Billy into turning over every last penny we had. Showed him a gold nugget the size of a walnut."

Ezra clenched his hands into fists. "And no doubt a map showing a vein of gold running right here."

"If I was you, mister, I'd skedaddle while you've got time and fresh horses. There's at least fifty of us with claims to the same land. I expect it's worthless, but that ain't gonna stop my Billy or any of them others from killin' each other over it. What else we gonna do?" And with that, she turned her back on him and disappeared into her snow-coated tent.

Ezra cursed himself for a fool. He'd brought his gun and extra ammunition, of course, but not enough. Not for this. He couldn't go back to Washington, and he couldn't stay here, not when he was outgunned.

He was in a fight to the death, and he was going to lose.

———————————

Caroline handed the letter back to her father. "And this is why you forbade me from campaigning against the Dawes Act? And from being with Raymond?"

"It is." Papa crossed to the fireplace and tossed the envelope into the flames.

"Then you have nothing against Raymond personally?" Caroline's voice trembled with hope, fear, and desire.

Papa stared into the fire. The slope of his back felt like a wall between them. "Personally, no." He turned around, his face almost as gray as the day she visited him in the hospital. "You know I love you and want only what's best for you, don't you?"

"Of course. Raymond is the best—"

"He's a good man, I grant you that. But consider carefully what you're longing to say right now." Papa strode back to her side and pulled her into a one-armed hug. "You once thought Edward Harrow was the best man for you. I'm grateful you've let go of him. Now take that lesson and apply it to Raymond Cooper. Is he a good man? No question. But is he the best man? For you? Before you say yes"—her assent was cut off—"disabuse yourself of any naive notions within that romantic heart of yours. Think, Caro. Think long and hard about what life with Raymond Cooper will mean for you, for me, and for your children."

A protest rose within her breast. She whirled to face him. "Papa, how dare you—"

"I beg your pardon for interrupting, but before you accuse me of prejudice, remember that I asked you to do the same with Edward Harrow before allowing him to propose to you." He tapped her nose.

Her indignation popped like a soap bubble. "You did. I'm sorry for assuming the worst."

"However, you must understand that there are those who will be cruel beyond imagination should you overcome Raymond's objections." Papa pointed over his shoulder with his thumb. "He's currently in my office coming up with reasons why you two can never be together."

"But—" She pressed a hand against her aching heart. "But you think he loves me?"

Papa's smile was part tender, part patronizing. "I do not think it, dear girl. I know it." He patted her cheek before walking out of the library, leaving her with a whirlwind of thoughts and emotions.

Molly's words played over and over again, particularly the ones about dangling happiness before Raymond then snatching it away because she wasn't up to loving a man like him.

A man like him.

Hm.

There *were* no other men like him.

What Caroline hoped to see in Edward Harrow she'd found in Raymond Cooper. With a bit more fire in his belly, yes, but from a desire for fairness and justice. She could live with that. But could she live in Wyoming? Raymond said the nearest fort was a three-day journey. She'd never lived more than a three-minute walk from anywhere.

More to the point, could she overcome her need for approval from others enough to love Raymond well?

She bowed her head. *Lord, I need Your wisdom to guide me. You know my heart. You know its fickle nature and how I've allowed it to rule over me in the past. You also know my desire for faithfulness. I know Raymond would be faithful to me, but Lord, can I be faithful to him?*

Caroline wiped away tears wetting her cheeks.

Molly says it will take a remarkable woman to love Raymond as he deserves to be loved. I have no great faith in myself, but I have great confidence in You and in Your faithfulness.

And in that moment, she felt peace wash over her troubled soul. God never asked her to rely on her own faithfulness. She was to rely on His. Raymond was His precious son as much as she was His precious daughter. They were both scarred and frightened, but with God's help, they could walk the path to healing together.

"Thank You, Lord," she whispered.

A small click alerted her that someone was coming. She wiped her cheeks again, pinching them to add some color, then turned to face the doors and whatever came through them.

Raymond walked in, his posture ramrod straight, with a determined set to his jaw.

He was here to tell her goodbye.

She held up a hand to forestall him. "Before you say a word, please let me say something."

He stopped and narrowed his gaze.

She pressed a hand against her galloping heart. "I've been thinking and praying about what a future with you means."

His eyes widened, and he opened his mouth.

"No. Please let me finish." She licked her dry lips, praying for just the right words. "You have my heart. I've made that painfully obvious. What I don't know is how seriously you've taken that because of. . .well, so many things. Edward is one. He's behind me now, in case you were wondering. How could he hold a candle to you?"

Pink crept into Raymond's cheeks.

"You and I"—she waved a hand between them—"come from very different worlds. That's also painfully obvious. But does it mean we can't forge a new path together? I believe we can because, at our cores, we are the same. It's just the circumstances of how we grew up that separate us."

"Caroline—"

"Please. As much as I love hearing my name on your lips, you must let me finish." She took a shaky breath. "I'm terrified that I'm not good enough to love you well. I'm afraid I will crumble under the pressure of either this city or your family ranch. But I know the one who is faithful to complete the good work He has started in me." Caroline took three steps forward, bringing herself within touching distance of him.

It was now or never.

She took a shuddering breath and summoned every ounce of courage. "I won't say this again, because I've learned that my trust must be in God rather than men. If you say no to this, I will survive. I won't be—and I don't think you will be—as happy as possible, but that's the risk we take."

Raymond shook his head. "Don't—"

"Please ask me to share your life." She cut him off before he crushed her last hope. "I promise to put my trust in the God who loves us both to teach me how to love you and be faithful to you for as long as we both shall live." She placed her hand on his heart. It beat like a hummingbird's wings beneath her fingertips.

He pressed his hand over the top of hers.

She tried to read the emotions on his face, but it was difficult to see through the tears in her eyes. She allowed herself to hope until he pulled her hand away from his chest.

"Caroline," he whispered her name with such tenderness, it sliced her heart in half. "I love you too. There's no point in denying it. And I too have thought and prayed about any future you and I might have together."

"So. . . ?" She said she wouldn't ask again, but every fiber strained to hear him propose.

Raymond dropped his gaze to their hands. Then he let go and stepped back. "No."

EPILOGUE

"What?"

Caroline smiled at her daughter's horrified reaction.

"You never told me that? I always thought Papa proposed to you"—Penelope pointed at the lone tree in the yard—"right there. At least that's the story you've always told me."

Raymond opened the screened door and stepped onto the porch. "I did. And, if I remember correctly—which I do—what I said when we were back in Washington, DC, was, 'No,' followed rapidly by, 'not yet.'"

"I was getting to that." Caroline shooed her husband back into the house with a wave of her hand. He blew a kiss at her before disappearing. "Oh, I love that man."

"Mother?" Penelope's brows rose in the exact way her father's did when he wanted an explanation.

"You remember that part about my silly notion that I'd lost my one and only chance at love when Edward Harrow broke our engagement?"

Penelope nodded. "What an idiot."

Caroline laughed at her daughter's defense of her. "Quite the opposite, in fact. He knew before I did that, though there were plenty of things drawing us together, there were some irreconcilable things pushing us apart."

Granny E nodded her head and pointed at Penelope. "Your father was afraid of the same thing."

Grace picked up her tea and winked at Caroline. "I remember the day you arrived. I was sure you'd be on the first train back out of here."

"I almost was." Caroline chuckled. "I'd never seen anything like"—she waved her hand at the landscape—"this."

Penelope craned her neck to look around. "I don't understand."

Grace took a sip of tea and set it back down on the table. "That's because you grew up here. This is home to you."

"Go on with you two." Granny placed an extra biscuit on Penelope's plate. "You've teased the poor girl enough. Just tell her what you're meaning to, straight out."

"All right then, here it is." Caroline reached across the table to grip her daughter's hands. "Just because you love someone doesn't mean you can live with them."

"What?" This time, Penelope's tone of voice held disbelief.

Caroline sat back and raised her hands in a helpless gesture. "I'm as hopeless of a romantic as you'll ever meet."

Granny and Grace both grunted in agreement, the love and life the three of them had shared tempering the irritation Caroline had felt in her younger years at their ready agreement with her silly romantic notions that had gotten her into so much trouble as a new bride.

Caroline kept her focus on her daughter. "But love in real life, unlike love in some of those novels we've all read, doesn't overcome *eeeverything*." She drew the word out with dramatic flair. "It can overcome a lot when you mix in patience and determination, but what if I'd arrived here already married and discovered I couldn't survive the isolation of the ranch? I'd only known town life with its nearby stores, restaurants, endless parties, and short carriage rides to visit with friends. This life is very different, and your father needed to know that I wouldn't up and run away or wither and die here."

Penelope looked troubled. "I'd never thought of that."

"So he made a bargain with me. Remember, I was fighting for my chance to convince him we belonged together while he"— Caroline tilted her head toward the front door—"was fighting against me. He told me he'd marry me if I could survive for a full year out here."

"We never thought she'd make it." Granny gave Caroline a grin. "Never been so happy to be wrong in all my days."

Raymond poked his head out the door. "Me too." He disappeared as fast as he'd come.

"He's making sure I'm telling it right." Caroline shook her head with mock disapproval.

"You're the self-proclaimed hopeless romantic." His voice carried from the house to the porch. "Not me."

"I prefer hope*ful* romantic these days," she called over her shoulder. "Don't you have a case to win? Quit pestering me, husband."

His rich laughter floated on the wind, quite a difference from his days in Washington, DC. He'd found his place of influence here, fighting to earn respect among both the Shoshone and Arapaho people so he could defend them in court. While he never went back to Harvard, he had earned a law degree and successfully defended Indians and whites alike. He'd become so well known, he'd been summoned back to the nation's capital to testify on legislation modifying the General Allotment Act to rectify some of its injustices.

Granny picked up her teacup. "Love is a choice you make every day."

Caroline nodded. "But to be fair," she qualified, "love is much easier when you choose someone who shares your values, your faith, and the way of life you want to lead. That's why it was so wise of your father to insist that I live here through all the seasons before he agreed to marry me."

The sun turned red, casting an orange glow over the landscape. Caroline had come to love the long, slow sunsets. She'd found her life here, had even overcome fainting at the sight of blood enough to help deliver babies, splint broken bones, and sit with the dying until their last breath.

"I found that something more my father always wanted for me." Caroline leaned forward and reached out her hands to her daughter. She waited for Penelope to grip them before saying, "And now it's time for you to find your something more, whatever or whoever that turns out to be."

AUTHOR'S NOTE

Please know that I used the term "Indian" rather than "Native American" throughout this story to reflect historical accuracy. However, I used it with a great deal of fear and trembling over the effect it might have on modern sensibilities. I have no wish to offend anyone, least of all our Native American brothers and sisters, so I hope you will forgive me.

Senator Henry L. Dawes and Senator Henry M. Teller (on whom I based Gerald Forrester) were real men in the same political party with very different ideas on how to best help Native Americans. While writing this novella, I found myself sympathizing with both men and their motives. Only in hindsight and by talking to several Native Americans do I see where Senator Dawes' logic failed.

The tragedy of the Dawes Act is how it was interpreted, including forced "civilization" by taking children away from their parents, educating them in the white man's ways, and forbidding them from speaking their own language or practicing their traditional cultural rituals. And much of it was done by Christians. I weep over that.

Many years ago, I heard a sermon about how the United States was founded on religious freedom. But within that was an underlying assumption that America was the new Promised Land because, after 1600+ years without a nation of Israel on the map, God needed a new nation of "chosen people" to fulfill His promises. Thus, anyone occupying American land was the equivalent of a Philistine and needed to be wiped out. It reminded me of Abraham and Sarah "helping" God keep his promise of a child to them through Ishmael. Oh, how much trouble we cause ourselves and every generation after us when we don't believe God's Word!

As I said in my dedication, I am indebted to Cherelle Garner for sharing the ramifications of the Dawes Act on her immediate family. She is my sister in Christ but also my sister by blood, for we all go back to the same ancestors. I can't undo the damage she's suffered, but I pray this story blesses her.

Thank you for reading. I look forward to hearing from you at www.BeccaWhitham.com.

BECCA WHITHAM is an award-winning author, paper crafter, and "Baba" to three, adorable grandchildren. She follows her husband of almost forty years to wherever the army needs a chaplain. In between moves, she writes stories about the redeeming power of true love. She's a member of American Christian Fiction Writers and winner of the 2018 Spur Award. Contact her at BeccaWhitham.com.

PENELOPE

By

KIMBERLEY WOODHOUSE

This novella is lovingly dedicated to two of my favorite reader ladies:
Diane Housel and Lesley Hayden–Artis
From the first time I met you at Fiction Readers
Summit back in 2019, I knew you were kindred
spirits and I wanted to know you better.
Every time I see you now, it's like a party.
What joy you bring to me and the Christian Fiction community.
Thank you for your precious support, your
encouragement, and your friendship.
This one is for you.

CHAPTER ONE

———— ◆●◆ ————

1910

The Rocking K Ranch

About twenty miles south of Thermopolis,
Wyoming, along the Bighorn River

The last few weeks at home had been some of the best of her life. Not only had Penelope heard from Great-Grandma Eleanor about the beginnings of the ranch and their life out here when there had been nothing else, but several rich stories about her great-grandpa Wildcat and his life among the Shoshone and what it had been like to scout for wagon trains were shared from his journals. The love the two shared was most beautiful even if it started out as a marriage of convenience.

It gave her hope that her agreement to wed Nicholas would turn out full of love as well.

Her grandparents made that hope even brighter. Grandpa Winfield cared for Grandma Grace when she thought she was a monster and unlovable. He saw past the scars and loved her for who she was and always told her she was beautiful inside *and* out. Their marriage too had started out as one of convenience.

All her life, Penelope had been surrounded by family and love. Her great-grandparents who decided to plant roots in this magnificent state. Her grandparents who carried on the dream and built the small homestead into a thriving ranch. And then her parents, Raymond and Caroline, who fought together against the Dawes Act and returned home to continue the legacy of love.

While she longed to fall in love like her parents had, it could still happen with Nicholas. . .couldn't it?

One thing kept niggling at the back of her mind. The more she wrote about her family's stories, the deeper her connection to the ranch and her family history grew. In proportion, the thought of moving across the ocean produced a deep dread. That was the one negative in this whole plan. How could she leave this place? And the people?

Perhaps she could convince Nicholas to come out here to visit. Once he saw the ranch for himself, he might like it enough to stay.

Penelope cringed. He was quite the gentleman and used to all the amenities of the city, that was for certain. But he had reiterated time and again that he was completely fascinated with the Wild West.

She stood to her feet and paced the room, tapping her pencil against her palm. Of course, if they were to continue with their plan—to write Westerns—it might be better for them to actually live in the west. Another good argument she could bring up with her fiancé.

Maybe she should start planting the seeds for the idea now in her letters. After all, she had been writing him almost every day. It couldn't hurt.

Mail out in Wyoming was still a bit slow, and she hadn't received anything from him yet. Although she had received a packet from his father yesterday. The new contract had been executed and sent to her. Mr. Allen was pushing for a wedding as soon as she was done with the book so that all the legalities would be in place for the upcoming publications.

Publications!

Her dreams were coming true. Her name was going to be on a book! On multiple books! She bounced on her toes and wanted to pinch herself to make sure she wasn't dreaming. After allowing herself several minutes to revel in the excitement, she spun on her heel and went back to her little writing desk.

Stacks of papers filled every nook and cranny. At this rate, she had enough material to write an entire book about each generation. Somehow, she would need to condense it into a more manageable read. But at least she had all the stories, all the details, all the vibrant life out on the page.

The sound of a wagon rolling up outside made her put her pencil back down and peer out the window. Diane and Lesley, two older women who were their closest neighbors, sat on the bench seat, while a man she didn't recognize sat on the wagon bed with his legs dangling off the back.

Penelope's curiosity got the best of her, and she raced for the front door. She flung it open and greeted her friends. "My two favorite neighbors." With a laugh, she rushed to the wagon.

"We're your *only* neighbors for ten miles, but we'll take it." Diane laughed along with her, set the brake, and tied off the reins. "Lesley and I wanted to see if you had any more for us to read to—"

"And we brought you a visitor," Lesley interjected.

Penelope had already forgotten about the man in the back. But he'd hopped down, grabbed two large leather satchels, and headed for her. "Name's Jason Miller, Miss Cooper. Mr. Allen sent me."

"The photographer!" She put a hand to her cheek. "I've been

so caught up in my writing that I'd forgotten you were coming."

"Don't worry about it. I'm sure I can find a place to stay"—he surveyed the wide-open spaces—"somewhere." His lips turned up into a smile that brightened his blue eyes.

"I don't think you'll be finding a fancy hotel out here, young man." Diane waited for him to offer her a hand down from the wagon seat.

"I don't need anything fancy." He assisted her to the ground and then lifted a hand to Lesley next.

The two older women grinned from ear to ear. "I like this one." Diane threw a thumb over her shoulder as she headed toward Penelope.

"Me too." Lesley nodded and the feather on her hat bounced as she walked.

"It will be fine. We have plenty of room here on the ranch. I just forgot to remind my mother." It was a good thing her mother was the ultimate hostess and could handle just about anything the world threw at her. Penelope gestured for her guests to follow her into the house. She would make sure they were comfortable in the living room before informing her mother they would have a temporary lodger. Once everyone was seated, she smiled at the small group. "Wait here for just a moment, and I'll fetch us some refreshments."

As she headed toward the large kitchen at the back of the house, she caught Mr. Miller's gaze. The amusement in his eyes was unmistakable. But whether it was caused by his ride with her animated and delightful neighbors *or* her own forgetfulness, she wasn't sure.

Jason listened to Diane and Lesley—as they'd introduced themselves, he didn't even know the women's last names—chatter on about the stories from Penelope and how they couldn't wait for the next installment.

Miss Cooper must be an awfully good writer to have these women so engrossed. Even more so to have the likes of Nicholas Allen interested in publishing her stories. But something wasn't sitting right with Jason. Penelope Cooper was nothing like he expected after the junior Mr. Allen had hired him for this job. Why would a beautiful young woman like *her* wish to marry the likes of him? Did she know nothing of his reputation back in London?

"What do you think, Jason?" Diane pointed a look at him.

Oops. He hadn't been listening to them. "I'm sorry, I was off in my own thoughts. How can I be of assistance?"

The two chuckled and tittered back and forth.

Lesley waved a hand at him. "Oh, you do beat all, young man. We were simply asking about Westerns—novels—do you think Penelope's will do well? She's quite precious to us, you know, and we wouldn't want anything to happen to her."

If he told them what he knew of the business-savvy Allens, that might encourage them that book sales could do well, but then again, it might also make them think twice about their sweet neighbor marrying into the cutthroat publishing family. At a loss for how to answer honestly, he murmured, "I really like Westerns."

"Oh good." Diane's smile was wide, with lines crinkling up around her eyes. Jason couldn't help but smile back. "They are my absolute favorite. Lesley's too. Penelope writes the best ones we've ever read, and right now she's writing the story of four generations of her family. She's got more than fifty other stories that are simply the best."

"The very best we've ever read. And we are quite well read." Lesley's chin lifted ever so slightly. "From the classics to newspapers from all the major cities, we've read it."

He raised his eyebrows and couldn't help but let his grin spread. These two were a delight. And a handful, for certain. "Then if your opinion is that, I'm sure I will agree. You two definitely seem to know what you're talking about. As to Miss Cooper's stories, that's why I'm here."

Diane patted his arm. "Of course. You're here to take pictures."

Lesley stood and walked a small lap around the room before coming to stand before the couch where Diane and Jason sat. She put her hands on her hips and fixed her gaze on him. "What kind of pictures are you planning on taking? Nothing untoward, I hope. It has to be the very best and with the highest reputation for our Penelope." Her eyes narrowed.

Putting on the most serious face he could muster in the midst of their scrutiny, he held back a chuckle and supplied, "Nothing untoward. I promise. It will all be of the beautiful scenery here in Wyoming. The ranch. The family. That sort of thing."

"Good." Lesley lifted her chin another notch. "We'll have to preview these pictures, of course."

"Of course." Diane nodded.

He dipped his chin along with them. "Certainly. It will be my pleasure to get your feedback to make sure I truly capture the essence of Wyoming."

"Good." Lesley gave a slight wiggle of her brows to her friend. "Then we can allow you to stay. When we first heard of this big British publisher wanting our girl's stories, we were hesitant. Had our guard up. As I'm sure you can well understand."

"Yes, ma'am." He bit the inside of his cheek. These two ladies made him miss his own grandmother.

"Well"—she sat down and looped her arm through his with a pat—"since you are such a gentleman and genuine, you've helped to put our minds at ease."

With a lady on each arm, his heart swelled. "Thank you. I won't take that for granted. I promise."

Diane's face turned very serious. "Be sure that you don't, and you'll stay on our good side."

"Oh," he sent her a conspiratorial look, "that settles it. The last thing I'd *ever* want to do would be to get on your bad side."

His two companions laughed along with him. At least he'd made two friends.

"You come over anytime you want to chat. We'll fatten you up."

Before he could respond, the door swung open. "Mr. Miller." A beautiful, older, blond woman entered the living room and held out her hand. "Welcome to the Rocking K Ranch. We are so glad you've come to help out with Penelope's project. I'm her mother, Caroline Cooper."

He stood and took her hand, kissing her knuckles. "Lovely to meet you, Mrs. Cooper."

"I have a guest room prepared, and you are welcome to stay as long as you need."

"That is most generous. Thank you." Over the woman's shoulder, he noticed Penelope. In stark contrast to her mother, her dark hair and dark eyes studied him. What did she see? Did he measure up?

CHAPTER TWO

A rooster crowed outside, and Jason bolted upright. Never in his life had he heard such a thing so close and so *loud*.

The boisterous rooster decided once wasn't enough and repeated his resonant cry. Apparently directly outside Jason's window.

So much for sleep. He kicked off the blankets and swung his feet to the floor.

Last night it had taken him a long time to stop thinking about all he'd seen and heard his first day. He wasn't certain what time he finally fell asleep, but it was well after dark.

All his life, he'd lived in the city. London, New York, Philadelphia. His dad had worked in the magazine business and had gotten him involved with photography at a young age. Jason couldn't imagine doing anything else. He loved being behind the camera.

Every once in a while, he'd been sent out on an assignment to capture the beauty and landscapes of America. But never had he ventured this far west.

It had gotten under his skin. In a matter of days. He loved it.

The vastness of the frontier. The magnitude of the mountains. The tumbleweeds. The lack of large cities bustling with people.

The incredibly clean and clear air.

The ladies had spoken of hot springs to the north of the ranch, and that would be the first thing on his list to explore the next time he had a day to himself.

Penelope Cooper's family was large and talkative. When they all gathered together, it was quite the crew. Especially when you added in all the cowboys who worked on the ranch and were "part of the family" as Mr. Cooper stated.

He'd never seen anything like it but instantly felt at ease. Like he was home.

All the crazy tales he'd heard about the Wild West were outlandish now that he was here. He couldn't help but want to applaud Miss Cooper for wanting to write *real* Westerns that captured the essence of life out here.

Even though he was exhausted, excitement rippled through him as he dressed and splashed water on his face. Today, he was told he'd get to follow the cowboys around on the ranch and he could capture whatever he wanted in pictures. And that he could ask whatever questions he liked. It would be a great adventure.

One thing was certain. There weren't any facades out here.

It was like a breath of fresh air.

He exited his room. The scent of coffee blended with something sweet and delicious made his mouth water.

"Good morning, Mr. Miller." Penelope greeted him with a smile as she filled glasses at the table with milk. Her dark hair was piled atop her head and a crisp white apron covered her deep pink dress. "Did you sleep well?"

Always one for the God's honest truth, he wrinkled up his nose. "Not long enough, but that was all my own doing. I had a difficult time turning off my enthusiasm to be here."

She laughed along with him and continued her way around

the table. "I'm glad you are enthusiastic but sorry you didn't get enough sleep. Rest assured, I'm sure the men will wear you out and you won't have any trouble finding sleep this evening."

"I'm looking forward to it. And I'm sure you're correct. I'll hit the hay tonight and feel right as rain tomorrow."

Several others joined them in the kitchen, cutting off their conversation. Disappointment made its way up his spine. But he didn't have time to analyze it as the hubbub of breakfast began. While it was nice to have a big meal to start the day, it would have been nicer for a bit more time with Penelope.

Now where did those thoughts come from? She was his boss's fiancée.

The crowd grew and filled in the large wooden table. The blessing was given, dishes were passed, and everyone dug in.

Questions were lobbed in his direction from family members, and he did his best to answer them. Especially from Penelope's two younger brothers, Michael and Andrew. Those two talked faster than anyone he'd ever heard.

They wanted to know everything from how a camera worked, to how long it took to take a photograph, to what his favorite photograph of all time was.

In between bites, he answered and tried to keep up with all the platters as they passed over and over again around the table.

This crew could eat.

No wonder it took four women to prepare the meal!

Before he'd swallowed his last bite, all the men began to rise, and each spoke their thanks and goodbyes to the women around the table.

Jason jumped to his feet and swigged the last of his milk, not wanting to miss a thing. "Thank you." He nodded at Penelope and her mother.

"Have fun!" Mrs. Cooper called after him. Laughter followed.

He grabbed his bag on the way out the door and trailed the men out to the corral.

"You're accustomed to riding?" Mr. Cooper—Penelope's father—threw the question over his shoulder as they walked. The man's black hair hung in a braid under his cowboy hat.

"Yes, sir." He skipped a step or two to keep up. "Probably not as much as you, but I know how to ride." More than anything in this moment, he wanted to impress the man. Why, he wasn't sure, but the thought of letting the rugged man down wasn't something he was about to do. Especially not on his first day out with him.

A horse was saddled for Jason, and then each man mounted his own animal.

Jason did his best to keep up with the pack and then followed Mr. Cooper and his foreman when they split off from the group.

Mr. Allen had informed him that Penelope Cooper came from a family that had lived in Wyoming for four generations and that there was Indian blood in her family from her grandfather or great-grandfather.

What Jason hadn't expected was to see that her father appeared to be full-blooded Indian himself. Not that it bothered him one bit. He believed God made all men equal, so the color of a man's skin or his heritage didn't amount to a hill of beans to Jason. But he knew the Allen men and their reputation. Prayerfully, they wouldn't take advantage of Miss Cooper. And if the junior Mr. Allen was going to marry her, he must respect her family. Jason grimaced. Hopefully that was true. He shouldn't judge the Allens by all the rumors he'd heard over the years. He really didn't know the men other than the occasional assignment when they gave specific instructions.

His horse moved a bit under him as they started up an incline.

Jason pulled himself out of his ponderings. Wouldn't be good to take a tumble because he wasn't paying attention.

He followed the ranch owner and foreman up a ridge where they could look down at the ranch from above. Green grass rippled like the ocean before them, with clusters of cows dotting the fields. Evergreen trees looked to create a natural boundary on the west side of the ranch's massive acreage. A river wound around the southeast boundary, rippling in bursts of white caps. But most magnificent of all were the mountains. The craggy bluffs rose like granite slashes against the cloudless blue sky.

Jason's jaw dropped. "Wow."

Mr. Cooper's mouth widened into a grin. "It's breathtaking, isn't it?"

"That, sir, is an understatement."

The owner of this beautiful ranch leaned over his saddle horn. "I figured this would be the best spot for you to get your first photographs."

Jason nodded, still taking it all in. "It's perfect, sir. Thank you." Dismounting lickety-split, he pulled out his equipment and set things up while the two men stared down at him from their mounts. "I'd love to get a shot of you two as well."

"Sure." Mr. Cooper smiled, but his eyes seared into Jason. "And then we can chat about the publishing company you work for and the man who wants to marry my daughter."

CHAPTER THREE

―――◆•◆―――

With her Bible in her lap, Penelope watched the sun rise through the window in her bedroom. Today was her "day off" in the kitchen for breakfast prep, and she was lingering over the Psalms. Chapter five, verse three was one of her favorites. She whispered the words to the rising sun. "My voice shalt thou hear in the morning, O LORD; in the morning will I direct my prayer unto thee, and will look up."

In the months she'd spent in New York City, her time in the Word hadn't been the same. Instead of hearing pots and pans clanging in the kitchen or the lowing of cattle, she'd been constantly beside herself trying to keep her focus while the noise in the always busy and bustling streets kept her jumping. Every moment seemed to have a new sound. While it was interesting and unique, it had been a constant distraction.

She'd learned to write in the afternoon with music playing on the Victrola and the noise of her typewriter drowning out the world around her.

It was thrilling to think that she would soon be published. And married.

She chewed on her bottom lip. The latter should probably be

the most exciting thing in her life to look forward to, but it wasn't.

Her first night back home had seen the most intense discussion she'd ever had with her family over her engagement. Everyone *seemed* to be supportive. But there had been a lot of personal questions. A lot of heated debate about the wisdom in her marrying a relative stranger and moving across the ocean. A lot of hesitance voiced in love.

In the end, her parents told her it was her decision to make, but she better make sure to bathe the entire thing in prayer and lay it at the Lord's feet. No one wanted to see her hurt or unhappy.

Penelope read the verses before her again, the words giving her a deep sense of comfort. Her parents were right. No matter how much she wanted to be published, she needed to seek the Lord regarding her engagement and wait on Him. "I'm directing my prayer to You, Father God. I'm looking to You for wisdom and discernment. As much as I long to be published and get my stories out into the world, I don't want to go against Your will. Right now, it seems You opened this door for me. Should I keep walking through it? If not, please show me." After pouring out her heart for several minutes, she closed her Bible, set it on her dresser, and prepared to greet everyone at breakfast.

Opening her door, she smiled. Today was the day she would give Mr. Miller—Jason—her tour of the ranch. For the past three days, he'd followed the men around from morning until evening. Each night he returned with a beaming grin and covered in lots of dirt and grime. She wasn't sure what the men were showing him, but at least he seemed to enjoy it.

Today, she hoped it to be different. She wanted him to see the ranch through her eyes. So he could understand her stories and take photographs that would help the readers in the big city get excited about the upcoming memoir and her Westerns.

Well, they were technically going to be *Nicholas'* and hers. But her name would be on there. That meant a great deal to her.

The thought of Nicholas cooled her exuberance a bit. She'd written him a dozen letters since she came home, and there hadn't been a single peep from him in return. Of course, he could be traveling. Perhaps even over in Europe. But he at least could have told her. They were going to be married soon, after all.

Not that he told her much about his life. Every conversation they'd had was about their future together—mainly about their stories. In all honesty, ninety percent of their chats had all been about her stories. How he would advertise them. How they would be the most notable couple for writing together.

Then he would read. She would write. He'd give her suggestions on what to change and how to turn each short story into a short novel.

Clatter from the kitchen broke through her thoughts. Never mind about Nicholas. She pasted her smile back in place and walked into the kitchen. Breakfast at the Rocking K Ranch always boosted her spirits.

An hour later, she and Jason were out on their horses, roaming the vast pastures. She showed him some of her favorite views, and it was pleasant to sit in silence and watch him work with the camera equipment.

"So. . ." He packed up the wooden tripod and camera after taking another picture. "What got you into writing?"

Staring out at this land she loved so much, she inhaled deeply. The smells of the ranch were so familiar to her. Grass and leather. Hay and horses. Even the smell of the cows, while unpleasant at times, was a sign she was home. She glanced at Jason. "As if this place wasn't enough fodder for my imagination, my mother says I could make up a story about anything. And I did. Especially if

I was in trouble." She chuckled.

Jason's deep laughter joined with hers. "Ah, the weaver of a tall tale, huh?"

She shifted in the saddle. "Yes, indeed. And it didn't take long for me to learn how to make them more believable so much so that my parents had a hard time discerning the truth."

"Oh boy." His gear packed, he lifted himself back up onto his horse.

"Over time, I learned that lying to my parents about what actually happened was wrong. But my mother encouraged my storytelling for good things. She showed me that I could honor God with my gift of story to help show people the love of Jesus."

His nod to her was thoughtful. "I have to admit, I haven't been around a family—or anyone really—that is so open about their faith like yours."

She narrowed her gaze. "Are you not a man of faith, Mr. Miller?"

"Oh, I definitely am, Miss Cooper."

Giving him an annoyed expression, she shook her head. "I thought we agreed when you first arrived you would call me Penelope."

"We did." He winked at her. "But you broke the agreement first, when you just called me Mr. Miller."

"Touché." She prodded her horse into motion, and they took a slow and steady pace down to the river. "Tell me about your faith, *Jason*."

"My grandmother was the one who taught me about God and His Son. She died when I was only seven, but it stuck with me. What has made it difficult is trying to learn and grow in the society in which we live. There's so much division—between classes, between denominations, between people in general—and it seems like for too many that faith isn't a relationship. It's a duty.

Go to church on Sunday. Give in the offering. Feed the poor.

"I'll be honest, I got stuck in the same pattern. Got busy with life, and so I pushed God down on my list. I kept going to church, but it was all the same. People were there for appearances like it was just a show. Last year, I lost a friend to a horrible illness. In his last weeks, he wrote individual letters to his family and friends challenging each one of us to forget about all the cares of this world and focus on what was truly important. It shook me to my core, and I made God my priority again. The only problem is, the more time I spend in the Word, the more I crave deeper teaching. I still haven't found a good church where the preaching stirs me to action like my friend's letter did."

Tears pricked her eyes. "Jason. . .I. . ."The words got stuck in her throat. She swallowed them down. "Thank you for sharing from your heart with me. It's so easy to get caught up in the busyness of the city, isn't it? I mean, we are always busy here at the ranch, but you are correct. It seemed much harder to keep my focus in the right place when I was there."

"Sounds like something you and I both need to work on before we go back. Of course, I'll be going back to New York, but you'll be moving to London." He grimaced a bit and tilted his head. "Believe me, London is even busier. Especially since you'll be writing book after book." He shifted his gaze to her for a brief moment, and she couldn't decipher the look in his eyes. He turned back to the view in front of him before she could say anything.

More than she wanted to admit, she wished she knew what he was thinking. "While you're here, would you mind telling me about London? I've never been, and I'd like to be prepared."

"Of course. But first, I want you to finish telling me about how your love for storytelling grew and how you became such an accomplished writer."

Her heart softened, and she gave him a broad smile before looking back toward the river. "My parents encouraged me to write stories to tell my great-grandparents each day when we visited. Since they were older, we brought them dinner every evening when they couldn't come to the main house. I was a busy child—as my mother tells it—and it helped to keep me occupied and focused. My great-grandpa was the first one who helped me understand the love for stories. He'd get so excited about any story I'd tell him and then he'd ask, 'What happened next?' and so the stories continued to blossom and flourish. He'd ask me questions that would help my imagination grow. When he passed away, I didn't tell another story for over a year."

"I'm so sorry for your loss. He sounds like quite the man."

"Oh, he was. I wish you could have known him." She swallowed the lump of emotion in her throat. "So then, Great-Grandma Eleanor continued the tradition. The whole family watched me become far too sullen in my grief and missing my great-grandpa. One day after church, she took me for a picnic and helped me dig up the part of me that I'd buried with him. Every day after school, I'd head straight to her house and tell her all about my day. Then she'd have me write her a story while she made cookies or baked bread. When she was done, we'd eat a treat and I'd read her my story. Those are some of the best memories I have."

Jason's expression was contemplative. "Sounds like your family was key in bringing you to this point."

Her head bobbed up and down, tears stinging her eyes. "Yes. I wouldn't be who I am today without them. All of them."

So how could she even think of leaving them. . .forever?

CHAPTER FOUR

———◆•◆———

J ason stared up at the ceiling as he tried to get his brain to catch up with his weary body and prepare for rest. Another long day at the ranch had filled his heart and his soul with more than he ever dreamed he needed or wanted for that matter. Until he'd come out west, he didn't know what he'd been missing.

Oh, he'd felt the hole in his life—not knowing what it would take to fill it—and poured himself into his work, which hadn't been difficult. Allen and Tate Publishing had kept him busier than he'd ever been, but it couldn't diminish the longing inside him.

Ever since his friend died last year, he'd thought the longing had been for a deeper relationship with the Lord. And it had been. But the restlessness he'd felt only proved to him that he wasn't doing exactly what God wanted him to do, and he had no idea how to figure out what that was. God definitely gave him his talent. His eye for photography was recognized worldwide. But if he was supposed to give that up and serve the Lord in another way, he wanted to be willing.

Then he'd been assigned to come out to Wyoming.

This.

This was *where* he was supposed to be.

It might only be for a short time, but when this job was over, he at least had a frame of reference. On his trip out west, he'd asked the Lord what He had for him next. He'd fasted and prayed, waiting on the Lord's answer.

Plainer than the nose on his face, the facts were clear to him now. He'd go wherever God wanted him to go. Do whatever He wanted him to do.

Perhaps coming out to the clean air of Wyoming had cleared his mind so he could hear the Lord without any other hindrances.

The conversations with Raymond Cooper the last few days hadn't hurt either.

Penelope's father was an incredible man. A man who loved the Lord and his family.

Jason had been concerned that first day out on the ranch with the man's questions that were straight to the point. But in all honesty, he had been able to tell the man about how large the publishing company was. It was world renowned. So that part of his answers was good. But when the older man pushed about the man marrying his daughter, Jason had no other choice but to be honest.

He didn't know where Mr. Nicholas Allen Jr. stood on faith now. He didn't know about his current circumstances or beliefs. All he had to go on was his reputation in the past. And as a wealthy man in London, there was a lot to his reputation from before.

The positive thing Jason could say was that when the senior Mr. Allen had sent Jason out on the job, he'd expressed his relief that his son was focused on settling down now and had found an honorable bride for himself.

Mr. Cooper had read between the lines. He understood the truth. What he would do about it was between him and his family.

Jason could sleep peacefully, knowing he'd been honest without slandering a man he barely knew. Hearsay was never a good thing to share. Gossip plain and simple.

He shifted in his bed onto his side and thought about the other questions Mr. Cooper had posed. None of them had been intrusive or inappropriate. Simply a man wanting to ascertain if giving his daughter in marriage was the right thing.

In this day and age, it was good to see the respect this family had for one another and their decisions. Penelope was twenty-two years old. She was an adult. It was clear her family supported and respected her, knowing that they had raised her to be able to make wise decisions.

But would Mr. Cooper step in if Nicholas didn't ever come to Wyoming and ask for his daughter's hand in marriage? That puzzled Jason.

If he were a father and had a daughter as amazing as Penelope, he'd have a hard time allowing her to marry a man for the chance to get her work published and then send her across the ocean to perhaps never see again.

He couldn't imagine what the man's prayers were like with that heavy weight hanging over him.

Jason sighed and flopped onto his back again. It wasn't any of his business. No matter how much the family had welcomed him here.

It was best for him to do his job to the best of his ability and enjoy the time here as much as he could. God had a plan. Jason needed to rest in that.

He closed his eyes. As weary as he was, he couldn't stop his mind from drifting to the dark-haired, dark-eyed daughter of the Rocking K Ranch.

London

"It doesn't matter to me one whit what you *thought* would be a good idea." Father narrowed his gaze at him. "We've expanded the company, and there will be no more of your risk-taking." He stood and straightened his waistcoat.

"Father—"

"No more, Nicholas. I've made up my mind. The best thing you've done in the past ten years is find that western woman and her stories. I won't have you messing this up."

Messing it up? It was *his* life after all. At first, the thought of becoming a renowned author himself was quite appealing. Even the thought of marriage was appealing. Settling down. At least for a few days. But as soon as he'd arrived back in London, he realized how much he'd have to give up. A lot more than his father even knew about.

"It's time for you to clean up your reputation throughout the city. Don't think I don't know about all your secrets."

"Father, in my defense—"

"I won't listen to another excuse. You are almost forty years old. Unless you want my *majority* shares of Allen and Tate to be given to Tate's son when I die, you will do what I say. Plain and simple." He turned and faced the window.

Rage bubbled in Nicholas's chest. Edmund Tate was a bore and a notorious penny-pincher. If that man got Father's shares, Nicholas would find himself without the funds to hire a hackney, much less live as he was accustomed. He clamped his lips together rather than spewing the words that he wanted to say to his father's back. Inheriting the publishing company was the only good thing from his father. And he needed the money. He had a reputation to maintain among the elite.

Maybe putting up with a little wife wouldn't be so bad. Besides, she would do all the work for their books. He wouldn't have to invest much time. Now that he wouldn't be doing the acquisitions either, he'd have more time for his own. . .pursuits.

Father's shoulders rose and fell. He half turned. "Miss Cooper's Western novels will reach an entire new audience. One we desperately need to reach if we wish to grow as projected. Her writing is brilliant. Now, I'm trusting you to bring all this to fruition."

"Yes, sir." He pasted on a dutiful smile.

"I'm not trying to rain on your parade. As a young man, I was wild and raucous as well. But you aren't young anymore. Stop acting like it and do your duty. Sales will be better if you give up your dalliances *and* the gambling. Accept the future that is before you. I can't tout you two as the darling husband and wife writing duo if you are always off gallivanting around."

The senior Allen's plans were set. Decisions had already been made. That meant Nicholas would have to swallow his opinions if he wanted to have control of Allen and Tate eventually.

"Do I have your word that you will take this seriously? We agree about what has to be done?" Father stepped closer to him.

"Yes, sir." Best to just agree to it and move on. For now. "I want the best for the future of Allen and Tate."

"Good, good." The first genuine smile he'd seen from his father since he showed him Penelope's stories spread across the old man's face. "I'm glad to hear it. I expect you to work with Miss Cooper and the editors to get the story of her family in tip-top shape in time for a fall release." Father clapped son on the back.

"Of course."

"And the wedding? Is everything on plan with her family?"

"I'm working on it."

"Get it done. The sooner the better." With that, Father walked back around his desk and sat down. "That will be all."

Dismissed. Just like one of the servants. "I'll see you at dinner." But his father didn't respond or even look up.

The man had been a titan in the publishing business for so long, he didn't have any relationships anymore. Only people to boss around.

Nicholas exited the grand office and took the long hallway back to his wing of the Allen mansion. He didn't like the idea of changing his ways. Even if Miss Penelope Cooper was beautiful and talented. If it meant getting what he wanted in the long run, perhaps he could make the sacrifice and at least keep up appearances of a happy marriage and family.

At least until the company was his.

Then again, his father wasn't getting any younger. If something were to happen to him, it wouldn't be unheard of. . .

The thought made him pause. Was that the solution?

Nicholas paced the hall outside his sitting room, the thoughts taking root in his mind.

It wouldn't be that difficult.

He could still marry the Cooper woman. Take her stories, and slap his own name on them. As his wife, she wouldn't have the right to say anything.

The plan could work.

Get rid of Father.

Take over the company.

Have Penelope do what she loved and write the books.

Allen and Tate would publish them under his name and make a fortune. The company would thrive.

He could do whatever he wanted at that point. Best of both

worlds. He wouldn't have to work like a slave like his father did to keep things running. The board could do that.

The more he thought about it, the more he smiled at the success that was within his reach.

One thing stood in his way—his father.

CHAPTER FIVE

———◆◆———

Taking the well-worn path to her great-grandparents' small log home, Penelope took her time gathering her thoughts.

The legacy left to her by her family was phenomenal. She wouldn't change a thing.

Except maybe that her great-grandmother wasn't sick and could stay with them on this earth indefinitely. And she'd wish for her great-grandpa to still be alive.

But other than that, she couldn't ask for anything else.

Well. . .perhaps for guidance in her situation.

She'd spent more time on her knees lately—which was a good thing—but the answers hadn't come.

After Great-Grandma Eleanor had spent days telling all the stories to Penelope, she'd needed rest. But now it was a good time for Penelope to sit with her eldest relative and pour out her heart. If ever any of them had godly wisdom, it was Eleanor Manning.

When Penelope reached the door, she lightly tapped and then entered the home. Great-Grandpa Ray had built this beautiful cabin for them back in 1860. Eleanor never wanted to move to what she called "the big house" even after her husband passed.

Thankfully, the distance between the homes on the ranch

wasn't great. It was a simple five-minute walk.

Oh, the memories Penelope had of visiting this home as a child. It was always full of love and good food.

The silence that greeted her in the once bustling home now made her heart ache. It would be devastating to all of them to lose Eleanor, even though they would wish to rejoice that she had gone on to be with her Savior. It would still hurt a great deal.

She entered her great-grandmother's room.

"Is that my Penelope-girl?" The hushed words were barely audible, but they brought such a smile to her face.

"Yes, it's me." She pulled up a chair, sat, and gently took the older woman's frail hand in hers. "I came for a visit. Just you and me."

"That sounds lovely." A light cough shook her shoulders. "Help me sit up a bit?"

"Of course." It took a bit of maneuvering, but once she had her great-grandmother sitting upright, she was able to smile into the eyes of her loved one. "A sip of water?"

"Yes, please." Great-Grandma Eleanor's voice cracked. After several good swallows, she leaned her head back. "Now, what's on your mind?"

Where should she start? "I have a bit of a conundrum."

An eyebrow lifted in response.

With a big breath, she ventured on. "I'm struggling with my decision to marry Nicholas." There. She'd said it and let out a whoosh of air. "I know I was confident of it all when I telegrammed and wrote to the family with the details, but now that I'm home and have had more time to think about it, I'm floundering. I mean, I'm very excited about his father's publishing company contracting my stories, but is that a reason to marry? It is the fulfillment of my dreams." She tilted her head back and forth as she weighed her options. "Nowadays, it's the best route for me as a woman, and it does seem like God opened this door for me, but. . ." She let the thought linger for a moment.

"No buts, Penelope. Do you love Nicholas?" Her grand-mother's words were strong and sweet.

"I care about him. He's my friend. Just like you and Great-Grandpa Ray when you got married. And look how happy the two of you were. So there's hope for love, right?"

"There's always hope when God is the center."

Inwardly, Penelope cringed. Nicholas' faith wasn't like hers or her family's. Every time she'd brought it up, he said all the right things but quickly changed the subject. Well, it didn't matter. *She* could make sure that they committed to put God first. "Do you think I should marry Nicholas?"

"That, my dear, isn't a question I can answer. I *can* say with confidence that I believe God opened this door. I'm not certain where the door will lead, but He brought you home to tell the story. He's the author of all, and He gave you this gift. You keep seeking Him and seeking to use your gift for Him, and He will show you the way."

Penelope chewed the corner of her lip. Her grandmother spoke the truth, but the truth didn't make the waiting any easier. She picked at a loose string on her skirt. "The other thing is. . .London is a long way from here."

A soft laugh echoed from the bed. "That it is. But trains and steamships have shortened the distance. Don't let that stand in the way if you are supposed to go."

"You aren't making this easy."

More laughter from the bed. "My job isn't to give you all the answers. I wish I could make it easy, and I wish I knew the future, but I don't. What do your parents say?"

Penelope let her shoulders slump. "That's the thing. They haven't said much. Although, I know it's coming because I see the wheels in Dad's head turning. Mom has been gracious and loving and supportive. But there's always been people around when we talk. I'm sure they are waiting for a time when we are alone to give me their opinions. They have told me that it is my decision to make, which makes it even more difficult."

"They are being wise in holding their words."

"What do you mean?"

Great-Grandma Eleanor closed her eyes for a moment and then opened them again. "They are taking time to pray and think about it before rushing to judgment. That's always good, especially when it is their little girl they are talking about. No matter how old you get, Penelope, you will still be their little girl. It's hard to release the girls into God's hands and set them free."

She took a moment to digest the words. What would her parents have to say once they had time to think and pray over it? Should she ask them?

Probably not. If she pressed before they were ready to talk, that might only bring out the negative. And she had enough trouble getting over all the negative thoughts herself. "Now that you mention it, I can't imagine what it must be like for parents. I'm having a hard enough time with this decision—even though I already made it. I just don't want to make the wrong choice or be selfish in my choice. I wish to honor the Lord in all that I do."

Great-Grandma Eleanor squeezed her hand. "That's the best you can do."

"Will you do me a favor, Great-Grandma?"

"If I can."

"Would you keep this between you and me? I don't want to put anyone else in the family in turmoil if they think I'm struggling with my decision."

"Of course, dear. But promise me you won't keep it from them for long. Having a family of prayer warriors behind you is exactly what you need right now."

"I promise." Penelope grinned.

Her great-grandma shifted, and a wry smile lifted her lips. "Now tell me all about that photographer—Mr. Miller? Your grandma Grace tells me he's handsome as the day is long and has a smile that will melt butter."

"Grandma Eleanor!" Penelope felt the heat rushing to her cheeks. The handsome Mr. Miller hadn't escaped her notice either. But *that* was a complication she didn't need right now. Not when she was engaged to be married.

"When do I get to meet him?" She winked.

CHAPTER SIX

———◆◆◆———

Out of the corner of his eye, Jason glimpsed Penelope on her horse. The days on the ranch had raced by, and he'd taken more photographs than he'd ever thought he would on this trip, but he felt like he was just getting started. "Where to next?" Hopefully, he didn't sound too schoolboyish eager. But he'd come to realize something—he really enjoyed spending time with her.

She pursed her lips and glanced around. "I feel like I've taken you all over the place already, but there's so much ground to cover, especially if we need multiple pictures for each story."

"I'm at your disposal. Besides, they gave me several weeks to get the job done right. It may seem like we've taken a lot of pictures, but we haven't even scratched the surface, have we? I'm eager to see whatever you envision for the novels. Some of the pictures may not turn out, so that's why I take multiples. More is better in this case." He clamped his lips together before he rambled any further.

She shifted her gaze to him and sent him a wide smile. "I knew we were of the same mind. It makes it so much easier to talk about what I see when I'm writing the stories. You have done an incredible job capturing that."

"It's been my pleasure. And your family is amazing. I'm growing rather fond of them."

She wiggled her eyebrows at him. "My grandma Grace apparently told my great-grandma about you, and now she's hankering to meet you. So I would say that the fondness is mutual."

"Oh boy. Do I want to know what she said?"

Her eyes crinkled at the corners as her lips upturned, amusement clear on her face. "Let's just say it was good and leave it at that."

He overexaggerated a swipe of his brow. "Whew. I wouldn't want to get on the bad side of any of the women at the Rocking K."

Her laughter bubbled out, and she tipped her head back. "I haven't had this much fun in ages."

"I'm glad to hear it. My sister always tells me that I'm dull, so now I can write to her and tell her that I've been declared fun."

Their laughter mingled together and floated up into the sky. What he wouldn't give to stretch his time here. This ranch and the area had seared itself into his heart. And Penelope was fast becoming a good friend. His heart pinched. She was just the kind of woman he'd always hoped and prayed to find. But he had to shove those thoughts away. She was betrothed to his boss. He shook his head.

"What's wrong?"

He jerked his gaze back to her, feeling the heat fill his neck and face. "Nothing."

"I don't believe you for one second, Jason Miller. All of a sudden, you frowned. What is it?"

Clearing his throat, he tried to come up with a response that was honest but didn't give away what he'd been thinking. That would be disastrous. And he wouldn't dishonor his boss. "I truly love it here, and I don't like the thought of leaving this place."

Her eyes warmed. "It does my heart good to hear how much you love the ranch." She released a sigh. "I do too. It's hard to imagine leaving it behind."

For several moments, they sat in heavy silence. He hated that he'd brought up the subject and dampened both of their moods. "Look, I didn't mean to sadden you." What could he do to fix this? "Can you tell me about the hot springs up in Thermopolis? You talk of them a lot, and I must admit it's hard for me to imagine."

As she turned back to him, her smile beamed once again. "That's a perfect idea, Jason."

"What is?"

"We should go to Thermopolis. I write about it in many of my stories. You'll *definitely* want to get lots of photographs there." She glanced down at the watch on her shirtwaist. "We should spend the rest of the day out here, and I'll have one of the men prepare the skiff for us and take us up tomorrow. Does that sound good?"

"A skiff?"

"It's a small boat. We have to go up the river to get to Thermopolis. Otherwise, it would take days to go around the mountain."

"Oh." Up the river? In a skiff? The shock he felt was certain to be all over his face.

She playfully waved a hand at him. "What's wrong? Are you afraid of water?"

"No. Not water so much." He lifted his hat and scratched at his head.

"Well then, what is it?"

"I can't swim."

Walking down Fifth Street in Thermopolis, Penelope told Jason about the history of the area. "In 1896, a treaty was made with the Shoshone and Arapaho. The hot springs were given to Wyoming with the stipulation that the hot springs would be available to all for free."

"That's pretty amazing." He shoved his hands into his pockets and strolled casually beside her. "Did they abide by the treaty? Are they still free?"

"They are. I'll take you to the State Bathhouse in a little bit. The McGannon Sanitarium is right beside it, with forty beds. But it's quite the walk from here."

The other men from the ranch had dispersed to take care of their business and had agreed to meet them back at the skiff at four that afternoon.

"I don't mind. Giving my legs some exercise on firm ground is exactly what I need after that boat ride with my knees tucked up to my chin. Although, I wasn't envious of the effort the guys had to put in to get us up here. No wonder there were three of them rowing."

Their trip up the river had been full of excitement since the water could be quite fast this time of year. But he'd held on tight and even laughed several times as they got sprayed.

It had been fun to watch him. "I ran away from home once when I was little and thought I could row myself up the river." The memory made her laugh. "I didn't get far before my arms tuckered out and I'd actually gone backward rather than forward."

"What happened?"

"My dad swam out into the middle of the river and rescued me. He never scolded me or punished me, but he told me that if I wanted to try to run away again, I should ask for help." She hadn't thought about that time in so many years. Her dad's face was clear in her mind, and she couldn't help but laugh at the stubborn little girl she'd been.

"That would have been fun to see. Little Penelope Cooper trying to run away when she already lived in the middle of nowhere." They walked a little farther. "The town is really nice. Do you come up here often?" He stopped in the dusty street and turned toward her. "I mean, that was quite an adventurous trip." The laughter in his eyes made him look like he was up to mischief.

"Only once in a while. It's much faster to come up the river than to take the time to ride all the way around the mountain. But if the water is running too quick—especially during spring runoff—we don't dare risk it. Personally, I don't mind getting a little wet. It's fun. But most of the other ladies in my family prefer to take the long way around the mountain."

"I can't blame them." His lips twitched. "I was pretty worried about my camera equipment staying dry."

"Well then, you better prepare yourself for the trip back. It will be *much* faster going downstream." She quirked one eyebrow at him.

"Is that a challenge, Miss Cooper?"

"Perhaps we should go to the hot springs now, and I can teach you the basic elements of swimming. Just in case." It was way too much fun to tease him.

He put a hand to his chest. "You wouldn't dare dump the boat over on purpose and risk my life and limb, now would you?" The exaggeration in his voice played along nicely with her scheme.

"Maybe I would, maybe I wouldn't." She shrugged. "Best you should be prepared."

"I look forward to it."

CHAPTER SEVEN

---•••---

The day had been one of the best ones she'd had in a long time. Penelope curled her feet up under her on the settee in the parlor and sipped her hot chocolate. What had been a luxury when she was a child was now a mainstay for evenings by the fire.

All day, she'd bantered with Jason. Shown him around Thermopolis. Sat back and watched him take photographs of anything and everything.

As promised, at the hot springs, she'd taught him some basic elements of swimming, but they hadn't had a lot of time and had raced back to meet the men with the skiff. The ride home had been full of laughter, lots of water spraying in their faces, and Jason rejoicing that his camera equipment was still dry when they returned home.

All in all, it had been a nice break away from everything.

She hadn't thought about everything entailed with her contracts, all the writing and work to be done, or Allen and Tate. She hadn't thought about moving to London.

She hadn't thought about Nicholas at all. Not one bit.

With a grimace, she took another sip. Was that so bad? That she didn't think of her betrothed even once?

"Penelope?" Her mother's voice broke into her thoughts. She gazed up to see Mom and Dad enter the room holding hands. It was so sweet to see how much her parents loved each other.

Her mother sat beside her. "Mind if we join you for a bit before we turn in for the night?"

"Not at all." Penelope scooted over a bit. "It's been too long since it's just been the three of us."

"Gracious. I can't even think that far back. Once your brothers came along, we've been busy corralling them ever since."

She laughed along with her mother. The poor woman had lost several babies after Penelope. It wasn't until she was nine years old that their family had been blessed by the twins. Now at thirteen, the two young men were taller than she was and beginning to fill out their broad shoulders. One of these days, they wouldn't be wiry beanpoles that could climb up anything but strong young men who could help Dad shoulder the responsibility of the ranch.

In that moment, the thought of not being here to watch them grow up made her stomach drop. Would she miss seeing her brothers marry and have children? Would they never know their Aunt Penelope? Would her children never know her family?

As the depth of everything her decision meant washed over her, she swallowed hard.

"Your mother and I would like to speak to you." Dad's words sliced through her melancholy thoughts.

"Oh?" Her stomach knotted. Whenever a conversation started that way, it sounded ominous.

"We wanted to take plenty of time to pray for you and Nicholas about this big step in life you're taking. And we needed some time to see you for ourselves again and make sure you were happy. Now that we have a bit of time alone, thanks to your brothers spending the night at Grandma Eleanor's, we'd like to discuss the future."

"All right." She swallowed and braced herself, not knowing what was about to come. Would they tell her she couldn't marry Nicholas? Or would they give their blessing even without meeting him?

"First," Mother patted her knee and then straightened her shoulders, "we'd like to hear the full story about how you met Nicholas and how all this transpired. Every detail. We promise to listen to everything before we ask questions."

Penelope nodded. While she'd telegrammed and written her parents about it, they deserved to hear the entire account from her directly. With a deep breath, she dove in. It took her the next twenty minutes to tell them everything.

Silence followed for a brief second, and Penelope watched her parents looking across the room at each other. She couldn't decipher what their unspoken communication meant, so she waited.

"Does Nicholas know Jesus as his Savior?" Dad's first question *would* cut to the most important factor. The factor that she had pushed to the back.

She knew better. She did. But her parents deserved the truth. With a wince, she plowed ahead. "I admit that I should have asked that question first and foremost. It was selfish of me to follow my dreams first rather than take that into consideration." The hot chocolate that had tasted so delicious earlier now made her mouth feel like cotton. "That being said, I know that Nicholas and his father do attend church. They both have expressed how much faith means to them, and they want their children to know God."

Another look passed between her parents.

Mom licked her lips. "Attending church, words of faith, and wanting their children to know God are a far cry from a relationship with the Lord, dear."

"I know that, Mom." Feeling scolded, her tone sounded like a whiny child.

"We know you do." Another knee pat from her mother. But it wasn't over.

Dad leaned over his knees and placed his elbows on them. "Logically, I can understand you wanting this marriage because of the publishing business. I can. It's an incredible opportunity for you, and we want your dreams to come true. But as your father, I'm still struggling to release you into the hands of a man that we don't know. I know you are friends. Since he is a man of wealth, I would assume that he would take care of you. However, we don't know these things for certain because we've never met him."

As much as she wanted to argue and be defensive, she couldn't. He was correct. But the thought of giving up her dreams stabbed her in the heart. Surely she and Nicholas could make a good marriage out of their friendship. He'd even said he cared for her. That could blossom into love while they accomplished publishing and writing together. It could work. It had to. At this point, all other options for publishing here in America were closed. The many rejections from publishers in New York had made that fact obvious. "I understand your perspective, I do. But don't you think it's pretty clear that the Lord opened this door for me? Isn't that why you all sent me to New York in the first place?"

"Dear, we sent you to follow your publishing dreams. Not to marry a man who would take you across the ocean." Mother grimaced. "I'm sorry. I shouldn't have said it that way. Of course we see how this does seem like an open door. But what if it's not the door you're thinking it is?"

"What do you mean?" Penelope studied her mother. If there was a way out of this where she could write her stories and still stay in Wyoming, she'd love to see the path laid out.

"We are simply asking you to continue praying about this." Dad sat up straight and released a long sigh. "We realize you have already committed to this arrangement and have signed a contract for your books. But in addition to prayer, we have a request."

"I will keep praying. I promise." The least she could do to honor her parents was to listen to what they had to say. It's not like she hadn't had her own doubts. "What is your request?"

"Before we agree to this, as your parents, we'd like Nicholas to come out here and see us. Even if it's only for a day. I believe a true gentleman would do as much." Her father's eyes snapped even in the dim light. This wasn't a request that came lightly. He was expecting his future son-in-law to show him some honor.

"I'll send a telegram first thing in the morning."

"Thank you." But her dad still didn't look satisfied.

Mother placed her hand over Penelope's and squeezed it gently. A sure sign she was prepping her for something else.

"There's one more thing." Dad's lips had turned into a deep frown.

"Yes?" Her voice cracked. When she was a child and he took on that expression, it normally meant she was in big trouble.

He stood up and clasped his hands behind him. "I don't wish to participate in hearsay or gossip, but since we have yet to meet Mr. Nicholas Allen Jr., all we have to go on is what others know of him. Mr. Miller is an employee of Allen and Tate, so I had no qualms asking him what he knew of the man who wished to marry my daughter."

Her mouth went completely dry. "And?"

"He was hesitant to say anything negative—I could tell— which made me respect him even more. Jason admitted that he didn't know the junior Allen well, but he had heard of his reputation back in London."

Something inside her began to boil. "What did he say?"

"It wasn't good, Penelope. And that's all you need to know."

London

With gloves on his hands, Nicholas wrapped the hemlock leaves in paper and then wrapped the packet in another sheet of paper just to be safe. He tucked the packet under the seat in his carriage, looked around him to make sure no one had seen him, and then climbed up to drive. It would be a three-hour journey home, but it would be worth it.

Never in his life would he have thought that he could stoop to this level of deceit. But it had to be done. Father had forced his hand, and it was the only way out.

Besides, the senior Nicholas Allen had lived a long and fruitful life. He'd grown Allen and Tate into a magnificent and massive business.

From here, without the shackles his father insisted on restricting him with, Nicholas would be free to do what he pleased. He could still have a magnificent moneymaking publishing house.

He could have everything he wanted.

It was a good plan.

He'd even settled into the idea of marrying Penelope. If her novels turned out to be as popular as Father anticipated, Nicholas would be set up for life. There was no way he would give up the moneymaking beauty he had at his fingertips.

Their butler in New York had sent word that her letters were piling up. He'd have to deal with that at some point. Perhaps tomorrow.

After he poisoned Father tonight.

CHAPTER EIGHT

——◆◆◆——

Jason loaded his camera gear onto the horse. Today, he planned to wander the ranch and take whatever photograph took his fancy. He'd originally wanted to spend another day with Penelope, but she wouldn't even meet his gaze at breakfast, and the dark circles under her eyes attested to a lack of sleep. Perhaps she wasn't feeling well.

He shouldn't be thinking about spending time with her anyway. She was engaged to his boss. He was here to do a job, and that was it. The reminder was getting harder and harder to swallow.

Although, the longer he thought and prayed about it, the more he felt the Lord tugging him out west. How that would manifest, Jason had no idea, but he wanted to be open to the Lord's leading.

Once everything was secure, he shoved his left boot into the stirrup. Pulling himself up to mount, he heard footsteps behind him.

Stomping footsteps.

Of the lady variety.

Oh boy.

He situated himself in the saddle and turned.

Penelope. Her brown eyes looked like his coffee, deep and rich in the morning light. Her dark hair was piled high on her head today. However, her hurried march out to the corral had caused several strands to slip from their pins around her face.

She was beautiful.

And spitting mad.

"What did you say to my parents?" Her words were low but harsh. She peered over her shoulder.

Jason looked toward the house from the corral. They were a good twenty yards away, but she obviously didn't want anyone to hear whatever it was she had to say to him. He took a calming breath and dismounted. He stepped closer to her, and the scent of lavender teased his nose. "You'll have to give me some context. I've spoken to your parents a lot in the couple weeks I've been here." He smiled but doubted it would calm the storm that clearly raged in her.

She crossed her arms over her chest and whisper-shouted. "What. Did. You. Say. To. My. Father. About. Nicholas?"

Oh. Mr. Cooper and his wife had spoken to Penelope. Jason softened. "Not a lot, Penelope. I promise. Your father asked some very tough questions, and I had to answer honestly. Rest assured, I told him that what I knew of my boss's—your fiancé's—reputation was only hearsay. I've never witnessed anything but the business side of things."

"You've heard what, exactly, about Nicholas?" Her voice cracked, and the steam behind her anger dissipated a bit.

"It isn't fitting for me to speak what I've heard in front of a lady." Yes, he was trying to delay the inevitable, but it was a true statement.

Her chin lifted a notch. "I can handle it, Jason. Please."

Jason studied her for several moments. This would not end well, no matter how much he softened the blow, but he had to be honest. "Understand that a gentleman's reputation in London is only spoken about with other gentlemen. Ladies are not normally privy to these kinds of details."

"That's what concerns me. I have a right to know, especially since I'm about to marry this man." Her eyes glistened with unshed tears.

Jason's heart broke a little. This might be her undoing. Could he be the one to inflict pain on her? He hated the thought. Closing his eyes, he took a quick breath and prayed for the Lord to guide his words. "If what is said about his reputation is true, he's had many mistresses over the years. Women he never intended to marry. He gambles and drinks a good deal." Brevity was best in a situation like this. That was the best he could do.

Her shoulders rose and fell with her breath. Shock and then hurt flitted across her face before she shuttered her expressions. "This is well known within gentlemen's circles?"

"I'm afraid so, yes."

"Does his father have the same reputation?"

"No." He swallowed. "It is quite well known that his father abhors his son's behaviors and has covered many indiscretions so they wouldn't get published in the papers. Nevertheless, it is still talked about." Reaching toward her, he touched her elbow. "I'm sorry, Penelope. Truly, I am."

"It's fine. I appreciate you telling me." But a single tear slipped out.

He wanted to wipe it away, but it wasn't his place. What could he do to make things right? "If it helps, I have heard that Nicholas senior has been saying for several years that if his son was going to inherit, he had to change his ways. Perhaps he's already made a significant turnaround in his life. Then he met you."

She nodded ever so slightly but didn't say a word.

Jason stood there and watched her. What he wouldn't give at this point to be able to fix this. To ease her pain. Penelope had become a good friend. Over the past few weeks, they'd enjoyed each other's company and talked about everything. Except Nicholas. Jason sighed. At least she knew the full truth now. It was up to her what she wanted to do with it.

With a quivering chin, she eyed him. "Thank you, Jason. I know that wasn't easy." She cleared her throat. "And I apologize for being so angry with you when I first came out. It wasn't your fault—I had no right to be so harsh with you."

He chuckled. "Oh yes, you did. And I understand that completely."

It seemed to break through her wall. She relaxed her arms and let them hang at her sides. A sad laugh escaped her lips. "I need to pray about this, but I can't say that I'm not hurt by his deceit about his past. A marriage of convenience with an honorable man is one thing. But now? I don't know. The only thing I know for certain is that Mr. Allen Senior said that there wouldn't be any publishing of books unless I married his son. Maybe he had hopes that *I* could be the one to straighten out Nicholas Junior."

"Perhaps. But that isn't a burden you should have to bear."

She clasped her hands and began to fidget with her fingers. Turning her face away, she looked toward the mountain. "It's heartbreaking to think that all my hopes and dreams for my stories are tied up with this man and my upcoming marriage to him."

"You don't have to marry him, Penelope. Not if you don't want to. There will be another way to get published. The Lord is faithful. If He's given you this gift and this dream, then He will make a way."

Her dark eyes turned back to him. Clear and confident. "You're correct. And right now, I don't *want* to marry him. But I still made a commitment and signed a contract. The right thing to do now is to ask Nicholas his true intentions. I'll send a telegram and wait for his response. The honorable thing for *him* to do is be honest with me."

Penelope turned on her heel and headed toward the house. She stopped abruptly and half turned toward him again. "Thank you, Jason, for your honesty. It takes courage to share difficult things that people might not want to hear. You're a good friend."

The tear sliding down her cheek didn't escape his notice.

He'd hurt her, and there wasn't anything he could do to fix it. It stabbed him in the heart.

CHAPTER NINE

———◆◆◆———

Penelope had sent a telegram to Nicholas ten days ago, asking him to come meet her parents. She made it clear her father required it before they wed.

No response.

Which was enough to get her temper simmering. Why hadn't he written? Why wouldn't he respond even to a telegram? Even if he was in London, his butler in New York City always made sure that correspondence made it to the Allens.

Now she'd sent another telegram. Marked it as urgent. They needed to speak immediately.

Still no response.

Two days had passed since the second telegram, so she'd sat down this morning and written a long letter. In it, she detailed her father's request and also her feelings about what she'd learned of his reputation in the past. She gave him the full opportunity to explain and show her that he'd changed. If he had and if he came out to meet her parents, she would follow through with her commitment.

Plain and simple.

All the weeks they'd worked together, he'd never made her

feel insignificant or beneath him. He definitely hadn't seemed like the Nicholas that had the reputation Jason shared. But then again, perhaps it was all a facade. How was she to know?

God, I need Your help more than ever. Please show me the way. Help me put my selfish desires aside.

And she had for the most part. She wasn't about to marry a man who wasn't faithful to her, convenient marriage or not. Her stories could wait.

Staring out the window of her bedroom, Penelope crossed her arms over her chest and lifted her chin. Jason was right. There would be another way to get published. If God wanted her to be, it would happen.

In the grand scheme of things, the stories should be put aside for now. Keeping God first was most important. And if she were going to marry someone, it had to be for the right reasons. It had to be to a godly man. Someone who would love her and the gifts God had given her. Her mother, grandmother, and great-grandmother were all strong women who loved Jesus. And their husbands loved them just the way the Lord had made them—flaws and all. She knew their marriages hadn't been without struggles, but together, each marriage had blessed the next generation with example after example about what it meant to love God and love others.

Penelope suddenly had the insatiable urge to gather with the women in her family. An idea was brewing.

She grabbed her shawl with a smile and ran into the kitchen.

Two hours later, Penelope sat in a chair next to Great-Grandma Eleanor's bed. Grandma Grace was seated on the other side, and her mother was in a chair at the foot of the bed. They'd made a cinnamon swirl cake and had brought it warm from the oven.

She got up from her seat and walked over to the windows.

Pulling open the drapes, she allowed the sun to warm her face. With a deep breath, she turned to them.

"I'd like to ask you all about marriage."

Great-Grandma Eleanor smiled from the bed and waggled her eyebrows. "My favorite subject."

Grandma Grace giggled. "Mama!" She covered her mouth.

Penelope's mother just sipped her coffee and shook her head.

"I'm not dead yet, Grace, and your father was the love of my life. I think youngsters need to see more of what a real marriage is like—and what it should be." Great-Grandma Eleanor coughed into her hankie. "I've told you the story, Penelope. You know we didn't initially marry for love. Life was difficult, and we had to survive. But when we poured ourselves into loving God and loving each other, it was the most beautiful thing ever." She pointed a bony finger.

"That's exactly what I'm asking about." Penelope took her seat again and straightened her shoulders. "I may have been hasty in my decision. There was so much excitement to get my stories published, and Nicholas offered a way. It seemed like God was opening the door. But then his father thought it would be even better if Nicholas and I married." She took a sip of her coffee and bolstered herself for the next part. "We are friends. We worked well together in New York. He was charming and wealthy. But...I've since come to learn that he's had a reputation in the past. A reputation that makes me rethink my decision."

Grandma Grace's gaze narrowed. "Does he still have this reputation?"

Penelope sighed. "That's what I'm trying to ascertain. He could be a changed man. From what I saw in New York for the couple months we worked together, I didn't see anything of it. But it's his reputation in London that is the problem. And that is where we would be living."

"The real question is whether this man has dedicated himself to the Lord. Nothing else matters if that isn't the case." Great-Grandma Eleanor's words were soft and loving.

Penelope stared at the woman who'd been a spiritual mentor in her life. All the women in this room had. But when the twins came along, it took all hands on deck to manage them and the ranch. So the women of the Rocking K Ranch had divided up special times for Penelope.

Grandma Grace took her for an hour or so a day and taught her all about gardening and cooking. It didn't matter how big of a mess they made, they'd laugh and create and clean up the mess.

Her mornings were spent with Mom, who taught her all about etiquette, manners, managing a home, and did all her lessons at home, including French and Latin.

Then there was her time with Great-Grandma Eleanor. She taught her how to crochet, quilt, and sew. But it was always more than that. They set out to study the entire Bible together. And they did it. It took six years—especially with all of Penelope's questions—but when they completed it, they started over again. The second time through, she'd grown up quite a bit and their discussions grew deeper.

As Penelope looked around the room at each woman, she yearned to raise her children like this. Surrounded by godly family. By people who would pour into one another and help each other through the toughest of times.

If she married Nicholas—that wouldn't happen.

She drew in a long breath, "I don't know enough about Nicholas to know where he truly stands with the Lord." With a shake of her head, she shared her heart. Everything became clear. "I don't know why I needed to talk about marriage. It's easy to see that I shouldn't marry Nicholas. Books or no books. I want a godly husband. And I want to be here. In Wyoming." In that moment, it felt like a huge weight fell off her shoulders.

Smiles around the room greeted her.

Mom stood and walked over to her. "I know that wasn't easy, dear. But we are here for you, and we are praying."

"And who says we can't talk about marriage?" Great-Grandma Eleanor giggled.

Grandma Grace winked at Penelope. "Exactly. I agree with Mama."

Penelope felt a blush heat her cheeks. "Well, since I don't exactly have a beau, I think that might be a little hasty." She took a bite of cake to sort her thoughts. "There's one thing I'm struggling with."

"What is it, dear?" Mom gripped her hand.

"I truly felt like God opened that door for me in New York when all the other ones were closed. I guess—I guess I'm confused by that."

Grandma Grace set her fork down and cleared her throat. "Who said that God hasn't opened a door for you? Maybe you were simply looking at the wrong one."

CHAPTER TEN

———◆●◆———

It was Jason's last morning at the Rocking K Ranch. As he'd done every morning since arriving, Jason ate breakfast, saddled his horse, and spent hours riding the ranch and taking as many pictures as he could. At some point, photographing this ranch had ceased to be a job. He'd fallen in love with the land, the family, Pene— No. He couldn't go there. She was an engaged woman, off limits. They were only friends. And the best thing he could do was capture her home in a way that honored the generations who had built this beautiful living testimony to love.

His heart pinched. The thought of her marrying Nicholas Allen Jr. turned his gut. But it wasn't his place to say anything. Even though Penelope was the most incredible woman he'd ever met. Even though he loved Wyoming and this ranch.

His job wasn't here.

It was time to head back to New York.

If he wanted to be respectable in all his dealings, he needed to stay out of Penelope's life and allow her to follow wherever she felt God leading.

He just wished it led to him.

Horse's hooves sounded behind him.

Jason turned his own mount and couldn't help but smile. Penelope.

She rode up beside him. "I was looking for you." Her smile was warm.

It did funny things to his insides. "Oh?"

"I wanted to apologize again for taking out my anger on you last week. I shouldn't have charged after you and accused you of anything. You only spoke truth and, sadly, you got the brunt of my emotions." Her nose crinkled and she grimaced. "Will you forgive me?"

It was the cutest thing he'd ever seen. "There's nothing to forgive. It was completely understandable."

"Friends?" Her smile was back.

Friends? His mind echoed her question. He wished for more, but he couldn't. Instead he smiled back, hoping she wouldn't notice the strain of it. "Of course."

"Care to ride for a bit?" Her horse shifted slightly, and Penelope swayed with the movement.

Jason studied her face for a moment. Something was different. She was much more relaxed today. The tension that had clouded her features the last few weeks was gone. He had no right to ask her what had changed. But he was glad to see it, nonetheless. "I'd love to. I just finished." He tightened his grip on the reins.

She frowned. "Finished? As in finished for today or the whole job?"

His heart flipped. Was that disappointment he heard in her voice? Did she hate the idea of him leaving? "I've been here for weeks. Yeah, sadly, I think I'm finished with the job. I should probably head back to New York tomorrow."

"Well, that's a disappointment. We have all enjoyed having you around."

He tipped his head as they began a slow descent of the ridge. "I have to say I'm disappointed too. Wyoming has grabbed a piece of my heart."

"I'm so glad you like it here." She stared out over the horizon. "I can't imagine anywhere else I'd rather be."

"This is definitely where you belong, Penelope. It's an amazing ranch. Your family is incredible. If I had known about this place sooner, I would have come out here and settled."

"It's pretty unique. Sometimes it's difficult to be so far away from everything, but we make up for it in a million other ways." Once they were back on level ground, she pulled her horse to a stop. She toyed with the reins in her hands for a moment, her eyes fixed on the ground. "I wanted to tell you that I've telegrammed Nicholas and have written him a letter. I don't think God is calling me to marry him and move to London."

His eyebrows shot up under his hat. "Really?"

Penelope looked up, and their gazes locked. Her face was the prettiest shade of pink Jason had ever seen. "If I don't marry him, there are no book contracts. But my dreams don't have to die. You were right about that. If the Lord wants my stories to be published, He will make a way. But marrying the wrong man isn't the way to do it."

The wrong man? Jason's shoulders relaxed, tension he didn't realize he'd been carrying easing in an instant.

As they stared at one another, Jason could only hope that she felt a tiny amount of what he was feeling. But what if she didn't?

He licked his lips. "I've been praying for you. And I will continue." They allowed the horses to graze. "Have you heard from Nicholas?"

She shook her head. "No. At this point, I don't know if I will." With a shrug, she smiled. "And I'm okay with that. But I'm not going to marry him. I'm not going back to New York."

———————

As she rode next to Jason on the way back to the main house, Penelope's heart ached.

He was leaving tomorrow.

They'd talked for hours today, and it had been lovely. One of the best days of her life, if she were to be honest.

Not because anything magical happened but because she realized she had a best friend in him. They'd laughed and shared childhood stories. They'd talked about scripture and where the Lord was pruning each of them. They'd talked of dreams.

He understood her.

He understood the Penelope from the Wyoming ranch with all the heritage and legacy that came with it. But he also understood the Penelope that was the dreamer and writer—the one who longed to share her stories with the world.

Never had she had a relationship like that.

She studied his profile as they rode.

But she hadn't shared what was truly in her heart. Of course, it had only become apparent today. It was like her eyes had been opened after a long sleep.

"Thank you for today, Penelope." Jason's words broke through her thoughts. "I can't imagine a more perfect last day here." His smile beamed at her, and her stomach flipped.

He was a handsome and rugged man. But that wasn't what she saw. It was his eyes. And the truth in them. The caring. The understanding.

Jason Miller held a piece of her heart. Plain and simple. "It has been a perfect day, hasn't it?" She longed to say more, but until she heard from Nicholas and things were resolved, she couldn't do that to Jason. It wasn't fair. "Would it be all right if we wrote to one another?"

"I would like that." His smile slipped a little. "But I have no idea where my job will send me next. So don't get mad if I don't respond right away."

"I won't." That's right. His job. For Allen and Tate. She cringed inside.

They rode up to the house, and Mom ran out with a paper in her hand. "It's from Nicholas."

Penelope dismounted and her stomach dropped. He'd finally responded?

She took the paper as Jason and Mom watched her. As she read the words, her other hand covered her mouth. Short and to the point. But no response to anything else. To none of her letters. He expected her to simply comply.

"What's wrong?" Mom's voice was soft.

Penelope lifted her chin and tried not to spit the words. "His father has died. He won't be coming to Wyoming. And he's sending tickets for me to go to London. For the wedding."

CHAPTER ELEVEN

———◆◆◆———

The train puffed its way into the station and Jason's heart sank. He was leaving Wyoming. He was leaving the Rocking K Ranch. He was leaving Penelope.

Last night, he hadn't slept a wink. Instead, he'd prayed and made a few decisions. After that, he wrote Penelope a long letter.

He wasn't sure she would ever read it. But hoped that she would.

Only time would tell.

A whole wagonload of the family came to see him off, but everyone had errands to attend to before his train left, so he'd taken his things to the station to sit and wait.

He'd spent a good bit of time praying, and now the closer the time came for his departure the thought of leaving was even harder.

"Jason." Penelope walked briskly toward him with her hand over her heart. "Goodness, I didn't think my errands would take me that long."

"I'm glad you made it." He smiled warmly at her. If only he could tell her everything in his heart. "It won't be long before I have to board."

"I know." She gripped her drawstring purse with both hands.

"But I sent a telegram to Nicholas sharing my family's condolences for the loss of his father and also telling him that the wedding was off."

He raised his eyebrows at that. "Oh?"

"I don't know why I ever thought it would work. I feel at complete peace about my decision. I just wanted you to know. I hope that doesn't cause difficulty for you since you were sent out here for this project. For me."

"Don't you worry about me, Penelope." He pulled the envelope out of his coat pocket. "I'll be just fine." He braced himself with a deep breath. "Here. I'd like you to have this."

She took the envelope, a quizzical expression on her face. "What's this?"

"A letter." He covered her gloved hand with his own. "But you can't open it now."

"Why not?"

"Once Nicholas confirms your wedding is off, you can open it."

"Why? I thought we were friends." She stepped closer. Lavender teased his senses again. He would never associate that flower with anyone else but Penelope.

"We are friends." He pulled his hand away as the rest of her family approached. "That's why I wrote you the letter. But I need you to wait to open it. It's the appropriate thing to do." He dipped his head and stared into her eyes. "Will you do that for me, please?"

"Yes." The whispered word washed over him. Her mouth tipped up to one side in a bittersweet smile. "Thank you."

"For what?"

"For the letter. For your friendship. I—"

"All aboard!" the conductor shouted.

The rest of her family reached him. "Have a great trip!"

"It was great to have you here."

"You're welcome back anytime."

"Come again when you can stay longer."

Lots of hugs were given him, a basket of food, several other wrapped gifts that he was told to open once the train was underway.

He caught Penelope's gaze over the head of her grandma. A single tear slipped down her cheek.

London

"Mr. Allen, that is unacceptable. You are in no way ready to take over this company. Neither will the board allow you to fill your father's spot."

Nicholas came out of his chair. "I don't care what you think the board will allow. It is in my father's will that I am to take over the company after he's gone. I inherited his majority shares."

"That's what you think is in your father's will?" The chairman of the board leveled a smirk at him and leaned back in his chair. "I take it you haven't seen the updated will, have you?"

He narrowed his gaze. What? No. His father wouldn't have.

But yes, he would have. The man never wanted him to be able to succeed. He slammed a fist down on the table. "Show me this updated will."

"It will be read this afternoon. You already knew that." But the man couldn't look more pleased with himself.

Later that afternoon, Nicholas had calmed himself and entered the lawyer's offices with a broad smile. He couldn't allow anyone to think that he didn't know exactly what he was doing.

But the reading of the will did not go in his favor.

The stipulation Father had put in his will was recent. Very recent.

Nicholas would not be allowed to take his father's seat as president of Allen and Tate unless he married Miss Cooper, settled down, and worked with her to publish the new Westerns. One every three months.

"Of course, you may continue on in your current position in the company and work your way up if this isn't acceptable." The chairman of the board eyed him.

Nicholas surveyed the room. Every board member was present. Every one of them despised him, and he knew it. No one wanted him to take over Allen and Tate except him.

"What about my father's money?" He didn't care if it sounded callous. Perhaps there was enough for him to leave all this behind and start over without this pretentious board hovering over his shoulder at every turn.

The lawyer took off his glasses and speared him with a look. But Nicholas stared back. "Well?"

Father's lawyer went back to the document. "The main house will stay in trust until you marry, settle down, and fulfill your father's list." He slid another paper out and gave it to Nicholas.

He glanced at it. Then wadded it up. Father wanted him to give up everything and become a respectable citizen, husband, and father. More than anything, he wanted to throttle his father's neck. Maybe he should have done that rather than poisoning him.

The lawyer didn't seem to care that he'd wadded up the paper. "You will inherit your apartment here in London, but all other properties are to be sold and the proceeds given to the ten different charities your father has listed."

Of course his father would do that to him. The properties were worth a fortune. This was ridiculous. "What. About. The. Money," he said through clenched teeth.

It was the lawyer's turn to smile at him as he set down the will. "You will not inherit any money, Mr. Allen. Your father has decided to invest some of it back into the company to provide scholarships at Oxford. The rest of it will also be given to the charities your father entailed."

Not what he wanted to hear.

"Well, I guess the only choice I have is to marry. And that's already planned. So gentlemen, I will see you at the wedding."

The chairman stood up and walked over to him. "This wire came for you earlier. Sounds like there won't be any wedding." He clapped him on the back and went back to his seat.

Every eye in the room was on him.

He read the wire. When he glanced back up, he knew that everyone else had read it too. They were probably all waiting to throw a party as soon as he gave in. Well, that wasn't about to happen.

"This isn't over."

CHAPTER TWELVE

———◆◆◆———

One whole day since Jason left, and Penelope had wanted to rip open the letter a hundred times already. But she'd agreed to wait.

She missed him.

She took her time walking the long path back from Great-Grandma Eleanor's house. The visit had been a quiet one. Her great-grandma had slept almost the whole visit. Not that Penelope had much to say.

Regret had filled her over and over that she hadn't taken more time with Jason. To chat. To know more about him. And now that he was gone, she couldn't.

They'd promised to write one another, but she was afraid to try and put words on paper, especially with how she was feeling right now. She'd probably become a blubbering mess.

When she reached the house, she went straight to her mom and hugged her.

"What's this melancholy all about?" Mom took Penelope's face between her two hands.

"I. . .miss Jason."

"Ah." Her mother nodded.

Dad burst through the front door. "I am about to go to London and meet this Nicholas fella face-to-face. And he won't like it." He thrust a paper at Penelope.

You cannot back out. STOP. You will be in breach of contract. STOP. I expect you in London in two weeks. STOP.

Heat rushed to her face like her hair was on fire. Breach of contract? That's all she was to him? Rage boiled within her, and she raced to her room and searched in her trunk for the contract. Grabbing the offending papers, she brought them out so her parents could help her sort through them. "Here. You have a law degree. What should I do?" She crossed her arms over her chest, certain her father could find a way through.

Dad read through the contract, his face getting darker and darker as he went. "You're not in breach of anything." He stood up, grabbed his hat, and headed out the door. "I will take care of this Nicholas Allen. And unless he wants you to own part of his company, he'd better leave you alone. For good."

———————

Back in New York, Jason turned in a good portion of the photographs to his supervisor. The ones of Penelope's family and more specific ones of the ranch he left out. But the picturesque views of Wyoming could be used for any number of different things since Penelope wouldn't be giving her stories to Allen and Tate. They were good photographs, and he was proud of the work he'd done, but he didn't want to compromise the Coopers or invade their privacy when the family story wouldn't be published.

Back at his small desk in the New York offices of the publishing company, he wrote out his resignation. It had been easy to make the decision. He didn't want to work for them anymore and hoped to find a job where he could journey out west and stay there. What mattered now was that he was done here. Done.

After packing up his meager belongings in the office, he dropped them off at his small apartment and then headed straight to a friend.

The air here wasn't fresh like Wyoming. And the noise was almost hurtful to his ears after weeks out on the wide-open ranch land. As he walked the few blocks to Bruce's office, he didn't even want to stay here. Nothing was here. Nothing of value. Nothing that he wanted to continue. It was definitely time for a life change. And he knew what he wanted.

He pulled on the giant glass door trimmed in brass and headed for the elevator. Bruce had worked for the largest newspaper in New York City for more than ten years. Maybe he had some ideas of a fresh start for Jason.

CHAPTER THIRTEEN

———◆•◆———

Nicholas drained the rest of the amber fluid in his glass and threw it into the fireplace.

"Anything I can do, sir?" His butler, George, appeared in the doorway.

"Leave me be!" he roared.

He grabbed the papers off the table next to his chair. Penelope's father just *had to have* a law degree from Harvard. Starting with the top sheet, he wadded it up and threw it into the fire as well. And then the next page. And then the next. And the next. Until the fire hungrily ate every one.

The man thought he could sue Nicholas for threatening his daughter and lying about her being in breach of contract.

It would be laughable if he wasn't so desperate to find a way out of this mess.

Everything had been going according to plan. He was going to inherit everything.

But no. He had to meet Miss Penelope Cooper in the bake shop, and she ruined his life.

Well, he wasn't about to let that happen.

He'd ruin her. Somehow. He'd find a way around this. He

always did. Nicholas Allen Jr. wasn't about to let anyone stand in his way—

Loud banging sounded at the front door.

"What now?!" he screamed and stood to his feet. Wobbling from all the alcohol he'd consumed, he steadied himself with the side table as George hurried to answer the incessant knocking.

His butler opened the door. Multiple voices rang out, and the cacophony of stomping feet on his marble foyer made his ears ring.

Then, the constable stood before him, with his tall, domed hat almost reaching the top of the doorway. Several uniformed men stood behind him.

"Mr. Nicholas Allen Junior. You are under arrest for the murder of your father, Mr. Nicholas Allen Senior."

His legs went out from under him. "What? I didn't murder my father...." But his words were slurred. How had they found out?

"Let's get you down to Scotland Yard. We have all the evidence we need."

"But...I was supposed to have all the money...." Nicholas began to sob. He curled up into a ball. It was just a bad dream. He'd had too much to drink. When he woke up in the morning, it would all be over. He closed his eyes and put his hands over his ears.

Somehow, he was lifted off the floor, and he floated for a while.

Until he was thrown into the back of the police carriage and locked behind a barred door.

The breeze was gentle, stirring up scents of grass and wildflowers. Penelope sat on a large boulder, her thoughts on Jason as she watched the rippling current of the river. There'd been no response from Nicholas. And why would there be? Dad's letter and legal expertise had given the publisher's son no other option. There would be no wedding. No lawsuits.

She was free.

Which meant, per Jason's stipulations, she could now read his letter.

The cream envelope sat in her lap untouched. Nerves bubbled in her, and she huffed out a breath. She was being ridiculous. Days ago, her impatience had almost been unbearable. But now, now that she was free to read whatever this letter contained, she hesitated. Penelope took a deep breath, trying to settle her mind.

The truth was, she was afraid.

Afraid she'd pushed him away while trying to figure out what she was doing with Nicholas. That he only wanted to be friends. That she'd misread the tenderness and care he'd shown her again and again.

Shaking her head, she picked up the letter and slipped her finger under the seal. Speculation was silly when the truth was right in front of her. Yes, they were friends. But they had a deep connection. They each felt it, she knew that deep down. *Lord, I hope that he feels the same way as I do. That he at least cares for me and wants to see if there is something between us. But if he doesn't, help me. I'm done trying to do things my way. I want Your will.*

Penelope unfolded the thick sheet of paper and began to read.

Dear Penelope,

Over the last few weeks, I've been admiring you and appreciating your friendship more than you could probably ever imagine. In all honesty, I had to keep reminding myself that you were engaged to my boss.

If you are reading this letter, then that means you are not marrying Nicholas Allen Jr.

I believe God brought me out to Wyoming for several reasons. One: to see the West and the beauty here. Two: to meet you and your family. And three: for Him to work in my heart and give me direction.

My hope is not to jump ahead before I'm supposed to, so I will simply say this:

Penelope, you are an amazing woman of God. It has been my honor and privilege to get to know you, and I am proud that you call me your friend.

But if, perhaps, like me, you feel more than friendship, please write as soon as you can. I'm not sure where the Lord will take me once I'm back in New York.

> *I hope that it's back to you.*
> *With love, your friend,*
> *Jason*

Wanting to squeal with glee, she threw her hands up to the sky and released her exuberance. She lifted her skirts and ran as fast as she could back to the house.

She had a letter to write.

CHAPTER FOURTEEN

———◆◆◆———

It had been two weeks since word came of Nicholas' arrest. Penelope had received a telegram from the chairman of the board of Allen and Tate.

Sitting at her little desk under her bedroom window, she stared out across the ranch. It was hard to believe that her one-time fiancé had murdered his own father. All for money, it seemed.

The gentleman she'd met in the bakery that day was nothing like the real Nicholas, apparently. Thankfully, God had spared her from a horrible mistake.

Last week, a new contract had arrived in the mail from the publishing company. They still wanted her book about her family's legacy. And they still wanted the Westerns.

This time, she'd had Dad look over the contracts first and see if they were on the up and up. But even after he approved them, she couldn't bring herself to sign them.

As politely as she could, she turned them down. Of course, she wrote a lengthy letter expressing to the board how much she appreciated the offer, but after the actions of Nicholas, she didn't feel right about it. A telegram had come yesterday wishing her the best of luck and hopes that she would consider them in the future.

It was all she'd needed to bolster her spirits.

This morning, she'd typed for four hours straight, determined to get the rest of her family's story down on paper so she could read it to Great-Grandma Eleanor before she passed.

Doc had come yesterday and said she probably only had a few weeks left. To which Great-Grandma Eleanor had responded, "Praise God."

Penelope pulled her gaze back from the window with a smile and went back to the story. She'd love to give this gift to her family—whether it was published or not.

She hadn't heard from Jason but prayed for him every day and wrote him a letter each evening and mailed them every few days.

He was probably on another assignment and very busy with his work, but she wanted him to know she was thinking of him. . .and cared for him.

By midafternoon, her shoulders and back were screaming at her. Penelope stood and picked up all the pages she'd written today. With a pencil behind her ear, she began to read and walk.

She made it out the front door and heard a commotion.

Glancing up, she couldn't believe her eyes. "Jason!"

He dismounted his horse and walked toward her. Penelope put her papers on the porch chair and sprinted down the stairs. They met in the middle, and she jumped into his arms. He smelled like horses and was dusty from his ride, but she didn't care. He was here and he was holding her. She closed her eyes and fought tears. *Thank You, Jesus.*

———————

Holding Penelope in his arms was the best thing Jason had ever felt. As he swung her around, he whispered into her ear, "I hope you know that I love you."

She pulled back, and he set her down on her feet. Those eyes of hers were bright with tears. Happy tears, judging by the smile on her face. "You do?"

"I do."

The sound of a door slamming open and footsteps were signs that almost the whole Cooper clan was coming to see them. Jason knew their moment was about to end. Better take advantage of it while he had the chance.

"I might as well do this the right way, since everyone is here." He got down on one knee. "Penelope Cooper, will you marry me?"

"Yes!" she squealed and gripped his hand.

He stood back up and nodded at Mr. Cooper. The man nodded back.

As the whole crew watched, Jason connected with each member of the family and smiled. "I've taken a job with a large newspaper, and they want me to do a photographic series of Wyoming, the Grand Tetons, and Yellowstone National Park. It's an assignment for the next few years, so I'm hoping we can get married and have our home base here and travel back and forth."

Caroline Cooper clapped her hands together. "That's wonderful news! They can get started on a cabin for you two right away, can't you, Ray?" She patted her husband on the shoulder.

"Yes, ma'am." The man simply grinned at his wife.

"And for you, Penelope. I have another surprise."

She gazed up at him with love in her eyes. "Really?"

He handed her a thick envelope.

Her brow dipped into a V as she took it and opened it up.

No one said a word as she scanned the pages.

She covered her mouth and hugged him tight and then looked at her family. "It's a contract to write Western serials for the newspaper. Under my own name. For the next *five years*."

"And I have it on good authority that a publisher is interested in your family's story—Legacy of Love."

"It's almost too good to be true." She laid her head on his shoulder, squeezing his hand tightly.

Grandma Grace walked forward and covered each of their hands with her own. "I told you that God had opened the door. You just had to walk through the right one."

EPILOGUE

---◆◆◆---

Ten years later

1920

Wyoming

Penelope gazed out on the ranch from a window in the second floor of her home. Her husband was chasing their kids around the little yard he'd fenced in for them. Jason and her father had built onto the little log cabin they'd first moved into all those years ago. Not only did each of their three children have their own bedroom, but she had a small room to call her workspace.

Funny how things worked out. She'd insisted to Jason that she didn't need a space, thinking she'd be able to keep a little desk in their bedroom. But as their family expanded and the noise grew in volume as the kids aged, she'd been so grateful for this special room. Nap times had been her great escape into her fictional world.

After Great-Grandma Eleanor went home to Jesus, Grandma Grace and Mama had helped her with the children so she could write, much like they had done with her when she was younger.

Her brothers and their families also provided a lot of entertainment, especially when she had a deadline closing in. Juggling ranch life, family, chores, and writing had been an adventure, but they'd made it happen.

Once Jason had fulfilled his contract to the paper, they'd hired him specifically to do photos for the covers of her books and for the advertisements.

They stayed plenty busy, and God provided for them every step of the way.

Grandma Grace had been right. Penelope simply had to walk through the right door.

A wagon stirred up dust on the road from the east and drew her attention.

Perfect timing. She couldn't help but smile. Diane and Lesley. The women who had cheered her on and encouraged her in her writing for more than a dozen years. They claimed they were her biggest fans, which always set her family into a competition with them. It always ended in laughter and lots of smiles.

It had been a while since their last visit. She raced down the stairs and into the kitchen. The new scone recipe she'd tried just for this occasion had turned out beautifully. Penelope's mouth watered as she set them out on her prettiest dishes.

"Yoo-hoo! It's just us, your biggest fans!" Diane's singsong voice floated in from the porch.

"Come on in!" Penelope called from the kitchen and licked the orange glaze off her fingers.

Lesley was the first to enter, her hat boasting *four* feathers that bounced and bobbed with as much enthusiasm as the older woman. "My dear, you have outdone yourself." She dropped her copy of Penelope's latest novel on the worktable. "It's simply perfect. I can't tell you how many times I held my breath and couldn't wait to turn the page."

"I agree wholeheartedly." Diane pulled out a chair and took a seat. "I truly didn't think you could do anything better than the serials you wrote for the paper. For seven years you kept me enraptured and pining for the next issue. But this?" She pointed to the book with a raised eyebrow. "It's even better."

"That's because"—Jason entered from the back door—"my wife gets plenty of fodder from all of us. She'll never have an excuse to run out of ideas." He planted a kiss on her cheek and wrapped his arms around her waist.

Penelope could feel herself blush all the way down to her toes but loved the feeling of being in his arms.

Her older friends chuckled. Lesley winked. "That *must* be why she's a bestseller."

"I have to admit, I was shocked that they contracted more of the serials and the readers seemed to eat them up. But I have so many stories yet to tell. I'm enjoying writing the novels."

"Say," Diane chimed in, "maybe your next book should include two lovely ladies in the prime of their life. Women who love to read."

"Yes," Lesley nodded, "women with wisdom and quiet, meek spirits."

Penelope watched the two. Everyone kept a straight face. For about ten seconds. Then the laughter filled every crack and crevice in the room.

Diane wiped at a tear in the corner of her eye. "That was brilliant, Lesley. Simply brilliant."

Penelope shared a glance with Jason, and he sent her a nod and left the room. Oh, how she loved that he could read her like that. "I *would* like you to read my next story. It still has some fine-tuning to do, but I think you'll get a kick out of the characters."

Jason reappeared and set a stack of typed pages tied with twine in front of the ladies.

"Oh, goodie!" Diane picked up the pages and turned to Lesley. "We could read it aloud and take turns."

"Splendid idea." Lesley peered over her shoulder.

Diane untied the twine and lifted the first page. "Oh my." She put a hand to her throat.

" 'For Lesley and Diane, with much love.' " Lesley read the words aloud.

Penelope's smile stretched as the two women stared at the page and then looked up to her. "It's about two sisters who run a ranch all by themselves and get caught up in a murder mystery."

Tears glistened in each of the women's eyes. Diane's jaw dropped ever so slightly while Lesley closed her eyes and shook her head.

"We've never had such an honor." Lesley walked around the table and hugged her. "Thank you."

Conversation was light and full of laughter as they ate scones and drank tea. But the two hurried out soon after, saying they couldn't wait to start reading *their* story.

As the wagon rolled away, Penelope watched from the porch and waved.

Jason joined her. "Those two are my favorites. They were my first real introduction to Wyoming." He took her hand and squeezed.

She led him down the steps of the porch, and they strolled around the house together. "I have a surprise for you."

"Good thing I love surprises." He turned her to face him and pulled her close.

Her heart kicked up a notch. Gracious, what this man did to

her even after ten years. "Would you be up for asking my father if he would help you add on to the house?"

"What. . .you're finally realizing that you need a larger space to work in? I've been telling y—"

She stopped his words with a hand over his lips. "It's not for me." She gazed at him for a long moment, waiting for him to get the hint.

His eyes widened. "Oh. . .you mean?"

With a quick nod, she sucked in her bottom lip. She loved how excited he got every time they were expecting.

Jason threw his hat in the air and picked her up off the ground, spinning in a wide circle. "I love you, Penelope Miller."

"Forever and always, Mr. Miller." Her laughter echoed around the yard as their children came running.

Maybe one day, her grandchildren and great-grandchildren would pass down their legacy of love just like she had.

It was a dream come true.

ACKNOWLEDGMENTS

First, I have to do a shout-out to the crew of this novella collection. When I first asked Mary if she would like to do something together, we were at an RWA conference. (Gracious, that was years ago. . .yikes.) We've been friends for a long time, and she is one of my favorite authors, so I knew it would be fun. Darcie, Becca, and I have also been friends for many, many years. We've been in critique group for so long that we know each other's strengths and weaknesses. These three friends have made this collection possible. Thank you. I love you all.

To the team at Barbour—what a joy to work with you again. I can't even count right now how many books we've done together. Thank you for bringing this family legacy to life.

To my hubby, Jeremy—You. Are. The. Best. I love you more every day.

And most importantly, to God be the glory!

Readers, we love you and thank you for journeying with us to the Rocking K Ranch.

Kimberley Woodhouse is an award-winning and bestselling author of more than twenty-five fiction and nonfiction books. Winner of the Carol Award, the Holt Medallion, the Reader's Choice Award, Selah Award, and Spur Award. A popular speaker and teacher, she has shared her theme of "Joy Through Trials" with more than two million people across the country at more than two thousand events. A lover of history and research, she often gets sucked into the past and then her husband has to lure her out with chocolate. Kim and her husband of thirty years have two adult married children. She is passionate about music and Bible study and loves the gift of story. You can connect with Kimberley at www.kimberleywoodhouse. com and at www.facebook.com/KimberleyWoodhouseAuthor.

MORE ROMANCE COLLECTIONS FROM BARBOUR PUBLISHING!

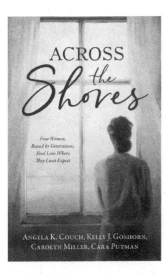

Across the Shores

Despite the years and miles that separate them, four women are linked by a gold pendant and a shared faith in God. In New South Wales, 1851, Josephine follows her brother on a hunt for gold. Caroline is determined to start fresh in Baltimore, 1877, even while hiding the scars of her past. Anna's wayward brother seeks refuge in Canada, 1905, dragging her along on the journey. In the Outer Banks, 1942, Lauren is determined to find her missing brother. Each woman's faith will be tested even as love meets them on the shores.

Paperback / 978-1-63609-519-6

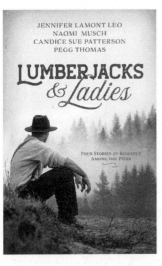

Lumberjacks and Ladies

Struggling to remain independent in the 1800s, four women reluctantly open up to help—and love. Winifred finds herself running the family lobstering business, stubbornly rejecting help from a local lumberjack. Elizabeth cooks for a logging crew, spurning the men's advances, until reoccurring gifts capture her attention. Maggie seeks a husband—in name only—from the logging camps, but the man who answers her letter is a heart-touching surprise. Carrie will not sell her timberland and allows the banker's nephew to sign onto her logging crew to ferret out the reason she is losing money at an alarming rate.

Paperback / 978-1-63609-140-2

JOIN US ONLINE!

Christian Fiction for Women

Christian Fiction for Women is your online home for the latest in Christian fiction.

Check us out online for:

- Giveaways
- Recipes
- Info about Upcoming Releases
- Book Trailers
- News and More!

Find Christian Fiction for Women at Your Favorite Social Media Site:

 Search "Christian Fiction for Women"

 @fictionforwomen